A Betrayal in Belgium

An Elspeth Duff Mystery

Ann Crew

To MY GOOD FRIENDS
CHARLOTTE & PETER

Ann Crew

ACE/AC Editions
All rights reserved.
ISBN-13: 9798438361275

Library of Congress Control Number: 2022906671

Independently published through Kindle Direct Publishing, a division of amazon.com

anncrew.com

elspethduffmysteries.com

Also by Ann Crew

Praise for *A Murder in Malta:*

"Each main character has a rich backstory with enough skeletons in cupboards to provide grist for a number of future novels.

An often compelling . . . excursion through exotic locales featuring unusual, complex characters."

— *Kirkus Review*

List of Major Characters

Elspeth Duff, special security advisor to the Kennington hotels

Sir Richard Munro, Elspeth's second husband and member of the British Foreign and Commonwealth Office (FCO), on assignment to the European Commission in Brussels

Eric, Lord Kennington, Elspeth's employer and owner of the Kennington hotel chain

Pamela Crumm, his business partner and Elspeth's friend

Magdelena Cassar, Elspeth's titular aunt in Malta

Roger Bouchard, security officer at the European Commission

Bernard Debock, manager of the Kennington Bruges hotel

Frans Bootds, head of security at the Kennington Bruges hotel

Martinus, a concierge at the hotel

Mateo, mysterious money lender or possibly a code name for the same

Dagmar de Saint Phalle, a Scandinavian beauty

Alexandre de Saint Phalle, her husband, chairman of Magna World Enterprises

Hans and Poul, her young sons

Pedar Johanssen, Dagmar's first husband who died tragically in a skiing accident

Viktor Novikov, owner of TransEuropean Ores

Hélène, his French wife

Jean Luc, their son

Ulrich Müeller, president of Amalgamated Scrap Metal
Brokerage

Helga, his wife

Kristin, his daughter

Raffaello and Giorgio, two young men of interest

Police Captain Schrott, of the Bruges police

Lizzie Craig Foxworthy, Elspeth's estranged daughter

Karlene Clare, Lizzie's nanny

Peter Craig, Elspeth's son

Detective Superintendent Tony Ketcham, Elspeth's
friend at Scotland Yard

**Eduardo Tomàs Costa da Silva, Jorge Xavier Morilla
Figuiera, and Wilhelm Vogler,** associates of Helga
Müeller in Portugal

A member of the Sûreté in Paris.

1

Sir Richard Munro watched his wife Elspeth Duff take off her ruby earrings. She was sitting half disrobed in front of the mirror of her dressing table and eyeing him curiously. They had just arrived back at their flat in Kensington from a diplomatic reception held at the Belgian Embassy in Belgravia.

"What did Madame de Saint Phalle mean when she asked if *Le Chevalier Richard* knew about Mateo?" she asked turning to him.

"Did she speak in English or French?" he asked.

"French, but I'm certain I understood correctly." She pressed her lips together and looked at him with raised eyebrows.

"To whom was she talking?"

"I couldn't see. I had my back to her and could only hear her words. When I turned round, the person she was addressing was no longer there."

Richard had learned over their three years of marriage to pay attention to his wife's inquisitive mind. Her question about Madame de Saint Phalle involved a secret that only a handful of people in the world knew and a person he was charged to find. Yet Elspeth had picked up a passing reference to the secret that she should not have heard. Nor should Madame de Saint Phalle have spoken of it.

Dagmar de Saint Phalle was a delight to see, with

high Scandinavian cheekbones, almost white-blonde hair, clear pale skin, and inviting liquid blue eyes. No man could walk into a room without feeling her cool sexuality. Yet she was not for the taking. Richard had heard that beauty often covers an uneasy soul, but Madame de Saint Phalle was not a troubled person but a troublesome one.

Dagmar's outspokenness was the nemesis of the diplomatic services. Richard had conferred with the security officers at the European Commission and the Foreign and Commonwealth Office about this, but they always have cautioned him to tread lightly. She obviously had used her beauty to marry wealth, status, and power. Her husband, Alexandre de Saint Phalle had tentacles throughout the loftiest governmental and financial circles in Europe and also in the Russian Federation.

Richard had never met Alexandre de Saint Phalle, but in Richard's recently acquired post as a special advisor to the European Commission in Brussels, he knew he soon would. His new duties at the commission included tracing laundered money that passed among the shady financial moguls in the European Union. In that capacity he was bound to turn over the paving stones of the rich and unscrupulous and unearth the grubs underneath. How successfully he could help eradicate them without disrupting the avenues of trade within the European Union was his newest challenge, one he anticipated with excitement. He had no idea at the time that Dagmar de Saint Phalle's remark would put Elspeth in physical danger.

"What did she mean?" Elspeth asked again. "And who is Mateo?"

He reached over to undo the clasp of her ruby necklace and kissed her exposed shoulder.

"Are you brushing me off?" she said with a grin.

"I am," he said.

"Can I wheedle it out of you?" she said, looking sideways and up at him.

"Not this time."

Under no circumstances could he reveal what Dagmar meant. What did he know about Mateo? At this point too little. Mateo was an unknown agent possibly in Portugal. The name had just surfaced in clandestine emails that were being monitored by Interpol and funnelled to Richard's secure site. He could think of no reason Dagmar de Saint Phalle should know about Mateo unless her husband was somehow involved. Alexandre de Saint Phalle bore watching.

Richard hated keeping things from his wife. She had read law at Cambridge and had worked in both public and private investigation and security matters for a number of years. He trusted both her insight and intelligence. In the past he had assisted her in several of her cases, but since their marriage she was loath to become involved in his diplomatic life. This attitude had changed since the recent affair in the Outer Hebrides, however. If only he could let her in on what little he knew about Mateo, he would have done so without hesitation.

Later after slipping on her silk pyjamas, she came to bed. He breathed contentedly as she rolled over to him.

She did not sigh and relax into his arms as she usually did.

"Who's the beauty? Madame de Saint Phalle?" She added the name, although it was not necessary.

"A very dangerous woman."

"As a predator of men?"

"As a woman who talks too much."

"Perhaps she is lonely. People who talk too much often are."

Richard did not agree. Lonely people were often shy. But Elspeth was a keen observer of people, and he might have to reconsider his assumption.

"In your work have you ever heard of Alexandre de Saint Phalle or Magna World Enterprises?" he asked her.

"No, I don't think so. Should I have?"

"If you were in international finance, you would have. De Saint Phalle as chairman of Magna World Enterprises controls a fair share of the precious metal exports from the former Soviet Union into continental Europe. He is making a push to expand into the UK but is meeting with strenuous objections from the government here. Dagmar is his wife."

Richard hoped he had not said too much. A mind like Elspeth's could easily have questioned what sort of metals, but she seemed satisfied at least temporarily with his explanation. She touched his cheek lovingly and turned away from him fluffing her feather pillow.

"Good night, dear Dickie," she said, with fatigue in her voice and was quickly asleep.

Richard turned away from her but could not sleep. Why was Dagmar asking about him? Was there a link between Magna World Enterprises and Mateo? If so, Richard's job had just become harder.

Elspeth's curiosity returned in the morning.

Richard heard her rise but did not follow her down from the loft of their flat which served as their bedroom and into the kitchen until he smelled that Elspeth was microwaving bacon. He dragged on his dressing gown and padded down the stairs. Elspeth had laid out the table. *The Financial Times* was waiting by his place and *The Times* by hers.

Her put his arms around her and kissed her neck.

"Fried or scrambled?" she asked.

He knew she prepared fried eggs badly, cooking not being one of her skills. He chose scrambled and offered to make his own.

Once seated and taking a piece of toast from the rack, she asked, "Who is the Mateo Madame de Saint Phalle mentioned last night? Is he Spanish or Italian?"

He evaded her query, although he understood it. "Both, I think or neither," he said. "We're not sure. Even if we were, I couldn't tell you."

"Can you tell me about Dagmar?"

"She's very beautiful."

Elspeth cocked an eyebrow. "I noticed. But who is she behind the beauty?"

"Alexandre de Saint Phalle's wife."

"Dickie, you're quite impossible when you get secretive. You told me that last night. She must have a history beyond her marital status, riveting face, and magnificent clothes."

"One has a hard time getting beyond that," Richard said smiling.

She let out a groan of frustration. "Be cagey, if you must."

"Meaning you will try to find out?"

"I might," she said biting into her toast, 'but only because you won't tell me."

He knew that in her job she had the contacts to do so, but he did not tell her anymore.

They conversed about the daily news. Finally Elspeth rose.

"I'm taking the Eurostar over to Paris today. If all goes well, I'll be back in London late this evening."

"Why not take a diversion and come through Brussels? I need to go there for the week." Richard kept a small flat in the Belgian capital and home of the European Union. He frequently stayed there, although in his new assignment he could spend a great deal of his time in London. "Surely Eric and Pamela can spare you for a day," he added, mentioning her employers.

"But can you spare a day when you get there? You're always so busy in your new position. When will you be back in London?"

"At least by the weekend."

"I can try for Brussels but let me ring you when I get to Paris. I'm not yet sure of my schedule there."

When Elspeth went upstairs to ready herself for her trip, Richard went to his computer. His small office in their flat served him well on days when he planned not to cross the Channel and did not want to brave traffic into Whitehall to his office at the FCO. He found little of

6

pressing interest in his electronic mailbox. He switched to his secure site and sent the rudiments of Elspeth's overheard conversation the night before to Roger Bouchard, the security officer with whom he frequently liaised at the European Commission. The response was immediate.

Richard—Meet me when you arrive in Brussels this afternoon. At fourteen hours? My office? Telephone me when you get here for confirmation. —Roger

Now fully dressed in her professional clothes, which were as striking but more severe than her evening clothes the night before, Elspeth entered his office. Richard looked up and smiled with approval. His wife was a handsome woman and often dressed to highlight her deep cobalt blue eyes, light brown hair, and graceful carriage. She did not have Dagmar de Saint Phalle's beauty, but few women did. Richard could not imagine being married to a goddess such as Dagmar. He liked the way men admired Elspeth when they met her, but he did not want them thinking of undressing her. He preferred keeping that privilege to himself.

She bade him goodbye but with a grin that disturbed him. He hoped she would not get up to one of her tricks and try to hunt down Dagmar, or worse Mateo.

Roger Bouchard rose from his desk at the European Commission and insisted on ordering coffee, which Richard did not want. They made a perfunctory pass at pleasantries before Richard brought Roger back to the business at hand.

"Have you turned up anything more on Mateo?" Richard asked.

Roger shook his head. "We are not certain that Mateo is a real person. His name may be a password for an *organisation*." He pronounced the last word in the French way.

"Can you connect him or it to Magna World Enterprises?"

"No more than to any other large European firm specialising in precious scrap metals."

"Scrap weapons grade uranium or plutonium?"

"Are you suggesting, Richard, that Magna deals with these substances?"

"One thinks of North Korea and Iran wanting these metals, but there also are terrorist elements within the European Union who would pay dearly for access to them. Firms like Magna have channels already set up to import metals from the former Soviet bloc. Others have responsibility to monitor this, but my job is to watch the money. The name Mateo indicates money transfers of some sort, legal or otherwise. I want to know as much information as you find on Mateo, be he a person or an organisation."

Roger Bouchard bobbed his head.

Richard poured cream in his coffee but refused sugar. "I want to set a trap," he continued, "and I want your cooperation. Reading through the reports, I can find three firms who might be involved with Mateo. All three have access to spent radioactive fuel. They operate under the mantle of respectability, but there may be employees in their midst even at the highest levels who use legitimate avenues of trade for illicit gain. I have targeted three: Magna, Trans-European Ores, and Amalgamated Scrap."

Roger looked doubtfully at Richard. "The big three. If they are hiding anything, one can bet they have buried it very deeply."

Richard smiled conspiratorially. "I'm not going to challenge them. I'm going to recruit their services to find out if there is any skulduggery."

"Any skull . . .? I do not understand."

"Any wrongdoing. I plan to pit one against the other."

"And how will you do that?"

"With the permission of the president of the EC, of course, I want to bring the heads of these firms together in a single room and explain our problem with the illegal transportation of high-grade metals and the money involved in it. If they all are above board, they may be able to help us. If one is not, then I'll try to weasel that one out."

"The weasel is a small animal, yes?"

"A very underhanded one," Richard added. "I wonder how much is left in my budget for this year. I have a brilliant idea if we can afford it."

*

Elspeth Duff was grateful for the speed with which she could get to Paris because Pamela Crumm had set up her first appointment at the new Kennington rue du Faubourg Saint-Honoré hotel for eleven o'clock. The meeting was routine and lasted through lunch. Although her job as one of Eric Kennington's top security advisors had occasional moments of great excitement, often she was involved in the everyday workings of the international boutique hotel chain. She had sat for most of the morning, first on the train, then in the taxi, and finally in the meeting. Her legs and back were protesting, and she needed fresh air.

She had an hour and a half before her second appointment and made excuses to the manager of the hotel. She strode out to the main entrance to the hotel, was greeted by the head doorman, whom she knew previously from the Kennington Mayfair, and turned down the fashionable avenue. Although the early October sun was shining, a brisk wind came round the corner and hit her. She pulled her scarf more securely around her neck.

In the press of her business in Paris, Elspeth had forgotten Dagmar de Saint Phalle's ill-spoken comment until she saw the woman fifty yards ahead of her. Dagmar was walking with intentional strides, obviously with a destination in mind. Elspeth paused and then followed her. They had spoken pleasantly at one point during the evening before, when Elspeth was making every effort to be responsive to her husband's diplomatic connections, a task she still did not relish. Perhaps she could find a common ground in browsing through the shops that lined the street and she and Dagmar need not dwell on the party at the Belgian Embassy in London the night before.

When Elspeth had no sooner set her pace, one just fast enough to catch up with Madame de Saint Phalle, she stopped short. Elspeth became aware that someone else was following Dagmar. Elspeth had been trained in the art of surveillance, and to her schooled eye a man behind Dagmar moved forward when she did and then paused and stepped into a doorway or between cars along the street when a possibility existed that Dagmar might look around. After several minutes, the man nodded almost imperceptibly to another man across the street, and they exchanged locations. The switch took place several times. Each time the men would slightly change their appearance, a different hat, a mackintosh taken off, sunglasses put on or removed. A bystander would not have noticed if unlike Elspeth they were not educated to see them.

Elspeth drew back and started a surveillance of her own. With her haute couture clothing and dignified bearing Elspeth could easily pass for a wealthy middle-aged European woman. She smiled inwardly at her own deceit.

Elspeth did not have a camera, but she had learned years before to correct this deficiency with mental imaging which later could be translated into words and put into an acceptable image by a forensic artist.

The first man was in his thirties, Elspeth estimated, was about six feet tall and looked southern European. He had pocked olive skin, spiky black hair, which he smoothed down later, and a straight nose with a hint of a hook at the bottom. He might have been considered handsome if he were made up and photographed in the right way. He carried a tote bag with various accessories, a scarf, eyeglasses, a baseball cap, and a windcheater.

His accomplice was younger, perhaps by about ten

years, shorter, and less attractive. His hair was nondescript brown and cut short. He had a two-day trace of a beard, a style Elspeth had never liked. The accomplice started out in a black raincoat, which he shed. He was wearing jeans and a plain black, long-sleeved tee shirt. He had two different styles of sunglasses. Elspeth took mental notes of their facial features, the length of their noses, the shape of their eyes and chin, and the distance between the features. She also studied the shapes of their ears, although she could only just see their outline from a distance. The top of the second man's left ear was torn.

Dagmar seemed oblivious.

Elspeth slowed her pace so that she could watch the men. There was a rhythm between them, as if they had performed their surveillance dance many times before. No one else on the street took note.

Dagmar disappeared into Hermès. The two men paused outside, one on each side of the avenue. Elspeth brushed by the one near the door to the house of fashion and entered into its interior. She had visited the shop several times before and knew her way about. She found Dagmar at the men's tie counter.

"Madame de Saint Phalle?" Elspeth said to the air behind Dagmar.

Dagmar turned and looked at her. For a moment Elspeth thought she might not be recognised. Elspeth did not like using her title by marriage and did not feel comfortable using it now. Should she introduce herself using her own name or her married one?

"Lady Munro," Dagmar exclaimed, saving Elspeth

from making that decision. "What are you doing in Paris? But, of course, the British Embassy is just down the road. Are you here with Sir Richard?"

"No, I have just come for the day to do some shopping," Elspeth lied.

"I'm buying a tie for my husband. Which one do you think, the red or the blue?"

"They're equally nice," Elspeth said without prevarication. One could hardly go wrong with an Hermès tie.

"Have you had lunch?" Dagmar said after telling the man at the counter that she would take both ties.

"Unfortunately yes or I would suggest we eat together." Elspeth did not have enough time even for a coffee before her forthcoming appointment at the hotel.

"What a pity. You must ring me the next time you are here in Paris." Dagmar did not offer a way for Elspeth to do so.

Later, back in London, Elspeth called Richard and in passing mentioned the surveillance in Paris.

"Are you certain?" Richard asked.

"Quite."

Richard frowned. "Do you have any ideas of why?"

"The most common reason would be that her husband wished to catch her with another man. The fair Dagmar may be cheating. Since I know so little about her, this is only a guess," Elspeth said. "It's not my affair, thank goodness."

"It may be soon," Richard said.

Elspeth sat up straight from the sofa where she was

sipping her after-dinner coffee. Richard sounded conspiratorial. She could imagine him smiling with just the corners of his mouth.

"Come clean, Dickie. What are you plotting? And don't tell me it has to do with Pamela Crumm. You two always are up to something."

Pamela Crumm was the business partner of Lord Kennington and was responsible for the day-to-day running of the many Kennington hotels around the world. She also was Elspeth's closest friend in London. Richard and Pamela, however, had plotted behind Elspeth's back several times before, which always annoyed Elspeth. Her friend and her husband usually had Elspeth's welfare at heart, but Elspeth felt she could manage on her own. She was not always right.

"Have you been to the Kennington Bruges?"

Elspeth shook her head. The Kennington Bruges was one of Lord Kennington's more recent acquisitions and had had no security problems to date. Elspeth hoped it would stay that way. She found working in countries where she had no knowledge of the language difficult, even if much of the population spoke English. Lord Kennington insisted that all his staff members, even the ones in the kitchen, speak some English. If Elspeth had to go beyond the confines of the hotel, however, she frequently needed someone to go with her to translate. What a bother that she was not one of those people who could become fluent in a foreign language easily, although she had an ear for British, Canadian, and American accents.

"Pamela tells me it's a small hotel and well suited

to what I have in mind," Richard said.

Elspeth asked him suspiciously. "What is your interest?"

"I need somewhere to meet three of the top precious scrap metal dealers in Europe. All of them are extremely rich and they need to be treated accordingly. I have asked Pamela to set up a meeting there."

"I'm sure they have adequate security," Elspeth said.

"Pamela thinks so. Elspeth, I want you to come to the meeting as my wife, not as a security advisor to Lord Kennington. The wives of the dealers are going to be asked along as well." He paused. "Including Dagmar de Saint Phalle."

Elspeth swallowed. She did not like official diplomatic duties because she did not want Richard to compare her with his first wife, Lady Marjorie, who, in Elspeth's eyes, was the consummate diplomatic wife. Elspeth thought she could never reach such heights of perfection. She worried that Richard would view her unfavourably, and in the first three years of her marriage to Richard, she had refused to be drawn into Richard's official life except on rare occasions. After their confrontation in the Outer Hebrides the preceding March, however, Elspeth decided to take a more active part in Richard's professional life. She still did not enjoy doing so because of her own inner doubts. No second wife likes to fall short of the first one. Elspeth felt she often did. Members of the Foreign and Commonwealth Office would remember Lady Marjorie. Elspeth wondered how many of Richard's party at the

Kennington Bruges would have known Marjorie too.

Elspeth held up her chin. "What will be my function? Am I to act as hostess?" The thought terrified her.

"No," Richard said.

Elspeth suspected he was reading her thoughts.

"Just come as yourself. You may not think so, but many people find you absolutely smashing."

"Liar," Elspeth said. "With Dagmar de Saint Phalle there, I can easily fade into the background."

Elspeth had no doubts about her appearance. She stood five feet seven inches tall, eight inches shorter than her husband, which allowed her to wear the high heels that were currently in fashion. When Elspeth was eighteen, she had been taught deportment by a French countess and had shed the ragtag existence of her youth in the Scottish Highlands. At that time, with the help of her titular aunt, the famed Maltese pianist Magdelena Cassar, Elspeth had learned to dress with classically good style and always have her hair styled simply but expensively. Her designer clothes were her one vanity. Yet she found her jaw too strong, her nose too sharply chiselled, and her strongmindedness too apparent.

Richard chuckled. "Dagmar may take people's breath away, but my dearest one, you never need apologise. Beauty such as Dagmar's is probably a curse."

"I expect it is. One has a hard time getting beyond it. I suspect even her husband can't trust her, if it is he who is having her shadowed."

"Do you think it might be someone else?" Richard

asked.

"She could be being followed because she is Alexandre de Saint Phalle's wife."

"I don't understand," Richard said.

Elspeth's devious mind went to work. "Kidnapping, extortion, blackmail? I can think of any number of scenarios."

Richard laughed. "It's just as well you are on the right side of the law," he said. "The criminals of this world would love you."

"On occasion many of them at the hotels hate me. It's an occupational hazard," she said.

Richard became serious. "But you will come, won't you?"

She bit her lower lip. She did not want to lie to him. He would not like that. She wanted to make him happy, but felt she often failed to do so. When she disappointed him, she could see it in his eyes, although he seldom expressed it verbally. If only he would face her down. At times when he was saddened by her, he smiled at her like a patient parent.

"I'll come," she said. "I'm sure you have already arranged with Lord Kennington and Pamela that I will be given the time off." Then a thought struck her. "If it is time off," she added. Later she remembered these words.

"I have set up the meeting for the middle of this month. It's hard to get the schedules of three busy men, particularly rivals in business, to agree on a common time. The enticement of the Kennington hotel, all expenses paid for them, their wives, and older children and the weekend dates seems to have clinched the time.

Just a few more details need to be finalised."

"All expenses paid? Who's paying?" Elspeth asked. She had seen the final bills of many guests.

"I have enough in my budget at the European Commission to cover it. This meeting could be one of the keys to my mission there. I received concurrence from the head of the European Commission this afternoon."

"Will there be security beyond the normal hotel coverage?"

"Roger Bouchard could be there, if I choose to include him."

"With his wife?"

"I forgot to ask if he has one."

Elspeth grinned. "Security people are always discounted," she said. "Tell me other than Dagmar and Alexandre de Saint Phalle who is attending."

"Viktor Novikov, who is head of TransEurope Ores based in Marseilles, his wife and son, and Ulrich Müeller, President of Amalgamated Scrap Metal Brokerage in Hamburg, his wife and daughter."

"And what will my job be?" she asked. "To entertain the wives, I suppose," she said.

"That's what I had in mind. Have you visited Bruges before? I understand it is a gem of a city."
"Never," she said, "although I've always wanted to."

"Good. I've arranged for a guide for you and the other wives."

"Certainly. Dickie, aren't you going to ask me to probe them for information?

Richard shook his head. "No, consider it a holiday," he said. "I hope the company will not be deadly."

Or end up dead, Elspeth thought perversely.

2

A small, tightly built man bustled forward as Elspeth and Richard entered the lobby of the Kennington hotel.

"May I introduce myself? I am Bernard Debock, manager of the hotel," he said.

"We are the Munros," Richard said in reply, but he did not give his title.

The manager had done his homework. "Yes, Sir Richard and Lady Munro. You are welcome. Let me show you to your rooms."

The suite faced a canal below and the line of trees along its edge. Elspeth admired the shady street in front of the hotel which had few strollers, but a motor launch filled with tourists passed by silently, probably because of the double-paned windows.

"I hope these rooms are satisfactory," Bernard Debock said. "Ms Crumm has asked that we make arrangements for your upcoming meetings, Sir Richard. I hope you and your wife will be comfortable." He gave no indication that he knew who Elspeth was within the ranks of the Kennington Organisation.

Cagey Pamela, Elspeth thought, but she wanted to believe Richard and consider their stay as a wife who was on holiday whilst her husband was at work. Elspeth wondered how Lady Marjorie would have acted, but then fiercely put the image out of her mind. She must stop her insecurity over being in public as Richard's wife.

"Do you think Pamela told Mr Debock who I am?" Elspeth asked her husband later.

"I asked her not to," Richard said. "You're not on duty. Enjoy yourself."

Elspeth was not comfortable meeting new people when she was away from the protective mantle of her job or her family. She was never sure why. She knew how to make small talk. She was Cambridge educated and had travelled extensively in the recent years of her life. Her aunt, the pianist Magdelena Cassar, had taught her about music, always an easy topic of conversation with guests who stayed at Kennington hotels and at the few diplomatic receptions Elspeth had grudgingly consented to attend. Elspeth had lived in Southern California for over twenty years and mingled comfortably with Americans, including Hollywood stars. She interacted with Europeans, Asians, Africans, and Australians with equal ease, but mainly in her job. Socialising for her was a learned art not a natural proclivity. On top of that, now she would have to play the role of Richard's wife. Since their marriage most of her time with Richard had been cherished moments alone. Could she present herself as Lady Munro and not feel awkward the whole time, wondering if she were matching Lady Marjorie's standards? Would Richard be measuring her? Would she let him down? Inwardly she groaned.

Richard continued. "Elspeth, my dearest, I must go make arrangements. Will you see to the unpacking?"

Richard said.

"Like a good wife?" she said with a half-smile.

Elspeth's cousin Biddy had chided her at the end of the affair in the Outer Hebrides to be a 'good wife' to Richard. The admonishment had struck at a tender chord.

Richard looked at her askance. Then he laughed and looked mockingly down his long aristocratic nose. "Like a good little wife."

How easily Richard could defuse her anxiety with his quick wit. And how often he had to do it.

"Let's meet for drinks downstairs in the bar at six. You can meet the members of the party then," he said as he departed.

The only person in the bar Elspeth recognised, other than her husband, was Dagmar de Saint Phalle. She was sitting by the window overlooking the canal and a man was looming over her possessively. Elspeth estimated he was as tall as Richard, but the resemblance stopped there. The man's face resembled that of an eagle, beaklike and hostile. His eyes, like the bird, were almost yellow. His hand, which rested on the back of Dagmar's chair, was like a claw. He did not take his eyes from Dagmar when Elspeth entered the room. He watched Dagmar look up at Elspeth. Only then did he follow the direction of her eyes. His eyes rested on Elspeth without kindness. Elspeth suppressed an inward shudder. Dagmar started to rise, but his hand went down on her shoulder and prevented her from doing so.

Richard must have seen this interaction because he

came across the room towards Elspeth and gently took her arm.

"Come and meet Alexandre de Saint Phalle," he said blandly but she could hear his caution. "The others have not yet come down."

Dagmar remained seated but Alexandre turned as Richard and Elspeth approached.

"This is my wife, Alexandre. Elspeth, Alexandre de Saint Phalle."

The hand that had held down Dagmar took Elspeth's hand drawing it to his lips. The old-fashioned gesture had no warmth.

"Lady Munro," he said, clipping his words.

What would Lady Marjorie have done in this situation?

"Monsieur de Saint Phalle," Elspeth said. "I met your wife at the Belgian Embassy in London several weeks ago but did not have the pleasure of seeing you there." She did not mention their encounter in Paris.

His eyes looked down at her. "I saw you there, Lady Munro. Do you always wear such fine rubies?"

Elspeth was taken back.

"They are gifts from my husband," she said without further explanation. Richard had given the necklace to her on her birthday in the first year they were married, the earrings in the second, and the bracelet the following Christmas. Rubies were her birthstone, for which she was grateful as she loved their flare. Disconcerted by the directness of Alexandre de Saint Phalle's remark, she was thankful she had not brought the jewels to Bruges.

A commotion across the room broke the tension of

a the moment. Dagmar looked up hopefully but then disappointment crossed her face. Her husband was watching her. Who did Dagmar think would come through the door? Three people entered. A large, balding man with a neatly trimmed beard led them. Elspeth was reminded of Edward the Seventh. A woman of a comfortable size, quite obviously his wife, was just behind. She had her arm linked through that of young woman, who resembled her but who was slender and pretty. No woman, no matter how young, however, could compete with Dagmar de Saint Phalle.

Richard was still in possession of Elspeth's arm and guided her towards the new arrivals. The man seemed to know him.

"Elspeth, meet the Müellers. Ulrich, we have met but I do not know your family."

"Good evening, Sir Richard. They are happy to come here with me. My wife Helga and my daughter Kristin." Herr Müeller spoke with a guttural accent.

"Come and meet the de Saint Phalles, who have preceded you here," Richard said.

"I know Alexandre from business and have heard of his beautiful wife," Ulrich said.

His wife nudged him merrily.

They crossed the room, which was beginning to fill with other guests.

Richard whispered in Elspeth's ear. "I have met Ulrich, but I do not know Viktor Novikov. Watch the door for me and see if a likely candidate appears."

Their wait was short. A man with a broad Slavic face came into the bar and looked around. He spotted

Dagmar. He smiled and nodded to her. Her flush was so slight that only someone watching her closely could have seen it. Elspeth did and she thought Dagmar's husband had as well. Dagmar turned her eyes away and stared out through the window at the canal.

The man bounded across the room. Alexandre de Saint Phalle's eyes followed him.

"Alexandre, it is a pleasure to see you again" the man said. He extended his hand but Alexandre did not take it. The man frowned and shook his head. He turned to Ulrich Müeller, who did shake his hand. Ulrich once again introduced his family.

"Are you alone, Viktor?" Ulrich asked.

"No, my wife and son are here, but as always they are late. You must be Sir Richard. And your wife?"

That moment of silence that comes after new people are introduced was filled only by the chatter of the other guests in the bar. Elspeth suspected that Lady Marjorie would have known exactly what to do at such a time so was relieved when Richard intervened.

"There is no need to rush," he said and waved to the waiter. "Let's have something to drink. Dinner is in half an hour."

Talk of the weather and their respective flights to the airport at Brussels filled the next few minutes and the initial awkwardness passed.

Richard drew Alexandre de Saint Phalle into conversation. Viktor Novikov engaged the Müellers. Elspeth took a seat next to Dagmar, whose beauty did not cover her uneasiness.

"Have you noticed how the raindrops make circles

in the water then eventually overlap? When they do, each circle loses its completeness and everything becomes muddled," Dagmar said, her eyes fixed on the canal, where a passing shower was falling.

Elspeth tried to think of an appropriate response. "When I was a child," she said, "my cousins and I loved to skip stones on the lochs near my home in Scotland. That way the circles were spread out in a row. But, yes, eventually they did merge with each other or got lost if the wind came up."

"Do you have children, Lady Munro?"

"Two, but they are grown."

"I have two young sons, five and seven years old. I fear for them."

Elspeth's professional mind clicked in. "Fear?" she asked.

Dagmar shook her head and fell into silence. Their drinks arrived to break her uneasiness.

"Do you plan to do any shopping here?" Elspeth asked after accepting her wine glass.

"I have been here before. The lace is exquisite but not to my taste," Dagmar said.

She went silent again.

Elspeth could not think of what to say next. Instinctively she reached out and covered Dagmar's hand with her own. Dagmar turned over her hand and gripped Elspeth's but suddenly dropped it when Alexandre de Saint Phalle turned around. His eyes locked on hers. She stared back. Elspeth was not sure if Dagmar's look was of defiance or apprehension. Certainly there was no love in her face.

Hélène Novikova chose this moment to make her entrance. Elspeth drew in her breath and saw Dagmar stiffen. Hélène was not as beautiful as Dagmar, but she was arresting. Her sculpted dark brown hair fell shoulder length and in front had a white streak, so white that it must have been natural. To Elspeth's trained eye, Hélène's clothes could only have come from the best of French couturiers. Her frock's classic lines shouted quality—and money.

A young man with straight dark hair that matched Hélène's but shorter was walking behind his mother as she made her way to the corner when Richard's party was gathered.

"I am late," Hélène said with a beguiling French accent. She offered neither apology nor explanation. "You do not know my son. He is named Jean Luc."

Jean Luc seemed oblivious to his mother's late arrival. He must be inured to it. He looked at the party members and his eyes lit on Kristin Müeller. He moved away from his mother and to Kristin's side. Soon he was flirting and Kristin laughed. It proved to be the only bit of levity in the party that evening except the struggling attempts of Helga Müeller to amuse the guests at dinner with light-hearted stories of her childhood in the American sector of West Germany.

"Dickie, I'm afraid I let you down. I had no idea how to raise the gloom at dinner," Elspeth said when they were back in their rooms.

He laughed. "You did wonderfully," he said. "Viktor Novikov has often outfoxed de Saint Phalle in their business. I knew that when I set up the meeting. I plan to use their edginess to my advantage."

"I think Kristin and Jean Luc will entertain themselves, but the women?"

"I fear I'm counting on you. The men's rivalry seems to have filtered down to their wives. Away from their husbands they may relax. I have set up a private carriage tour in the morning for the four of you. Will you find that difficult? Jean Luc and Kristin have been invited to join you, but I doubt they will go."

Elspeth did not want to admit to any shortcoming. "I'll do my best," she said. "How would Marjorie have done it?"

Richard came round and took Elspeth by the shoulders. "Marjorie is dead, and I love *you*," he said. "You seem to have no idea of how well you always handle yourself."

"Awkwardly," she said.

"No, my dearest. Your grandmother would have approved of you this evening."

Reference to Elspeth's grandmother was an old joke between them. When Richard had first met Elspeth when she was fifteen, she was a bratty, brainy, and ragtag girl, whose grandmother, the seventh Countess of Tay, was trying to instruct her in the finer arts of etiquette. Elspeth had rebelled at the time but the lessons had stuck.

"Besides," he added, "you were the handsomest woman in the room."

She leaned forward and kissed him. Dearest Dickie!

3

When Richard had chosen Alexandre de Saint Phalle and Viktor Novikov to attend his meeting, he knew there was bad blood between them. He had purposely added the affable Müeller as an antidote. Yet last night's dinner had done nothing to clear the air between the two rivals. Richard doffed his hat to Helga Müeller for her attempts at jollity and to Elspeth, whose consummate good manners had smoothed over the many rough patches during the meal. Only the two young people seemed oblivious to what was going on around them.

Richard had booked a private room for their weekend meetings and had asked that a breakfast buffet be set out there Friday morning. He wanted to start their meeting early and not have the men be distracted by their families.

De Saint Phalle came first and drew Richard into a corner. De Saint Phalle kept looking at the door as he spoke.

"Don't trust him, Sir Richard. He is a snake," Alexandre whispered out of earshot of the waiter who was waiting patiently by the food.

Richard did not need to be told who de Saint Phalle thought the snake was. His antipathy towards Viktor Novikov was apparent. Richard's many years in the diplomatic corps had taught him the skills of appeasement and he answered tactfully.

"Fortunately we are not here to conduct any commercial business. I'm merely gathering information that may be useful in tracking laundered money across Europe. I want to hear from Ulrich Müeller and Viktor Novikov as well as you. Certainly you are at liberty to contradict Viktor Novikov if you find what he is contributing to our discussions is false."

"Rest assured I will," de Saint Phalle snorted.

With those words, the door opened and Herr Müeller came in. Unlike Alexandre de Saint Phalle, who was dressed in a tailored suit and conservative blue tie, Ulrich was in an open necked shirt and woollen Bavarian jacket. He greeted the other two men jovially, coming over and shaking both their hands exuberantly.

"I see breakfast has been laid out. The famous Kennington buffet!" He went round to the sideboard and began filling his plate with two smoked salmon eggs Benedict à la Kennington, several rashers of crisp bacon, fresh fruit, and two different kinds of hot rolls. He spooned out some peach jam and put a large portion of butter on his plate. He seated himself and got the attention of the waiter standing patiently by the food.

"Coffee with hot milk and some orange juice would suit me nicely. And bring some brown sugar."

"It is on the table, Herr Müeller, if you please" the waiter said. The members of service staff in Kennington hotels were instructed to learn the names of the guests they would be serving.

Ulrich tucked into his meal and invited the other two men to join him. Richard chose scrambled eggs, fruit, and toast. He had eaten many Kennington hotel breakfasts before and was not enticed by the richer choices. Alexandre eyed the food and finally selected a croissant and several freshly sliced apricots. Richard asked for tea and Alexandre an espresso.

The appointed hour for the beginning of the meeting came and Viktor Novikov had not yet appeared. Richard disliked lateness but disguised his impatience by ordering another cup of tea.

Novikov arrived fifteen minutes after the scheduled start of the meeting and explained his delayed arrival. "Hélène wanted me to share her breakfast in the room. Since this meeting is to be informal, I trust you all do not mind."

Richard kept his composure. There was no purpose in stirring up ill feelings so early in the meeting.

Alexandre, however, took the bait.

"Are you assuming our time is worth nothing?" he challenged.

Viktor Novikov snarled. "And what else had you planned to do with your time this morning, undercut one of my deals?"

"Gentlemen," Richard pleaded. "There is no need to . . ."

The meeting had started badly. Richard tried to bring it on track. He cleared his throat.

"I had hoped we could begin our discussions by clearing up a matter of concern to me. Then we can get on with our meeting. Do any of you know an agent called Mateo? I think he may be a money launderer in Portugal."

Richard watched the faces of the three men. De Saint Phalle shook his head, but Richard did not trust his blank expression. Novikov stared defiantly at Richard and set his jaw. Müeller laughed.

"The mysterious Mateo," Müeller said. "His reputation is known to me and I expect to Viktor and Alexandre as well. I have never contacted him although his network has tried to approach me."

"About what?" Richard asked.

"About shipping spent plutonium into Germany. I never touch the stuff."

"And you, Novikov. Has his network approached you?"

"No," Viktor said.

Richard did not like the shortness of his answer.

"Liar," de Saint Phalle said. "You worked with him last year after I told him to go to hell."

Novikov blanched. "Sir Richard, I hope you will not take Alexandre's words as true. He is attacking me because he thinks I have slept with his wife. That also is not true."

"Viper," Alexandre de Saint Phalle hissed.

Richard rose and slammed his fists on the table, a device he found effective because of his height. "Gentlemen, we are here to discuss money laundering. I hope we can keep personal affairs out of our conversation."

"Waiter, will you fill our cups and then leave us. I'll call you if we need anything else."

The waiter's act of replenishing their coffee and tea seemed to bring down the emotional tension in the room.

The men settled down to work. Mateo's name was not brought up again, although Richard planned to get Ulrich Müeller aside and learn more later about Mateo approaching him. As their conversation continued, Richard watched Viktor Novikov and wondered if Alexandre de Saint Phalle's accusation was real. Would a woman be attracted by Viktor's Slavic face with its wide cheekbones, pale blue eyes with the hint of Asia in their shape, and clipped blond hair that was beginning to recede? Richard saw a middle-aged man with the beginning of a paunch, which he covered with a red tartan waistcoat. Richard was Scottish, but he did not subscribe to the wearing of tartans by clan members only but wondered why Viktor had chosen such a bright example from the many subtler patterns. Richard could not see Viktor's sex appeal. He must ask Elspeth if Viktor had any. Or perhaps had Viktor seduced Alexandre's wife as a way to snub his rival? Dagmar once again was in the middle of a controversy.

*

Elspeth kissed Richard goodbye with a heavy heart and wished him well at his morning meeting. She dressed with her usual care and made her way down to the breakfast room. She found Dagmar eating alone.

"May I join you?" Elspeth asked.

"Good morning, Lady Munro. Please do. Helga Müeller has just left to go for a hearty walk, as she called it. "I shall enjoy finishing my breakfast with someone less enthusiastic."

Elspeth selected a light breakfast from the buffet and asked the waiter for Kenyan coffee, a speciality that

Lord Kennington had especially grown for his hotels. She returned to Dagmar's table. She noticed that every man who entered the room gawped at Dagmar.

"One gets used to the staring. I cannot help my looks," Dagmar said. "When I was young, I tried to hide behind baggy clothes, but it didn't help. Now I enjoy what God gave me and often use it to advantage. Is that shameless of me?"

"Not at all," Elspeth said. She had used her own appearance as a tool on occasion. Elspeth's next question was from her heart.

"Do you enjoy the role as your husband's wife?"

"Alexandre insists. I would prefer to be at home with my sons, but I suppose I must earn my keep."

Elspeth was not sure how to respond. She felt idiotic went she repeated, "Earn your keep?"

Dagmar smiled revealing white, straight teeth. "My job is to be Alexandre's wife. Hans and Poul are not his but he provides for them lavishly. I was married before, you see, but my first husband, Alexandre's closest friend, suffered a tragic skiing accident. Alexandre and Pedar were together at the time. Alexandre married me soon afterwards. I did not love him, but he gave me and my sons a place in the world. I repay him by being the best wife I can, although some days I would like to flee back home to my parents' farm in Denmark and forget the world Alexandre lives in. But I stay quiet and earn my keep for the boys. Do you earn yours?"

Elspeth was amazed by Dagmar's candour. Dagmar's face was almost expressionless as she spoke.

"I have my own career apart from Richard," Elspeth

said. "Our marriage is a second one for both of us. We were married over three years ago, and there are no young children involved, which makes things easier for us. We are apart frequently, although Richard particularly asked me along on this trip. I suppose this weekend I am earning my keep." Elspeth did not say what her career was. "Tell me about your children," she continued, hoping to be treading on less risky ground.

Dagmar's face changed, its beauty becoming filled with sweetness. She talked lovingly about her children until Helga Müeller burst through the door. "The guide is waiting for us in the lobby! He is very handsome." She grinned from one round cheek to the other. Dagmar looked up in the air and Elspeth could almost hear her silent groan.

When the three women reached the lobby, the concierge met them with a note scrawled on a piece of heavy stationery bearing the crest of the Kennington hotels and the motto 'Comfort and Service'. Hélène Novikov declined the invitation for the morning tour. She pleaded fatigue from her trip to Bruges. Elspeth doubted it. Marseille to Brussels was not a long flight and Bruges was less than ninety kilometres away from the airport.

"The two young people have already gone out, Lady Munro. They said they would make their own way," the concierge explained. "They said not to wait for them."

*

The men broke in time for lunch at one. Richard had arranged with Elspeth that they all should meet in the dining room on the ground floor, but he went briefly up to his and Elspeth's suite. When he arrived there, he sensed that her morning had not gone smoothly. He exchanged glances with Elspeth, who raised her carefully shaped eyebrows in appeal. Had he asked her to do too much? He was well aware of her aversion to her current role, but so far she had been perfect in it. Now she did not look happy, which pained him. Elspeth could describe little of the sites they had seen to Richard in the few moments they had alone in their rooms before lunch.

"Dagmar was followed again," Elspeth told Richard. "By the same surveillance team I saw in Paris."

"Are you sure?"

"Yes. I pretended to want to turn back several times to look again at something I had just seen. We double backed several times. Each time Dagmar's tail found something interesting to study nearby."

"Did Dagmar seem to notice?"

"No. Both she and Helga Müeller must have thought me rather strange, but I held on to my right as a Scotswoman to be a bit flighty. I imitated my mother."

Richard laughed out loud. "That's the first thing that has amused me all day."

"How is the conference going?"

"Turgidly. If I get through the weekend without Alexandre de Saint Phalle and Viktor Novikov killing each other, I will consider my efforts a success. Thank God for the presence of Herr Müeller."

"Have you learned anything?"

"Some things that are a bit promising."

"Who Mateo is?"

"Somewhat peripherally. I think Ulrich Müeller knows. I plan on getting him to tell me more. But you're not supposed to know about all that."

"If you won't tell me, I can always go to Dagmar. We've become quite chummy," Elspeth said, glancing sideways at her husband.

"Vixen," he said. He kissed her. "Keep an eye on your chum. Her being shadowed may have nothing to do with this weekend, but Dagmar is always a worry."

Elspeth put her arm through her husband's as they left their suite. Perhaps acting the part of a diplomatic wife was not so awful. And it was nice to see Richard at work and be at his side.

Little did she know what waited for her downstairs.

4

The lift stopped on the floor below to collect other guests. Richard and Elspeth stood towards the rear, their hands entwined behind Richard's back. Elspeth rested her head against the mirrored wall behind her and wished the ride would go on forever. When the lift reached the ground floor, they let the other passengers get off first.

"Shall we ride back up and then come down again," Elspeth said with a grin.

Her fantasy, however, was broken by the intrusion of a man in a dark suit and tie. His name badge identified him as Frans Bootds, Head of Security for the Kennington Bruges.

"May I speak to you, Ms Duff? Ms Crumm in London said I should contact you," he said.

Ms Duff, the name Elspeth used professionally. Not Lady Munro.

"Sir Richard, I think you would like to be along. Please will you come to my office in the back?" Frans Bootds said.

The security office in the back rooms of the hotel reminded Elspeth of many other Kennington hotels. Banks of security camera monitors lined one wall. A man sat monitoring all public parts of the hotel. Frans's small office was beyond.

Frans offered seats to Richard and Elspeth. He sat

on the edge of his desk chair and picked up a pen. Then he put it down and straightened it. Elspeth could tell he was tense.

"I am sorry to disturb your stay, but a matter of grave concern has happened. I called the security office in London at once. They told me, Ms Duff, that you were staying here," Frans said. "Your good reputation comes before you."

"What's happened?" Elspeth asked.

He fiddled with his pen again. "One of the kitchen staff found a dead body behind the hotel near the rubbish bins. He was strangled by a tie."

"Do you know who he is?"

"He is one of the guests. His name is Alexandre de Saint Phalle. I believe, Sir Richard, he was one of your group."

Elspeth drew in her breath. She heard Richard blow out his.

Elspeth spoke first. "Strangled?"

"His tie was tied around his throat, but he must have been hit first. His head was battered — is that the right word?"

"De Saint Phalle," Richard said. "Are you sure?"

"Yes, Sir Richard. In a small hotel like this, we get to know the guests' names on the first day they are here."

"Who identified the body?" Richard asked.

"I did," Frans said. The kitchen worker came immediately to me after she found the body. She is a sensible woman and did not panic, but she was very upset. We sent her home but told her to say nothing. I told her I would question her later."

"Did you go out to see the body? Is it still there?" Elspeth asked.

"Yes to both questions," Frans answered. "I had the body covered with a blanket and some plastic because it is raining on and off. Then I called the security in London, who told me to get the police. Ms Crumm called shortly after and told me to contact you."

"I want to see the body," Elspeth said. She abhorred the thought and looked up at Richard for support. She had not come to Bruges in her official capacity, and she did not want to take control.

"Did you by any chance take photographs?" Richard asked.

"I took several with my mobile," he said. "The body is not pleasant to see."

"Have the police arrived yet?" Elspeth asked.

"They are in the back with the body now. I told them to leave everything undisturbed until I could reach you. The police here know how to be silent."

As Frans Bootds was talking, Elspeth was by habit mentally plotting her next moves.

She turned to both the security officer and her husband. "First let's see the body. Mr Bootds, Frans, I want you to deal with the police. Explain to them that you will be handling the case but that I am visiting from the Kennington Organisation in London. Tell them I will not interfere with their investigation, but that I will be reporting directly to Lord Kennington on their progress. I do not speak Flemish and will need you to translate."

"As you wish, Ms Duff. Most of Bruges police

speak good English, but I will translate if you need me."

She continued. "In the meantime, I want to make inquiries of my own among the guests here. If I can assist the police in any way, please let me know, but I think I'll be most helpful talking to the people in Sir Richard's group. Above all, do everything you can to keep this out of the press. Lord Kennington will insist."

"I understand," Frans said.

Elspeth hoped he did. Eric Kennington detested any adverse publicity on the running of his hotels. At least the murder had been outside of the building. She hoped it was in a place that was easily reachable from the outside so that anyone could have accessed it. She took a deep breath. "Now let's get the unpleasantness over with."

They rose. Richard took her by the arm. She was grateful for it. She looked up at him with thanks and then drew her arm from his. He would understand that she was no longer playing the part of his wife. She felt the familiarity of her normal job flow through her and felt relieved that she now could do what she did best.

The body was lying by a large bin in an enclosed area behind the kitchen. The only external access to the area was by way of a solid steel gate, which was chained and padlocked and a solid steel door in it for pedestrian traffic. Was the gate scalable? Elspeth judged that a fit person might be able to climb over it but with difficulty.

Viewing a dead body is never easy. Elspeth had been called to do so several times in her career but always disliked the task. As reported, one of Frans's staff had laid a blanket and a large piece of plastic over the corpse. A uniformed policeman pulled the covering back for Elspeth and Richard to see.

Other than in films, Alexandre de Saint Phalle's body was the first one Elspeth had encountered that had been badly beaten. He had massive contusions across his cheekbones, which were not applied by a makeup artist as they did in Hollywood. His nose was no longer long and hawk-like but a crooked version of its former self. Several teeth were missing, and his yellow eyes stared lifeless at the rain clouds above. One ear was bloodied. A blue Hermès tie that Elspeth recognised had been used as a garrotte in what appeared to be the killer's final guarantee that Alexandre de Saint Phalle would not rise from his wounds.

Elspeth's stomach retched. She tried not to show her feelings but was thankful Richard said, "I think we have seen enough. I'm sure the police photographer will record what is needed." The man obviously in charge of the police investigation came up to them and spoke in passable English.

"I think you do not need to see more," he said.

"Thank you," Elspeth said, knowing the image of Alexandre de Saint Phalle's face would not leave her for a long time. She turned away and wanted to be sick. Instead she raised her head and met Richard's gaze, which were looking with concern at her.

"Shall we go in, Richard?" she said.

They did not speak or touch as they took the lift back to their suite. When they arrived, Elspeth ran to their bathroom and threw up. She wished she had been less inclined to nausea when faced with such unpleasantness.

Wiping her mouth and taking a sip of water, she returned to the sitting room.

"Oh, Dickie, I was trying so hard to be the perfect diplomatic wife. Now this."

He laughed. "Somehow, my dearest one, I think you are going to be a lot happier investigating the murder than you would have been escorting the wives around on another excursion." He seemed to sense her feelings. "In all fairness to the group, we need to tell them that de Saint Phalle has died. But I don't think we need to go into details yet. Do you want me to make the announcement at lunch?"

Elspeth was relieved but did not want to say so. Instead she said, "That would be brilliant, Dickie. It's a job I always hate. But let me see if I can talk to Dagmar first. I'll go down to the lobby and see if she is there."

The interview would be painful for Elspeth, but she owed it to Dagmar. She sensed that Dagmar was more vulnerable than Richard had previously made out.

He hugged Elspeth for a long moment, and they left their suite with their arms about each other. She pressed close to Richard. They once again made their way down to the ground floor. The entire group, including Hélène and the young people were gathered just outside the private dining room. Jean Luc Novikov seemed to be entertaining them all with an amusing story. With a glance at Richard, Elspeth approached Dagmar.

"May I speak to you privately for a moment," Elspeth said, drawing Dagmar apart. Elspeth led her to a cluster of chairs in a corner of the lounge. Elspeth took Dagmar's hand.

"I have bad news for you. Your husband was found behind the hotel. He has been assaulted and did not survive the attack. I'm sorry to put it so brutally."

Dagmar's hand went cold and the little colour she had in her face left it. Her ice blue eyes registered no emotion. They held Elspeth's without blinking.

Finally she said, "Are you sure?"

"I've seen his body. It's not a pleasant sight. The head of security at the hotel has identified him for the police and Richard and I have confirmed it."

"Why would you do that?" Dagmar asked.

"I work for the Kennington hotels—in security. That's my job, Dagmar, aside from being Richard's wife. I know this must be very difficult for you. Would you like to go to your room?"

"Yes, I think so."

"I'll have some lunch sent up."

"I'm not too sure I could eat," Dagmar said. This was the first moment that Dagmar seemed to register any feeling.

"Would you like me to come with you?"

"No. I would like to be alone."

"I understand," Elspeth said, trying to imagine what it would be like to be told one's husband had been brutally murdered.

She rose and put out her hand for Dagmar. Dagmar took it, her hand still chilly. They took the lift to the first floor and approached the de Saint Phalle suite.

"We will need to talk later," Elspeth said.

"I need a little time to get adjusted," Dagmar said as

she put the room card in the lock of her door.

After she left Dagmar, Elspeth wondered if she had done the right thing. If Dagmar had been involved in the murder, would she now have time to destroy the evidence? Elspeth almost turned back to the suite but at the last moment did not. If Dagmar had no complicity in the murder, she should be given time to grieve.

5

Richard watched Elspeth take Dagmar across the room. He knew Elspeth so well that although she bore herself with her usual grace, her jaw had tightened and her back stiffened. He quickly gathered the others into the private room off the main dining room he had booked for their lunch. A buffet had been set out, mixing continental, traditional English, and local Belgian foods. Several soups were offered as well. After the group had chosen their food and wine had been poured for them, Richard rose from his place.

He cleared his throat. "I need to explain the absence of the de Saint Phalles," he started. "There has been an unfortunate accident. Alexandre de Saint Phalle was attacked behind the hotel. He was beaten by his attacker or attackers and was killed."

Everyone stopped eating. Some gasped; others frowned. No one spoke.

"The police have been contacted and are investigating," Richard continued. "Also hotel security has been alerted." He debated whether he should tell the group about Elspeth's position or not. He decided that for the moment he would not. "You're all free to ask any questions, although little is known at the moment."

Viktor Novikov was the first to react verbally. "This is an outrage," he said. "I always thought Bruges a safe city. And a Kennington hotel safer still."

"The murder did not take place in the hotel,"

Richard said. He did not elaborate. "But undoubtedly you all will be questioned. I'll let you all know as we learn more. The police have promised to keep us informed."

Ulrich Müeller had lost his cheerful countenance. "Alexandre? Murdered? But this is impossible," he blustered.

The others remained silent.

At this moment, Elspeth came in the room. Richard saw that she was looking bemused. She looked up at him and raised an eyebrow.

"My wife . . ." he began.

Elspeth shook her head almost imperceptibly.

He changed what he was about to say. "My wife has told Mme de Saint Phalle."

"She is resting in her room and has asked to be left alone," Elspeth said.

"*La pauvre chérie*," Hélène Novikova said. "The poor dear. She is so beautiful but so doomed. But her husband . . ."

Viktor Novikov put a warning hand on his wife's arm. "That is quite enough, Hélène."

His wife laughed almost hysterically. "And you, Viktor, what do you think of Alexandre now that he is dead? Do you forgive him of all his sins?"

"Now is not the moment to bring up the past," Viktor said.

"*Maman*," Jean Luc said. "You should not say anything you will regret later."

Hélène did not heed her son's advice. "I regret nothing about Alexandre de Saint Phalle. He deserves to be dead!"

The room turned silent. The only sound was the rattling of the rain against the windowpanes.

Helga Müeller sat stoically. A false smile was pinned on her face. Her daughter fidgeted in her chair.

Richard broke the silence. "I suggest that we leave matters to the police at this point. Gentlemen, I want to continue our discussions this afternoon. Ladies, you may wish to rest or, if you are still willing to go, your guide will be available for a shopping tour," he said.

"Jean Luc and I have other plans," Kristin said.

They all resumed their meal. Ulrich Müeller and his wife returned to the buffet for more food. Hélène took another glass of wine. Viktor pushed his food about on his plate. The young people put their heads together.

Elspeth went to the buffet and served herself. She declined wine and asked for tea. When she was settled, she spoke quietly to Richard.

"I want to question Helga and Hélène, separately if possible. After lunch, will you have a minute before you go back into your conference? Can we meet in our suite? I want to talk to you about the men."

Richard trusted Elspeth's judgement, particularly when it came to security matters. He nodded quickly.

When the meal was nearly ending, Richard rose again. "I know all of you will have questions about Alexandre de Saint Phalle's death. Before coming in to lunch, I spoke with the head of security here at the hotel, and asked him if our group could be disturbed as little as possible. Of course de Saint Phalle was a guest of mine and of the European Commission, so I feel a great deal of responsibility for making the rest of your stay here safe and comfortable. My wife has agreed to assist you, ladies, while I will continue meeting with Novikov and Müeller. I hope this arrangement is acceptable to you all."

Heads nodded.

As everyone finished their meal, Richard said. "Gentlemen, shall we meet at half past two back in our conference room?"

Richard had been concerned about Elspeth ever since the affair in the Outer Hebrides. He felt she still regretted the injury to him on Lewis. Indeed, she did bear some guilt, but he had long since forgiven her. Shortly afterwards her titular aunt, the renowned Maltese pianist Magdelena Cassar, had died, leaving Elspeth devastated by her loss. Richard knew that during the previous summer, Elspeth had gone about her duties for the Kennington Organisation but with a heavy heart. She had tried to balance them with the demands of Magdelena's estate, which were complicated and far from settled. Major changes take their toll, Richard thought. His transfer from being British high commissioner in Malta to his current role in the European Commission had shifted his base of operations from Ta'Xbiex to Brussels. Magdelena's death and then Elspeth's being needed in Malta to help work out the complexities of Magdelena's bequests had been taxing. Elspeth had been on an emotional rollercoaster since April, but she always raised her strong chin and carried on.

Richard did not want to ascribe Alexandre de Saint Phalle's brutal death to act as a cure for the hurt in Elspeth's life, but it offered an absorbing distraction and seemed in the last two hours to have taken her out of her doldrums. Should Richard be thankful for this? He thought so despite the circumstances.

Elspeth was animated when they returned to their suite.

"I may have missed something, but I saw a great deal of animosity among the people downstairs."

"I quite agree. But do you think one of our players, as we might call them, was involved in Alexandre's murder?"

Elspeth's look challenged him. "Don't you?" she asked. "Do we know the whereabouts of any of the group before lunch? Your meeting had adjourned and we women had come in an hour before. There was plenty of time for any one of them to murder Alexandre."

"None of them seemed to have any injuries to their faces or hands," Richard said. "After seeing Alexandre's body, don't you think they might?"

"If they used fists, yes, but they may have used something else. I'm not a pathologist, but the blows inflicted on Alexandre's face seemed too severe for an attack with mere human hands. I will be interested to see what the police pathologist has to say."

Elspeth had a point, one Richard should have seen.

"Do you think a woman could have inflicted such blows?"

"Helga Müeller probably could have on a good day and Hélène perhaps in a temper. I took Dagmar's arm when I told her about her husband. She spends many hours in the gym every day I would guess. Her arm could have been made of steel. The women are no freer of guilt than the men."

"Would they have a motive?"

"Dickie, didn't you say Dagmar was trouble?"

"I think I said troublesome. She always seems to be on the edge of something dangerous."

"And the others?"

"I can see no reason why Helga Müeller would want Alexandre dead, but Hélène seems to be nursing some kind of bitterness towards him."

"I am going to find out what it is. In the meantime, see what you can discover from Viktor and Ulrich."

"Viktor already has expressed his personal dislike of Alexandre. Also Alexandre accused Viktor of trying to seduce his wife."

"Then the Novikovs need investigating. But, Dickie, do you think any of hostility between the Novikovs and the de Saint Phalles has to do with their businesses as well as their past personal relationships?"

"Your guess is as good as mine."

"It's good to have you along on this investigation. See what you can find out this afternoon. Oh, thank you, my dearest Dickie," she said.

6

After Richard left the suite, Elspeth made her way down to the first floor and wrapped on Dagmar's door.

"It's Lady Munro," Elspeth said through the door. She heard the chain taken away and the latch being released. She had expected to be turned away. Instead Dagmar's response to her knock was welcoming.

"Lady Munro, do come in," Dagmar said. She did not look grieved. "There still is some coffee in the thermos they sent up with lunch. Will you have some?"

Although Elspeth did not want any, she accepted. She watched Dagmar as she poured out two cups.

Elspeth looked around the suite's sitting room. Outer clothing, newspapers and magazines were strewn everywhere, but there was no sign of Alexandre's possessions. Elspeth had not suspected that Dagmar was the untidy sort and wondered if Alexandre had been.

"Thank you for coming," Dagmar said. "I needed someone to talk to. How odd it is that when there is a death in the family, so many people turn away."

Elspeth took a swallow of her coffee, trying to balance her words between her dual roles as Richard's wife and a security advisor to the Kennington Organisation and to Lord Kennington personally. She decided in favour of the latter.

"May I call you Dagmar? Please call me Elspeth. I of course feel sympathy for your loss but . . ."

"Don't, please." Dagmar said. "Alexandre was a bastard."

Elspeth choked on her coffee.

"You are shocked, I can see," Dagmar said. "He was. Why should I pretend? No, I didn't kill him, if that is your next question."

Dagmar's words did not fit her calm, beautiful face. Her expression was benign and her words spoken softly not angrily.

Elspeth decided not to respond directly. "I came to Bruges a bit under false pretences. Richard asked me here to play the role of his wife, but I have other connections to the Kennington hotels. As I told you earlier, I work for Lord Kennington as a roving security advisor to help in situations like Alexandre's death." Elspeth skirted the word murder. "Would you mind terribly if I assume that role now?"

"You seem very discreet, Elspeth. Ask what you want."

"Dagmar, you speak perfect English. Where did you learn it?"

"Denmark is such a small country that most Danes are multi-lingual. I also spent two years in an English boarding school. I hated it but I learned English. I also speak French, Italian and German. I have a good ear and speak them all with ease. I have been told I don't have an accent in any of them. I also understand Russian although I don't speak it well. This gives me the advantage too of being able to eavesdrop when people expect me not to understand."

Elspeth regretted the common British assumption

that everyone should speak English and therefore few Britons, including herself, were fully fluent in other languages.

"And where do you live?"

"In Paris. Alexandre wanted to be taken for French. He even changed his name to de Saint Phalle. His real name was Alexei Petrovsky. Hardly a noble name is it? He didn't tell me about this until after we were married. He legally changed his name when he fled from East Germany in 1977."

Elspeth cocked an eyebrow in puzzlement.

"Oh, it was quite an adventure story. His father was Russian and a KGB advisor to the Stasi. His mother worked for the secret police as well. Not a background that Alexandre wanted, so he reinvented himself. Still until the unification of Germany he was terrified the Stasi would come for him."

"Did they?" Elspeth asked.

"Several times he said he thought he was being followed, but nothing came of it."

"Did he get back in touch with his parents after the reunification of Germany?"

"Not that I know of. I think he wanted to drop all ties with Germany—East, West, or unified. He pretended not to speak German or Russian, although naturally he spoke both, except when we went to Moscow."

"Dagmar, do you know that you are being followed?"

"Followed?"

"Yes. Two men are shadowing you. I saw them

when we met at Hermès in Paris and again this morning. Do you have any idea of why they might be following you?"

"It probably was Alexandre's doing. He was always afraid I would run off with another man," she said.

"Did you ever consider it?"

Dagmar shook her head. "I know how best to provide for my sons. I did not love my husband, but he treated Hans and Poul as if they had been his own."

"Did he have any children of his own?"

"No."

"Then you are his next of kin."

"He said his parents were dead. He also had a brother in East Germany. I don't know where he is now. Alexandre had no contact with him after he came to the West, as far as I know."

"Do you inherit?" Elspeth asked. She felt asking would not be offensive as Dagmar so obviously was not grieving.

"Alexandre always told me the boys and I would be well off if anything happened to him. but I don't know the terms of his will."

"Do you know what will happen to his business interests?"

"Magna World Enterprises has a Board of Directors. I assume they will carry on. Elspeth, may I leave Bruges now? I see no reason for me to stay and I am anxious to get back to Hans and Poul in Paris."

"The police will want to see you," Elspeth said. "They will tell you if they wish you to stay. May I ask you one more thing?"

"Certainly."

"Do you have any idea who may have killed your husband?"

"At least ten people come to mind and that is without thinking. He was a powerful but not a loved man. But then again there are at least ten men he would have murdered without compunction," Dagmar said after taking another sip of her coffee. "Viktor Novikov is one of them."

Elspeth wanted to sympathise with Dagmar but she could not. Dagmar seemed too detached. What was she hiding?

"Why is that?" Elspeth asked.

"Alexandre did not like to be bettered," Dagmar said, adding more sugar to her cup and indelicately licking her coffee spoon. Elspeth could not decide if the gesture was coquettish or absent-minded. Probably the latter.

"And did Viktor better him?"

"Frequently, and not always just in business."

Elspeth frowned and waited for Dagmar to explain, but Dagmar did not volunteer anything further. Was this what Richard had meant when he described Dagmar as 'troublesome'?

"Are you suggesting that Viktor was responsible for the attack on you husband?"

"Why not? Viktor is no nicer than my husband was. They lived in a cutthroat world. Only the hardest of men in it survived at all."

But Alexandre de Saint Phalle had not survived, Elspeth thought.

"Can you think of anyone else in particular?" Elspeth asked. "Someone who might be here in Bruges?"

The corners of Dagmar's mouth twitched. "Try Hélène Novikova."

"Victor's wife? Why would she want to murder Alexandre?"

"He spurned her. She isn't used to that. She's rather a bitch. She wanted an affair with him in order to spite Viktor, I think. Alexandre laughed in her face and told me the whole thing afterwards. My husband was not always a nice man, but he was loyal to me." Had Dagmar said this with the great confidence of the super beautiful? Elspeth wondered.

"It sounds very vicious," she said out loud.

"It is. One always has to be careful. So much is always at stake. One slip can cost millions of euros."

"Is it all about money?" Elspeth asked.

"No, it's about power, not money. They all have far more money than they can spend. Sometimes I find it indecent. I would have left Alexandre and gone back to my family's farm in Denmark if I could have provided for my boys there. Now it looks like I can."

Dagmar appeared to be a woman of contradictions. She wore her designer clothes the way wealthy people who stayed at Kennington hotels did. Elspeth could not imagine her on a farm. She played the part of Alexandre's wife but she said she did so because it provided safety for her sons. She looked demure but was muscular and spoke viciously about both her murdered husband and his associates. Yet she said she trusted his loyalty to her. She also seemed to have the temperament to kill her husband but there was no proof yet that she had.

Elspeth wanted to get to know Dagmar better, not because she liked her but because she was high on the suspect list. But she did not want Dagmar to think she could be considered a murderer. Consequently Elspeth held off asking Dagmar where she had been between the time they had returned to the hotel from their morning tour and when she had come down for lunch.

"Dagmar, will you come out with us to go shopping this afternoon?" Elspeth asked. She wanted to see Dagmar's interaction with Hélène Novikova, assuming Hélène would agree to come along as well. Also Elspeth wanted to know if the surveillance team still would be in evidence now that Alexandre was dead.

Elspeth went next to Hélène and Viktor's suite. She tapped on the door. Jean Luc opened it as if he were expecting someone else—Kristin perhaps. His face registered disappointment.

"Is your mother in?" Elspeth asked.

"She is lying down," he said.

Elspeth suspected that Hélène spent a great deal of time lounging in bed.

"Will you tell her I'm here?"

"Come in," Jean Luc said. "I will tell her."

Hélène appeared five minutes later in a peignoir that must have cost thousands of euros and would have fit on a nineteen thirties Hollywood set. Feathers wrapped her beautifully made-up face. Was she expecting someone? Certainly she knew that Viktor would be tied up in his meeting all afternoon.

Unlike her son, Hélène seemed detached. Elspeth wondered if it was her title. She deplored its influence. In the past she had only used it when she wanted to seem arrogant or needed it for effect, but now it was useful. Still, Elspeth explained her dual role to Hélène.

Hélène laughed. "So you are a titled lady detective. I did not think they existed outside of books."

"I don't usually use my title when I am working. It confuses people who do not understand our British system and would interfere with my work," Elspeth said feeling defensive. She had an inkling that Hélène liked putting people in that position.

"I would like to ask you a few questions if I may, Madame Novikova. I see you used the Russian form of your name."

"It has a mystique." Just like Elspeth's title.

"Are you Russian?" Elspeth couldn't be sure from Hélène's facial features, which must have been sculpted by at least one plastic surgeon's knife.

"No, French."

"Have you been married to Viktor long?"

"My son, Lady Munro, is twenty years old. And, yes, he was born after Viktor and I were married. I married him in 1984, twenty-five years ago. I was very young at the time."

Elspeth could not judge the veracity of this last remark but doubted it.

"Was Viktor already in the precious scrap metal business at that time?'

"Why do you ask? Does this have something to do with Alexandre de Saint Phalle's murder?"

"I don't know as yet," Elspeth admitted.

"I met Viktor when he came out of the Soviet Union to Paris as an aide to a communist trade official. I was working as a simultaneous translator for the French Ministry of the Economy, Finance, and Industry at the time and was assigned to translate for Viktor and his superior at a trade show. I helped Viktor escape and we were married soon afterwards. In those days he was a very attractive man. He has not aged well. His work keeps him from staying fit."

Another woman who does not like her husband, Elspeth thought, and she was happy that her own marriage was a loving one. Dear Dickie, she thought, and smiled.

Hélène frowned. "Do you find Viktor unattractive?"

"I have only met him twice and then only briefly and therefore cannot say," Elspeth said evasively. She had dealt with enough middle-aged men who were losing their youth to long hours of work and bad eating habits to pay little attention to the resultant damage to their figures. Elspeth judged a man or woman on their intelligence and commitment to life, whatever form that took. She had even admired criminals for their cleverness if not their honesty. She was likely to judge Hélène's seemingly idle lifestyle more harshly than her husband's active one.

"Why are you asking me about my background, Lady Munro? Surely it has no bearing on Alexandre de Saint Phalle's death. I hardly knew him."

Flags went up in Elspeth's mind. She remembered Dagmar's earlier words.

"I had supposed that the world of the leaders in the precious scrap metal business would be small. Am I wrong?"

"The men know each other. We wives are left out. I prefer it that way. People like Alexandre and Dagmar de Saint Phalle are not, how shall I put it, *raffiné* — refined. Dagmar was raised on a farm in Denmark; one can almost smell the cow manure. And Alexandre's background is surrounded in mystery. I suggest that you could solve that mystery and then you will find his killer."

Elspeth gave as pleasant a smile as she could muster. "My job is not to find the killer. That task belongs to the police. I merely want to make sure that all the guests in the hotel are safe and secure and that members of my husband's party will have no more unpleasantness. I want to ask you a few more questions, if I may?"

"Where was I before lunch you mean?"

Elspeth nodded.

"Viktor and I had breakfast together and then I went back to sleep. I woke about eleven and took my time getting dressed and putting on my makeup. I always like to look my best when I go out. Viktor came in after his meeting and we went down to lunch together. I have no witnesses except the room service attendant who came to get the breakfast things. Jean Luc had gone out with the Müeller girl."

"Do you remember what time your husband came

61

back to the room?" Elspeth asked.

"It must have been about half past twelve. I had just finished dressing."

"Where do you and your husband live?" Elspeth said, although she knew the answer.

"Most of the time in Marseilles. We also have flats in London and Moscow."

"Moscow?"

"Yes, Viktor often has business there and it is easier to have a flat than go to a hotel. I go with him in the summer but never in the winter."

"Are you involved in his business?"

"Only on occasions like this one. Strictly socially."

"Madame Novikova, do you know someone named Mateo?"

"What an odd question. I once knew someone in Madrid by the name of Mateo Sanchez, but it was a long time ago. I haven't been in contact for years."

Elspeth thought Hélène was telling the truth about Mateo, but she doubted she was being completely honest about her relationship with Alexandre de Saint Phalle. Elspeth wanted to watch Hélène's interaction with Dagmar and therefore asked Hélène to join them on a shopping expedition that afternoon.

"The men will be involved until half past five according to my husband. Why not join us? I always am looking for clothes. It is a weakness of mine."

"Your frock is quite beautiful. Did you get it in Paris?"

"No, I had it made in London by my French dressmaker. I will tell him you admired it." Elspeth said.

"Will you come? We are meeting in the lobby at three."

Elspeth left the Novikovs's suite and ventured down the corridor to where the Müellers were staying. No one was there. Her interview with Helga Müeller would have to wait. Somehow Elspeth thought that Frau Müeller was the least likely person to be involved in Alexandre de Saint Phalle's death, but Elspeth was an experienced enough investigator not to eliminate any suspect at this point.

It was now half past two. Elspeth returned to the suite she shared with Richard and phoned Pamela Crumm at the offices of the Kennington Organisation in London.

Pamela answered her private line with her clipped tones. "Pamela Crumm here."

"It's Elspeth. What a terrible mess here."

"How are you, m'friend?" Pamela asked. Although Pamela was technically one of Elspeth's employers, events over the last ten years of Elspeth's time at the Kennington Organisation had led to a close friendship between them. "Deep in murder again I hear. Tell me about it," Pamela said.

The relating of the facts did little to lessen Elspeth's queasiness. "Pamela, I am not sure what role you want me to play here. I have told Frans Bootds that I'll question the female members of Richard's party. Richard has agreed to deal with the men. I have this premonition that the murder could possibly relate directly to the interaction between the Novikovs and the de Saint Phalles and their past dealings together."

Elspeth recounted the details of her two interviews.

"Do you think Viktor killed Alexandre? It sounds possible."

"I don't know honestly. I don't want to implicate him if he's innocent. But any one of the women could be guilty too. Dagmar had no love for her husband. She sounded as if she were doing servitude to provide for her sons. Hélène is a puzzle. She appears to be a lady of leisure, but she has a keen ear for languages and was a professional simultaneous translator at one time— between Russian and French anyway. She's not beautiful the way Dagmar is, but she is glamorous. I wonder what she does with her time."

"I'll find out what I can about the Novikovs and the de Saint Phalles," Pamela said. She was an inveterate follower of international gossip.

"I'm sure Richard had them vetted through security at the European Commission," Elspeth said.

"Not for scandal, though. Let me see what I can dig up in that department." Elspeth could almost see her friend's eyes sparkle.

"Ring me when you know more. I'll tell Eric you are on the trail," Pamela said. Eric was Lord Kennington, head of the Kennington Organisation.

"At any rate, Pamela, Dagmar de Saint Phalle is being shadowed. I want to find out why."

When Elspeth rang off from London, she called the Müeller's suite. No one answered. Where was Helga Müeller?

7

Richard was a man who liked order, particularly in his diplomatic dealings. One of the reasons he had been given his knighthood was his ability to facilitate compromise among hostile parties in difficult situations around the world. He listened well and used what he heard to bring disagreeing parties together to find a workable solution. He prided himself that he seldom lost his temper. He did only when he had been stretched to the limits of patience. His wife was more likely to bring out his irritability that anyone else, although he loved her dearly and had for a long time.

Even before Alexandre de Saint Phalle's death, Richard had no intention of engaging the last two men whom he had called to Bruges in any confrontation. Their morning session had come close to Viktor and Alexandre exchanging blows, albeit verbal ones. Richard had deflected them by insisting they stay with the business at hand, and the end of the morning session had been productive. The three rival entrepreneurs had explained to Richard the intricacies of the precious scrap metal trade. Before de Saint Phalle's body had been discovered, Richard had planned an afternoon agenda that included the illegal shipment of precious scrap metal, the movement of spent radioactive material from the former Soviet Union into western Europe and the precautions taken to keep the material out of the hands of terrorists. By design he was saving the use of money laundering by any illegal shipments until the next day's session.

De Saint Phalle's murder, however, changed everything. If Alexandre's death were the result of the morning's unpleasant exchange between him and Victor, Richard needed to find out why. He suspected that the animosity between Viktor and Alexandre was not new.

When they re-convened at two-thirty, Richard's two guests appeared tense. Viktor kept adjusting his collar, as it were too tight about his fleshy neck. Richard saw a bead of sweat settle on a boil was rising at the back of his hairline. Ulrich was more jovial than he had been in the morning, but his laugh seemed forced, and his attempts at humour verged on tastelessness.

Richard thought the best way to clear the air was to face the fact of the murder directly.

"Gentlemen," Richard said, "I suggest we deal with Alexandre de Saint Phalle first."

Both of the other men's heads nodded slowly, almost in unison.

"You both have dealt with him in the past," Richard said. "I think it would be useful if each of you told me about your experiences with him, particularly in light of who his enemies might be or if you know of any reason why someone would wish to accost him outside the hotel."

Neither man volunteered to go first.

"Why don't we start with you, Ulrich?"

Ulrich's good humour dried up. "Alexandre de Saint Phalle was not an honest man. I have not had many dealings with him in the past, but his company outbid mine several times. I suspect that he provided bribes to those responsible for awarding the contract. But he was subtle. I can prove nothing. I hate dishonest business tactics and do not stoop to using them despite de Saint Phalle."

"Did you know him personally?" Richard asked.

"I have met him several times before."

"Do you think he was dishonest in other ways?"

"*Ja*, I think he wanted profit the most. He did not let anything get in the way of that."

"Including money laundering?" Richard asked.

"*Ja*, that too. The banks in Switzerland must be bursting with his illegal gains," Ulrich said, laying his arms across his stomach and twisting his chubby fingers together.

Richard turned to Viktor. "Do you agree?"

"For sure. But Alexandre was very careful and his name was at least as important as his profits. He wanted to be accepted into European high society. That is why he married a beautiful wife and why he kept a lavish dwelling in Paris, flats in London and Rome and a villa in Provence. In the current economic downturn, he must have lost a great deal of money on his property. But they were for show mainly. I expect Dagmar will keep them until their value returns. She knows the worth of a euro."

"Do you know Dagmar well?" Richard asked. He tried to sound bland but remembered that Viktor had accused Alexandre of thinking Viktor had tried to seduce Dagmar. Although Richard would have preferred that personal issues be kept from their discussions, the murder had changed things. Murder was a personal thing.

"Well enough," Viktor said. "One can only trust Dagmar so far."

"Will she take over Magna World Enterprises?" Ulrich asked.

Viktor laughed. "Not our beautiful Dagmar. She has no head for business other than gossiping about it. We all know not to tell anything to Dagmar that one didn't want to see the next morning in the scandal sheets. Dagmar has a nose for finding out the most interesting things and then broadcasting them. But she doesn't always get things right."

Richard remembered Elspeth's overhearing Dagmar asking if he knew about Mateo. Where did that information come from?

Richard wondered why Viktor had skirted the issue of his closeness to Dagmar. A woman of Dagmar's beauty would naturally attract lovers. Richard wondered about her faithfulness and if it had any connection, fidelity or not, to her husband's murder. After all it seemed that Alexandre had made arrangements for Dagmar to be followed. Richard suspected that each person he asked would have a different take on Dagmar. At this point it would be disastrous for Viktor to admit to an extramarital affair with her. The implications would be too great. Richard, therefore, decided to move on.

"This morning I mentioned Mateo, which seemed to provoke anger on de Saint Phalle's part. Do either one of you know why?"

Ulrich answered first, which annoyed Richard. Now Viktor would have time to formulate his answer.

"Mateo is not a good thing," Ulrich said.

Richard was puzzled. "You speak of Mateo as a thing not a person. Is that right?"

Ulrich nodded. "Mateo is a code word for a network of bankers who launder money. No one knows who the head of the network is. He is always called Mateo although that cannot be his real name. Nominally they work out of Portugal, but most of us suspect the powers behind them are in the Russian Federation."

Richard turned to Viktor. "Do you agree?"

Viktor smiled slowly. "I think Herr Müeller is trying to implicate me because of my Russian background. I agree that Mateo, which I can confirm is a codename not an actual person, nominally works out of Portugal. I also agree that the head of the network is not in Portugal. Personally I suspect the Cosa Nostra in Sicily."

"You both said you had been approached by Mateo," Richard said. "Tell me about how?"

Ulrich volunteered first again. "I still say the head of Mateo is in the Russian Federation. Two years ago, when Mateo first came to my attention, a man using the name Mateo Rodrigues, came to my offices in Hamburg. He implied that he would offer me over a half a million euros to carry a lorry load of scrap copper from Ukraine to Hamburg. The price offered was too high, even for a large amount of copper. I was suspicious and turned him down. I keep my business above board. I cannot afford to make irregular shipments from the east to west Europe. One slip and I would lose the good name I have spent many years building."

"And you, Novikov? How were you approached?"

"In the same way, only the shipment was high-grade steel alloy, the price three quarters of a million euros for a single shipment from Georgia across the Black Sea to Turkey and then on to Italy. I, like Ulrich, declined and for the same reason."

"And Alexandre de Saint Phalle? Can you be certain he did get involved with Mateo?"

"Alexandre would do anything for a euro, particularly if he thought he could get away with it. Two years ago he had several setbacks, mostly because of me. Suddenly his business rebounded without plausible explanation," Viktor said.

"And you think he took Mateo's offer?" Richard asked.

"For the amount of his financial recovery, I would say he accepted to take more than one shipment."

"Do you know about this, Müeller?"

"I heard about it," Ulrich said.

Richard sat back in his chair. "The European Commission was aware that shipments of weapons grade uranium could be seeping into Europe. Terrorist restrictions had made this increasingly difficult, both in terms of payment and transportation. Are your shipments from the former Soviet bloc carefully checked when they come into the EU?" Richard asked.

Both men nodded.

"But customs officials can be paid to overlook one or two containers—particularly if the bribe is high enough. De Saint Phalle would not be above that," Viktor said.

"Do you have proof of that?' Richard asked. "It is a dangerous accusation, and de Saint Phalle is not here to defend himself."

Viktor rose and went to look out of the window. Ulrich wiped the back one of his hands on his sleeve nervously. Neither answered Richard's question.

In frustration Richard said, "Enough about de Saint Phalle. We have other things to discuss."

At five Richard returned to the suite that he and Elspeth were using. She had not yet returned from her shopping expedition. Consequently Richard decided to find Frans Bootds and see what further news there was from the police.

Although Richard trusted Elspeth's investigative skills implicitly, he felt responsible for the welfare of his group. The information he had gathered from Ulrich and Viktor was inconclusive. Was de Saint Phalle really such a rogue? Was it his connection to Mateo that provoked his murder? Was Mateo based in the Russian Federation, in Portugal or in Sicily? And how much should Richard tell Frans Bootds or the Bruges police?

He had been involved in several of Elspeth's cases before and had watched her purposely withhold information from the police. In almost every case she justified this by saying she was protecting the guests at the hotel. She admitted that once she had let a guest, who obliquely admitted to fraud, leave one of the Kennington hotels and the country where it was located. Elspeth had not informed the police because she could prove nothing. Richard was not sure he approved.

He found Frans Bootds in the lobby talking to the concierge. By Kennington standards the lobby was small but as lavishly appointed as the larger ones. Frans was at the reception desk.

"Sir Richard, I am glad you are here. I have a report from the police. Will you please come into the security area?"

When they were settled in Frans's small office, Frans picked up a file that sat alone on his desk, opened it and took out a single sheet of a paper, which he studied quickly.

"I am fortunate that the captain at the police and I have worked together before. I was in the police for a short while and trained at the police academy. I did not like the work, which was often outside. I am susceptible to colds and a policeman with a red nose who sneezes often is laughed at. I prefer the work here, which is almost always indoors and dust free. What is more the pay is much better." He took out a handkerchief and wiped his nose, as if as a precaution. "Let me tell you what the police have found, since the report is in Flemish."

"I would be thankful if you would," Richard said.

"The coroner believes that the death was caused not by the beating but by strangulation. The victim was probably beaten until he was unconscious. A hard object, like a piece of lumber or a cricket bat, was used. Since this weapon was not found, the police conclude that it was thrown in the canal and by now could be floating up to the North Sea. The police will look for it but do not have much hope. The medical examiner said there were small red dots in the victim's eyes that are consistent with strangulation. The tie would suggest it too and appears to be the victim's own."

"Do the police say if any suspicious people were seen in the area?"

"They are making enquiries."

"Where is the body now?"

"In the police morgue. They want to do a complete postmortem, which will be done in Brussels. The captain said it would take at least a week."

"Will you ask the police when the body will be released? I don't want Madame de Saint Phalle to be distressed by any delay."

"Do you know if Madame is religious? Perhaps we could bring in a priest."

"I have no idea. Let's leave that to my wife—to Ms Duff," he added at the end. "But please ask the police when all of the people in my party will be able to leave Bruges."

"Of course, Sir Richard. Please convey what I have told you to Ms Duff. She is a very famous person in our department."

8

Hélène Novikova, as seemed to be her habit, was late. Dagmar, wearing a bright blue frock and colourful jacket and scarf, had avoided any sign of mourning in her dress or countenance. She was sitting in a corner of the lounge flipping through a copy of Paris *Vogue*. Helga Müeller materialised shortly after Elspeth reached the lobby, although Elspeth had not been able to reach her by phone to arrange a time for the shopping expedition. Still, Helga seemed eager to join the group when she heard the plans.

"I expect I never will see my daughter again," she said with a chuckle. "But Jean Luc is a handsome boy. I do not blame Kristin. She was taught by the nuns and I think likes her new freedom from them. It could be a Romeo and Juliet romance, as my husband and the Novikovs are not on good terms."

Dagmar caught Elspeth's eyes and shrugged. Elspeth wondered at what. Helga Müeller was undoubtedly warm-hearted, and certainly a romance between Kristin and Jean Luc did not concern Dagmar. But why Dagmar's disdainful gesture? What possible difference could it make to her? Elspeth once again thought that she did not like Dagmar.

Twenty minutes after the appointed time of their meeting Hélène appeared. She was dressed conservatively but expensively in black, which set her in contrast to Dagmar's peacock blue frock and Frau

Müeller's practical woollen suit. Elspeth was glad that she had chosen a grey tweed skirt and long jacket, which did not clash with the other members of her group. A discerning eye would recognise the fineness of the cut of Elspeth's sober choice.

Elspeth had made enquiries about the finest shops in Bruges, surmising that at least two of her three companions would prefer shopping for clothing and that the third would come along because of her happy disposition.

No sooner had they left the hotel than Elspeth spotted the two men shadowing Dagmar. Elspeth reached in the pocket of her coat where she had put a small camera. She was determined to get digital images of the men before the afternoon was out. At first she did not mention their presence to Dagmar. Elspeth wondered if she should confront the men directly but deferred her decision until later in the afternoon. She could possibly speak to them without the other women noticing. If they were in Alexandre de Saint Phalle's employ, as Dagmar had suggested, did they know that he was dead? And if they were not his henchmen, what then?

Elspeth watched Hélène and Dagmar. Their greeting was polite but stiff. When they left the hotel, Hélène let Dagmar go first through the door followed by Helga and Elspeth took up the rear. The weather had cleared, and the blue sky promised no further rain.

Elspeth became so fixed on the men following Dagmar that she forgot her duty as Richard's wife. Dagmar came up to her as the other two women entered a shop displaying lace and silk scarves.

"Elspeth, you seem distracted."

Elspeth bit her lower lip. "Sorry. Let's go into the shop. Then I want you to look through the window. Do you see the man with the black jacket and baseball cap? Do you recognise him?"

Dagmar laughed. "Are you playing sleuth?" she asked in a way that annoyed Elspeth.

Elspeth had no idea if the two men following Dagmar had anything to do with her husband's death or if they represented any danger to Dagmar, but Elspeth could not dismiss their potential for harm. As much as she disliked Dagmar, she could not shirk her duty to the Kennington Organisation or her obligation to Richard.

"He's one of the men I saw in Paris when we met at Hermès," Elspeth said.

"I thought you said there were two men," Dagmar said peering out of the window. She squinted. Elspeth wondered if she were short-sighted.

"Have you seen the man before?" Elspeth asked.

Dagmar frowned. "It's hard to tell with the baseball cap. He looks vaguely familiar."

At that moment the man took off the cap and ran his hands over his short black hair, which for the moment was parted in the middle. Dagmar narrowed her eyes again. She glanced sideways at Elspeth. She opened her mouth as if to speak and then shut it again. Then she shook her head.

Elspeth watched Dagmar. Why was she denying any knowledge of the man whom she apparently knew?

"Are you sure you don't recognise him?"

"Shall we join the other ladies and look at the

lace?" Dagmar said.

"You go on. I'll be with you in a moment."

Elspeth was glad that the Kennington Organisation had provided a decent but small camera. She hoped the glass of the shop window would not obscure the image. She took five shots and checked them. Only one caught the man's face fully. He had olive skin, dark eyes and a beak of a nose. His eyebrows grew together. He could have been Italian or Spanish. Elspeth guessed him to be about thirty years old, but in Elspeth's middle age the young looked younger and younger. And he definitely resembled the man on the rue du Faubourg Saint-Honoré.

The man slipped away.

When the women left the shop, Elspeth watched for the second man she had seen in Paris. She could not see him even though the streets were not crowded. A group of tourists listening to a guide extol the virtues of the old city of Bruges in German passed. Then Elspeth saw him, tagging along. He was out of place in the ageing group, although he had a camera slung around his neck. It was the rucksack that gave him away—and the wrap-around mirrored sunglasses.

Throughout the afternoon Elspeth watched the two men carry out their surveillance dance. First one cut in and then the other. They changed their appearances slightly each time with a cap, a jacket, or a change in hairstyle, and found clever places to stop and hide when the ladies moved in and out of the shops. Elspeth was never able to get a clear photograph of the second man, but she got two more credible ones of the first one. She would have Frans Bootds print the three clear shots out for her and circulate them to the concierge staff and the doormen at the hotel.

Only Helga bought anything, which she explained would make wonderful gifts for her half-blind grandmother who was approaching ninety-five. Elspeth hoped these purchases reflected no judgement on the quality of the lace, which was exquisite. The other women browsed but were not tempted. Dagmar seemed slightly bored, her mind undoubtedly on other things. But throughout the afternoon she showed no signs of grieving.

They returned to the hotel after stopping for tea in an open-air plaza. The clock above the receptionist showed it was now half-past five. The women were about to take the lift to the suites when Elspeth saw her husband coming out of the back rooms with Frans Bootds. Richard motioned her over to where they were standing.

As Elspeth left the women, Helga Müeller turned to Dagmar. "We have not talked all afternoon. Come to our suite for a drink before dinner please. At six-thirty?"

Dagmar looked directly at the German woman. Elspeth could not read the exchange between the two of them. She assumed that Helga had offered the invitation as a kindness, but the expression on Dagmar's face was hostile and unfriendly, which Elspeth would have expected. Dagmar was such an enigma.

Elspeth had no time to speculate further. Calling out to the women that dinner was at half-past seven, she hurried across the lobby and joined Richard and Frans.

Richard spoke to her in low tones and explained what the police had reported.

"So the tie was final the murder weapon," Elspeth said. "I wonder why the murderer used Alexandre's tie. Is it some sort of message? Dagmar bought a blue tie at Hermès when I saw her there. Was it the same one?"

Neither Frans nor Richard had an answer.

"Keep us informed, Frans. Does anyone cover for you at night?" Elspeth asked.

"Only the woman who monitors the security cameras. She calls me if there is any problem. I live nearby."

"Have her let me know too about anything unusual, anything at all. Also have her call me if any member of our party moves about during the night," Elspeth said. All Kennington hotels had security cameras that monitored all the public space, the corridors in the guest area, the public entrances and exits and the employee areas. No guest could leave their room without security knowing of it. Only those in the guest rooms escaped the prying nose of the closed-circuit cameras. Lord Kennington was adamant about the security of his hotels, but he ordered the tapes destroyed soon afterwards to protect the privacy of his guests. Elspeth had utilised the tapes before, however, when there was malevolence about.

"Also, Frans, I took some photographs today," Elspeth said. "I will email them to you as soon as I return to our rooms. I want all your staff to be on alert to see if the man in the photographs is lingering outside the hotel or comes into the lobby. What time do you leave?"

"At six. I will see you get the photographs before that."

When Frans Bootds left them, Elspeth said to Richard. "Do you need a breath of air after your meetings all day?" Then she whispered, "I want to talk to you about what I learned today."

As they left the hotel, the wind caught her hair and sent it merrily about her face. They stood at the edge of the canal, and Richard reached up and brushed her hair back from her face. His tender gesture sent a surge of warmth through her and somehow made things right, despite all that was happening around them. She looked up at his long, thin face and saw that all was well between them and past difficulties forgiven.

Elspeth launched into her tale of Dagmar's surveillance that afternoon. "The men shadowing Dagmar were obvious but she shrugged them off. Do you think Alexandre always had Dagmar followed?"

"It's likely," Richard said. "It may have been for her safety and not her waywardness. Does Dagmar strike you as a loose woman? I have known her for several years and think not. Men fall in love with her beautiful face, but I have never seen her reciprocate."

"I may be oversensitive after the murder, but I keep feeling Dagmar is at the centre of it."

"And not de Saint Phalle's business activities?"

Richard relayed the comments from Ulrich and Viktor regarding Alexandre's supposedly nefarious activities.

"Do you believe them?" Elspeth asked.

"Not completely, but why would both Müeller and Novikov think de Saint Phalle was dealing in the illegal transport of nuclear fuel if there was no truth in it?"

Elspeth shook her head. Richard smiled down at her and touched her cheek. "What are you thinking, my foxy one?"

"We have three separate reasons for Alexandre's murder," she said, smiling back at Richard. How glorious it was to trust him again after the fiasco on Lewis.

"Three? I thought there were only two— Alexandre's complicated business dealings and the personal entanglements of his wife."

"Or simply a random act," Elspeth said. Such a thing was always a possibility. "But if that's the case, how did the murderer get into the trash enclosure behind the hotel and then get away? Perhaps you are right and there are only two reasons. Which makes all those remaining of our party suspects except one."

"Who are you excluding?"

"Helga Müeller. To date she has no motive."

"You said you had not talked to her. If you do, perhaps you'll find a reason she might want to kill Alexandre. Frau Müeller seems approachable enough. She may give you more insight about her husband's relationship to Novikov and de Saint Phalle."

"What concerns me, and often does, is that no one is speaking the whole truth. Did you think, Dickie, when you brought the three men and their wives together, that the result might be murder?"

"Usually it's you, my dearest, that gets me involved

with murder," he said with a little laugh. "Now the tables are turned. But let's discuss strategy. The sooner we find the reason for the murder, the sooner we all can leave here. We have a unique position to question our four suspects. Let's watch their interaction at dinner. It may provide some insight."

Kristin and Jean Luc did not appear at dinner, but the others did. Elspeth noticed that Dagmar had not changed out of her peacock blue frock, but Hélène had changed from black to brilliant mauve, as if in competition with Dagmar's gaudy but chic fashion statement. Helga had changed from the comfortable tweeds to an equally comfortable-looking silk suit.

Richard had made arrangements for them to eat in an alcove off the main dining room, so that they could order from the hotel menu but converse with a degree of privacy. He had been sensitive enough to ask for a round table so there was no distinction of place. Elspeth and Richard discussed the seating arrangement beforehand. Elspeth sat between Viktor and Dagmar, Richard between Dagmar and Hélène, leaving Ulrich beside his wife and opposite Dagmar.

Conversation began generally. The weather and prospects for it being clear the next day occupied their time after they all ordered. No one mentioned the murder. Perhaps it was not a suitable dinner topic, but it must have been on everyone's mind. The dinner arrived punctually, as it always did in a Kennington hotel dining room, with one waiter for each guest. As the seven around the table began to eat, conversation languished.

Elspeth looked up at Richard and wondered if he was expecting her to take the lead as hostess. He returned her look with an expectant smile. It must have been the same smile he gave to Lady Marjorie multiple times over their thirty years of marriage. Elspeth found this almost unconscious gesture on his part unnerving. She felt she was expected to be the diplomatic wife again, a role she increasingly disliked. Why had she agreed with such alacrity to this weekend in Bruges? One could always discuss the wonders of the food, but that would get Elspeth no closer to the murderer. Yet this was no place for interrogation.

Elspeth gave Richard what she hoped was a look crying for help. Her grandmother had taught her to talk to the person to one side of her for one course and then during the next course turn to the person on her other side. Since meals in the twenty-first century abbreviated courses to three or four at the most, Elspeth wondered if this rule still applied. She decided to make her own rules and turned to Dagmar, leaving Viktor to Helga.

Children were always a safe topic, but it was exhausted before the starters were finished. Dagmar fell silent. Was this the time to turn to Viktor and let Richard take over with Dagmar? But he was deep in conversation with Helga discussing sailing. Ulrich seemed interested in their conversation but was adding nothing. Was he merely avoiding joining in his wife's cheerful inanities? Elspeth glanced briefly at Viktor who was smiling at the talkative Helga. Elspeth had no choice but to continue her efforts with Dagmar.

Dagmar's face did not move. She stared across the

table at Helga but did not appear to be listening to her. Elspeth remembered the day her fiancé had been killed at Cambridge almost forty years before. She recalled the frozen feeling of loss inside. Yet as she watched Dagmar, she could not see any true anguish. Dagmar's eyes were filled with intensity, but Elspeth could not read the reason behind them. A sharp memory perhaps? Something about Alexandre that had nothing to do with Helga Müeller's chatter?

Elspeth's speculations were interrupted by the arrival of the main course. Masterfully Richard turned from Helga and Ulrich Müeller to Dagmar, who looked politely to him. Elspeth watched her husband's skill in bringing Dagmar out of her shell. Soon she was responding politely to Richard's questions.

Elspeth turned to Viktor. He glanced back at Dagmar and raised an eyebrow.

"She is not sad that Alexandre is gone, I think," he said in a hushed tone.

Elspeth pressed her lips together. "What makes you say that?"

Elspeth had not noticed before that Viktor Novikov had small, spattered acne scars along his cheeks.

"Dagmar despised Alexandre," he said.

"Are you sure?"

"Lady Munro, I circulate frequently in the top echelons of business and diplomacy in Europe. Your husband and I have met on occasion, but before this weekend I never had the pleasure of being introduced to you. I see you're watching everybody, and I am too. I can guess that you love your husband and that Ulrich

Müeller tolerates his wife, but before de Saint-Phalle died, there was friction between him and Dagmar."

And I wonder what your relationship is with your wife, Elspeth thought.

Viktor went on. "Dagmar tends to be outspoken when she is slightly tipsy. Alexandre detested this. Dagmar didn't seem to care at all. In fact she seemed to delight in saying things that would provoke Alexandre. He would take her away when she became like this, but frequently the damage was done. Dagmar seems to be watching her drink tonight perhaps because she no longer has anyone to annoy. Don't be deceived by her beauty. She uses people's response to her as a weapon to punish her husband."

"But why would she want to punish him?" Elspeth asked, hoping her voice was quiet enough that the others would not hear.

"Because she thought he had been responsible for her first husband's death."

Elspeth frowned, which seemed to prompt Viktor to tell the story.

"Pedar Johanssen, her first husband, and Alexandre were great friends and often skied together. Dagmar was deeply in love with Pedar, and Alexandre was deeply in love with Dagmar. About four winters ago, when Dagmar and Pedar's children were very young, Pedar was lost under an avalanche in the French Alps. Alexandre was skiing with him but came away unharmed."

"But that proves nothing," Elspeth said.

"No, as you say, it proves nothing. Dagmar was left

with her sons. Alexandre quickly stepped in. Dagmar married him but she never trusted him."

"You seem to know Dagmar well," Elspeth said.

"As well as anyone still alive I expect. No, we were not lovers. But I have been her confidant for many years. It has worked to my advantage in business. I was Pedar's friend too."

"Am I being presumptuous to ask if Dagmar hated Alexandre enough to do him harm?" Elspeth asked.

Viktor laughed out loud, causing the others at the table to look up.

"I have no idea, Lady Munro," he answered and changed the topic.

The meal passed uneventfully after this, but Viktor's words had roused Elspeth's curiosity, Had Dagmar killed Alexandre? She might have if Viktor's words were true.

After dinner as they were leaving the dining room Viktor suggested they all move on to a bar outside the hotel for a nightcap. Hélène perked up but the Müellers declined.

Dagmar said, "How inappropriate, Viktor," and turned to the lift.

Elspeth caught Richard's eye and he shook his head slightly. Elspeth pleaded fatigue and joined her husband. They took the lift with Dagmar, leaving the Müellers behind. Dagmar did not speak as they rose above the lobby and wished them a curt good night as she reached her floor, which was one below Elspeth and Richard's.

When they reached their suite, Elspeth flung open the door to the narrow deck, although the room was perfectly heated. Below she heard a reedy woman's voice singing.

"Sur le pont d'Avignon
On y danse, on y danse
Sur le pont d'Avignon
On y danse tout en rond.
Les belles dames font comme ça
Et puis encore comme ça.

Sur le pont d'Avignon
On y danse, on y danse
Sur le pont d'Avignon
On y danse tout en rond."

The beautiful women go this way and that way, Elspeth translated. The childhood song was followed by an hysterical laugh. Elspeth could not tell if grief or relief caused it, but it definitely was Dagmar who was singing on her balcony below.

9

In the middle of the night, 02:17 on the clock at Elspeth's bedside, the phone gave out persistent bleats. Elspeth reached for it instinctively. On the other end of the line a female voice said, "Security here. Ms Duff, Madame de Saint Phalle just left her room. She keeps looking round, as if she wants to make sure she is alone. She is approaching the lift now. She has a coat with her."

Elspeth sat bolt upright. "Thank you. I have my mobile which I will keep on vibrate. Keep me posted." She gave her mobile number to the woman from security and tore the bedcovers back. Richard rose from his side of the bed. He yawned.

"What's happening?" he asked.

Elspeth explained. "I'm going after her."

"Who?"

"Dagmar."

"Not alone," he said.

Both dressed hurriedly. Elspeth normally carried dark casual clothes and trainers with her for this sort of emergency as well as for an occasional foray into the exercise room, but since she had not anticipated being on duty over the weekend, she settled for the trouser suit and flat shoes in which she had travelled. She glanced over at Richard, who was struggling with a navy-blue pullover that Elspeth recognised from the few times she had been on his boat.

She laughed although she did not feel any levity.

"Do you care for an evening stroll, my dearest?"

"Lead on," he said.

"Dagmar will have left the hotel by now, if she is up to some sort of mischief," Elspeth said. "Why do you suppose she was acting so furtively?"

"Take my arm, Elspeth. I can say you are suffering from jet lag, couldn't sleep and needed a brisk walk."

"With one hour time change? Who are you going to tell that to? The doorman is too well trained to ask."

"Anyone else who wants to know," he said with a chuckle.

The doorman did not ask, but he proved valuable. He obviously knew who Elspeth was.

"Did you see Madame de Saint Phalle leave the hotel?" Elspeth asked.

"Yes, Ms Duff. She left just a moment ago."

"Did you see anyone else? Was she joined by anyone?"

A night doorman's duties in a small hotel like the Kennington Bruges could not be particularly stimulating. Yet Lord Kennington insisted that his night help while on duty be alert. The doorman drew one of the photographs Elspeth had taken earlier from an inner pocket of his uniform.

"When Madame de Saint Phalle left, this man followed her. He had been waiting across the street outside the hotel for the last hour or so. When he arrived, he spoke to a younger man, who had been waiting in the same spot all evening."

"Thank you, Jan," Elspeth said, eyeing his name badge. "I want you to watch to see if anyone else comes out of the building, particularly the Müellers or the Novikovs. Do you know them?" This last question was superfluous, as the staff in the front of the hotel were required to know all the guests.

"Of course, Ms Duff."

"Ring security if they do come out," Elspeth said. "Now, Dickie, how about that walk you promised me."

Despite the late hour, the streets around the hotel were not completely dark. The ornate streetlamps along the way and at the crossroads gave off beams of light that reflected on the wet cobblestones and sent herringbone patterns across the ripples which the wind had caused in the nearby canal. Pathways in the narrow grassy strip between the road and the water were lit by low lights which reflected on the barrier wall.

They crossed the deserted street and followed Dagmar along the city streets until she entered a large park. At first they could not see her, but, as their eyes grew accustomed to the half-light along the path lined with trees and benches, Richard pointed across a flower bed surrounded by low growing hedge. Dagmar was ahead of them. She was walking swiftly, and the man who was her shadow was following closely behind. She was dressed in dark clothing, but her head was uncovered and her light blonde hair unmistakable. He was dressed in a black tracksuit and trainers, which had a reflective edge on the heels, marking his steps behind her.

Dagmar turned abruptly and faced him. He nearly ran into her.

He was at least a half a foot taller than she, yet she

did not seem afraid. She raised her finger at him, the way a schoolmistress would, and began to shake it up and down.

Elspeth and Richard moved nearer to them but stayed in the shadows. They could hear Dagmar's voice. Elspeth could not understand them although she could hear the words. She turned to Richard, who whispered "*Schweizerdeutsch,* Swiss German."

"What are they saying?"

Richard shook his head. "I can only understand some of the words. I think she is accusing him of something. He seems contrite."

"Even his body language tells that," Elspeth said with a small chuckle. "I wouldn't want to be at the receiving end."

Dagmar seemed finally to make amends with the man. She turned her face to the light of one of the high lampposts. In the illumination her beauty shone out. The man was obviously enraptured. Dagmar spoke quickly to him and then moved so that her back was facing Elspeth and Richard. They could no longer hear her words. They felt emboldened to walk out into the lit path and follow Dagmar and the man whose voices were now muffled. The two of them stopped by a stone torso of a woman identified as Koningin Astrid. Soon they were in deep conversation but spoke softly. No hint of their words was blown back to where Richard and Elspeth stood in a deep shadow. Dagmar and the man spoke for several minutes, back and forth, like a ping-pong volley. Sometimes he shook his head and at others nodded. Finally they seemed to reach some sort of an agreement.

Dagmar held out her hand and shook his, and then he sprinted away. She turned to a nearby pond and stared into it for a long time. Then she turned back towards the hotel.

Richard took Elspeth by the arm, his finger to his lips. Elspeth could think on only one way to hide their identity. She threw her arms around Richard and kissed him. By the time they broke from their embrace, Dagmar was past them. They followed her and watched her enter the hotel. Elspeth hoped her ruse had worked.

The doorman was obviously waiting for them.

"I hope you enjoyed your walk Sir Richard and Lady Munro," he said.

They nodded and smiled but did not reply.

When Elspeth was roused in the morning by the wake-up call she had requested the night before, she pulled Richard's arms around her and sighed.

"Wouldn't it be nice if we were here on our own and there had been no murder?" she said.

He kissed the back of her neck. "Dearest Elspeth, murder does seem to follow you round like an unseen spectre."

"Mmm," she said. "But Alexandre de Saint Phalle did die here, and I must get up and deal with it. What are your plans today, Dickie?" she asked, rolling over and returning his kiss.

"You tempt me to stay in bed, but I could hardly justify that to the European Commission. Suppose I wrote in my report: Saturday morning I made love to Lord Kennington's roving security advisor."

"That might spice up the report a bit," Elspeth said.

He brushed his fingers along her nose, tapped its tip and laughed. "I rang the security office in Brussels yesterday to tell them what happened, but it was after four in the afternoon on a Friday and everyone seems to have gone home. So we have until Monday to clarify things. I plan to question Müeller and Novikov more thoroughly about de Saint Phalle. I think I will do it one-to-one. And you?"

"I want to find out what Dagmar was up to last night."

"Do you think she will tell you?"

"I'm not sure. I still don't understand Dagmar. Her beauty is distracting."

"And the other women?"

"I think I'll tackle Frau Müeller first. She seems the most detached from everything that has happened here and may therefore have some unemotional insights. I'm already tired of Hélène's barbs."

Elspeth and Richard found the Müellers just as they were emerging from the breakfast room. Elspeth whispered to Richard, "I'll see if Helga will have coffee with me in the lounge. I can get a bite to eat later."

Helga beamed at Elspeth's invitation. They settled in a corner where they could not be overheard. Helga ordered a hot chocolate and Elspeth a cappuccino.

"Are we off on another excursion this morning?" Helga asked.

"If anyone is up to one," Elspeth said. Because of her lack of sleep, Elspeth hoped no one was, but the look on Helga's face said otherwise. "Neither Madame de Saint Phalle not Madame Novikova is down yet," Elspeth added.

"*Ach*, that's so. I never sleep in. One wastes a perfectly good day by getting out of bed late."

Unless, thought Elspeth, one was out until all hours of the night. She was thankful the hot drinks came. Elspeth sipped hers and stifled a yawn.

"Frau Müeller, last night was not the time to talk about Alexandre de Saint Phalle's death, since Madam de Saint Phalle was present. But would you mind if I asked you a few questions this morning?"

"Of course you may ask," Helga said.

"Do you know the de Saint Phalles well?"

"Not well but a little."

"Tell me about them."

"One does not trust Dagmar with a secret. She likes to gossip. And men always talk to her. Her beauty always attracts men, but I think she does not like it."

"Doesn't like her beauty?"

"It caused trouble for her with Alexandre."

"Was he jealous?"

"He was always watching her. I would not like that from my Ulrich. A husband must trust his wife."

"Did he have reason to be jealous?"

Helga took a long swallow of her chocolate and then smiled crookedly. "I think not. Dagmar may be indiscreet with words, but I think she is—was—faithful to Alexandre. He did not think so. Many men had ideas about Dagmar. But I have no knowledge that she ever took up with anyone except Alexandre after Pedar died."

"You knew Pedar?"

"*Ja*. He was a good man, but he, how do you say, strayed."

"Strayed? Had lovers?"

"*Ja*."

"Are you sure?"

"*Ja*. Not women lovers."

"He was gay?"

"Everyone knew this after a while. He was very handsome. He and Dagmar made a beautiful couple and had two fine boys. I do not think Dagmar knew when she married Pedar, but later he was very open about it. I think she was relieved when Pedar was killed in the avalanche."

"Did she marry Alexandre on the rebound?"

Helga laughed deeply. "*Nein*, Lady Munro. She married Alexandre because she no longer loved Pedar. Dagmar loved Alexandre."

"Loved Alexandre," Elspeth said, parrot-like. "What was Alexandre like?"

"Alexandre? He came from a Russian family with ties in East Germany."

"Yes, I had heard."

"He wanted no one to know, but I tricked him."

"How is that?"

"He said he did not speak German. I said something behind his back, in complicated German. Something to do with his business and his cheating. He turned to me with a very red and angry face. Wasn't I clever?"

Not particularly Elspeth thought. Helga had used a common ruse.

"Why is his being a Russian important?" Elspeth asked. "Did it make a difference in his relationship with Dagmar? Did she know?"

"She must have."

"How long were they married?"

"Three, four years, I do not remember."

"And?"

"Alexandre lied about his background because he did not want people to know about his business dealings with the Russian Federation. He used his family's background to make connections. Ulrich used to swear about it because he thought Alexandre knew members of the Russian underground and had access to plutonium. Ulrich says Alexandre used his contacts to bring the fuel to the west illegally. But I do not know anything about this."

"But you know about Dagmar."

"*Ja*. I think everybody knows about Dagmar."

"What do you think she will do?"

Helga laughed again. "Hélène Novikova will tell you Dagmar loves pigs and will go back to her family farm in Denmark. I think not so. Dagmar will soon find a new stepfather for her boys. She likes being the centre of attention."

"Frau Müeller, I think the others will not be coming down soon. Will you forgive me if I do not join you this morning? I didn't sleep well last night. I'll let the guide know you will be alone, unless Kristin and Jean Luc wish to join you."

"Those young people do not think about an old person like me, but I will take the guide. I want to see the church with the Michelangelo statue and I do not think Dagmar or Hélène will."

Elspeth rose and made her way to the breakfast room. Richard had left and there was no sign of any other of Richard's guests.

Elspeth ate quickly and lightly. She left the room and was about to turn into the security office, when a young male voice she did not recognise spoke to her.

"Lady Munro, may we speak to you?"

Elspeth turned to find Jean Luc with Kristin beside him.

"Have you had breakfast?," she asked.

Both nodded.

"We have been walking about the town since seven o'clock and had coffee at a café along one of the main canals. I didn't want my mother interfering," Kristin said.

"My mother would not be up, so there was no difficulty there," Jean Luc said with a grin. "But Kristin and I have been talking, and we think there is something you and Sir Richard should know. May we speak to you in private?"

"Come into the back rooms of the hotel," Elspeth said. She led them behind the reception desk, past the monitors, and into a small conference room off the security office. A marker board on the wall had the floor plans of the hotel and the names of various hall porters marked in the locations they were to staff that day.

Jean Luc's eyes widened. "Are we allowed in here?"

Kristin became still.

"It's the safest place I can think of," Elspeth said and explained her position in the Kennington Organisation. "What is it you wanted to say?"

"It is about the murder of Monsieur de Saint Phalle. We saw something that could be important," Jean Luc began.

"We are not sure," Kristin added.

Elspeth looked at the two young people. Murder was never pleasant, but in her experience, death was easier for people as they grew older.

"Tell me about it," Elspeth said as gently as she could manage.

Jean Luc looked at Kristin as if seeking her permission to speak. "Yesterday morning we walked together towards the Koningin Astrid Park. We did not want to go with the older people on the tour. It was raining on and off. During one rain, we took shelter under the bandstand which was covered. When we were waiting for the shower to clear, we saw two men talking. They were speaking *Schweizerdeutsch*. I do not understand this language, but Kristin could understand most of it. Tell Lady Munro, Kristin."

"I could make out most of what they said. The older one, whose name is Raffaello, was begging the younger one, named Giorgio, to help him with 'her'. Raffaello seemed upset, but Giorgio kept saying no. He said he did not want to do what Raffaello was asking him. Raffaello said something I could not completely understand, but something about a brother's love. Giorgio then went away. We thought he was angry. He got wet in the rain but did not seem to care. Raffaello shouted at him that he was a coward."

"You said Raffaello was upset. Was he angry too?" Elspeth asked. Angry enough to commit murder, she thought but did not say.

Kristin glanced over at Jean Luc, and then continued. "No. It was more like they had a fight about his girlfriend. That kind of upset you know. At one point he said, 'I love her, don't you understand' or words to that effect. Upset like that."

"Where did this man Raffaello go after the harsh words?"

"He went towards the hotel and Giorgio followed him," Jean Luc said. "That is why we thought Sir Richard ought to know. In case there is any danger to our parents."

"Did Raffaello have any weapon? A gun? A stick or cane?"

Both the young people shook their heads.

"Do any of your parents have any worries about their own safety?" Elspeth asked.

Jean Luc pursed his lips. "My father is Russian. He fears that the Russian security police, the old KGB, may be watching him. He is very careful when he returns to Russia to do everything, how do you say, by the book. My mother laughs at him sometimes and says he is paranoid."

"Do you think so?" Elspeth asked.

Jean Luc seemed to relax. "Not my father. He's fearless, I think. He escaped from the Soviet Union when he was younger. My mother helped him. She was very brave when she was younger, but I think my father's money has made her lazy."

"And you, Fraulein Müeller? Do you think there is danger to your parents?"

Kristin shook her head. "My mother tends to poke her nose into everything. But danger to my parents? I think no. They are too happy to attract for danger. I wish they would pretend to be less *lustig*, jolly. Sometimes it is embarrassing to me. My mother drags me all over Europe when *Vater* is away. My parents have small flats in Paris, London, Rome and a small villa in Portugal near Oporto. My mother says we own the properties and must use them. I think it is a waste of money to have so many homes. I prefer the south of France, but we have no home there."

She looked shyly at Jean Luc as she said this. Elspeth suspected this preference was new because she remembered the Novikovs lived in Marseilles.

"But you both think that Raffaello poses a threat. Why do you think so?"

"In the past I have seen him watching the hotel. He would walk past it and then turn around and walk past it the other way."

"Describe him," Elspeth said. Now she was curious.

Jean Luc took the lead "He looks Italian. His name suggests that anyway. But he may be Swiss since they spoke in Swiss German. He had green eyes. I noticed them particularly. He was maybe one hundred seventy centimetres or so tall, my height, and slender."

"His eyebrows grew together, which made him look sinister," Kristin added.

Elspeth froze inside. Raffaello must be one of the

men who were following Dagmar, the one she had spoken to the night before in the park. Now at least she had a name for him. The other man must be his brother, named Giorgio. That was a start. She wondered if Dagmar knew who they were or if she had approached Raffaello last night because Elspeth had told her that she was being followed and wanted to confront the men who were doing so. Was Raffaello still about? Elspeth could approach him, she supposed, and ask him what he had seen at the time of the murder. What excuse could she give? Or should she tell the police? It might be best to talk to Raffaello first.

"Have either one of you seen the two men before?"

"I saw them at the airport when we arrived in Brussels," Jean Luc said.

"Did you arrive at the same time, Kristin?"

"We came in on a different flight. We met Jean Luc's father in the lobby when we arrived," Kristin said.

"Jean Luc, what were the two men doing in the airport?" Elspeth asked.

"I only remember Raffaello's green eyes. They were staring at Madame de Saint Phalle." He reddened. "Any man would stare at her. Raffaello was not the only one," he added.

Kristin frowned and glanced at him sideways.

"Did you see the two men outside the hotel this morning?" Elspeth asked, amused by Kristin's disparaging look.

"I wasn't paying attention," Kristin said.

"I may have seen them. Like Kristin, I did not pay much attention."

"If you think of anything else, let me know. I'm responsible, you see, not only to all of you but also to Lord Kennington, who is the owner of the Kennington hotels. He doesn't like things like this going on near his hotels," Elspeth said. She stood and smiled at them.

"This is amazing," Jean Luc said as they left the security office and walked past the monitors. I had no idea you could see everything that goes on in the hotel."

"It's for the guests' protection only," Elspeth said with a kind laugh. "We don't monitor for anything else."

"Have you ever used this to catch someone doing something illegal?" Kristin asked.

Elspeth smiled. "Occasionally."

When they reached the lobby, Elspeth took her leave of the two young people and made her way to the breakfast room for another cup of coffee. She wished she had Richard to talk to but assumed he had long since disappeared into the conference room. She did not know what time he would be through with his meetings with the two other men in the party. Perhaps she could best use her time to find and question Raffaello, but her plans went astray when Dagmar dashed into the room.

"Oh, Elspeth," she cried. "I am in mortal danger."

10

Before getting his breakfast Richard watched Elspeth take Frau Müeller by the arm and make her way out into the lounge. He wished he knew which part she was playing, his wife or security advisor to Lord Kennington. She was ambivalent about the former role and preferred the latter. The murder gave her an out, but still he wanted her to be comfortable beside him in diplomatic situations. He thought about his first wife for a few moments and sighed. Marjorie would not relish a murder the way Elspeth appeared to do. If only he could convince Elspeth that she was doing magnificently at his side, but he could feel her tension at the meals they ate together with his group. He had no idea why. Elspeth's manners were impeccable. She stepped in when things became awkward, perhaps only slightly less quickly than Marjorie would have, but Marjorie had been trained from birth to be a diplomat's wife.

Richard remembered Elspeth's youth, her exuberance, and reckless spirit. Even Elspeth's first marriage had been unconventional. But one could not tell now. He only knew of her current discomfort because he had known her for so long. Despite her normally excellent posture, her back had straightened when she had led Helga Müeller into the lobby and the tone of her manner had changed from banal politeness to competence. Her eyes seemed to take on a new lustre. No one else would have noticed the change but Richard did and relaxed. He was ready to face Herr Müeller.

Ulrich like Richard watched his wife. Richard could not read his expression. Was he checking up on her? Why?

"Join me while I have breakfast," Richard said.

Ulrich turned from his wife and headed towards the buffet. Richard was grateful that Ulrich was willing to fill his plate once again so that they could have a one-to-one conversation. They found a quiet table near a window overlooking the canal.

"I do like Brugghe," Ulrich said, giving the German name to the city. "So few cars. One can look across a street and see what is on the other side." He took a large mouthful of sausage.

Richard buttered his toast and added thick-cut marmalade, which he knew was especially made in Dundee for the Kennington hotels. Being married to an employee of the Kennington Organisation had many compensations.

"Herr Müeller, our negotiations here are important to the European Commission's understanding of the precious metals trade, but I feel you, Novikov and I cannot proceed comfortably until we have cleared up Alexandre de Saint Phalle's murder. It will always be in the room with us until we do."

Ulrich Müeller bobbed his head up and down several times. "*Ja*. I agree."

"May I ask you some questions before Novikov joins us?"

Müeller nodded again and put down his knife and

fork.

"How well did you know Alexandre de Saint Phalle?" Richard asked.

"He was a rival in business, so I watched closely everything he did. I did not know him personally only in business. We went to many of the same functions for people in our trade, but I did not know his wife well."

"Do you know Novikov personally?"

"A bit more than de Saint Phalle."

"How is that?"

"He came to Hamburg to visit my operations there. At one time we talked about merging our firms, but it did not work. Viktor and Hélène stayed with me and Helga at our home outside Hamburg, and we became acquainted a bit."

"Do you think Novikov had anything to do with de Saint Phalle's murder? They didn't seem on good terms yesterday morning."

"Viktor can be, what is the word, volatile. That is one of the reasons I decided that our partnership would not work well. Also Viktor is Russian. I do not know if he can be trusted. We Germans do not think the Russians are always honest."

"Do you think Novikov's anger towards de Saint Phalle could have led to murder? De Saint Phalle's death involved a beating. Do you think Novikov could have been responsible?"

Ulrich cut into another sausage before answering. "When Viktor visited us in Hamburg, he said he did not like de Saint Phalle and suspected him of illegal dealings. I never knew of any, but Viktor was certain that Alexandre used contacts in the Russian underworld. I took Viktor's word for it."

"Then Novikov's possible attack on de Saint Phalle yesterday had some substance?"

"I do not know from my own knowledge."

"Do you think there was anything between Novikov and Madame de Saint Phalle?"

"Perhaps Viktor made up this—to provoke Alexandre. That is like Viktor. But there was bad blood between Alexandre and Viktor. I do not know what caused it."

"Do you think de Saint Phalle's murder had to do with his business or his personal life?"

Ulrich had his mouth full and did not answer at once. He shook his head back and forth and his double chin under his beard waggled.

"I do not know," he said through the bits of food in his mouth.

Richard wanted to believe him. Richard considered himself a good judge of men, and Ulrich Müeller struck him as being above board, or at least as above board as a successful businessman can be in the modern world.

They finished their meal in more general conversation. Ulrich told several amusing stories about his business, which made Richard chuckle. By the time they rose from their meal, Viktor Novikov had not appeared.

Richard said, "It looks like Novikov has once again been lured into having breakfast with his wife in their rooms. Let me call up and see if he ready to join us. I don't want to waste all our time on the murder. We do have other work to do."

As they took the lift to the first floor, Richard asked as casually as he could, "What do you make of Dagmar de Saint Phalle?"

"She is an unhappy woman."

"Why unhappy?"

"Because she cannot settle down. I think something is always bothering her."

Richard wondered at the German's observation. Richard had watched Dagmar several times at diplomatic receptions. He had tried to see beyond her beauty. Because he was so deeply in love with Elspeth, he had no desires in other directions. That Dagmar was unsettled had never occurred to him.

"Are you attracted by her?" Richard asked Ulrich.

Ulrich laughed out loud. "No man is so blind that he cannot see her assets, but I am comfortable with my Helga."

"What do you think is bothering her?"

"Her husband."

"Why do you say that?"

"Whenever I met Dagmar, she was always trying to impress Alexandre, trying to show him that she was clever."

Richard thought of the night at the Belgian Embassy in London and what Elspeth had told him about Dagmar's comment about Mateo. Elspeth had not seen whom Dagmar was addressing, but obviously Dagmar was either gossiping or had another reason for the comment? Was she talking to Alexandre or someone else? If it was Alexandre, was she trying to impress him with her knowledge about Mateo? Damn Mateo, whoever or whatever he or it was. Richard did not like uncertainty.

When they reached the conference room, Viktor Novikov was there, waiting for them. Richard wanted to speak to him alone. He turned to Ulrich.

"Will you give us about fifteen minutes?"

"*Ja*. I will go and see what Helga is doing this morning."

Once alone with Viktor, Richard invited him to have some coffee and they settled at one end of the conference table.

"I want to discuss Alexandre de Saint Phalle with you, so that we can get the question of the murder settled—at least enough that we can continue our discussions without his ghost being present. From your comments yesterday, you obviously knew him personally."

"Unfortunately," Viktor sneered.

"And you did not like him?"

"Not at all, but don't take that as an admission of guilt. I may have not liked him, but I would not have murdered him."

"Who do you think did?"

"Dagmar?"

Richard eyed Viktor. Was his comment meant to be provocative or did he truly believe Dagmar was involved?

"She hardly seems strong enough to have beaten him to death."

"Wasn't he strangled with his tie as well?"

Richard nodded. But how did Viktor know about the tie? He was sure that when he had told the group about the murder that he had not mentioned the tie.

"Are you suggesting that Dagmar was strong enough to attack her husband?"

"Or that she had someone do it for her. A crazed lover?"

Viktor's suggestion sounded devious, Richard thought, but he did not know why.

"So you think Dagmar has that effect on men? Do you have any knowledge that Dagmar has 'crazed lovers'?"

"Dagmar is the most virtuous woman I know, but she is like Helen of Troy. Men want to possess her."

Richard held Viktor's eyes. "Did you?"

"Alexandre may have suggested that yesterday. He was the jealous type. No, I love my wife and she has been too important in my life for me to be unfaithful. She isn't as beautiful or young as Dagmar, and she is the mother of my son, but she helped me escape from the Soviets. Besides, when Dagmar isn't there, Hélène is considered the beauty in the room. But a man can fantasise when Dagmar is about. I think Alexandre knew most men did."

"You suggested that Dagmar might hire assassins. Why? Didn't she have everything she could want in her husband? He gave her a lifestyle that few are fortunate to have."

Viktor roared with laughter. "Poor rich little Dagmar. She had everything but only cared about her sons' welfare and not her own. Everyone said that is

109

why she married Alexandre after her first husband was killed."

"Could she have killed de Saint Phalle because she thought he had been responsible for her first husband's death?"

"Beautiful Dagmar always wanted to be in the middle of things. Now she is," Novikov said without answering Richard's question.

"Is there any reason why de Saint Phalle would have been killed because of his business activities?"

"It's always a possibility. He dealt close to the edge, particularly when he lost a get deal of money several years ago. That's when he got involved with Mateo, I think."

"Would Mateo have killed him?"

"The organisation? Possibly. Mateo is in the shadows all the time to people in our trade. Could the people in Mateo's organisation have killed Alexandre? No one knows enough about them to know for sure. I haven't been very helpful, have I?"

"Where were you after our meeting yesterday morning?"

"I went up to see Hélène."

"Which she will confirm?"

Viktor smiled crookedly.

Richard felt he was getting nowhere. Viktor's cynicism was unproductive. Further probing elicited nothing.

Viktor stood up and poured himself another cup of coffee. Richard scribbled some cryptic notes, enough to remind him of his conversations with both Ulrich and

Viktor. He needed to share the information he had just discovered with Elspeth and see if she could make any sense of it.

11

"Mortal danger?" Elspeth said to the distraught Dagmar.

Dagmar's face lacked makeup and was streaked with tears, although neither condition detracted from her beauty. Instead she seemed to be enhanced by real emotion.

"This!" Dagmar gagged. She held out an envelope engraved with the Kennington hotel logo. The envelope had been ripped open. Inside Elspeth found a piece of ordinary copy paper printed with the words "BE WARNED". The message was computer generated.

Elspeth read the words twice and said, "Where did you get this?"

"Room service brought it up on my breakfast tray."

Elspeth turned over the envelope. There was no name written on the front. She asked, "Did the man from room service say where it came from?"

"I didn't open it until he left," Dagmar mewled.

"I'll find out. But in the meantime, do you have any idea who might have sent it to you? Or what he or she was warning you about?"

"Alexandre," she sobbed.

Elspeth did not like the histrionics in which Dagmar was indulging. Rather than comforting Dagmar, she breathed out audibly. "Warning you about Alexandre or warning you about something to do with his death?"

"Warning me that I am next," she moaned.

"Have you been threatened before?"

Dagmar retracted her lips, bore her straight white teeth and flared her nostrils. Next she frowned. Elspeth was not certain if this was fear or dramatics.

Dagmar was silent for a moment, obviously considering her answer. Elspeth waited.

"Have you?" Elspeth said again.

Finally Dagmar said, "Not directly."

"Indirectly?"

"Alexandre was often," Dagmar said. "Sometimes the threats mentioned the family. I was afraid for my boys."

"And for yourself?"

"If anything happened to me, what would become of my boys?"

"Did you and Alexandre make any provisions for their safety?" Certainly any loving parent would have, Elspeth thought, particularly a family as wealthy as the de Saint Phalles.

"They are guarded in our home in the sixteenth *arrondissement* in Paris. There is always a policeman at the door after Alexandre was shot at three years ago."

Alexandre had been the target of a murderer before, but in what circumstances? Elspeth thought.

"He was coming home from his office," Dagmar said as if reading Elspeth's mind. "The police said it was a random shooting but the next day he received a paper just like this one. The same words."

"In English?" Elspeth asked.

"In French," Dagmar said and translated. *Soyez averti*. That was when Alexandre became worried."

"And the police did nothing?"

"No, they never found who shot at Alexandre, but Alexandre had influence with the chief of police of our district. Many rich and important families live in our building. The chief sent the guards to our house."

"Are the guards still there after all this time?"

"Yes. That is why I can leave Hans and Poul and travel with Alexandre. I feel they are safe. I also thought we were safe here at the hotel, but now I know we are not."

Elspeth took a deep breath. Lord Kennington would be distressed that a guest of his had uttered these words, particularly one prone to gossip. Elspeth was glad that she and Dagmar were out of earshot of any other guests.

"I'll take personal charge of this if I may. Dagmar, stay in your room this morning. I will alert the hall porter on your floor not to leave the hallway outside your room unattended. And don't let anyone in, no one but me. Do you understand? Now let me take you up there."

When they reached Dagmar's suite, Elspeth asked if Dagmar needed anything before she left.

Dagmar shook her head.

"Remember, don't open your door to anyone except me, not even room service or other members of our party," Elspeth said on parting. "I'll be back soon. Try not to worry about the note. It is meant to frighten you, but what it has actually done is alert us. May I keep the note?"

Dagmar docilely nodded to Elspeth, who tucked the note in her jacket pocket. Elspeth had many more questions for Dagmar, but now was not the time to ask them.

When Elspeth made her way back to the breakfast room, she no sooner had set her cup of coffee on her table when a waiter came over to her and presented her with a creamy white and engraved Kennington hotel envelope addressed by computer. 'Lady Monroe', it said.

Noting the misspelling, she tore it open. Inside was a single sheet of white copy paper with the words "BE WARNED."

Elspeth swallowed. Her toast and fruit no longer held any appeal. She pushed them away and rose.

"Is there something wrong with your food," a waiter standing nearby asked.

"No, it's quite up to the usual Kennington standards. But tell me, who gave you this envelope?"

"The concierge brought it to the dining room."

She thanked the waiter and bolted from the room. The concierge was standing at his desk, discussing walking tours with a guest Elspeth did not recognise. Elspeth did not want to seem impatient, but she thought the guest would never settle on which tour to take. She often admired the patience and courtesy of the Kennington hotel concierges, but now was not one of those times.

Finally Elspeth got the concierge's attention. No one was near, so she felt she could speak directly. She held up the envelope.

"Can you tell me who gave this envelope to you?"

The concierge pursed his lips. "It was left on the

counter a few minutes ago. I didn't see who put it there."

"Who was in the lobby at the time?" Elspeth asked.

The concierge looked chagrined. "I stepped out for just a moment. I did not see."

Elspeth knew that Lord Kennington insisted that the concierge's desk be covered at all times.

"I asked the receptionist if she would fill in for me for a moment," he said as if in apology.

Elspeth said nothing about the lapse. Instead she walked over to the reception desk and asked the woman on duty.

"I was keeping an eye on the concierge's desk but also, at this time of the morning we are often busy with checkouts. I didn't see anyone there, Ms Duff, but I may have been distracted."

"Then someone could have passed the desk and left something on the counter?"

The receptionist looked sheepish. "Martinus was gone for only a moment."

Elspeth made her way to the back rooms and sought out Frans Bootds.

"Frans, I want you to find out who gave an envelope to room service to be delivered to Madame de Saint Phalle this morning." She decided not to let the security man in on its contents. "Have you heard anything more from the police?"

"Nothing, Ms Duff."

"When you see the police captain, ask if anyone was lingering about the back of the hotel yesterday afternoon. Get a description if you can."

When Elspeth made her way back up to the rooms

she and Richard shared, she felt an odd sense of relief. Now she was being truly useful and doing something she knew how to do well. She took out her mobile and rang Pamela Crumm in London. Although it was Saturday, Pamela was at her desk.

"Pamela, I don't like this case. I feel a bit of an interloper, having come here under different pretences, as Richard's wife and not a Kennington employee. I'm trying to find a way to deal with Richard's group that combines both roles."

"And having trouble with it, m'friend?" Pamela said. "But you must have known this would happen sometime."

"Honestly, I don't like the dual role. I'm trying to be tactful as Richard's wife, but . . ."

Pamela chuckled. "I thought you were always tactful."

Elspeth groaned. "When I have authority, I can be subtle but also assertive. I'm trying to figure out how to be that here in my professional capacity without Richard making me feel I have overstepped my boundaries."

"I've always found Richard reasonable. I don't understand why you don't. Is it Lady Marjorie's ghost? I thought you had exorcised that."

"I'm sure he's making comparisons."

"He probably is Elspeth. Let him. I assure you that you won't come up short. In the meantime, do you want me to call the manager? Let's see, that's Bernard Debock. I'll tell him you have full authority there to conduct any investigation you see fit."

"A call might help, but the hotel staff all know who

I am and Frans Bootds, the security head here, is being fully cooperative." Elspeth laughed. "It's Richard's guests that concern me."

Elspeth told Pamela of her interviews with Helga Müeller, her daughter, Jean Luc Novikov, and Hélène. Only at the end did she mention the warnings.

"I'm sure you'll get to bottom of all this," Pamela said with more confidence than Elspeth was feeling. "By Monday morning I'm certain I'll be able to tell Eric the case is solved."

With these words Pamela ended the conversation and asked Elspeth to stay in touch. Elspeth was one of the few people in the world who had Pamela's home telephone number and that of her private mobile. Therefore Elspeth had no excuse to exclude Pamela from what was happening in Bruges, and if necessary to rely on her as backup. In the end, their conversation did little to boost Elspeth's mood.

Elspeth glanced at her watch and considered her next move. She needed time alone to think. Slipping on her mackintosh, she went down the back stairs in order to avoid meeting anyone in the lift. She let herself out the kitchen door to the hotel. The door gave out to the rear areas of the hotel, including the rubbish area where Alexandre's body had been found. Elspeth was loath to revisit the scene of the crime but knew it could give her some insight into what happened there on the morning of the murder.

A shower had just passed and the ground was wet. The faint image of the chalk marks that marked Alexandre's last resting place lingered on the tarmac.

Elspeth noted that the entire area was fenced off. One large set of steel gates, crowned with spikes, guarded the access to the side street. A pedestrian door in the gates was secured with a steel sheet and a heavy padlock and chain on the inside. Three doors came out of the hotel: the alarmed exit door from the stairs which could only be opened using a key card, a double door from the storeroom, and a wide door into the kitchen. The staff entry must have been on the street beyond. Elspeth calculated that the smooth brick wall surrounding the area must have been four metres high and not easily scalable.

How then did Alexandre's murderer get into this area? And how did he or she leave? Had both victim and perpetrator come from the inside of the hotel? They could have used their room entry cards, but they could not have known they only allowed them to exit but not to enter. Had they come together or separately? Elspeth disliked both alternatives. An outside job would have been more palatable but far less possible.

When the body had been discovered, Elspeth had not taken careful note of its surroundings. Doing so now offered little insight. All had been restored to order, as one would expect at a Kennington hotel. But to Elspeth the vision of Alexandre's body, blue tie twisted profanely about its neck and its face smashed, blotted out everything else. The tie with the Hermès logo. The one Dagmar had asked Elspeth to help choose in Paris.

None of it made sense unless Dagmar was the murderer. But how would she have gained entry back into the building? Or Alexandre for that matter? Had one of them propped open the door?

Elspeth reluctantly turned back into the hotel, this time choosing the door into the kitchen. The kitchen was in immaculate order, the chefs and staff hard at work preparing lunch and baking for the tea service. Elspeth would ask Frans Bootds to question all of them during the lull before tea. She debated whether she wanted to be present and decided not. None of them had any apparent motive. Mentally she made a list of questions for Frans.

Next she went to Bernard Debock's office. He was just coming in from the public rooms and greeted Elspeth warily.

"Lady Munro, or should I say Ms Duff, how may I help you? London called me and said I am to do everything you require."

Elspeth smiled at the formality of the small man. No manager liked receiving a call from the head office no matter how friendly. Because a call from the top echelons of the Kennington Organisation was always daunting, she felt she needed to reassure him.

"I'm very happy with the help Frans Bootds is giving me," she said. "I'll be asking for more assistance but first I wanted to clear it with London and with you. I never intended to be anything but a guest when I arrived for the weekend." Elspeth regretted the last statement because it sounded apologetic. Giving away her personal anxiety was not helpful.

"Frans is at your service," the manager said. "Please let me know what else my staff can do."

"Since Alexandre de Saint Phalle was attacked at the back of the hotel, I want Frans to question the staff, particularly those in the kitchen, about any unusual activity in the back area of the hotel yesterday morning. I want to find out if any of the guests made their way out to the rear, or if anyone else who was not on the staff for that matter. I would like you personally to question the staff member who found the body and the staff in the lobby who were there at the time of the murder."

"Of course," the manager said stiffly. Hotel managers were uncomfortable with deaths in their hotel and their uneasiness was compounded if it involved violence.

"I'll handle questioning the guests who have any connection to Monsieur de Saint Phalle. I would appreciate it if you put off the police until I do so. I have every faith in the police, but I think at this point I can discover more information than they can."

"Yes, Ms Duff."

"When the police arrive, please refer them to me. Tell them who I am but not why I came here initially."

Damn, Elspeth thought, I'm apologising again. She never would have if she had come to the hotel in her official capacity rather than her role as Richard's wife. She thought using her title only confused her role. She was glad Bernard Debock had dropped it.

"I would like to talk to the police before they question the guests. When they contact you, please set up an appointment with them for me. I'll need a translator if the officer in charge does not speak English. Frans Bootds will do very well."

Now she was sounding imperious, not a way to win the manager's good will. Elspeth had dealt with uneasy

121

managers before but never such a highly strung one.

"I'll keep you informed in every way I can. Has there been any coverage in the press?" Elspeth asked.

Bernard Debock shook his head. "I asked the captain of the police not to make contact with the press, but they will come eventually," he said.

"Yes, I know. Let's hope we can get this settled before there is a ghoulish splash in the Sunday papers."

Elspeth left the office feeling unsettled. She should question Dagmar again, but first she wanted to talk to Hélène, who might be able to shed further light on Dagmar and Alexandre de Saint Phalle. Richard had said Dagmar was troublesome and Hélène might know more of why.

She checked her watch. It was still only eleven and Richard said he would be tied up until noon. She wanted to talk to him. She shook her head, trying to think back on what all the members of Richard's party had said about Dagmar. Elspeth wished she had taken meticulous notes, but at the time it had seemed unnecessary. She went up to her suite and pulled some stationery from the drawer of the desk since she did not have a printer with her and did not want to go downstairs to the business centre to print out anything she wrote on her laptop. She labelled the sheet DAGMAR. She was still scribbling away in her large hand when she heard Richard put his key card in the lock of the door to their suite.

"Dickie dearest, we need to talk. Do you have plans for the group for lunch? I would think by this time they will be thoroughly sick of each other's company."

"Lunch today is on their own. I know I need a break and I am sure they do as well."

"Let's go somewhere outside the hotel? I have a great deal to discuss with you, and I want to do it where no one will be listening."

"Do you have anywhere in mind?" he asked.

"Let's walk into the centre of the city, to the main square, and see if we can find somewhere private to talk," she suggested.

They decided to walk to the large central square dominated by the old church spire that was ringing out pop favourites. Tourists abounded but seemed only interested in their guidebooks or hiring a horse-drawn carriage.

As they walked, avoiding the crowds along the way, Elspeth said to Richard, "I have made notes about everything people have said to me about Dagmar. I'm used to people having disparate opinions, particularly about someone as striking as Dagmar, but when I put everything here together, I find too many contradictions."

"I made notes as well, quick ones. Let's put them together with yours," he said. "Perhaps I can muddy the waters further."

She laughed and took his arm. Much as she defended her independence in their marriage, she felt a warm glow of companionship in the current crisis. Richard's unemotional nature in the past had sometimes annoyed her, but now that she saw him at work, she recognised that his strength of character and calmness served him well.

They found a small restaurant off the square with outside seating and few patrons at this early hour.

"Do you want me to tell you what I found out this morning or do you want to do so first?" he asked. "You seem bursting with eagerness."

"Do I?" she said, arching an eyebrow and laughed. "Dickie, I do love you!" Her outburst was so spontaneous that it surprised even her. He was obviously pleased and reached over for her hand.

"I promise to sit still until you tell me your news. It may or may not confuse things any more than they already appear to be," she said.

Richard reached in his jacket pocket and took out his notes. He deciphered them for her. "It's apparent that neither Ulrich nor Viktor liked Alexandre de Saint Phalle. According to both, Alexandre was involved in some deep dealing with Mateo. What confused me, however, was the degree of intimate knowledge they professed. On the night we all first met here, didn't Ulrich say he had never met Dagmar before? Still he seemed to have strong opinions about her. He said Dagmar was always trying to show Alexandre that she was clever. How would he know if he had never met her? He called Dagmar unsettled, but he disclaimed close personal acquaintance with either her or Alexandre. Do you really believe that rumour alone could give Ulrich these strong opinions?"

"How odd," Elspeth said. "Helga seemed to have a great deal of knowledge about Dagmar and her past as well, but it contradicted so completely what the others said that I doubt anything she said was true."

Elspeth told Richard of her conversation with Helga about Dagmar, Pedar and Alexandre.

Richard drew his long face longer. "Could she have been making it all up?"

"I usually can read people fairly well. She sounded genuine. The only people who can lie so successful are people who believe their own lies, sociopaths usually. Somehow our jolly Frau Müeller doesn't strike me as being one. If she is, I've been totally taken in. Dagmar seems more likely to be lying."

"Are you sure?"

Elspeth shook her head. "The only thing certain is that everyone is lying—a little bit anyway, if for no other reason than to protect themselves."

"Are you suggesting any one of them might have committed the murder?"

Elspeth paused, wine glass in air. "Yes, I suppose I am—even or especially Dagmar herself. She has the most to gain."

"Does she? Neither Ulrich or Viktor seemed sad to hear of Alexandre's demise."

"For business reasons only?" Elspeth asked quizzingly.

"For Ulrich, yes, I think so. Viktor is another matter."

"Do you believe what Viktor said, that Alexandre had thought Viktor had tried to seduce Dagmar and perhaps succeeded?"

Richard raised his eyebrows and looked down his long nose, which made him look censorious, but his eyes were twinkling, which made Elspeth chuckle.

"Alexandre was a man of complexity," he said seriously. "I wonder if even Dagmar knew all the ins and outs of his life and of his feelings about her," he said. "A woman of Dagmar's beauty evokes all sorts of responses, from jealousy by women to lust by men. We have both heard various stories about her relationship with Alexandre. She claims she didn't love him but was loyal to him because she needed him to protect her children. What did you say she called him?"

"A bastard," Elspeth said with a grin.

"But at the same time didn't Viktor tell you that Alexandre was loyal to her and had spurned Hélène?" he said.

"He did. Strangely Viktor claims he was Dagmar's confidant for years, one assumes up until the time she married Alexandre after her first husband died. Viktor confirms that Dagmar despised Alexandre and loved her first husband Pedar deeply. Viktor was on the edge of saying that Alexandre was responsible somehow for Pedar's death but refused to be drawn in when I suggested she might have been involved in Alexandre's murder. Then Frau Müeller comes along, says Pedar is openly gay and flaunted it and Dagmar loved Alexandre. Who should we believe?"

"No one," he said. "But what do you make of the warnings that came to you and to Dagmar? Do you think there's anything in them or that someone is trying to divert your attention from the real facts?"

"But who? And why the misspelling of your surname? Was that done on purpose to make it seem the threat came from someone who did not know the real spelling and therefore was not in your party?"

"Did anyone else get a warning?"

"Not that I know of, but Helga and Hélène would be the most likely. I need to talk to them as soon as I return to the hotel, but in the meantime I also need a quiet lunch with you and time for the facts to settle in my head."

12

Richard watched Elspeth as they ate and felt slightly guilty. As much as he knew she dreaded it, he had been comparing her with Marjorie. Although he had frequently told Elspeth that no passion existed in his marriage to Marjorie, Elspeth was clever enough to know that Marjorie had been a superlative wife for him during the years they had shared together in the diplomatic corps. Marjorie was naturally skilled in the art of tactfulness and stayed calm in every situation. Marjorie could entertain people from all over the world without ever making a gaffe. Some blamed her for being haughty, but she had inherited this trait from her upbringing as the daughter of the Earl of Glenborough, who had been British high commissioner to New Delhi when she was young. Richard knew that Marjorie's moniker at the FCO was 'Mouldy Marjorie'. Outside her role, she was old fashioned, but no foreign official had been able to fault her manners or presence.

In contrast, marriage to Elspeth had not always been easy. He had met her during his first summer at Oxford. He fell in love with her the day they met and had never ceased to do so. She brought out the best and the worst in him. He had always borne himself with dignity and prided himself on his steadiness. Elspeth often upset his calm. He was seldom rattled, but he sometimes became angry with her. Yet this negative side of his outwardly suppressed nature was countered by the deep physical and emotional responses she brought out in him. Their marriage had not been the blissful experience he had hoped for when he finally got her to agree to marriage. Elspeth was wilful at times, opinionated, and too quick to fault herself if there was any derision between them. Her calm exterior and professional manner belied her often expressed feeling that she was not good enough for him. No amount of reassurance could help, even after the events on the Isle of Lewis.

Richard knew that the weekend was a gamble and would tax her feelings of inferiority to Marjorie. The weekend had started badly for Elspeth. He could find no failings in her manner, but she had been stiff and unnatural. This distressed him because he had hoped in the future she would take her place at his side with ease. He knew she had tried but could sense her feelings of failure.

When Alexandre de Saint Phalle had been murdered, Elspeth's manner changed. She seemed to find her place, but that place was as a security advisor to the Kennington Organisation and not as his wife. He saw that this metamorphosis bothered her. After the affair in the Outer Hebrides the previous spring, she had somehow got it in her head that she should be 'a good wife' but obviously whatever that entailed made her uncomfortable.

Slowly he was coming to the conclusion that Elspeth would never replace Marjorie. His fantasy that she eventually might be able to had been dashed in the last two days. It was not that she had done anything wrong. Deep down he sensed she simply did not like the role in which he was casting her and never would. He would have to hide his disappointment.

Away from the hotel she relaxed. They ate their lunch, chatting companionably as they so often did when eating out. He wondered what other wife would be so casual in the face of a criminal investigation, but this was Elspeth's profession. Years ago she had ceased to be affected personally by the crimes or deaths of hotel guests who she knew only in passing. He knew the deaths that occurred in her private life, however, were deeply felt. Her fiancé had been murdered when she was a student at Cambridge and more recently her titular aunt, the great Magdelena Cassar, had died. Richard and Elspeth had been with her at the end. Afterwards Richard held Elspeth for a long time and soothed her deep dry sobs. Doing so helped his own grief. Yet when Elspeth was on duty, she seldom showed any emotion beyond concern for the smooth running of Lord Kennington's hotels.

"You seem deep in thought, Dickie," she said as their meal was served.

He reached over and put his hand on hers but said nothing. He was glad she had not read his mind.

"Will Alexandre's death ruin all your work this weekend?" she asked.

He considered her question. "I hadn't looked at things that way," he said.

"It might help," she suggested. "You said you had chosen Alexandre, Victor, and Ulrich because of the tension between them. The murder will probably exacerbate that."

He cocked his head and looked sideways at her. He was amused by her curious turn of mind. Marjorie never would have had such a thought, but Elspeth was right. He had already seen the tension increase in the interaction between Ulrich and Viktor that morning. Both were trying very hard to put the blame for de Saint Phalle's death on each other or someone else.

"I've already learned a great deal. I have no idea if the murder will contribute anything further or be distracting. Neither Ulrich nor Viktor has given me specifics, but they have provided enough information for me to follow up on when I get back to Brussels."

He waited until they had finished eating before he broached the other subject on his mind. He was aware it might upset Elspeth but he felt he had no choice.

"There is something else, my dearest," he said after they had ordered coffee. "Matters here have gone beyond the hotel and I think it's time that I had a security man from Brussels come in."

Elspeth drew back as if electrically shocked. She reddened and then went pale. She stared down at her beautifully manicured nails and then out to the street before replying.

"Are you saying that I can't do enough in my position at the hotel? Or is it that I am here as your wife and you don't want me to go too far? Or that my meddling will somehow compromise you?"

He could tell that she was angry underneath her quietly spoken words.

"Please, Elspeth, my very dearest. It's none of the

above. It's that I think this thing is bigger than Alexandre's murder."

"Things you cannot tell me? Am I not to be trusted? After all, Dickie, criminal investigation is my calling, at least as a security advisor to the hotels. And I can't take Marjorie's place obviously."

He had expected some reaction, but not such a stinging one.

"You are doing wonderfully," he said. "In both roles," he added.

He could tell from the storm clouds that crossed her eyes that she was not convinced. He tried to modify his words so that she would understand.

"I'm getting into very deep waters. I need someone from the EC who can back me up. I'm not at liberty to go into it."

He knew from her face that he was sounding pompous, which was not his intent.

"Frankly, I'm beginning to feel this whole weekend was a mistake," he continued. "At the beginning I felt there was hope that the relaxed nature of being outside Brussels in a luxurious place and with wives also present would make Alexandre, Viktor, and Ulrich loosen up. Quite the opposite has happened and now I have to mop things up."

"And my butting in has only made things worse. I begged you before we were married not to put me in Marjorie's place. You have, and I've been dancing between her role and mine and have fallen flat on my face. I'm not sure whether I should apologise or stomp out of here."

He could see fire in her eyes now. He never had been good with Elspeth when she got this way.

"It's not that way at all," he pleaded.

"Isn't it? Then what is it? I suppose I am not tactful enough, a fault I have sometimes been accused of by many of those I have crossed. But you know that about me. Why put me in the middle?"

"I hoped I hadn't. I'm sorry you think I have."

"Am I to play tour guide to the women this afternoon?" she challenged.

"No, my dear. Take the afternoon off."

"I can hardly do that. I may take the afternoon off as your wife, but I still have the hotel to consider. I may have disappointed you but I can't let Eric or Pamela down. I think now, Dickie, I will leave. I need to cool down."

She rose with her usual grace and crossed the restaurant patio without turning back. He made his excuses to the waiter who was bringing the coffee and asked for the bill.

13

It had been Elspeth's intention to return to the hotel and talk to Hélène and Helga before returning to see how Dagmar was. First she thought a brisk walk might calm her down. She hated scrapping with Richard, but he had rattled her confidence, and she needed some time to get it back.

She unfolded a map she had bought the day before and decided to go to the art gallery. A touch of northern Gothic art might fit her mood. Sin and redemption. No sooner had she approached the garden at the front of the gallery than she saw Kristin running towards her. Jean Luc was not in evidence.

Kristin arrived breathless at her side, her face red and sweating probably from running. "Lady Munro, I've been looking all over the place for you. The hotel said you had gone out and I might find you in the centre of town. Have you seen my mother?"

"Not since she left the hotel this morning."

Kristin regained her breath. "I was to meet her at a restaurant in the Burg for lunch, but she didn't arrive. She's usually very prompt. I'm worried because I found this on her bed."

Kristin handed Elspeth a Kennington a familiar hotel envelope addressed to Frau Müeller. This time the name was spelled correctly, even with the umlaut. Elspeth did not need to open it because she was sure of the message, but Kristin's eyes were imploring. Just as

Elspeth had expected the message read 'BE WARNED'.

Elspeth looked up. "Come with me," she said. "Let's go back to the hotel where we can speak without others hearing."

"Should I be afraid?" Kristin asked, although from look on her face she already was.

"This is one of several similar messages," Elspeth said, taking Kristin by the arm and propelling her towards the hotel. "I don't think your mother was targeted specifically." She hoped this would settle Kristin down.

When they arrived back at the Kennington Bruges, Elspeth considered taking Kristin up to her suite and then thought that Richard might have returned there. Instead she led the young woman back to the security office. Kristin seemed reassured by this.

"Tell me what happened," Elspeth said as they settled in the straight chairs around Frans Bootds's desk.

"Jean Luc and I were out and about this morning, but he needed to see his mother when we returned. He said she normally doesn't get up before eleven. She's very demanding of his time," Kristin said screwing up her face disapprovingly.

Elspeth remembered Frau Müeller's energy.

"I had told Mutter I would join her for lunch, and we set a time and place," Kristin said.

"At what time did you do this?"

"When she was going out this morning. It must have been about nine."

"Where did you go with Jean Luc this morning?"

"Out into the Koningin Astrid Park. We thought it

might rain and we took some hotel umbrellas. We just wanted to talk. He's a nice person. I enjoy being with him, but I don't think his mother approves. Jean Luc says it's not me; it's my parents. I think his father and mine had a business arrangement that fell through and there still are bad feelings about it."

Elspeth nodded. This tallied with what Richard had told her about Ulrich and Viktor on the way down the lift to lunch the day before.

"Were you with your parents when the Novikovs visited them in Hamburg?"

Kristin looked down at her hands, fisting them and knocking her knuckles together. Then she looked up innocently. Elspeth could not read the gestures.

"No. They came to Hamburg when I was still in boarding school in Switzerland," Kristin said finally. "I spent four years there. The school was rather posh and I didn't always fit in. I was glad to leave and hope to go on to university next year in the UK. I want to read medicine, perhaps at Edinburgh."

"Do you have brothers or sisters?"

Kristin shook her head and curled her tongue to her front upper teeth. She sighed.

"And you don't want to follow in your father's footsteps?"

Kristin grinned. "Neither my father's nor my mother's."

"Does your mother work with your father?"

Kristin laughed. "Don't be fooled by their jolliness. *Mutter* and *Vater* hardly speak to one another except on occasions like this. *Mutter* travels all over Europe trying to avoid him. She drags me along when I'm not at school. We get along most of the time because she is always busily doing things, goodness knows what. When we travel to our various homes, I usually just take it easy and let her buzz about. That's why today didn't seem extraordinary until I saw the note on Mutter's bed. What do you think it means?"

Elspeth wondered how much she should tell Kristin and decided that telling her more than was necessary put a burden on the young woman that she did not need.

"I think someone is playing tricks on us. I got a similar note. Sometimes in the hotels we get cranks who do these kinds of things. I fear our large party is rather obvious, and therefore may be a target of such tomfoolery. You're not to worry. I'll follow up on the warnings. Are you sure you got the right place for lunch with your mother?"

Kristin reached in the her pocket and pulled out a piece of paper. The name of a bistro, an address and a time was written on it.

"She gave this to me this morning. *Mutter* likes to be precise, as several times in the past we have missed each other. She doesn't like to be kept waiting. She always says she has important things to do, although I haven't a clue as to what. She just bustles around meeting all sorts of people. Frankly I find her busyness rather uninteresting. But that's *Mutter*'s way. Yet it's unlike her not to appear for a prearranged meeting for lunch."

"There probably is a good explanation," Elspeth said. "But let me look further into it. Let me know when your mother re-appears."

As they returned to the lobby, Elspeth said. "Why don't you go into the dining room and have some lunch," Elspeth said. "I see Jean Luc and his mother there."

Kristin held up her head. "I probably won't be welcome. The grand Hélène won't want competition."

"They also serve lunch in the bar," Elspeth said. "Try there. By the way, where is your father?"

"Off somewhere on the end of his mobile, I suppose. *Vater* and I don't spend much time together. He finds business more fascinating."

Elspeth could tell that the remark hurt. She rose and put her hand on Kristin's shoulder.

The young woman flung her arms around Elspeth. Elspeth touched Kristin's cheek and wiped away an unexpected tear. Elspeth thought of her own daughter Lizzie, from whom she was now partially estranged, and felt sorrow spread through her. Comforting Kristin did not take the place of being with Lizzie, who still resented that her mother had been responsible for uncovering a murderer who was a relative of one of her closest friends.

What concern could Kristin be carrying? Before Elspeth could ask, the young woman ran past her. Elspeth followed her towards the lounge, but not into the bar, where Kristin retreated. Elspeth was left with the warning to Frau Müeller in her hand.

Elspeth went around to the dining room where the weekend lunch buffet was set up and saw Hélène and Jean Luc deep in conversation. Elspeth decided not to interrupt them. She went instead to the concierge in the lobby, who this time was on duty.

"Martinus, did you see Frau Müeller go out this morning?" Elspeth asked.

"Yes, Ms Duff," he said and straightened his back as if in salute.

Elspeth smiled inwardly at his tacit apology for not being at his desk earlier in the morning.

"Do you have any idea where she might have gone?"

"She asked the way to a KBC Bank. I told her they were closed at the weekend, but she said she wanted a cash point. I told her there was one here in the hotel, but she was insistent that she wanted that particular bank."

"And where is that?" Elspeth asked.

He gave directions.

If Helga Müeller had gone out earlier that morning it was unlikely that she would have spent over three hours at a bank that was closed. Was she meeting someone there? Perhaps one of the people she 'buzzed' around with at the various Müeller residences in Europe? Helga did not seem the type of person to carry on romantic affairs. What other sort of business might she have? Elspeth began to wonder if she had been in crime detection too long. Did everyone have devious motives behind his or her actions? In Helga's case, Elspeth doubted it.

Checking her watch, Elspeth realised it had been several hours since she had checked on Dagmar, who was imprisoned in her room. Elspeth hurried over to the lift and punched the button for Dagmar's floor. She acknowledged the hall porter who was sitting at the end of the corridor leading to the de Saint Phalle suite. She noticed that he looked up from a newspaper as she stepped out of the lift. Had he been at his post the whole time Elspeth had been gone? And, if so, had he been vigilant? He smiled back blandly, as if he did not recognise who she was.

She hurried down the hallway and tapped at Dagmar's door. No response came. Something was wrong. She knocked again, more loudly. Silence greeted her. Damn, she thought. She made her way back to the hall porter.

"Did Madame de Saint Phalle leave her room?" she asked. The hall porter looked puzzled by her question.

"I didn't see her, but I just came on duty at noon," he said.

"Weren't you here when Madame de Saint Phalle and I came up about two hours ago?"

"No, Ms Duff. That was my brother. He is hall porter in the morning, and I take over in the afternoon."

"Did he give you any instructions?"

"Just to be particularly vigilant, but that is part of our normal job."

"And you didn't see Madame de Saint Phalle? You do know who she is, don't you?"

He smiled knowingly. "She is hard to miss, madam."

"Was your post covered the whole time?"

Elspeth was becoming exasperated by these momentary lapses in coverage at the Kennington Bruges. She suspected that a minute here or there was usual but today they could be critical.

"My brother left just when I got here. Had you thought of checking the security screens downstairs?"

Elspeth took the stairs down as rapidly as was possible in high heels. She did not want to wait for the lift. She approached the man monitoring the security screens.

"Can you play back the monitor on the first floor west hallway?" she asked.

"Frans would be a better person to ask," he said. "I don't want to leave my post."

At least someone didn't.

Elspeth went round to the security office, where she found Frans Bootds.

"Madame de Saint Phalle has flown the coop," she said in her haste.

Frans looked at her oddly. Obviously he did not understand the colloquialism.

"The coop?" he asked.

"Has left her room," Elspeth explained. "Can you follow her on the tapes?"

"No sooner said than done," he said as if to demonstrate that he did know some common English expressions.

He booted up his computer and soon the two of them were watching Dagmar peer out of her room to see if she was being watched. The hall porter was not to be seen. Dagmar took the emergency stairs that were just beyond her room. Frans picked up her image in the staircase and then again as she went out the back door into the alley where Alexandre de Saint Phalle had been struck down. She flourished a key card, went through the door without setting off the alarm, round the corner of the building and was lost to view. The time read 11:57.

"Could she have found a way out of the rubbish enclosure?" Elspeth asked. "I didn't see one earlier."

"The dustman would have come about that time. The gates would be open," Frans explained.

Elspeth took in a deep breath and blew it out in frustration.

"She could be anywhere in Bruges, couldn't she? Do you have any suggestions as to where?"

Frans looked at her blankly.

"Sorry," she said, shaking her head. She felt foolish at having voiced her anxiety. "I didn't want Madame de Saint Phalle to leave the hotel. She may be in danger."

"Have you thought to call the police?" he said.

"I fear I don't speak Flemish."

"The captain on the case speaks excellent English," Frans said. "If you would like me to make the call . . ." He left the sentence dangling, but somehow Elspeth felt he was uncertain why Lord Kennington's security advisor would be so tentative. Damn, she thought again.

"She can't have gone far," Elspeth said. "I want to try to find her myself. Before I call the police. After all, a guest walking out of a hotel is not a crime, even if she is the widow of a murder victim."

Ugh. She was still fumbling, which was unlike her usual manner when working.

"Thank you, Frans. I'll stay in touch."

Elspeth walked back into the lobby and out towards

the canal. She put on her jacket, which she had in her hand. Crossing the road, she looked to see if Dagmar's two shadows were lingering on the pavement opposite the hotel, but she did not see them. Had they spotted Dagmar as she left the hotel and followed her?

The wail of police sirens broke through the air. Elspeth heard them coming nearer. Afraid for Dagmar, Elspeth stood still and tried to determine where the police were going, but they came towards her rather than the other way around. She saw the blue striped cars pull into the street in front of the hotel and squeal to a stop by the wall bordering the canal. A yellow and red ambulance, bells ringing, joined them shortly afterwards.

Elspeth's distance vision was keen. She stood far back, slightly hidden by a tree, and watched the police activity at the protective wall along the canal. She recognised one of the uniformed policemen who had been at the murder scene the day before. Another policeman, who was in a wet suit, tilted himself over the wall and shouted something Elspeth could not understand. An officer pulled ropes from the back of one of the police cars and uncoiled them. Two others took hold of one end of the rope and threw it to the wet-suited man in the water. After a slow and laborious effort, they dragged a body from the canal.

Elspeth drew in her breath. Even from her far off observation point, she recognised the practical tweed suit, the dark blond hair, which now had come loose from its sensible twist, and heavy legs encased in support tights.

Helga Müeller.

Elspeth debated whether to return to the hotel and leave the police to deal with the body or to approach the policeman she recognised. She needed a moment to think what she would have to say to Kristin so chose the latter course. As she neared the crime site, a young policeman stopped her. From his expression Elspeth guessed he had not seen a dead body before. His face was ashen and his small Adam's apple worked up and down below his weak chin.

"*Halt*," he said adding some words Elspeth did not understand, but the meaning was clear.

"I know who the body is," Elspeth said into his extended palm.

"*Halt*," he said again, obviously glad to have a reason to turn away from the dripping body that now had been put on a trolley taken from the ambulance. No one had thought to cover it.

Elspeth saw a fresh gash above one of Frau Müeller's eyebrows, although the water from the canal had washed it clean.

"You go away now," the young policeman said in broken English.

Elspeth drew back but did not go away. "I know who the body is," she said again.

He did not seem to understand. A crowd was beginning to gather and three of the policemen were rolling out blue and white police tape to secure the scene. One of them recognised Elspeth. He waved to the officer in charge of the scene, the same officer who had uncovered Alexandre de Saint Phalle's face for Elspeth and Richard to see previously.

The officer came over to the place along the cordon where Elspeth was standing.

"You are the lady from the hotel, yes?" he asked.

"Yes," Elspeth said, almost shouting with relief. "I know who the body is. She is one of the guests from the hotel. Her name is Helga Müeller."

"I do not remember your name," the officer said.

By habit Elspeth had a card case in her jacket pocket. She brought it out and extracted her business card with the address of the Kennington Organisation in London and her professional title.

"Are you working with Frans Bootds?" he asked.

"I am."

"But where is the tall man who was with you yesterday?"

"He is back at the hotel," Elspeth said, although she did not know for certain. The policeman must have assumed Richard was in charge.

"Does he work for the Kennington hotels as well?"

"No."

"Then why was he with you when you came to see the body yesterday?"

Elspeth thought a moment before answering. She remembered Richard had taken her arm and therefore she needed to give more of an explanation.

"He is my husband. He is hosting a small conference at the hotel this weekend. Monsieur de Saint Phalle was a participant, as is Frau Müeller's husband."

The officer frowned. "Mrs Müeller is dead," he said. "Mrs Duff, will you go back to the hotel, please, and tell Frans Bootds what you saw. The captain will want to interview you and Mr Duff. Please wait there. We are busy here now."

Elspeth looked over and saw that someone had finally put a sheet over Helga Müeller's body, and it was being lifted into the ambulance. As quickly as they had come, all the police cars but one and the ambulance slid away. Three young officers stayed behind for crowd control, and soon the people watching turned away. Elspeth made her way back to the hotel and into Frans Bootds's office, where she found him at his computer.

"Have you found anything?" he asked, looking up.

Elspeth swallowed. "Frans, Frau Müeller was just pulled out of the canal. She has drowned."

"How unfortunate," he said, as if he had learned the words from a dictionary of polite terms. He said the two words without feeling.

"I think Frau Müeller's death may be connected with Alexandre de Saint Phalle's," Elspeth said.

"Was she murdered too? he asked.

"I don't know for sure but I think so."

"We must let the police do their work," he said. "Frau Müeller's death did not take place at the hotel. We have no responsibility."

Of course he was right, but Helga Müeller had been a guest at the hotel and a member of Richard's party.

"Technically you are right, but I want to follow up. I'll take charge of the investigation for the moment here at the hotel. You can carry on with your other work." Now she sounded overbearing, but she had the authority to override his decisions and knew he was aware if this.

Almost imperceptibly he shrugged. Elspeth was annoyed by his gesture because it smacked of defiance. She must try to find a more tactful way to deal with him in the future.

"I'll have to tell Ulrich Müeller and then his daughter. Leave that to me," she said.

He seemed relieved. "As you wish, Ms Duff," he said.

"I'll also keep London informed. Will you please let Mr Debock know? Tell him I'll be in touch once I talk to Lord Kennington's office."

He nodded, which Elspeth took for consent.

She made her way up to the Müeller's suite and wrapped on the door. Kristin answered her knock.

"Have you found *Mutter*?" she asked.

"May I come in?"

"Please do. Tell me, where is she?"

Elspeth looked into the intelligent but innocent face of Helga and Ulrich's daughter. Her blue eyes reflected eagerness that Elspeth would soon crush.

"It there anything wrong?" Kristin burst out.

"I'm afraid so."

"Did *Mutter* have an accident?"

"Yes. Kristin, I'm afraid she is dead."

Kristin's reaction was unexpected.

"What a relief," she said blowing her breath out through her teeth. She looked up at Elspeth and seemed to reconsider her words. "God rest her soul," she added. She pressed her lips together and looked up at Elspeth.

"May we sit down," Elspeth asked.

"I have forgotten my manners. Please sit. Tell me what happened," Kristin said. There were no tears in her eyes.

"The police found your mother's body in the canal. She must have drowned." Elspeth did not mention the wound she had seen above Helga's eyebrow.

After taking her seat on a large sofa, Elspeth turned to Kristin.

"I don't understand why you said your mother's death was a relief."

"I hated her," Kristin said with gritted teeth. "Is that unnatural?"

Elspeth drew in her breath.

Kristin continued. "Now perhaps I can get on with my life. Lady Munro, my mother was not a nice person."

"I see," Elspeth said, although she did not. "Then I suppose offering my sympathies to you is not in order."

"Are you shocked?"

"Not really. I've dealt with people's reactions to death many times. Each person reacts differently."

And, thought Elspeth, each person gives away more in their first response to hearing about a death than at any other moment. After that, one takes control of one's emotions. Nonetheless, Kristin's response was unusual. Perhaps it was her youth or her generation. Elspeth knew that her own children were more likely to expose their feelings than she had been taught was correct. It might have been that they were born in California, but youth in other places exhibited the same behaviour much to Elspeth's consternation. There might be some benefit to such openness, but Elspeth had found this was not always the case. Frankness often led to impoliteness, but the opposite could be true as well. Richard's closed-down feelings sometimes distressed Elspeth.

Elspeth thought of her own daughter, Lizzie. Would Lizzie say she hated her mother if something happened to her? She hoped not. Yet when she returned to London Elspeth decided she would do all she could to make things right in their relationship. Their estrangement had gone on too long.

"Kristin, I'll see that your father is told. Do you want to see him?"

"No!"

Elspeth drew back.

"Oh, I'm sorry. I shouldn't have been so abrupt, but you see anything we would say to each other would be hypocritical. My father, like me, will probably be relieved. I know you need to tell him, but don't involve me."

"Is there anyone you would like me to inform?"

"I'll find Jean Luc. He will understand," Kristin said.

Elspeth rose. "Kristin, you can always call me. I'll stay in touch."

"Thank you, Lady Munro. You must have children. I sense you are a good mother."

If only that were true, Elspeth thought.

14

By the time Richard left the restaurant, Elspeth was out of sight. He walked stiffly away through the colourful tables and into the main square but had no inclination to return to the hotel. His heart ached. How could he set things right with Elspeth if she was so defensive? He knew that she had always struggled with their relationship. He was intensely aware that she loved him, not just mildly but passionately. Elspeth was cool and controlled in her work, but her external barriers broke down when she was alone with him. When they were on good terms, when she opened up to him, she gave him prodigious amounts of love, emotionally and physically. Yet when they disagreed, she could be not only stubborn but also completely mistaken about his feelings for her. He was not bringing in the security man from Brussels because he doubted Elspeth's ability. She just was not privy to what he knew, and under the mantle of his security agreement he had taken when he joined the EC, he could not tell her. He could talk to Roger Bouchard freely where he needed to be circumspect with Elspeth.

Perhaps he could ask Roger if he could get clearance to tell Elspeth what he knew about Mateo and the threat Mateo posed to the countries of the European Union although not Mateo's specific identity. Money laundering was only the visible tip of the problem. Underneath lay the threat of weapons grade nuclear fuel getting into terrorists' hands. Viktor, Ulrich, and even Alexandre de Saint Phalle had indicated they knew of this, but on further questioning all their information came by way of rumour. They had not given any concrete facts, which is what he had hoped for. How much of what they had said was true? Richard wondered if he would ever find out the truth.

If he told all this to Elspeth, would she soften?

Fatigue and fear hit him, his back exploding with tension. The last time he had felt this way was when he knew he was walking into a diplomatic trap in southern Africa, when, if he made an error in judgement, both he and Marjorie might not escape from the country with their lives and Her Majesty's government might lose its influence in a part of the world where a vicious coup was about to take place. But in that situation, the weapons were ageing rifles and sticks, not nuclear bombs. Perhaps he was getting too old for this sort of work because the situation in Africa had excited him but the current situation did not. In Africa Marjorie had stayed calmly at his side and asked for nothing. She had not taken offence over his handling of the situation nor had she offered any advice.

He heard the wail of the police cars in the distance and wondered if they were allowed into the small streets so pleasantly devoid of cars. Probably, although their presence would be completely out of place. He gave the sound no more thought.

By the time he reached the hotel, the road in front of the hotel was quiet. He saw the police tape around a section of the wall by the canal. He gave it only a passing notice.

When he arrived at the front door, the concierge approached him. "Sir Richard, your wife has asked that you go to your suite as soon as you arrived. She will join you there."

Immediately? What was this about? he wondered.

"Thank you, Martinus," he said and hurried to the lift. It opened at the first floor and Elspeth stepped in.

"Dickie! You're back," she said with none of the animosity that had accompanied their disagreement in the restaurant. "There's been another murder. Helga Müeller."

She threw her arms around him and held him tight. "I was a bit of a fool at lunch," she had time to say before the lift opened on their floor.

The hall porter nodded at Richard and Elspeth as she disentangled herself from Richard. When they reached their suite and were out of earshot, Elspeth spoke again.

"Things are going desperately wrong, and it's all connected with our group. Dagmar has disappeared and now Helga is dead. The police found her body in the canal, but I saw a large wound on her forehead. She must have been struck and then pushed into the canal. I am also worried about Dagmar. Ulrich and the others need to be told. I have already talked to Kristin."

He took her gently by the shoulders. "I'll take care of telling them," he said.

"Then let me see if I can find Dagmar. Her disappearance is a bother. She must have escaped through the back door and fled through the gates when they were opened for the dustmen. I'm trying to think where she might have gone."

"Did she take anything with her?" Richard asked.

"We watched the tapes in the security office, and she had only her coat. She didn't even have a handbag."

"Did she seem frightened?"

Elspeth bit her lip. "No, I think she seemed angry."

What an odd emotion, he thought. He knew Dagmar was important to the purpose of his conference. She might know the true identity of Mateo if what Elspeth had overheard in London had any credence. Or she might only have been trying to tantalise the person she was addressing. She had spoken in French, which might be important. Troublesome Dagmar. Had Richard made a mistake in including Alexandre de Saint Phalle in his party? Or had Alexandre's presence really been vital to finding out about Mateo's identity? He wished he knew.

"How do you plan to find Dagmar?" he asked.

"If she doesn't have a handbag, she can't go far. I had hoped to follow the men shadowing her, but they have disappeared from the street and the drive around the hotel. I can wait until she returns and approach her, but I would rather think of another way."

She frowned the way she did when in deep thought and bit the corner of her lip. "You won't by any chance have her mobile number? She might have taken her phone with her."

He shook his head. "But wait, Viktor would have the number. He said they were old pals."

"When you see him, ask him. In the meantime, I have another idea. But first I must call Pamela and tell

153

her the latest. Dickie, this certainly isn't an easy weekend for any of us."

With those words she retreated into their bedroom to make a private call. He felt enormous relief. His Elspeth was back. She seemed to have forgiven him for summoning Roger Bouchard. Or had she simply put it in the back of her mind?

He needed to contact Ulrich and Viktor. They had a meeting scheduled for three o'clock; it now was only two. He decided to speak to Ulrich first. He rang the Müellers' suite but got no answer. He next called the reception desk.

"Of course, Sir Richard, we will be pleased to pass along the message, but I just saw him go into the bar. You will find him there."

Richard could hear Elspeth on the phone in the other room. He opened the door and pointed downwards. She nodded in understanding but pointed to her mobile. The expression on her face was pained. She must have been talking to Lord Kennington.

He made his way to the bar, where he found Ulrich Müeller sitting by the window overlooking the interior garden courtyard.

"Sir Richard, do join me," he said heartily. He did not seem to have not heard of his wife's death.

Richard called over the waiter and asked to have what Ulrich was having, although Richard was not particularly fond of beer, even one of the fine products of Belgian breweries. He felt the need for some fortification when he spoke to Ulrich about what the police had discovered in the canal.

"Even in such a small hotel, the Kennington management has created a jewel of a little garden. I have a garden and a gardener in Hamburg, but never have had such a success,"

"Müeller, I have rather bad news for you."

"Has my daughter fallen for Viktor's son, worst luck?"

"Your wife had met an unfortunate accident," Richard said.

"Impossible," Ulrich said. "Helga does not allow accidents in her life." He laughed at his wit.

"She fell, or more likely, was pushed into the canal."

Ulrich roared with laughter. "I would have liked to have been there to see her," he said after taking a large swallow of his drink.

Richard cleared his throat. "She did not survive."

"What is this?" Ulrich said rather too loudly. The three other people at the bar turned and looked at him.

"The police dragged her body from the canal and took her off about half an hour ago. I expect they will be here at any moment to question you."

"Question me? About what?"

"You will have to go and identify the body, although my wife has already talked to the police and told them who Frau Müeller was," Richard said.

"Was she sure? Helga looks very ordinary. Your wife may have been mistaken."

Ulrich's disbelief might have been more convincing if he had shown any concern at his wife's death, but he did not. He simply took another drink from his glass stein and licked the foam off his beard.

"Herr Müeller, I am sorry for your loss. My wife has spoken to your daughter."

"She will not cry," Ulrich said. "She did not get on well with Helga, if it is Helga who died."

Richard wondered if Ulrich would grieve. Perhaps once his denial had passed.

Richard rose. Ulrich looked at him sideways, but Richard could not read what was in Ulrich's mind. Richard thought how he would have reacted had someone told him Elspeth had drown. Despite his normal reserve, he doubted he would stay as outwardly unmoved as Ulrich.

"I'll understand if you don't come to the meeting this afternoon," Richard said and left Ulrich with his beer.

15

The Novikovs and the de Saint Phalles had adjoining suites on the first floor. On her way to Dagmar's rooms, Elspeth saw Jean Luc leaving the suite where he was staying with his family. Elspeth drew him aside and relayed the news of Helga's death.

"I think Kristin needs some care right now," Elspeth said. "She particularly asked to see you when I told her the news."

Elspeth watched Jean Luc's face. At first, he frowned, then he affected the smile of a lover. "I would like to do that for Kristin. Do you know where she is now?"

"She was in her family's sitting room when I left her."

"I shall go to her."

"Is your mother in?" Elspeth asked on an impulse.

"*Oui*. We have just finished lunch. She said she does not wish to go out as she finds Bruges a dull place."

"I hope she will not be upset by my company," Elspeth said.

"I think, Lady Munro, that she would enjoy talking to someone as distinguished as you."

Elspeth knew her distinction came from her title and this annoyed her. She tapped on the door and was bidden to enter. Lounging on the sofa, Hélène was in a pink peignoir and reading the Parisian version of *Vogue*. She did not rise.

"Lady Munro, not out and about with the others?" she asked.

Elspeth decided not to mention Frau Müeller's death. "I think we all have had enough of being tourists," she said. "Madame Novikova, did you receive any unsigned message in a Kennington hotel envelope this morning?

"Oh, that. I threw it away."

"What did it say?"

Hélène laughed. "BE WARNED. Warned about what? I have nothing to be warned about. If it had been addressed to Viktor, he would get anxious, but me? I am not worried by this. In any case I tore it up and flushed it away in the toilet."

Hélène may not be concerned, but Elspeth was. Two of the four people who had received the note were now in trouble. Helga was dead and Dagmar had vanished. The notes that at first seemed a prank no longer could be dismissed out of hand. Was Hélène in danger? And was Elspeth as well?

"Why would Viktor be anxious?" Elspeth asked, trying to put her thought aside.

"He is always frightened about the KGB or FSB as it is now. I don't know why but growing up in the Soviet Union affected him deeply. He sees the secret police around every corner."

"Do you think the warning you got has anything to do with Viktor being in Bruges this weekend with Richard and the others?"

Hélène laughed again. "Is everyone as paranoid as my husband?"

Elspeth was taken back by Hélène's blasé tone, but she was not about to explain to Hélène why. "Have you seen Dagmar today?" she asked.

"Dagmar? I saw her out of the window crossing the road just before lunch. She was coming from behind the hotel. Dagmar is dangerous, you know."

"Dangerous? Why do you say that?"

"She knows too much, or thinks she does."

"Did you notice if she met anyone when you saw her?" Elspeth asked, excited that she might now have a lead as to where Dagmar had gone.

"I did not see anyone. Dagmar took a map out of the pocket of her coat and kept looking at it. Finally she seemed to get her bearings and went off down the street."

"Which way?"

"Towards the centre of the city. She seemed agitated."

"Agitated, not angry?"

"Not angry I think," Hélène said. "With Dagmar it is hard to judge how she is feeling."

"Do you know her that well?"

"As well as I ever want to. I hope now that Alexandre is out of the way that she won't be coming to Viktor and, how do you say it in English, weep on his coat."

"Cry on his sleeve. Why would she do that?"

"She did when Pedar died, before she married Alexandre," Hélène said.

"Tell me about Pedar."

"He was the nicest man in the world, but he and

Dagmar often quarrelled."

"About what?"

"About Alexandre and the other men in Dagmar's life."

Elspeth was confused. Hadn't Viktor said Dagmar did not stray? What other men?"

"She even tried to seduce Viktor. He told me about it."

"And Pedar? Did he have other interests as well?"

"You mean other woman? No."

Elspeth wished Hélène would explain.

"Other men? Was he gay?"

Hélène's laughter bordered on hilarity. "I can tell you for certain he was not gay," she said. "But I think I will say no more. The problems in Pedar and Dagmar's marriage were all because of Dagmar. You must have heard how quickly she married Alexandre after Pedar's death. Dagmar has always brought trouble."

Elspeth heard the echo of Richard's words.

"Why is that?"

"Because to be so beautiful that every man falls in love with you always causes trouble."

"Did your husband fall in love with her?"

"A little but not enough to be unfaithful. I satisfied any passion that her beauty might have aroused," Hélène said. She raised her chin and gave Elspeth a defiant look. What did it mean? Was it boasting or challenging? Elspeth wished she knew.

"When I talked to you earlier you said Dagmar was so beautiful but so doomed. What did you mean by that?"

"Lady Munro, look at her life. Pedar dies and now Alexandre as well. What woman has two husbands die unnaturally and in the space of a few years? She will undoubtedly find a new husband quickly, but she will do this for her sons and not for herself. She may have loved Pedar but she certainly did not love Alexandre."

"Do you think Alexandre was responsible for Pedar's death?"

Hélène smiled. "No one will ever know now. That secret died with Alexandre."

"Was there any enquiry into Pedar's death?"

"Only a simple one. Pedar was killed in an avalanche. These things happen in the Alps. The police said it was an accident. But when there is an avalanche warning, only expert skiers go up on the mountain. Both Alexandre and Pedar were experts. Alexandre was behind Pedar. Did he set off the avalanche? It's not hard to do. Who will ever know?"

"But you think Alexandre did?" Elspeth said.

"My thinking proves nothing."

Hélène turned her head towards the window, and Elspeth could see the wrinkles in her cheeks that she had so skilfully tried to hide with her makeup. Could this woman really compete with Dagmar? Would Elspeth ever know? Dagmar had that kind of beauty that did not need cosmetics; Hélène at her age did.

Elspeth tried another track. "Do you know Frau Müeller well?" she asked, keeping the question in the present tense.

"Helga? A bit."

"Do you think that underneath the jolly front, she

has more depth?"

"That is hard to know. She seldom is with her husband when he comes to gatherings of people in Viktor's business. She travels a great deal, or so Ulrich says. Viktor and I visited their home in Hamburg, but I had a feeling Helga does not feel at home there, as if it was Ulrich's home and not hers. I feel sorry for her daughter."

"Do you know who Helga sees when she travels, what sort of friends or acquaintances she has?"

"Helga had a hand in every pie. Because of Ulrich's wealth, she can travel in the best European industrialists' circles. I believe she does. I have seen her once or twice when Viktor and I travelled to Portugal. I believe Helga has a flat there, quite a spacious one with a very fashionable address in Oporto. The Portuguese accept Germans better than other countries. Even now many people do not trust them. Old memories die hard."

"They do." Elspeth said. "Helga is so obviously German. I find it odd that she doesn't try to be more cosmopolitan."

"She could be, but I think she chooses not to be. Underneath Helga is like Angela Merkel, tough as one can be. Why do you ask?"

"Because she may be a link to Alexandre's murder," Elspeth said.

Again Hélène burst out with a laugh. Elspeth could detect the scorn in it.

"Alexandre and Helga. I think not."

"They certainly knew each other, didn't they?"

"Probably. Helga is everywhere. She is hard to

miss."

"But you think their acquaintance was only random?"

"Random? Probably."

But, thought Elspeth, the two of them were murdered within twenty-four hours of each other a few hundred metres apart. Random? Probably not.

Feeling she could get no more useful information from Hélène, Elspeth took her departure. Once in the hallway, she let out her breath. Hélène was not an easy person with whom to deal.

Elspeth resumed her journey towards Dagmar's suite. She spoke to the hall porter and told him to watch for Dagmar and ring her on her mobile if Dagmar came up on the lift. Then using her master key card she let herself into Dagmar's rooms. They were still in disorder. Dagmar had flung the clothes she had worn the night before on the floor and several magazines were thrown down by the sofa. The television was on but the sound had been muted. Elspeth made a quick reconnaissance of the sitting room, bedroom and bathroom. Neither Alexandre de Saint Phalle's clothes nor his shoes were left in the walk-in wardrobe. His shaving kit was not to be found in the bathroom. The only pieces of evidence that he had inhabited the room were three packed suitcases that were stowed in the corner. Dagmar's things, on the contrary, were strewn everywhere. Who had packed Alexandre's things? Doing so hardly seemed Dagmar's style.

Elspeth returned to the sitting room. She went over

to the telephone. The small leather folio with the list of house phone numbers and a writing pad was open by the handset and the top sheet appeared to be torn off. Elspeth picked up the pad and slanted it towards the window. She could make up the impression on the sheet. It read "R-ff-el-o". Raffaello? The letters were followed by what looked like a phone number. The beginning of the number was plus forty-one, which Elspeth recognised as the international prefix for Switzerland. She could only make out three or four of the numbers that followed. She was turning the pad back and forth to see if the numbers would become clearer, when she heard the door open behind her and only had time to drop the pad before Dagmar came in.

"Hello, Elspeth," Dagmar said. "How did you get in? I have been naughty and escaped. I could not stand being shut up here, no matter what the risk."

Elspeth was tongue-tied. She had no reasonable explanation for being in Dagmar's room other than that she was snooping. Furthermore how had Dagmar got passed the hall porter without him noticing? She thought quickly.

"I came to check on you. The door was ajar." It was a lie but the best Elspeth could do.

"I was certain I shut it before leaving. Perhaps the latch did not catch. What were you looking for?"

Elspeth temporised. "I was about to call the front desk to see if you were downstairs."

"I went down the backstairs so no one would see me," Dagmar admitted. "I could not stay shut up any longer with Alexandre's ghost here."

"Alexandre's ghost?"

"Not a thing in a white sheet. His psychological presence. Does that make sense? I feel his arrogance and at the same time his overbearing need for me. Do you have any idea of what I go through daily? Men pant like dogs when I get nearby. The only person who didn't was my first husband, Pedar. I had known him all my life. We played together as children when I was a gawky girl, all teeth and bony legs. He laughed at my looks and told me he didn't care. I wish I had been born ugly. Then my children and I would be safe."

"Tell me about Pedar," Elspeth said.

"Pedar is the only man I ever loved. He had many faults, but I knew them all, just as he knew mine. When we were together, we laughed much of the time. I look back at the years of our marriage as the happiest time in my life. If only he had not died."

"Dagmar, I'm not too sure how to ask this delicately. Did Pedar like other men? Frau Müeller told me that he did. I want to straighten this out."

Dagmar's face paled. "That woman! What she wants is to control everyone. Don't be fooled by her jovial exterior."

"Then you know Helga?"

Dagmar answered indirectly. "Helga turns up far too often like the bad penny."

Turns up, Elspeth thought. Not turned up. Dagmar had been using the present tense without thinking, and so she could not know that Helga was dead.

"Did what she said have any truth in it?"

Dagmar looked Elspeth directly in the eyes. "Do

not believe Helga. She is a liar. She told you that about Pedar because she wants you to think badly of me."

Elspeth was not certain if Dagmar was asking for a compliment but she thought not. Beauty might intoxicate others, but Elspeth could see no reason why Helga would cast rumours about Dagmar that would discredit her first husband. What was Helga's motive? Elspeth could think of none.

"Why?" Elspeth asked genuinely.

"Helga Müeller is a menace," Dagmar said. She looked sideways at Elspeth and raised her beautiful eyebrows conspiratorially. "I wondered if your husband invited the Müellers here not for what Ulrich knows but for what Helga does."

"Does she know anything that might be life threatening?"

Dagmar suppressed a smile. "If Helga's life is threatened, I would say she deserves it."

"Why do you dislike her so much?"

"You just told me one reason, her accusations against Pedar. She needs to seem important."

"That hardly fits her image," Elspeth said.

"Have you been taken in?"

Elspeth shook her head, not so much in denial as in puzzlement. She had no idea why Helga Müeller needed to disparage Dagmar's first husband.

"Where did you go when you left here?" Elspeth asked.

"To a church and then into the centre of the city."

"Did you meet anyone in either place?'

Dagmar looked cagey. "What do you call them,

'shadows'? They still are following me, although I don't know why. I approached them and told them Alexandre was dead and there was no reason for them to continue."

"Them?"

"Raffaello and his brother Giorgio."

"Do you know them?" Elspeth asked.

"After you told me that they were following me, I made it my business to know. I went out of the hotel and confronted them."

"Did they say why they were following you?"

"They didn't know."

"Who was paying them?"

"I assumed it had been arranged by Alexandre. That was the sort of thing he might do. He always was terribly jealous. Raffaello said they were hired by a detective agency in Zurich and given an unlimited budget to see where I went and whom I met. The agency had told him about the meeting this weekend here in Bruges and where we would be staying. The agency had not yet instructed Raffaello and his brother to stop and that Alexandre would no longer pay them. They are tiresome men, Raffaello and Giorgio. Raffaello is boastful and like all men a bit lustful. Giorgio would do anything his brother asked him, I think. They both annoy me and make me laugh. They cannot be very good at reconnaissance if you saw them right away."

"I was trained to spot surveillance, but you're right, they're not very good. I wonder if they were told to be obvious.'

"So I would be careful, I suppose," Dagmar said.

"Is there any chance that someone else other than

Alexandre might want to have you followed?"

"No. Why would anyone? I have no enemies and try to lead a blameless life."

Elspeth was curious. "Why do you fear for your children?"

Dagmar smiled in the soft way mothers do. "They are the centre of my life. I am afraid only in a general way. Since they lost their father, I must act as both parents for them."

"Didn't Alexandre help?"

Dagmar frowned and lowered her eyes. "I thought he would, but things didn't work out that way. Alexandre was jealous even of them."

Elspeth sat back and wondered if she should broach the subject of Dagmar's late-night tryst with Raffaello, wondering if that was when Dagmar confronted Raffaello. Dagmar seemed in a talkative mood, and Elspeth might not find her that way again, particularly once she heard of Helga Müeller's death.

After a moment's pause, Elspeth asked, "What did you and Raffaello talk about last night in the park?"

Dagmar grinned. "So you did see me. I wasn't sure. Do you often go about kissing your husband so passionately in public?"

The way Dagmar spoke irritated Elspeth. Kissing Richard had been a ruse, but nevertheless, it was dark and a time for lovers to wander about without being spied upon.

"You must love him a great deal," Dagmar said.

Elspeth had not thought that her kissing Richard had been so passionate. "I do love him,' she replied

168

honestly but wished the conversation had not turned in this direction. But she supposed it was her own fault for hiding behind Richard's embrace. She wondered if this surprised Dagmar. Richard's demeanour was normally dignified and even perhaps a bit stiff, but that did not make him unlovable.

"Have you been married long?" Dagmar asked. "The blush of new love does not seem to have diminished."

Now Elspeth was thoroughly provoked by Dagmar. "Over three years," Elspeth snapped and then wished she had not. "We both were married before," she added although she did not know why it was any of Dagmar's business. Yet Dagmar could not find fodder for her gossiping without being forward.

The interview was proving unproductive, and Elspeth decided to end it. She rose from her seat and said, "Call me if you can think of any other reasons why someone would want to kill your husband. The police may be round again today for further questioning. I suggest you not go out again." Elspeth wanted to add a scathing 'for your own good', but that would be spiteful, and she was on duty. Dagmar did have a way of nettling people. After she left, Elspeth realised that Dagmar had not answered the questions Elspeth had asked about Pedar and about her conversation with Raffaello the night before.

Elspeth made her way down to the lobby, where she met Frans Bootds and Bernard Debock. A woman about Elspeth's age in a severe black business suit, crisp white shirt and with her black hair tightly pulled back was walking through the lobby with them with a young, uniformed police officer in tow.

Bernard motioned to Elspeth, who joined the group.

"Ms Duff, let me introduce you to Police Captain Schrott. Captain, Ms Duff is here from London and is a security advisor from the Kennington Organisation who reports directly to Lord Kennington," Bernard said.

Elspeth wondered if he were sending a tacit signal to the police captain that Elspeth was a person to be reckoned with.

"My pleasure," Elspeth said, taking note of the captain. Elspeth had not expected a woman and then chastised herself for having the same bias that many of the people with whom she dealt did when they first met her. Captain Schrott was watching Elspeth through a pair of intelligent brown eyes, which gave off the slightest hint of sympathy as if in commiseration for their joint plight.

"I am sure we will deal well together," she said with only the hint of a Flemish accent. "Mr Bootds was just saying how pleased he was that you had taken charge of the investigation. How long will you be staying in Bruges, Ms Duff?"

Elspeth had assumed that she would only be staying for the weekend. She was expected back in London on Monday. She could, of course, extend her stay, if needed, but she was set to conclude a case at the Kennington Edinburgh that she had been working on for several weeks.

"As long as needed," Elspeth hedged. "But I hope

we can wrap things up here at the hotel as soon as possible."

"Shall we go into my conference room," Bernard Debock suggested. "We can talk there out of the guests' hearing. Ms Duff, do you think your husband should be in on our meeting?"

Captain Schrott looked enquiringly at Elspeth. "Your husband? Is he in security as well?"

Elspeth explained. "Actually I came with him as a guest, as he is running a small meeting for the European Commission where he is seconded from the British Foreign and Commonwealth Office. Unfortunately Alexandre de Saint Phalle was attending that meeting and Helga Müeller's husband Ulrich was as well. But after the murders happened, our offices in London asked that I help out here. I have handled several murders before."

Bernard Debock jumped in. "We are happy Ms Duff is here and we can use her expertise. I will send one of my staff out to find Sir Richard."

"Sir Richard?" the captain asked.

"My husband, Richard Munro. I generally don't use his name professionally."

"What does he do at the European Commission?"

"He is a special advisor with ministerial rank to the President."

"And therefore he is quite important," the captain said. "What was the nature his business here? A Kennington hotel is a luxurious place for a meeting."

"Richard's idea was that if he brought the people he wanted to confer with together for a weekend, with wives and family invited as well, the men would relax, and he could get more information from them."

"About what?"

"May I answer that?" a deep baritone voice said.

Elspeth watched her husband open the door and come over to the end of the table where they were sitting. He smiled warmly at her and gave an almost undetectable wink. But then his face turned grave. Elspeth could see the strain growing on it.

"You must be the police," he said, "I am Richard Munro."

"I wasn't sure, Richard, how much I was allowed to tell the police. I'm glad you're here," Elspeth said.

Richard sat next to Elspeth and under the table touched her hand. Was he asking for her support or giving his to her? Probably both.

After Bernard Debock made introductions, Richard said, "Captain, what are we going to do about this problem?"

"Please forgive me," Bernard said. "I have other things to attend to. Ms Duff, be assured we will give you all the help you need."

Elspeth bit her lip. This was how it was to be, she thought. She wondered what Pamela Crumm in London had said to him that had put him on edge.

The captain, taking her cue from the manager, dismissed the uniformed policeman. "I hope now we can speak freely," she said when she was alone with Richard and Elspeth. "Too many people confuse things."

Elspeth silently agreed.

16

Richard could tell that Elspeth was worried, although she seemed thoroughly in control. He wondered how often she presented the world with her fierce intelligence and professional coolness when she was feeling anxious inside. In her job, probably always.

He turned to Police Captain Schrott, who was seated opposite him. He suspected that she worked hard to hide her femininity, but he sensed it was there hidden under her harsh exterior. She must have risen in the Bruges police by sheer competence and drive. Richard recognised this quality as the captain shared it with his wife.

"Captain," he said, "both Elspeth and I are totally at your disposal. My meeting here has turned out disastrously. The participants all are prominent in their field and have a great deal to contribute to the EC's understanding of the transportation of precious metals across Europe, including spent nuclear fuel. The EC is concerned that at least a few of the precious scrap metal dealers are in league with an organisation and possible money launderer called 'Mateo'. Brussels has been monitoring Mateo's movements, but we only have electronic confirmation of the organisation's existence. One of the things I had hoped to find out this weekend was who the head of the organisation is. EC security suspected it was one of the people attending my meeting. One must conclude that the murders are somehow connected to that fact. For the moment I hope that you will keep this information confidential. I only mentioned it to put you in the broader picture of why I invited this particular group to the Kennington Bruges. I know I can trust your discretion. Elspeth has been helping me question the various members of the group but to date we have found no indication of why both Monsieur de Saint Phalle and Frau Müeller were killed."

The captain sat watching Richard as he spoke. Her eyes made contact with his and held them steady. She showed no reaction to what he said.

When he was done, she said, "Are you then suggesting that we should not conduct our investigations beyond your group here at the hotel?"

"Had you thought of doing so?" he asked.

"The murderer struck just outside the hotel in both cases. We have criminal elements here in Bruges involved in the drug trade and in stolen property. Guests at the Kennington hotel could be easy targets. We cannot rule out our home-grown criminals," the captain said. "But I appreciate your concern that a member of your group could be involved."

"I think you should coordinate with Elspeth. She understands the Kennington hotels and their type of guests. She also knows the members of my party."

"I look forward to that," she said. "Before your wife and I begin, is there anything else you can tell me about Mateo? Why do you think he could be among your group?"

"We have an extremely competent security office in Brussels at the European Commission. Crime so easily crosses among the individual states when there is so little border control. Some crimes involve enormous amounts of money. We feel there is a strong link between money laundering and the illegal passage of nuclear fuel from the former Soviet countries into the EU nations and possible terrorists here. Alexandre de Saint Phalle may have been directly involved in those shipments. I don't know about the others, but our security department in Brussels is concerned about both Viktor Novikov and Ulrich Müeller. They both claim to be innocent of any wrongdoing, but they have made accusations and counter accusations against each other. I don't feel I've heard the complete truth. Yet I never suspected the meetings would result in not one but two murders."

"The tentacles of international crime are long and heavily intertwined, Sir Richard. We in Bruges have certain evidence that there are elements here that support terrorism and may be involved in money laundering. Can you be really sure that someone in your tight group is responsible for the two murders, or even if they were committed by the same person?" the captain asked.

It was an intelligent question, one which he could not answer. He turned to Elspeth and saw she was following their interchange with interest. Although her face was serious, he sensed his and the captain's interchange intrigued her. He would not have picked up her mood if he did not know Elspeth so well.

"We may be misguided," Elspeth said, "but two murders in twenty-four hours of people in a group that could harbour a criminal seems to indicate that someone in our group is responsible. I have been questioning the wives. All four of us received anonymous messages this morning that said, "BE WARNED". The words were computer generated but the envelopes came from the hotel."

"Do you have a copy of any of these?" the captain asked.

"I have my own and the one sent to Madame de Saint Phalle. Madame Novikova destroyed hers as she thought her husband would be upset. Helga Müeller's daughter opened the one meant for Frau Müeller. She may still have it. She showed it to me so I can confirm its existence," Elspeth said.

"But not the existence of Madame Novikova's," the captain observed.

"No, I only have her word.

"What do you think the message meant?"

"I have no idea, but my instinct tells me that the message was meant for only one of us."

"Frau Müeller perhaps?"

"In light of her murder, that seems plausible."

"You said the notes were delivered in hotel envelopes. Are these available easily?"

"To guests in the hotel, yes. Every room has a small supply of stationery and there is more in the writing room and the business centre."

"Therefore one would have to come into the hotel to get them if one were not a guest," the captain said almost to herself.

"Unless someone at the hotel supplied the envelopes to whoever wrote the message, which seems unlikely," Elspeth said.

The captain sat back, pushed her lips together, and frowned. "But a possibility. Ms Duff, let's form a two-pronged attack, you and your husband on the inside and my forces on the outside. I want you to tell me everything you learn which could point to the murderer or murderers. Sir Richard, I realise how delicate your assignment here is. I'm not concerned with the identity of Mateo and will leave that to you. Ms Duff can confer with me on matters in the hotel and leave you free to pursue your own investigations. I will concentrate on the outside elements and keep the two of you informed."

Richard was impressed by Captain Schrott's forthrightness, but he could sense that Elspeth was on her guard. Elspeth's theories on the warnings seemed sound, but she did not tell the captain about her interviews with the other wives. Richard wondered why.

Elspeth rose and extended her hand to the captain. "I'll stay in touch and let you know if I find anything conclusive."

Conclusive. What an odd word to use. Was Elspeth in doubt about what she had heard from Hélène and Dagmar? Why had Elspeth not mentioned Dagmar particularly as she seemed the catalyst for so much of the trouble between the husbands and wives?

Richard rose as well. "Yes, we will stay in touch."

"Will you let me know about the postmortem on Frau Müeller?" Elspeth asked as the captain turned towards the door.

"I will, Ms Duff. At this point we think she was drowned despite the blow on her head."

He expected Elspeth to escort the captain out, but

she did not. When he attempted to, Elspeth put her hand on his arm.

"Will you stay behind, Richard? I'm sure the captain may wish to speak to Frans Bootds before she leaves. Let me ring for him."

Frans must have been close at hand because he appeared almost immediately and led the captain off.

"Dickie," Elspeth said when they were alone, "you didn't tell me what you have learned about Mateo. May I know now?"

Richard once more wished he had cleared Elspeth's need to know with EC security. His original intent was to keep Elspeth out of his investigation, but she had been sniffing about it since the night at the Belgian Embassy in London. He felt he could no longer keep what he knew from her.

"My dearest snoop," he said touching the tip of her nose, "I'm afraid I have to come clean, since you are now so far involved to keep you in the dark would be unwise."

"You told the captain that you suspected that someone you had invited here was the head of the Mateo organisation. Who did you think it was?"

"Security in Brussels doesn't know. They have worked with Interpol, but Mateo is careful. In Brussels we agreed that a weekend such as this one would flush Mateo out, that one of the three men would reveal himself even if inadvertently."

"Have you any clue at this point?"

"I was leaning towards Alexandre de Saint Phalle,

but his murder points to one of the others."

"Are you thinking that Alexandre was murdered by Mateo?"

"It's possible," he said.

"What then of the warning to the wives?" she said, biting her lower lip. "Was it sent to warn Ulrich or Viktor that if one of them revealed Mateo's identity something would happen to his wife?"

"I had thought of that, but neither has said anything to implicate Mateo. When he was alive, Alexandre almost fell into my trap but then he was murdered. I wonder if Mateo meant to silence him before being betrayed?"

"Dickie, do you think at this point you should cancel the rest of your meetings? It could be dangerous to continue them."

"If I do, we are no closer to Mateo's real identity and the purpose of the meeting would be unfulfilled. I knew there might be some danger when I agreed to the weekend. That's one reason I suggested the wives and families come along, to lessen the threat. I had no idea Mateo would resort to murder."

Elspeth hesitated before she spoke again. Finally she said, "Do you think that Dagmar knows who Mateo is? If she does, she may be the next victim."

"She may know," Richard said. "Certainly in London she suggested she did. But Dagmar also has a habit of implying she knows something when she is only aware of the fringes of it."

"Which would put her in even more danger. If Viktor is Mateo, he has easy access to Dagmar as a past friend. I think we should warn her, don't you? She may not take our advice. She didn't take mine to stay in the hotel when she got the message with the warning. Instead she went out and talked to the two men who are tailing her."

"That sounds like Dagmar," Richard said.

"I am concerned that Hélène said that she thought Dagmar was doomed. Does that imply that she knows that Viktor means to hurt Dagmar in some way, or even kill her?" The question was rhetorical. Elspeth frowned deeply. "I wish I knew what was best to do."

Richard reached over to her and put his hand on hers. "I hope now you don't mind that I called in a security man from Brussels. As much as I respect your ability, my dearest, I do not want you to be killed."

"Why should I be killed?" she asked. Richard sensed her irritation.

"Because you know too much."

"Following your reasoning, Dickie, you are in as much danger as I. Now here's what I propose we do about it."

17

Elspeth had not completely formulated her plan when she spoke to her husband. He seemed unhappy when she suggested they break up and each follow a different line of inquiry. She proposed that Richard find Viktor and for safety sake engage him in a public place, perhaps the bar. She, on the other hand, would seek out Dagmar and see how much Dagmar was willing to tell her. Dagmar might consider Elspeth's rapid return to see her curious. Consequently Elspeth would have to think up a reasonable explanation. Elspeth thought warning Dagmar again would have no effect.

First she went around to Frans Bootds's office. He was busy sorting through a stack of papers beside his computer.

"Frans, we need to talk about what is happening here at the hotel," she said. She had already decided not to tell him about Richard's suspicions of Viktor Novikov. "Do you have extra security staff you can call on?"

"Two of my best people have a day off, but they are here in Bruges and I can call them if necessary."

Elspeth knew that the Kennington hotels paid well enough that extra duty was always an incentive.

"I want at least four people. Can you get that many?"

"I know I can get three, and count on me as well if I can help. My other duties are light right now," he said.

"Good. I'll clear all this with Lord Kennington's office, but I would like you to set up a meeting at, shall we say, five. That will give you two hours to pull together the team. If they can come at half past four, even better. I may need you all late into the night. You may want to get a rest before then." Elspeth knew there was a small bedroom behind each security office because such an arrangement was standard in Kennington hotels.

He smiled. "Or I can exist on strong coffee. If I can reach everyone, I definitely will follow your direction. Let me ring your mobile when I know when everyone can get here."

Elspeth took the lift to the first floor and made her way back to Dagmar's suite. She wrapped on the door. She was met with silence. Damn Dagmar, she thought. Where had she disappeared to now? She was about to give up her quest when she heard the noise of the door to the Novikov suite open. Dagmar stepped out. She was smirking. What was that about? Dagmar's visit to the Novikovs' rooms did not bode well.

Dagmar turned towards Elspeth. "Prying again?" she said.

Elspeth gritted her teeth but nodded towards Dagmar. "I have a few more things I would like to ask you," she said.

"About Alexandre? Haven't we exhausted that subject?"

"No, I would like to ask about Mateo."

Dagmar's face paled. "I have nothing to say," she said.

Elspeth decided to be direct. "But you know who he is, don't you?"

Dagmar threw her beautiful head back and laughed. "What makes you think that?"

Another evasive remark.

Elspeth decided to be direct. "Dagmar, two people in our group have been killed. I don't want there to be a third. Richard and I think the murderer may be Mateo and that he is here in the hotel. If you know who he is, for God's sake tell me."

Dagmar's colour rose. "What has God got to do with this? It seems to me that the murders were committed by a person or persons unknown not God." She laughed again, which irritated Elspeth further. Why would someone as beautiful as Dagmar be so perverse? Elspeth tried to think of a way to stay polite.

She drew in her breath and said, "Were you just seeing Hélène?"

"No, she and Jean Luc have gone out."

"Then you were seeing Viktor?"

"Lady Munro," Dagmar said formally, "Viktor has helped me in many situations. I have lost two husbands, and in both cases Viktor has been a comfort. I have few friends, but I count Viktor among that number."

"And did he comfort you?" Elspeth said.

"What we did is between me and Viktor, but to answer your question, yes, he did comfort me. You do not."

Dagmar's mirth had changed to rudeness. She obviously used this device to put Elspeth off, but Elspeth had more grit than Dagmar could ever know.

"My purpose, Madame de Saint Phalle, is to protect you, not comfort you, although I am sorry for your loss."

"Are you? I'm not. As I told you earlier, Alexandre was a scoundrel."

"Was he Mateo?"

"No. What an odd idea."

"Did he have dealings with Mateo?"

"I have no idea. He told me very little of his business transactions."

"When you were at the reception at the Belgian Embassy in London, why did you ask if my husband knew about Mateo?"

"Did I? I don't remember," she said with a coquettish grin.

She was obviously lying. Why? Did she know that Viktor was Mateo and was she shielding him? Or was Dagmar Mateo? What an odd thought. Neither Elspeth nor Richard had suspected that Mateo was a woman. Dagmar seemed an unlikely candidate, but not an impossible one.

"I remember," Elspeth said. "I heard you ask someone if *le Chevalier* Richard knew about Mateo. My French isn't terribly good, but I did understand what you said. Who were you addressing?"

Dagmar laughed again, this time rather shrilly.

"Your memory is better than mine then."

"It may be Mateo who is responsible for the deaths of your husband and of Helga Müeller."

"I just heard about Helga. You didn't tell me she was dead."

"No, I chose not to. Do you think Frau Müeller's

death is connected to your husband's?"

Dagmar became serious. "I have no way of knowing. Please leave me alone, Lady Munro. Haven't I suffered enough?"

Tears formed in her eyes. Elspeth wondered if they were real or practiced.

"I won't keep you," Elspeth said, feeling she would get no more from Dagmar.

"Thank goodness for that," Dagmar said. She turned abruptly from Elspeth and made her way down the hallway.

Elspeth watched Dagmar go and then made her own way slowly back to the lift and up to her suite, where she found Richard on his mobile. He was speaking in French, in which he was proficient, and from the little Elspeth understood he was adamant that the person on the other end get to Bruges even if it were on a Sunday. Elspeth had never heard Richard speak so forcefully before. He had often entered her professional world but she had seldom been a part of his. His manner, which was usually restrained, had become authoritative. That he was pulling rank was apparent.

He raised his hand to indicate he had seen her but went back to his business. Elspeth retreated into their bedroom and rang London on her secure line to Pamela Crumm's desk. As usual Pamela was working on Saturday afternoon.

"Elspeth, ducks, I was just thinking about you. Have you caught Alexandre de Saint Phalle's murderer yet?"

Elspeth groaned audibly.

Pamela said, "No complications, I hope. Tell me."

"I'm not too sure I want to. There's been another murder."

Elspeth heard Pamela let out a short burst of breath. "Who?" she asked.

Elspeth told her and added the details she had discovered so far, leaving out the search for Mateo, which Richard had told her was classified.

"And so everything happened outside the hotel. Eric will at least be grateful for that. But are you safe there?"

"Me?"

"You and Richard."

"I think the two of us are. I don't know about the others in the party. They're much more likely to be in danger."

"Can you or Richard think of a way of getting Richard's party away from the hotel?" Pamela asked. Her concern was for the safety of the hotel and all the guests other than Viktor.

"I can speak to Richard, of course, but I think his idea is to contain his party until the murderer is discovered. I just heard him on the phone. He is calling for backup from the security department at the European Commission."

"Extend our hospitality to whomever they send out, but despite all the organisation's resources, I am sure Eric will appreciate it if the EC does pay its own way. I already have given Richard reduced rates."

"You shouldn't have, Pamela."

"I'm very fond of your husband, Elspeth, and don't mind at all. I didn't tell Eric. Stay in touch."

When Elspeth returned to the sitting room, Richard was still on his phone.

"If I will be working on Sunday, why should security in Brussels be so averse to doing so?" he asked, this time in English. "Certainly this mission if important enough that a few hours of weekend work won't hurt anyone, particularly if the duty involves staying here at the Kennington Bruges. What security officer gets a chance like this every day?"

After Richard hung up, Elspeth smiled and went over to her husband. "In my eleven years working for the Kennington Organisation, I am still impressed by the enticement of the luxury Eric offers his guests, despite the seamy side I see in some of them."

He smiled. "Elspeth, I hope you realise why I have asked in EC security. You have to get on with your life and I mine. I'm certain the murders are connected to Mateo and not with the hotel, although they both occurred near here. I want you to feel free to move on."

"Pamela wants this whole thing settled as soon as possible. Eric doesn't like murders associated with his hotels, as you know."

It was Richard's turn to laugh. "And no paparazzi," he said. "I think Captain Schrott will be discreet. I liked her, didn't you?"

"I did. I wonder how much I should tell her about the undercurrents between Dagmar and Hélène, and among the others?"

Elspeth still felt that Dagmar and not Mateo should be the centre of the investigation, however much her husband disagreed with her.

"Elspeth, I think you should be discreet. Dagmar may stir up trouble, but she basically is harmless even if annoying. In any case she has suffered the loss of her husband and doesn't need to be badgered by the police. If you wish to continue your own investigations, do so. If you turn up anything, we can tell Pamela and Captain Schrott."

"How soon do you think you will adjourn your meetings for good?"

"Tomorrow afternoon as planned, but I'll be meeting Ulrich and Viktor in the morning separately. I didn't see Viktor this afternoon, did you?"

"He was with Dagmar or rather Dagmar was with him. Dickie, do you still think it wise to see Viktor alone considering that he might be Mateo and responsible for the murders?"

"It's a risk I must take in order to ferret him out."

Elspeth told Richard about the late night surveillance she had set up at the hotel. "This may be overkill," she said, "but, if something happens tonight, I don't want to be guilty of neglecting my duty."

He smiled at her in a way that she felt was condescending. The look reminded her so much of their days romping around Loch Tay when she was still in school and he a young student at Oxford that she chuckled and said, "Yes, Uncle Dickie, I know you don't approve."

He drew up his head and looked at her sideways. His eyebrows rose in an arrogant way and his glance slid down his long aristocratic nose. Then he burst out laughing as well.

"Elspeth, you are still a scamp at heart despite all your sophistication. Does this surveillance mean you will be up all night?"

"How could I miss another romantic night in bed with you, my disapproving darling? No, I just will be on call if anything happens. When is your security man scheduled to arrive?"

"He is driving from Brussels this evening and said he would be here about half past eight. His name is Roger Bouchard."

"Will he join us for dinner?"

"No, but I have invited everyone in our party to dine in a private room. I have confirmed this with both Viktor and Ulrich and will tackle Dagmar as soon as we are finished here. Let me deal with Dagmar this time and see if my manly charms work on her."

When Richard left the room, Elspeth lay down on the sofa but could not rest. She once had taken a class in meditation and had dropped it after the first session as the instructor had kept urging her to clear her mind. Elspeth's mind was constantly active and her attention always occupied. Much as she tried to still her mind, she could not. Nor could she now. Finally she rose, found her mackintosh and headed for the pavement in front of the hotel. A shower was passing so Elspeth took the umbrella offered by the doorman.

She crossed the wet cobblestones and set off at a fair pace in the opposite direction from where Frau Müeller had been fished from the canal. She rounded a corner and almost bumped into the two men who had been shadowing Dagmar de Saint Phalle. What were their names? Raffaello and Giorgio according to Dagmar.

Elspeth was on the point of speaking to them when the older of the two men, Raffaello, turned to her.

"I see umbrella. You stay at the Kennington hotel?"

His words gave Elspeth her opening. "I am," she said.

"You deliver a letter for me to one of guests please?"

Elspeth's curiosity was aroused, but she answered blandly. "You could leave it with the doorman, couldn't you?"

"No," Raffaello said. "He is not nice."

"Oh," Elspeth said, trying to sound only vaguely interested. "What has he done to make you think so?"

"He chase us off earlier."

"Why is that?"

"I think we are not grand." Raffaello held out a letter. His hand was in a leather glove that was scratched with age. His clothes looked slept in. "Do you know Madame de Saint Phalle? She is one of guests?"

"I have met her. Is the letter for her?"

"Yes. Please."

Elspeth took the letter, turned it over and saw Dagmar's name written on it. The hand that had addressed the envelope looked feminine and the envelope itself was one from the hotel.

Giorgio pushed his brother to one side and stepped up to face Elspeth. "Madame de Saint Phalle drop this letter," Giorgio explained, ignoring his brother.

"Do you know her?" Elspeth asked. She looked round at Raffaello who was glaring at Giorgio. "I have seen you following her, both here and in Paris."

Elspeth hoped that her boldness would not scare them away.

"It is our job," Raffaello said and added, "to protect her."

"Protect her? From what?"

"From danger," Giorgio said, jabbing his brother in the ribs.

Raffaello winced with pain.

Elspeth began to wonder if Giorgio was the more intelligent of the two. He certainly was being more circumspect with the information about Dagmar.

"She won't be in danger in the hotel," Elspeth said, hoping that was true.

Raffaello snorted. "She is in danger everywhere. She is very beautiful. It means danger."

"My brother sometimes get too involved with the people he follow," Giorgio explained. "How do you say it in English? He is daft. Shut up, Raffaello."

Elspeth thought Giorgio's joking tone hid something deeper. Perhaps fear? If Alexandre de Saint Phalle had hired Raffaello and Giorgio to follow Dagmar, they certainly faced losing a good job. Alexandre could no longer pay and Elspeth doubted Dagmar would either.

"I will see that Madame de Saint Phalle gets the letter. Where did you find it?"

Giorgio scowled at Raffaello and answered. "It the come out of her pocket there." He pointed towards wall alongside the canal.

The rain had begun in earnest, so Elspeth made excuses and headed back towards the hotel. She debated what to do with the letter. She wanted to read it before giving it to Dagmar. She surrendered her umbrella to the doorman and made her way to Frans Bootds's office. He was not there.

Elspeth looked carefully at the letter, which now soggy with rain. She tested the flap and saw the glue had come loose. She saw a letter opener on Frans's desk, picked it up and slowly lifted the flap. She drew out the letter. Inside was a computer-generated message on plain copy paper.

It read: 'I will not tell what I saw.'

Who had written it? What did it mean? And who had addressed the envelope? Dagmar herself?

Elspeth slipped the paper back in the envelope, sealed it and carefully put it in the pocket of her mackintosh. She needed to get a sample of Dagmar's handwriting. She picked up Frans's house phone, ran her finger down the list of extension's pasted on it and dialled room service.

"This is Elspeth Duff in security. Is the room service manager there?"

When he came to the phone, she asked if Dagmar had ordered anything from them in the last two days.

"I'll see Ms Duff. May I ring you back after I have checked?"

"Please. No better, if she has, will you please bring the order chits to me here in the security office."

The food service manager arrived five minutes

later.

"She ordered three different times," he said. "I have the signed chits here. I have not yet sent them up to the billing office. If you need them, will you return them to me when you are finished." His tone was deferential.

"Of course," Elspeth said, looking around the room. There was a copier in the corner. "Wait. Let me copy them. I'll clear it with the billing office that you will be sending copies not the originals."

The copier was a good one, as one would expect in a Kennington hotel. She handed the manager the sheets of paper which the copier had disgorged.

When he was gone, she laid the chits out on the small conference table in the corner of the room and drew out the envelope from her pocket. She stared at the four documents and then shook her head. She could not be sure if Dagmar was the person who had written the name on the envelope or if they held any clue to the two murders. She decided not to give this information to Captain Schrott for the moment. She found a stack of blank paper folders on the shelf behind Frans's computer and took one. She carefully laid the chits and the envelope in it. Then she let herself out of Frans's office. The security man who was monitoring the cameras around the hotel looked up as she passed.

"Do you want to see Frans?" he asked. "He went home to rest."

"No, it's not necessary," she said. "Tell him I'll talk to him when he gets back to the hotel."

Elspeth made her way back to her suite and found it empty. Richard must have been off seeing Dagmar.

Elspeth lay on the bed and tried again to empty her mind but found the effort was hopeless. She rose, went to the bathroom and turned on the hot water in the spa. Perhaps a good soak was the best way to leave the investigation to Captain Schrott. Yet Elspeth could not simply sink into the subtly scented bubble bath and let everything go. She wondered what Lady Marjorie would have done and then decided that there could be no comparison in a situation like this. Richard would just have to be disappointed that he had not found a new diplomatic wife. Having decided this she sighed and let her mind dwell on the caress of the hot bath.

18

Dagmar opened the door on Richard's first knock. At first she looked irritated but then her face relaxed when she saw him. Richard shook his head slightly and hoped she did not notice. Why would such a beautiful woman constantly have to resort to half-truthful gossip and disagreeableness? She so easily could let matters be. She had fortune and position as well as her astoundingly good looks. What quirk in her life had twisted her so? Surely she did not need to attract attention to herself by such unpleasant means. Or had she affected this manner as a means to deflect the attention that so quickly came to her because of her beauty?

"Sir Richard. Now this is a pleasure. I thought it might be someone else," Dagmar said.

"Madame de Saint Phalle," he said, "I have not expressed my condolences. Alexandre will be missed."

"Not by me," she responded. "Do come in. May I offer you a drink?"

"I won't stay. I came to invite you to dinner tonight. We will be dining privately so you don't need to worry about undue attention."

"Privately?"

"Just the members of our weekend group."

"Or what is left of them," she snorted. How like Dagmar.

"I don't want to end the weekend without our meeting all together one more time. I'm aware you may

195

want to return to Paris as soon as possible."

"If the police will let me. I had a call from a Captain Schrott who said she did not want me to leave Bruges until she had questioned me. I suppose that means I can't escape without being noticed."

"I have met the captain," Richard said. "She's intelligent and I think sensible. She'll understand that you wish to return to your children."

"I do. I am afraid they may hear the news of Alexandre's death through the papers or on the internet, although I have called our home in Paris and asked that the papers not be delivered tomorrow and that their nanny watch their computer use. Poul and Hans are sensitive children and they were fond of their stepfather. I want to be there when they are told of his death."

"I'm sure that if you cooperate with the captain she will be reasonable."

Dagmar smiled broadly. "Are you suggesting I might not be?"

"I'm certain you will."

She cocked an eyebrow, which Richard found alluring despite his love for Elspeth.

"Sir Richard, why is your wife constantly questioning me?"

"Didn't she tell you her position with the Kennington organisation?"

"Something about security, yes. But she seems to be going beyond that. Why is she so interested in Mateo? That can't have anything to do with the safety of the hotel."

He eyed her sharply. "What do you know about

Mateo?"

"That Mateo came here this weekend," she said.

"Then you do know who he is."

She shook her head and a strand of her ash blond fell down in front of her eye. She pushed it back.

"Alexandre said Mateo would be here."

"Can you confirm that he is?"

She suppressed a smile. "Are you suggesting Mateo killed Alexandre? And Helga Müeller?"

"It is a possibility," he said.

"It sounds like you suspect all of us. Is that what tonight's dinner is all about? To get all the possible murderers in one room and confront us like Hercule Poirot? Will you do the questioning or will your snooping wife?"

Richard winced at Dagmar's disparaging of Elspeth. He had watched Elspeth handle difficult cases and never had seen her be anything but polite, although sometimes her politeness had been modified by the word 'persistent'.

"Quite the contrary. I want to wrap up our meeting with a social event, a way for us all to unwind after all the tension of the last two days." Richard turned on all his diplomatic charm. "It would give me great pleasure to have you come, Madame de Saint Phalle."

"Sir Richard, how could I refuse?" she said with an impish smile.

"We are dining at a quarter past seven in the Van Dyke Room. I look forward to seeing you then."

Richard held back his annoyance. He made his way

next to the Novikov's suite. He squared his shoulders. He wondered if he could face Viktor and contain his suspicion that Viktor was the most likely candidate to be the head of the Mateo Organisation.

Hélène answered the door. She was dressed to go out, her coat in hand.

"Sir Richard, I was about to go out for a walk to clear my head. Viktor has told me all about Helga's murder. Is Bruges the city of death? I never really liked the place."

"I'm here to invite you and Viktor and of course Jean Luc to dine with me and my wife this evening."

As he was explaining the arrangements, Viktor came from one of the bedrooms.

"Did you say dinner? Hélène and I were planning an evening to ourselves. Our son has gone out with the Müeller girl again. I hope there is not any permanent interest there. She seems nice enough, but I do not want Jan Luc to associate with her father. Despite his happy manner, he is not a reputable man."

Reputable. What did Viktor mean? Was he trying to imply Ulrich was Mateo? Or was Viktor using diversionary tactics?

"I had hoped that both Jean Luc and Kristin will come to the dinner too," Richard said.

He smiled diplomatically. He felt that never having children of his own put him at a slight disadvantage in understanding the young.

"I have asked the kitchen to do something special for us all."

"All?" Hélène asked.

"Everyone in our weekend party."

Hélène snorted. "Dagmar as well? Is the grieving widow allowing herself a public appearance?"

"Be kind, Hélène. Alexandre's death cannot be easy for Dagmar," Viktor said.

"She hated him," Hélène said.

"You are mistaken," Viktor said. "Dagmar was always grateful for all Alexandre did for her boys. Yes, Sir Richard, we will be pleased to join you."

"While Madame Novikova has her walk, may I speak to you alone Viktor?" Richard asked.

"You sound ominous." Viktor said.

Richard cursed his own transparency. "I simply want to wrap up some details of our earlier discussion."

"Then come in. We can talk here without anyone interfering. Hélène, *chèrie*, off you go."

Richard knew he was taking a risk. Hélène's departure meant he had no backup if Viktor became violent. He wished now that he had told Elspeth that he was not only visiting Dagmar but also the Novikovs and Ulrich Müeller.

Viktor invited Richard to join him in a drink. Richard wanted to keep a clear head and therefore asked for a light whisky and soda. His intention was to sip at it. They settled in on one of the sofas in the sitting room.

"Other than the murders, what is so serious?" Viktor asked.

"Mateo," Richard said.

"Mateo? Haven't we already covered that?"

"Out of Ulrich's hearing, I wanted to ask you if you know who Mateo is. You said yesterday that you thought de Saint Phalle was involved with the organisation."

Viktor's answer was evasive. "So you suspect Müeller. That's a good assumption, although I have no proof."

"What do you know about the Mateo organisation that you haven't already told me?"

"I think I said that the Cosa Nostra might be behind it. They have their fingers in that sort of thing. With the internet so much has become possible and the brothers in Sicily must be experts by now at manipulating money transfers."

"You said that you were approached by Mateo. How was this done?"

"I met a man called Fernando Rodrigues at a party in Lisbon. He said he was from Mateo and asked to see me in my hotel the next day to talk about transporting metals from Kazakhstan to Essen. Ulrich and Helga Müeller and the de Saint Phalles were at the same party. Somehow I thought Fernando was connected with Ulrich."

"Did Fernando come to your hotel?"

"He never arrived."

"Did you find that odd?" Richard asked.

"Not very. I've had this sort of thing happen before. If the deal is shady, which I think this one was, sometimes the contact shies off at the last minute."

"But the man definitely said he was from Mateo?"

"Yes. I noticed that later he went over to Müeller after he spoke to me. I have no idea why. I couldn't hear what they were saying over the roar of the party."

"But he could have just been testing the waters to

see who was the most interested. Did Fernando approach Alexandre de Saint Phalle as well?"

"I didn't see him do so, but he may have spoken to him before he approached me."

"What do you make of Ulrich's suggestion that the Mateo organisation was run out of Moscow?"

"I think Ulrich was lying. He probably was trying to pin something on me since I originally came from the Soviet Union. Unlike de Saint Phalle, I did not think it necessary to change my name when I came out from behind the Iron Curtain. Sir Richard, I am an honest man. I run both my business and keep my personal life as blameless as I can."

Richard rubbed his chin. He wanted to ask Viktor about Dagmar but hesitated. He thought of Elspeth, who would have found a way to do so without being offensive. He realised his wife had skills in getting people to reveal their personal lives that he had not developed despite his many years in the diplomatic service. Even Marjorie would have feared to tread into the lives of Viktor and Dagmar, but Elspeth could.

He cleared his throat. He was surprised when Viktor spoke.

"I suppose you are wondering about de Saint Phalle," Viktor said.

"Of course. Do you think he had reasons to transport nuclear material from Kazakhstan other than to prop up a failing business? You seem close to his wife. Did she say anything?"

"If she had, I wouldn't have believed her."

"Why is everyone so hard on Dagmar?"

"Because she uses her cattiness to deflect people from her beauty."

"But you know her well. Isn't she a friend?"

"She was. After she married Alexandre, he insisted she see less of me."

Richard wished Elspeth were with them, but he improvised.

"Did she develop this cattiness, as you call it, after she married de Saint Phalle?"

Viktor cocked his head. "Now that you say so, yes, I suppose she did. Dagmar is a kind person underneath it all. Hélène is jealous of her because of her beauty, I suppose. Beauty is a curse not a blessing, don't you think?"

"Both, I suspect," Richard said. "It depends on how it is used. It's a pity Dagmar feels the need to counter her beauty with unpleasantness."

Novikov took a long drink of the vodka he had poured for himself. "Poor Dagmar," he said but did not elaborate. "Is there anything else I can do for you? If not, we will see you at dinner."

His dismissal was clear.

Richard made his way to the Müeller's suite, not knowing what he would find when he reached there. Kristin answered the door. Jean Luc was with her.

"Is your father in?" Richard asked.

"He is sleeping," Kristin said. "But come in. He always sleeps heavily during his afternoon nap. In any case, Jean Luc and I would like to speak to you privately about a matter that is bothering us. It's about my mother's death."

"How can I be of help?" Richard asked.

"Come in," the young woman said. "Would you like something to drink?"

Richard refused but accepted the offer to sit down. Jean Luc and Kristin sat opposite him. Jean Luc took her hand and interlaced their fingers.

Kristin began, "When my mother left this morning, she seemed agitated, which was unlike her. Because she was in such a state, I watched out of the window to see where see was going. She walked across the road towards the canal and then I lost sight of her. That was the last time I saw her. But that's not the odd thing. I think there may be a witness to what happened. There were two men waiting across the street from the hotel. They were chatting with each other but watching the hotel at the same time. The taller one watched my mother and then said something to the shorter one. The short one spread out his hands and shook his head, as if he couldn't believe what the tall one had said. The tall one laughed and then turned round and went in the same directions as my mother. Jean Luc and I have discussed this. If my mother died shortly after this, then the tall one might have seen how."

"Possibly," Richard said. "Can you describe the two men?"

Kristin gave an accurate description of Raffaello. Richard assumed the smaller man was his brother.

"My wife has spoken to both these men," Richard said. "I'll tell her what you saw. Would you be willing to tell this to the police?"

"We don't think it is that important," Jean Luc said, as if he disagreed with Kristin on the subject. "Lady Munro can judge. Maybe she should talk to them before anyone tells the police. After all we don't know what time Frau Müeller died."

"No, not yet. But thank you for telling me. Did you see anything else, Fraulein Müeller? After the taller man left?"

"He came back in maybe two or three minutes, not much longer than that. He was shaking his head. The younger man punched his arm as if to say, 'I told you so.' You know how close friends sometimes do."

"Are you sure it was just two or three minutes?"

"It couldn't have been longer. I had the kettle on to boil before I went to the window and it clicked off. Afterwards I went and made myself some tea."

Two or three minutes was surely long enough to confront someone, strike them on the head and throw them in the canal. Richard smiled inwardly at his thought. He was beginning to have the same suspicions as Elspeth.

"Thank you for telling me. I'll pass the information on to my wife."

At that moment the door to one of the bedrooms opened and Ulrich Müeller came out. He was wiping sleep from his eyes.

"I heard voices," he said in explanation. "Sir Richard, what a surprise."

Richard extended his invitation for dinner.

"Will everyone be there?" Ulrich asked.

"I have invited everyone. I hope they'll come."

Richard turned to Kristin. "I need to speak to your father alone. Can you find something to do downstairs? Go to the bar and put everything on my tab."

"With pleasure," Jean Luc said with a wide grin.

When Ulrich and Richard were alone, Richard again expressed his condolences. Ulrich shrugged. "Helga always put herself at risk. This time she lost."

"At risk? How?"

"She walked into places where she should not have gone," he said enigmatically. "And associated with people who did not wish her well. But that was her way. I did not try to stop her because she did not want to be stopped. Sir Richard, Helga and I were not on good terms. We only pretended to be when necessary. Most of the time we lived apart. It pained me that Kristin preferred to be with her and not with me. I love my daughter. Her mother tended to manipulate her in ways I did not like. But enough about that. What did you want to say to me?

Richard asked Ulrich the same question he had asked Viktor. "Do you know who Mateo is?"

"No," Ulrich said and crossed his arms tightly across his prominent belly.

"Not at all? Do you have any suspicions?"

"Viktor Novikov. That is one of the reasons I decided not to go into business with him."

"Are you sure?"

"No. It is just, how do you say, a hunch."

"You said you would not deal with Mateo, so you must have had some contact."

"Through a friend of Helga, someone she knew in

Portugal. Once I understood what the man wanted, I no longer wanted any contact with him."

"Yet you still think the power behind Mateo is in Russia and not Palermo."

"*Ja*, but I only suppose." Suddenly Müeller's English deteriorated.

"Then you can't help me."

"*Nein. Und* I think it is good if you and your wife leave Helga's death alone to the police."

Richard was puzzled. Ulrich seemed to have turned hostile.

"We will see you at dinner at seven fifteen."

Ulrich simply said "*Ja*."

Richard made his way back to the suite where he and Elspeth were staying. He found her soaking in the spa, reclined in an alluring position and reading a guidebook about Bruges. He leaned over and pecked her cheek.

"Mmm," she said. It's a pity we can't spend more time together here without having to mind your flock. The architecture is wonderful although much of the art a little too Catholic for my taste. Can we come back sometime after all this blows over?"

He sat at the edge of the tub and promised her they would.

"Shall I get you a drink?" he asked, knowing that the hotel would have put the sherry she liked and his favourite whisky in the mini bar. He returned to the bathroom and found her drying herself off. She slipped into a terry cloth robe with the Kennington crest on its pocket and wrapped her wet hair in a luxurious towel.

"Before I get dressed," she said, "fill me in on what Dagmar said." She listened attentively as he did so. He admitted to seeing the others as well.

"Would you like to take a walk before we go into dinner to see if we can find Raffaello and his brother?" she asked

"Yes, lady snoop," he said. "I suppose we need to attend to that."

He watched Elspeth dress, an activity that always brought back all the joy he felt in marrying her. Before he had become intimate with her, he never had seen a woman dress. His mother had her own apartments and he had never seen her less that fully adorned. Marjorie had always kept rooms of her own, and, although he had seen her in nightclothes, he never had seen her actually change her clothing. Elspeth shed her robe and began the process of putting on her undergarments without seeming to notice that he was watching her. He supposed that her casualness came from so many years in California with her first husband. She put on her clothing while talking to him and sipping her sherry. When she applied her makeup, lightly but expertly, she gave her full attention to it, however. When she was finished, she looked in the mirror and sighed.

"It will have to do," she said.

"You'll be the most magnificent woman in the room," he responded.

"That's hardly likely with Madame de Saint Phalle there, but you are sweet to say so," she countered.

19

Elspeth picked up her mackintosh, which she had thrown on the chair near the door into the sitting room, and saw the folder with an envelope addressed to Dagmar and the chits with it.

"What do you have there? Richard asked.

Elspeth opened the folder and explained the contents of the letter. Richard picked up the envelope and saw it sealed.

"Are you reading other people's private mail?" he asked with a half-smile and a glint in his eye.

"Dagmar will never know, but I suppose we ought to have this delivered before we go to find the men shadowing her. I'll leave it with the concierge. He needs to atone for past actions."

The evening air was fresh after a passing shower as Elspeth and Richard, arm in arm, stepped out of the hotel. Elspeth spoke to the doorman as they passed through the main doors of the hotel.

"Have you seen the two men who were lingering outside by the canal?"

He nodded. "Good evening, Sir Richard. Yes, Ms Duff. One tried to come into the hotel early this afternoon, but I told him to go away. He said he had something for one of the guests and he said he wanted to deliver it personally. Since you have given instructions to watch him and his brother, I did not let him in. The two of them take shifts watching the door. The smaller one is outside now, just behind the trees down the street by the canal."

"Well done," Elspeth said.

The doorman smiled in response.

Richard and Elspeth made their way across the road and went along the canal. They sauntered as if they had no particular business, but Elspeth kept her eye out for Giorgio. He must have seen her first because when Elspeth caught sight of him he ducked behind one of the trees. Elspeth spoke softly to Richard.

"He's over there. Let's wander that way but appear to be in a deep discussion. We can always use last night's ploy."

"Good gracious, was it only last night?" Richard said. "It seems a century ago."

"It does. Can you see him?"

Richard looked up and nodded. He put his arms around Elspeth's shoulder and led her along the wall by the canal, although it was still wet from the rain. Elspeth was grateful she had not yet put on her good shoes for the evening. She leaned her head on his shoulder and whispered in his ear.

"Let's act surprised. I hope he doesn't run away."

He did not. Instead he went further around the tree and hid himself, which he might have done successfully if Elspeth had not seen him first.

Richard led Elspeth towards the tree and leaned against it, pulling her to him. He winked at her.

"There's someone there, Dickie," she cried and gave a fake grimace right out of a melodrama. "I'm frightened!"

Richard held back a laugh but she could feel his body shake with mirth.

"There is no danger," a voice said. Giorgio emerged from the back of the tree.

Elspeth let out a long breath. "Oh, it's only you. I was a little afraid because of what happened here earlier. You are Giorgio, aren't you? Raffaello's brother?"

"Giorgio Burri. Raffaello Conti is my half-brother. And you, madam?"

"Munro," Elspeth said. "This is my husband Richard."

"Mr Munro," Giorgio said with a slight bow.

"Pleasure," Richard said in a most pompous way. Elspeth wanted to kick him for his stuffiness but instead she brought the conversation back to business.

"I saw that the envelope was delivered to Madame de Saint Phalle. Will you tell your brother? Or is he here so I may tell him myself?"

"He is sleeping," Giorgio said.

"While you keep watch?"

"I watch now. Is Madame de Saint Phalle good?"

"When I last saw her, she was well," Elspeth said. "Giorgio, I would like to ask you something in return for my favour to you. Did you see Frau Müeller, the German woman who was found in the canal, before she died?"

"We not see her when she murdered," he said. "That is very sad. I am sorry for daughter and her boyfriend."

"Did you see Frau Müeller earlier in the morning?"

He shook his head.

"Someone looking out the window of the hotel said that Raffaello followed her when she came out of the hotel."

"He see her, but Madame de Saint Phalle come out of the hotel and we go to work to follow her, to protect her."

"Where did Madame de Saint Phalle go?"

"Into the centre of the city, to main plaza. She had cup of coffee but first go to church, where she prayed."

"Prayed?" Elspeth said. Dagmar did not strike her as the sort of person who prayed.

"Is it the wrong word?" Giorgio asked.

"No, it is the right word."

"And after you started following Madame de Saint Phalle, you did not see Frau Müeller again?"

"The police just leave when we come back to the hotel," Giorgio said.

"Did Madame de Saint Phalle see the police?"

"I think no. She had no danger." His meaning was unclear.

"Will your brother be back soon?" Elspeth asked.

"At nine o'clock. He will say the same thing I say."

"Thank you, Giorgio." Elspeth said. "I am glad you are here for Madame de Saint Phalle."

Richard bowed and mumbled something, which Elspeth expected was intentionally vague.

When they returned to their suite to collect Elspeth's evening shoes and leave their coats, Richard asked, "What did you make of that?"

"I don't think he was telling the truth."

211

"Nor do I."

"I want to talk to Raffaello. He is more open than his half-brother."

"If you go out there tonight, I want to come with you."

"Won't you be busy with your man from Brussels? I think if all three of us go out, we will scare Raffaello. Besides, it's me who did the favour for him and saw that the letter was delivered. Dagmar should have it by now. I wonder what she will make of it and if she knows who it was from."

The dinner guests dragged in slowly. Kristin and Jean Luc were on time and Ulrich Müeller followed shortly afterwards. Hélène and Viktor came in fifteen minutes late. Elspeth could see Richard fidgeting. He drummed his fingers by his plate and finally called the waiter over.

"We will not wait for Madame de Saint Phalle. You may proceed with the first course."

They were halfway through the fish pâté with watercress served with a chilled white Bordeaux when Dagmar made her entrance. She was all in black but her frock was décolleté to the waist. Richard coughed as he swallowed his wine the wrong way. Ulrich looked startled and Viktor admiring. Hélène sniffed. Kristin looked away but Jean Luc stared and slowly smiled.

"Good evening everyone," Dagmar said demurely. "Am I late?"

Dagmar took her place between Ulrich and Viktor. She leaned over and touched Viktor's hand, with much of one breast exposed. Hélène watched her with gimlet eyes, which Dagmar chose not to notice. She sat gazing at Viktor but did not contribute to the stilted conversation.

Elspeth felt pained. What had been Richard's purpose when he set up this dinner? Did he believe that eating together would bring about harmony among them?

The boneless duckling thighs with figs came next with wild rice, and baked courgettes cooked with mushrooms and onions and topped with cheese. Because the food was rich, the servings were small. Everyone but Dagmar ate; Ulrich asked for more.

Having exhausted the weather, the food and the possibility of delayed travel arrangements, the party went silent. Even Richard seemed unable to prolong conversation in response to brief sentences from his guests. Elspeth rallied behind him with little success.

Dessert arrived. Small balls of chocolate and hazelnut ice cream with fresh raspberries drizzled decoratively with dark chocolate and garnished with fresh mint did little to sweeten the mood of the group. After an agonising hour, Richard rose.

"Because of the unfortunate events of the last two days, I have decided to end our formal discussions. I realise that the police may ask some of you to stay on, which I regret because I know you all have busy lives. I have asked Roger Bouchard from the EC security office in Brussels here this evening as a precaution. I will brief him on the events of the last few days. I don't think it necessary for him to question you as I believe my wife and I have already done so thoroughly. There is no need for this questioning to be duplicated. If there is anything more you would like to tell me or Elspeth, we will be available in the morning. You can ring our suite. Otherwise you all are free to go about your business when the police give you leave to do so. I hope the captain will not delay you too long. Now join me and Elspeth in the lounge for coffee if you wish. I would appreciate it if you will let me know when you are ready to leave the hotel."

Everyone nodded except Dagmar who shrugged becomingly.

As Elspeth walked out of the private dining room on Richard's arm, she whispered, "That was torturous."

"A bit," he responded, "I have been to more difficult dinners, however, and the food was truly up to the usual Kennington standards. What statement do you suppose Dagmar was attempting to make in that dress? It was quite . . ." he said with an intake of breath.

Elspeth laughed. "Outrageous?"

"Exactly. One never knows what Dagmar will do next."

Viktor and Hélène made their excuses, saying they were going on to a nightclub and would not join Elspeth and Richard in the lounge. Ulrich found a seat opposite them and ordered a brandy with his coffee. Dagmar disappeared.

Jean Luc came up to Elspeth. "May Kristin and I see you later, tonight not tomorrow?"

"What is it you want, boy?" Ulrich asked.

"Nothing important, Herr Müeller. It is about your

daughter's wish to go to Edinburgh to study. She thought Lady Munro might have some suggestions for her because the Munros are from Scotland."

"*Ach*," Ulrich said. "Kristin and this idea to become a doctor. It will pass like her other fantasies. Now that Helga is not here, Kristin should come home to Hamburg where she belongs."

"*Vater*, may we talk about this later?"

"*Ja*. Talk to Lady Munro if you wish. It can do no harm. You might like to visit the lochs someday."

Elspeth wondered what Kristin and Jean Luc really wanted to talk to her about. "Meet me in the writing room in an hour," she said. She wanted to make sure the night surveillance was in place before then.

Ulrich lingered over his coffee and brandy, asking for a second and third round. Elspeth thought he would never rise. Finally Richard, looking at his watch, made it happen.

"Müeller, forgive me, but I have an appointment shortly. He unfolded his long frame from his chair.

Elspeth was afraid that Ulrich would insist she stay, but he did not.

"I must go and see to packing our bags," he said and rose unsteadily.

When he was gone, Richard took Elspeth by the shoulders. "Roger Bouchard should be here at any minute. I know you have your arrangements to settle with Frans Bootds and need to see Kristin and Jean Luc after that. You must not go outside the hotel unless I come with you, even if it is late. Do you promise me, Elspeth?"

She bit her lip. She wanted to see Raffaello alone and ask him about Helga Müeller. "Mmm," she answered.

He looked sternly at her. "Promise me!"

She screwed up her face and rose on toes to kiss him. He did not give in.

"You may be in danger, despite what Giorgio says. Two people have been murdered, and you have been snooping round, maybe a little too much. I don't want you harmed."

"Then meet me at ten," she said. "But I want you to stay at a distance when I talk to Raffaello. You and Roger Bouchard can watch from the doorway. More than that I won't promise. Dickie, I handle situations like this all the time. Why do you suddenly think I need knightly protection?"

"Because you are here as my wife."

"And I have a job to do."

"Are you choosing one over the other?"

She raised her chin. "Yes, I suppose I am." She smiled, "But I won't go out until you can watch me. I'll concede to that."

"Good girl," he said with a chuckle.

She was annoyed by his remark, which she found patronising, but said nothing.

He looked deeply into her eyes and shook his head. "You really haven't changed in forty years," he said. "I should by now know better than to expect anything different from you, but you know I care very deeply for you and want you to be safe."

When Elspeth arrived at Frans Bootds's office, he and three other men were waiting for her. Elspeth gave her instructions.

"I want each of you to cover the guests in the suites assigned to my husband's party. The person most likely to leave this evening will be Madame de Saint Phalle. Monsieur and Madame Novikov have gone out, but when they return, keep an eye on them. Herr Müeller has probably gone to bed, since he had a great deal to drink this evening but still watch his rooms. Frans, I want you to follow anyone who leaves. If two people leave, phone me on my mobile."

It was just past nine when she finished giving her final instructions. She made her way back to the lobby, where she saw Richard sitting alone in the lounge. He obviously was waiting and she did not want to disturb him. Instead she went up to Dagmar's suite and knocked on the door. No answer came. She knocked again, this time more loudly. Nothing. Had Dagmar slipped out? With a smile, Elspeth hoped she had changed into a more suitable frock. Or perhaps Dagmar was tired of her game playing and had gone to bed with either a sleeping pill or a large glass of spirits.

Elspeth rang down to the security office and warned Frans Bootds. "I want you to put the guard on Madame de Saint Phalle's door immediately."

Then Elspeth returned to her own suite and looked longingly at the bed. The few hours of sleep she had the night before seemed an aeon ago. She called room service for a wake-up call at ten minutes to ten and reclined on the sofa in the sitting room. She was sound asleep when the call came.

Quickly changing her shoes and finding her mackintosh, she made her way back down to the lobby, wondering if Jean Luc and Kristin had approached her as Richard's wife or as a security officer. These double roles increasingly grated on her.

Jean Luc and Kristin were in the writing room, obviously deep in intimate conversation. They jumped apart when Elspeth approached and cleared her throat. Warmth filled Elspeth for she liked these young people. At least two members of Richard's party seemed to be hitting it off. She sat down alongside a leather topped writing table opposite them.

"Now tell me what you really want to talk about," she said.

Kristin giggled. "Was Jean Luc really so transparent?"

Elspeth nodded. "I have children of my own," she said as if this made her clairvoyant.

"We want to talk about our parents," Jean Luc said. "You already know that they do not get along. Part of the problem is their business competition, but another part is personal."

Elspeth cocked her head and waited for Jean Luc to continue.

"You know about the weekend my parents spent in Hamburg, yes?" he said

"A little," Elspeth said. "Were you there?"

"No, I was at university and Kristin was at school in Switzerland, but I heard my parents talking afterwards."

"I did as well," Kristin said. "The difficulty came

when Jean Luc and I discussed what each of our parents said about the visit. The two stories did not fit together. We want to tell you so you can let Sir Richard know. We think the differences are important."

Too many spiders on a web, Elspeth thought unkindly of the Müellers and the Novikovs.

Kristin took Jean Luc's hand as if for support. "You start," she said.

"I was home from university when my parents returned from Hamburg. I came into the library when I heard their voices in there. They were very, how do you say, agitated. My father was walking up and down and saying, "How was it possible to work with them? I suspect that Ulrich is covering for Mateo." I did not know who Mateo was, but my mother kept telling my father that he had made the right decision, that Ulrich Müeller could not be trusted. Does any of this make sense to you, Lady Munro?"

Elspeth nodded slowly. "A little, but, Kristin, how does this differ from what your parents said?"

Kristin looked up at Elspeth. "It was the spring hols. The headmistress at my school had made us promise to be diligent in our studies, particularly foreign languages. Probably because I was studying English, I was amazed when I heard my parents speaking in that language. Normally they speak in German to each other. I think they did not want the servants to understand. They walked under my window. My mother was scolding my father. 'Ulrich,' she said, 'you let Viktor walk over you. You must not allow him to.' My mother often scolds my father, although he does not like it. 'The business about Mateo, you must not let him always bring this up. He uses this to break off business with you. I think it is only an excuse. He came here to get your secrets. Now he can use the secrets to compete with you. You are foolish to let him.' My father was angry with my mother. This happens often when they are together. 'Stay out of my business, Helga,' he answered. 'Viktor knows very well who Mateo is.' He scoffed. Is that the right word? You see that Jean Luc's parents think my father is Mateo and my parents think Monsieur Novikov is. Do you know who Mateo is, Lady Munro?"

"Not yet," Elspeth whispered more to herself than to the young people. "But I think once I figure it out, I'll have a better idea who killed your mother and Monsieur de Saint Phalle."

"Do you think the murders are connected?"

"Yes, undoubtedly."

"Is it dangerous not to tell the police?" Jean Luc asked.

"I'm working with the police. My husband and I would prefer, however, that all of you who came as his guests this weekend be spared intense police interrogation. The police captain on the case thinks the murders were probably committed by people outside the hotel, criminal elements in the city."

"But you don't agree?" Kristin asked.

"I'm not sure," Elspeth said, although she was almost certain that the murderer was among their midst. "Thank you for telling me about your parents. And, by the way, if you would like to talk about Scotland, I would be more than pleased to do so."

Kristin smiled, "I suppose we should. Then if my father asks me, I can tell him honestly that we did."

"Why is your father opposed to your becoming a doctor?" Elspeth asked.

"He thinks it is not a proper profession for a woman. He has old fashioned ideas, unlike *Mutter*, who encouraged me to be independent."

"And you, Jean Luc, what do you think?"

He grinned. "Maybe I can find a course in Edinburgh for my postgraduate study."

"Then I must tell you a little about Scotland in the winter," Elspeth said, knowing instinctively that if Kristin and Jean Luc were in Scotland together, the dark days would not matter.

20

Roger Bouchard was late. Richard preferred promptness, a quality he admired in his wife and expected in others. Consequently Richard was not pleased when Roger came into the hotel at twenty past nine and made no excuse for his lateness. Richard was already unsettled by the events of the weekend. Elspeth might take murder in her stride as part of her job, but Richard was not used to such things in his. He rose and paced across the lobby to the front doors of the hotel. The evening doorman greeted him by name. Richard merely nodded at the courtesy and strode back into the interior of the hotel.

After he had done this three times, the doorman said, "Are you expecting someone, Sir Richard? If you wish to wait inside, I could see that your guest be shown into the bar or lounge, if you would like to wait there."

Richard said. "Yes, the bar will do nicely." But before going to the bar, he peered outside and saw Raffaello at his post beside the tree across the road. Raffaello was clad in a long anorak and had the hood up over his head to protect him from the passing showers. From his posture Richard suspected Raffaello was shivering slightly from cold.

Roger Bouchard sauntered into the bar, which further annoyed Richard. One did not saunter when on business. Roger's action smacked of his earlier protest at being called out on a Saturday evening.

"Richard," Roger said with a nod that was neither apologetic nor respectful. Roger turned to the barman who approached them and ordered a brandy. "Now what is so important that it could not wait until Monday?"

Insolence sat poorly with Richard and further exacerbated his mood.

"I have two murders and two strong suspects, both prominent men in the European business community. They will not wait until Monday before leaving the hotel, if the police allow them to do so. My wife, Elspeth, who is connected to the Kennington hotels' security department, is doing double duty here as not only my hostess and also as an informal investigator. I cannot allow this to continue. I want her to be free to carry on in the capacity as my hostess and not be distracted by the murders."

"Do the murders bother her?" Roger asked.

"Elspeth? No. She is quite used to murders," Richard said. He smiled inwardly, thinking that few men would say that of their wives with such equanimity. "She will undoubtedly tell you what she has learned and probably will want to continue with her own investigations. She can be a bit of a bulldog about such things, but in her capacity here as my wife I would prefer she be out of harm's way. Twice since I have known her, she had been attacked physically and grievously. In one case she had to be evacuated from Singapore to London and was in hospital for almost a month. It took six months for her to recover fully. I do not want that repeated here."

"Quite understandable," Roger said. He took a sip of the brandy the barman had brought and sighed contentedly. "Nice stuff," he said.

At a Kennington hotel, they would hardly dare to serve brandy that was not 'nice stuff'. Richard began to wonder why he had bothered to call Brussels. After all, despite his reluctance concerning her involvement, Richard trusted Elspeth's competence over Roger's, but he could not admit to Roger that calling him away from his weekend might have been a mistake.

"I need you here to coordinate with the police but at the same time to see that they do not disturb my guests," Richard said. "Captain Schrott from the Bruges police seems a reasonable person, but she is convinced the murderer or murderers come from the criminal fringe here in Bruges. She will share the postmortem reports with you and possibly anything else she finds if I request that she do so. Both Elspeth and I however think someone in our party may have some responsibility for the crimes. Elspeth has questioned the women and I the men, but we still haven't uncovered any concrete evidence. Captain Schrott may be right, which is why I need you. I cannot stay here beyond tomorrow and I think the others have the same issue."

"Are you saying you want me to stay on past tomorrow?" Roger asked.

"If necessary."

"But I have other work."

"Roger, you know how important it is for us to find Mateo. I had hoped this weekend would allow me to do so. And instead I have been faced with two murders of people who were supposed to supply me with the information. Do you really have anything that supersedes this?"

Richard raised his eyebrows and purposely looked down his long nose. Roger hesitated before answering.

"I can give it until Wednesday and then I must return to Brussels. Or perhaps I can arrange to conduct my business with Captain Schrott electronically, which will save your budget and probably my job. Even the temptation of staying here in this beautiful hotel cannot lure me from reality."

To the uninitiated the hotels did have an air of unreality, Richard thought, but through Elspeth he had seen the underside of them. It was not always pretty. At one time, he had tried to dissuade Elspeth from continuing on in her job, but she had made it a condition of their marriage three and a half years before that she continue on. He had never completely understood why.

He did need Roger Bouchard. If Roger could communicate from Brussels, so be it, but Richard wanted Roger to be in Bruges to meet everyone. Despite all the innovations in communication, Richard firmly believed that person-to-person meetings were the most effective. He planned to introduce Roger at breakfast the following morning.

Richard quickly filled Roger in on his suspicions that either Viktor Novikov or Ulrich Müeller was Mateo, and that Alexandre de Saint Phalle was murdered by one of them.

"And Helga Müeller? Why was she murdered?"

Roger swirled the brandy in its snifter and let out a

sigh, an action which signalled his disdain towards Richard. He wondered if Roger had heard anything he had just said or would remember it in the morning. Richard did not want to report Roger's lapses because previously he had found the man able to do his job. Perhaps what Richard was asking was just too difficult for him and he was afraid of failure. People who were good at a limited task, such as Roger's administrative duties, sometimes fell apart when their boundaries were stretched. Or perhaps he simply had had too much to drink.

Finally Roger said, "What time is breakfast?" Richard heard no concern in his voice.

Exasperated, Richard said, "We meet in a private room at nine. You can ask the concierge which one. I think we have done all we can this evening. The hotel has seen to your cases and you can get your room key card at the reception desk."

"I will finish my brandy and then do so."

Richard did not wait, as he knew Elspeth might slip out to see Raffaello and make the excuse that Richard was occupied when she went to do so. He bid Roger Bouchard goodnight and hoped the man would not order another brandy on his tab.

Richard caught up with Elspeth just as she was leaving their suite. She was dressed for the outdoors in her mackintosh and a hat that she had pulled down over her hair. She had changed into her flat shoes and carried a large torch.

"I'm coming with you," he said without greeting.

She must have sensed his darkened mood.

"Is something wrong?" she asked. She could just as easily have said 'Didn't I tell you that your man from Brussels wasn't needed'. He was thankful she did not. Instead she put her hand on his arm affectionately.

"Do you want to get your coat and hat? But please, Dickie, stay back. I have no idea if Raffaello will tell me anything, but I don't want to frighten him away."

Later riding down the lift, she asked, "Did you see Dagmar downstairs when you were waiting for Roger Bouchard?

He shook his head. "She wasn't in the bar or the lounge."

"Where do you suppose she has gone?"

"Could she simply be asleep? After all she was up as late as we were last night."

"I hope so," said Elspeth. "I wish I were in bed as well."

They greeted both the night concierge and the doorman. Neither had seen Dagmar. Frans Bootds and his team were nowhere to be seen. The lobby was empty except for the lone receptionist at the check-in desk, who was busy behind his computer. No stray guests were about.

When Richard and Elspeth stepped outdoors it was raining. The doorman offered an umbrella to them. Elspeth asked for two.

"Have you seen either of the two men who wait across the street?" she asked the doorman.

"One was there until the rain started," he said. "I

think he had disappeared into a doorway."

"Dickie, you stay here by the door, where you can be under cover. I'll go see if I can find Raffaello. Please don't follow. You will see my torch."

She plunged into the night. The beam from her torch lit up the bullets of rain. Richard could hardly make out Elspeth's torch beyond the halo of the lights from the hotel and the streetlights dimmed by the rain. He put up his umbrella and stepped into the road. The rain made a ricocheting noise like distant gunfire on the umbrella, but still above it he could hear a tremendous crack as if something had hit the ground.

He plunged into the darkness guided by the feeble light of his small torch. Please God let Elspeth be safe he whispered over and over again.

21

"Damn," Elspeth said to the dark. The rain restricted her vision, and she could not see beyond the light from her torch. The street lights were muted by the downpour and helped her little.

She called out, "Raffaello, are you there?" There was no answer. She tried again to no avail. She remembered that the fish market was about fifty feet down the road. She made her way there, stepping over the streams of water that were washing down the sides of the road. She stumbled over a small fallen branch and dropped her torch. It rolled into the gushing gutter and went out.

"Damn," she said again. A gust of wind caught her umbrella and reversed it. She fought with the spokes, trying to right it. Now thoroughly wet, she forged her way forward, hoping she could make out the silhouette of the fish market against the faint glow of the city beyond. She could only see a few feet in front of her. She called out again with no answer. She ventured on, finding her way more from memory than sight. The rain let up slightly and the concrete market stalls appeared as a black shadow against the night sky. Elspeth made her way towards it. She called out Raffaello's name again. She heard a faint groan.

She pulled her mobile out of her pocket and touched the screen. A light came on, which, though faint, revealed someone lying on the floor. Keeping the phone in her hand she knelt down by the body and shone the feeble glow on the face of the man lying there. He groaned again.

"Raffaello," Elspeth said.

He did not reply but he opened his eyes briefly. He obviously had been struck as his cheek was bleeding. Elspeth always memorized the emergency code of a country before entering it and she dialled 1-1-2. A voice came on and spoke first Flemish and then French.

"Do you speak English?" Elspeth yelled into her phone.

"Yes, madam," the voice said. "What is your emergency?"

Elspeth explained and then said, "I'll stay with him until the police come. They will need an ambulance."

"I will call the police station in Bruges. They will be there as soon as they can."

Elspeth heard someone approach from behind her. Fear rose in her. Both Alexandre and Helga had been murdered near here and now this. She put her phone in her pocket and kneeled into a squat with her arms over her head. The person's torchlight ran across her. She swallowed in terror.

"Elspeth, what the devil?" she heard a familiar baritone voice say.

She stood and rushed into Richard's arms. He held her tightly until her shivering subsided.

Finally she gasped, "Raffaello is over there. He has been attacked."

"I heard you calling the police. It's not safe here, my dearest. Come back to the hotel."

"No, I said I would wait. With you here, I don't

think the attackers will come back. Oh, dearest, dearest Dickie, thank you for coming," she said and held her arms tightly around his chest.

"Foolish girl," he said as if she were fifteen.

She ignored the remark. "I don't think Raffaello is in any condition to speak to me. I hope the police get here soon. I wouldn't like him to die. Maybe we were all wrong and Captain Schrott right. Raffaello's attack would suggest that."

In the distance the undulating wail of a police car broke through the rain. Richard did not let go of Elspeth.

"If we are going to wait, I want the attacker to be aware of both of us," he said. He straightened to his full height and kept his arms around her. "I picked up your torch from the gutter. It may not give any light, but it certainly can be used as a weapon."

"Do you think they will return? The men who attacked Raffaello?"

"Not now, not with the police coming. I expect they are long gone from here. Elspeth, did you need to take this risk?"

"I needed to talk to Raffaello."

Raffaello groaned again. Elspeth leaned down to him and whispered, "Tell me who did this?"

Elspeth thought he said "*ein Mann*", but she could not be sure.

"Did you know him?" she asked.

His eyelids flickered. "*Nein.*" He fell unconscious.

She looked up at Richard. "*Ein Mann* means one man, doesn't it?"

"Yes, but his voice was so soft I couldn't be sure

what he had said to you."

The sirens came closer and through the rain they could see the reflections of the blue lights. Shortly the beam of a spotlight caught them. Elspeth waved. The headlamps of a car cut through the downpour, the flashing lights now distinct. An ambulance followed behind. The police car drove through the flooding on the road and sprayed water in high jets. The ambulance made its more sedate way behind.

Captain Schrott was the first out of the police car. She had on a dark blue police mackintosh but was drenched by the time she reached the fish market stalls. Water ran from her hair down her cheeks and settled on her chin before dripping on her coat. She ran an impatient hand across her face and blew out the raindrops that had gathered on her lips.

"Sir Richard, Ms Duff, I want you to return to the hotel immediately. This is the third time the gang of criminals has struck here by the hotel. I cannot be responsible if you don't leave the crime scene now. It is too dangerous for you to stay. The police presence may attract some of your guests. Ms Duff, I advise that you warn the doorman not to let anyone go out tonight. Anyone who returns to the hotel I assume will come by taxi. Have the doorman take them inside as quickly as possible. I have been following this gang for a long time and now I think I am closer than ever before to finding them."

"But Raffaello?" Elspeth interposed.

"Raffaello?"

"Raffaello Conti, the man who is lying there."

"We will take him to the nearest hospital. I will have an officer go with you and take the information about him. But you two must leave." The captain motioned to a policeman waiting in the car. He rolled down the window.

She spoke in rapid Flemish, at which point the policeman looked out the window and pointed at the rain.

"My wife and I have umbrellas. Let me take one over to the car." Richard said, following his words with action. Elspeth put up her umbrella, which she had righted, and reluctantly left the stalls.

"I will see you in the morning," the captain said. "Don't leave the hotel again tonight."

Not wanting to parade the uniformed policeman across the lobby, Elspeth let them through the staff door, and let them into the kitchen area. The kitchen workers looked up from their work of making the breakfast pastries and breads. Elspeth signalled to them to resume their duties and escorted Richard and the policeman into the security office. Frans Bootds was there with his head on his arms on his desk and snoring gently. Elspeth's entry with the two men in tow roused him. He looked at Elspeth and smiled like a schoolboy caught disobeying the rules.

Elspeth took command. "Frans, there has been another attack outside the hotel. We need to put preparations in place to protect the comings and goings of the guests. All entrances and exits need to be guarded. For the moment, call your security staff off from watching the members of my husband's party and bring them here."

The policeman looked startled by Elspeth's authority. He must have wondered how a guest at the hotel could be so decisive.

"While you are gathering your staff, Sir Richard and I need to talk privately to the police officer in your conference room. Call me when everyone is assembled," she said.

Richard straightened up and cleared his throat. "This way, please," he said to the officer.

Elspeth followed the two men, her mind in turmoil. She had been convinced that the murderer was in the hotel, but now there was the possibility he was not. Had she been at fault to take command? Had she done this to avoid her duties as hostess to Richard's party, to settle back into a familiar role rather than trying to succeed at the one Richard had asked her to assume? Was she still that afraid of being Lady Marjorie's poor substitute? Or was she just being bossy, a trait Richard had often accused her of when they were young?

When they reached the conference room, she held back. Richard assumed his natural assertiveness.

The policeman spoke first, although Elspeth sensed he was uneasy. He took a slightly sodden pad of paper from his uniform pocket and opened to a blank page.

"Tell me what happened tonight," he said. His English was stilted but fluent.

Richard related the events from his perspective but did not say why he followed Elspeth.

"And you, madame, why did you go outside?"

"I wanted to speak to the man in the fish market who was attacked."

"What was his name?"

"Raffaello."

"And where was he from?"

"I'm not sure. Perhaps Switzerland. He spoke Swiss German with his brother."

"His brother? Who is his brother?"

Elspeth looked up at Richard who was staring at her. She wondered if he remembered the names Giorgio had told them earlier. She would have liked to evade the policeman's question, but with Richard's questioning look, she felt she could not.

"I spoke to his brother earlier today."

"Why, Ms Duff?"

"I thought he might have seen Frau Müeller's killer."

"Had he?"

"No. I went out tonight to see if Raffaello had."

"When it rained?"

"I didn't know it was raining so hard," she lied.

"You took an umbrella and a torch, no?"

"Yes, just in case."

"What do you know about Raffaello? What was his family name?"

"Conti."

"It was raining very hard with cats and dogs." He smiled, clearly pleased at his knowledge of the idiom. "How did you know where Raffaello Conti was?"

"I found him at the fish market. The doorman told me its Flemish name, but I have forgotten it."

The policeman smiled. "*Vismarkt*. It is close to English. Did the doorman see Raffaello? He was far away."

"Raffaello was watching one of the guests in the hotel," Elspeth finally admitted.

"The stalking?"

"No. I think the guest's husband wanted her followed, most likely for protection. The guests who stay here are well-to-do. The Kennington management won't be pleased that there is a gang of criminals working near here. Security is very important to the hotels. We cannot have our guests be afraid to go outside. I'm sure Lord Kennington will be highly concerned about the events of the last few days and the Bruges Police Department's inability to keep the streets near here safe."

Elspeth's words drew the desired effect. The policeman paled and coughed.

"You must speak to the captain," he said, as if the safety of the streets was her responsibility and not his. "We do not have this trouble often."

"I'm sure," Elspeth said. She was glad to have the pressure off of her. "Tell Captain Schrott that I would like a full report in the morning."

"Madame, I do not understand."

Elspeth softened. "I work directly for Lord Kennington, the owner of the Kennington hotels. You must appreciate with the prices he charges and the location he personally selects for his hotels, he expects safety inside and outside the buildings. I know Captain Schrott wants the same thing."

"She is one of the best captains. She will find the

criminals."

"Is there anything else you need from us tonight, officer?" Richard said. Elspeth expected he would accuse her of being too aggressive later, but that was the effect she wanted.

"No, I will tell the captain that you do not know about Raffaello, only his name," the policeman said.

"Let me show you out the back," Elspeth said, rising from her chair. Richard, shall we meet upstairs?"

Elspeth was chuckling when she arrived back at their suite.

"Sometimes, Elspeth, I find that the things that amuse you are quite appalling. Did you purposely put him off?"

"As quickly as I could. I didn't want him asking about Dagmar, who may well have been outside, or our other guests. As you know, both Eric and Pamela insist that we should keep the identity of the guests as confidential as is humanly possible. People with money or position feel a certain entitlement. Lord Kennington panders to that. The police often don't understand."

Richard finally smiled. He shook his head. "I think you are touched a bit by the devil. How did you know Raffaello's surname?"

"His brother Giorgio told me. Really, Dickie, I don't know anything more and I don't know exactly why Raffaello and Giorgio are following Dagmar. It may be all very well to say that they are there to protect her, but my sensibilities tell me they were shadowing her in order to tell Alexandre what she was doing. It's a different kind of shadowing."

"How is that?" he asked.

"The private investigator I trained under in Los Angeles before getting my private eye licence showed me how to shadow someone. It's really quite simple. Bodyguards work up close; tails try to hide from their subject."

"I'll remember that for future reference," he said. "You never know when it might be useful."

Elspeth scowled. She could not tell if he was serious or joking. His deadpan expression seldom gave him away.

"You never know," she said. She picked up a pillow on the sofa and hurled it at him. He caught it expertly but did not toss it back.

"We need to talk," he said, "but let's wait until morning. You must be as tired as I am."

"Oh, damn," she said. "I forgot to go back to Frans Bootds's office."

"Can't you do it by phone?"

"Perhaps I shall. If I do, it may give Frans back some of his dignity."

When Elspeth phoned him, Frans told Elspeth he had assembled his team and they were waiting for her.

"I won't be back down," she said without explaining why. "Have them watch all the entrances and exits, including the kitchen. I want someone to be physically present at each door in case anyone tries to slip out. Also have one of your men sit in the lobby and have them call you if any of the guests in my husband's party try to leave by the front. Let me know when the

Novikovs come in. You can ring me on our room phone."

After she hung up the phone, she sighed deeply.

"I hope," she said to her husband, "that we will not be disturbed."

"Except by the Novikovs' return," he said and took her in his arms, "My dearest one," he whispered in her ear, "now it's I who has brought mayhem to our lives."

The call came as they were settling in bed. Frans reported that the Novikovs had returned by taxi and went immediately to their rooms.

The next morning after rising, Elspeth said to Richard, "I slept the sleep of babes and feel much better. What do you have planned after breakfast?"

"Since it now appears that the murders were committed by someone outside the hotel, I'll tell everyone they are free to go."

"Including Roger Bouchard?"

"I want him to stay in touch with the police here, but he wants to do so electronically. I'm sure he will accuse me of dragging him away from his weekend and let the people in Brussels know his dissatisfaction. His department will not like my actions, but I still want Roger to meet all the people in the Mateo investigation. It could give him more sense of responsibility."

"Are you disappointed that you didn't find Mateo?"

"A bit. I still suspect Viktor but have no proof. If Mateo is either Viktor or Ulrich, they will know that the EC will be watching them closely. Our meeting here may act as a deterrent for Mateo's actions in the future."

"Hopefully. But I'm not convinced that you have failed here. We have a great deal of information. It just needs sorting. I wish the murders hadn't muddied things, but I still think there is a connection between the murders and Mateo."

Richard eyed her sharply. "You can't let it go, can you? Well, my dearest, if you do uncover Mateo, Europe will be a safer place."

"A lofty goal," she said. "Now let's get dressed and face your mob."

They were the first to arrive at the room set aside for breakfast for their group. Who shall I be this morning, Elspeth thought, Lady Munro or Elspeth Duff? She would try to perform her duties as hostess, but her mind was on Mateo and the murders. The others straggled in. No one looked happy, but they all came, including a long-faced Roger Bouchard. He looked as if he had a hangover and a grudge against Richard. Dagmar was dressed demurely in trousers and a jacket suitable for plane travel, but she announced she had hired a car to take her back to Paris. The others asked if they were free to go.

Elspeth surveyed the room, watching each individual face to see if any one of them showed relief after being let go. They all did except Kristin and Jean Luc, who whispered to each other at the end of the table away from the others.

The thrill of a Kennington breakfast seemed to have worn off. Even Ulrich Müeller's plate was less full.

When they all were finished serving themselves,

Richard rose. "The police believe that the deaths of Frau Müeller and Monsieur de Saint Phalle can be attributed to gang violence that has spread to this part of the city. I spoke to Captain Schrott this morning, and she asked that you all let the police know where you can be reached in the next few weeks. You are free to go once you have given this information to me."

Most sighed; Ulrich grunted.

Dagmar, however, could not let matters rest. "And that's all?" she said. "Nothing more? Nothing to soothe the grieving? No apology for police inefficiency? How like the Belgians."

Viktor rose at this point. "Oh, for God's sake, Dagmar, cut the dramatics."

"That's easy for you to say, Viktor. I noticed that no member of your family was hurt. Or is it that Hélène is too lazy to stir herself and get in harm's way?"

Hélène jerked up and Viktor glowered.

Ulrich stepped in. "I think we do not need to quarrel. It was a sad weekend for us all. It is best we all go home. Sir Richard, it was a pleasure to meet your good wife. Kristin, come."

"I want to say goodbye to Jean Luc. I'll be with you in a few minutes."

Viktor turned to Hélène and drew back her chair. "Come, *chèrie*. Sir Richard, Lady Munro," he said with a nod. "Jean Luc, we will be leaving shortly. Do hurry."

Dagmar stared at the Novikovs as they left.

"She is foul. I don't know what Viktor sees in her. The weekend was not a success, was it? Sir Richard, I know you did your best. Lady Munro, you were persistent but thank you for being so polite about it. Goodbye and safe trip."

She followed Ulrich Müeller and the Novikovs out of the room.

Jean Luc spoke hurriedly to Kristin. He took her hands and in an old-fashioned gesture kissed the back of both of them. Then he leaned over and kissed both of her cheeks. Elspeth could not hear what he said into her ear, but Kristin blushed, plainly with delight.

She came over to Richard and Elspeth. "Before I leave, may I talk to you again, Lady Munro?"

"I'll leave you two," Richard said. "I have things to attend to."

"Come and have another coffee," Elspeth said to Kristin. She felt her official duties were over for the weekend. She did not regret their termination.

"I expect my father will do very little in the way of a funeral. Neither of my parents are religious," Kristin said as she stirred cream into her cup. "I had planned to come to London next week. Will you be there? May I see you?"

"I'll be working in Edinburgh. Is there any chance you can take the train up there? It's a bit of a journey, but I can show you round if you like. Is it anything important?"

"I'm not sure. Something is not right about my mother's death, but I need to sort it out before seeing you in the UK."

"Here's my card. It has my mobile number and email. Don't worry that it is my business information. I check all my own messages."

"Thank you, Lady Munro. I wish my mother had been as sympathetic as you." She departed on those words. Elspeth was left wondering what it was Kristin was puzzling about and hoped her hesitance would cause her no harm.

Then Elspeth admonished herself for being so suspicious.

22

On returning from Bruges, Elspeth took a taxi to their home in Kensington but asked the driver to stop short of their flat near an ice cream shop. She knew her housekeeper would have left a meal for her to put in the microwave, but she had a sudden yen for the double chocolate ice cream laced with pecans. The shop made their own ice cream and the flavour was Elspeth's favourite. As she made the short walk to her flat pulling her case, she licked the ice cream in the cone and sighed at the pleasure over the double chocolate, the nuts and the satisfaction they gave her.

The sky was now darkening. She walked slowly, enjoying her treat and casually looking at the houses lining the street. Most of the occupants had drawn their curtains, but in one bay window she saw a woman and her daughter laughing. The mother embraced her child, and the child threw her arms around her mother, waiting to receive the kiss that was promptly given.

Elspeth stopped, trying to remember when she had hugged her daughter like that. Dear Lizzie, she thought, why are things still wrong between us? Elspeth had the year before implicated a relative of Lizzie's closest friend in a murder case. Lizzie had not forgiven her mother, although Elspeth had no choice in her actions.

Elspeth thought of Kristin Müeller, another daughter who was at odds with her mother. Kristin would now never have a chance to make things right with Helga, but Elspeth did have a chance to rectify her own maternal relationship with Lizzie.

She took the last bites of her waffle cone and wiped her fingers on her handkerchief. She unlocked the door to the flat and took her suitcase to the loft. Then she picked up her landline and dialled Lizzie's number. The phone rang six times. Elspeth was about to disconnect, when a voice came on the line. Tim, or was it his twin Tom, answered the phone with as much dignity as a five-year-old could muster.

"Foxworthy residence. May I assist you?" Tim or Tom stumbled on the esses. When he heard Elspeth's voice, he shouted, "Grandmother, where have you been? I miss you. I have a new engine for my train set. Will you come and see it?" Elspeth then knew it was Tom, who had always had a mania for trains and had an extensive model train track layout in the attic of their house in East Sussex.

"Dear Tom, I'll come as soon as I can. Is your mummy there?"

Tom dropped the phone and Elspeth could hear him scurrying off. She had not seen him for the last year. Sadness filled her. How could she choose the words to say to her daughter that would put things right?

"Hello, Mummy," the voice said on the other end of the line. Lizzie's voice was frosty.

Elspeth bit the corner of her lip. She swallowed.

"Lizzie, I want to make things better between us. Can we talk?"

"About what?" Lizzie said. "I really have nothing to say to you."

Elspeth tried again. "Would you consider coming up to London? You could bring the boys. I know Richard would be willing to take them to the Tower to see the yeoman, the ravens and the crown jewels, leaving us some time alone together."

"How is Richard?" Lizzie asked, without answering Elspeth's invitation.

"Lizzie, please. I have just had a case in Belgium where a daughter lost her mother. They were on bad terms. The daughter now has no chance to resolve things with her mother. I don't want that to happen between us. Please," she said again.

Elspeth heard Lizzie push her breath through her teeth. She knew daughter well enough to hear her resistance.

Elspeth tried again. "Or if a trip to London doesn't work for you, why not bring the children up to Biddy's farm on Loch Tay? They love playing with the animals and being taken out on the loch. Denis could do some fishing and we could talk. I'm sure Biddy would be happy to have us come." Denis was Lizzie's husband, and Biddy was Elspeth's cousin, Lady Elisabeth Douglas Forbes, who was unabashedly a farmer on the shores of Loch Tay in Perthshire. "We could all go together for the weekend or Richard and I could meet you there."

"What do you want to say, Mummy? No words will change what happened in Bermuda."

"No, they can't. But maybe . . ." Elspeth stopped. But maybe what? She tried to choose carefully her next words. "Maybe it's time for us to get beyond what happened there since we cannot change it."

Elspeth could hear the twins wrangling in the background.

"I'll think about it," Lizzie said.

"Please, my darling."

"Goodbye, Mummy. I must attend to the boys."

Elspeth sat a long time and stared at the phone. Well, she had tried. She thought of Dagmar, who had called her politely persistent. What worked in Elspeth's job, might just as well work in her personal life. She went to the kitchen and made herself a cup of tea. Then she returned to her home office and drew out a sheet of notepaper. She wrote three different letters before she was satisfied. In her large hand she addressed the envelope to her daughter.

Richard's call came in from Brussels as she was finishing the last draft. She still found the letter inadequate. She debated whether to show the letter to Richard but decided against it. This was her battle to fight, not his. She merely asked if he was free for the weekend to go to Scotland. When she rang off, she folded the letter, put it in an envelope and put a first class stamp on it. In order not to not lose courage, she stepped outside and put it in the red pillar-box at the end of her street. Hope lives eternal, she thought as she did so. Families often did heal old wounds. Please, Lizzie, understand that. Friends may come and go; families are permanent and good familial relationships a gift.

When she got back to the flat, she called Biddy and asked if she could come to Tay Farm and bring Richard, Lizzie, and her Foxworthy brood.

"Elspeth," Biddy said, "You're always welcome. I

hope this means you are making up with Lizzie."

Biddy the Wise. Biddy with whom Elspeth had played havoc in their youth but now was her closest friend and personal font of knowledge.

"I'm trying. She's still resistant."

"Do you want me to talk to her?"

"Would you? What would you say?"

"I'll think of something. I'll ring you afterwards."

"I'll be in Edinburgh the rest of the week, but you can reach me on my personal mobile number," Elspeth said.

"Chasing murderers again?"

Elspeth laughed. Biddy had once been involved in one of Elspeth's cases.

"This time it's just a swindler."

"Piece of cake," Biddy said. "When you receive Magdalena Cassar's money, have you thought of retiring?"

"Heavens, Biddy, what would I do with my time?"

"Be Richard's wife to start."

"I'm afraid I'm not very good at that. I've tried," Elspeth said clenching her teeth. "Please let me know about Lizzie."

When their call was finished, Elspeth sat back and frowned. In the years since divorcing her first husband in California, had she been selfish? Had she neglected her children? They were grown and had their own lives, but did they still need more of her attention? And was she disappointing Richard? She had no answers, but the thoughts dispirited her.

Elspeth spent Monday morning at the offices of the Kennington Organisation in the City of London preparing for her trip to Edinburgh. The comfort of her job swept over her. She felt competent and centred, unlike the way she had during her weekend in Bruges. The case in Edinburgh involved a complex scheme of fraud perpetrated against the hotel there. Elspeth knew she would have to spend long hours with the head of accounting and the head of security there, but she looked forward to the hard but hardly dangerous work ahead.

Still, deep down, the affair in Bruges bothered her. She hated cases without resolution. Her sensibilities told her that Captain Schrott might have been pursuing the wrong killers. She tried to turn her thoughts to the task ahead, but her mind would not settle.

Richard had gone on to Brussels from Bruges, with a promise to be home in London by Friday night. She was scheduled to take the noon train from King's Cross and hoped to return by Friday as well, unless Lizzie would come to Scotland.

All through the week, Elspeth expected a message from Biddy. Finally on Thursday Biddy rang her mobile and left a message saying she had convinced Lizzie to come to Tay Farm on Saturday. She would not bring her family as she anticipated a short stay. Once she got the message, she phoned Biddy back.

"What did Lizzie say?"

"Your daughter, Elspeth, is as stubborn as you are, but at least she agreed to talk. She's taking the noon train on Saturday and will stay for dinner. I urged her to stay the night, but she said it all depended on what happens when you talk."

"Oh dear. How like Lizzie. Richard and I will come up to the farm on Friday night, if that's OK with you."

"Perhaps we can talk before Lizzie arrives."

"I think that would be very helpful," Elspeth said.

The case in Edinburgh was routine for Elspeth. She had handled several swindlers before and was always amazed by their cleverness. The suspect was a sheik from Saudi Arabia who had come to Edinburgh with his four wives, all in burqa when they appeared in public. When Elspeth had gone to the suite they were staying in, the best in the hotel, she found the women in designer clothing, each with jewellery that screamed oil money and immaculate taste. With such riches, why would the Saudi want to defraud the hotel? Elspeth watched the husband and wives for three days before she discovered why. The swindler was the youngest wife.

Such cases were difficult to resolve. Elspeth did not want to contact the police, although the crime was prosecutable. The Kennington hotels always kept the police away if possible, particularly when wealthy or prominent guests were concerned. Elspeth thought carefully before she requested an audience with the sheik. She made sure the hotel manager was with her when she spoke to him in order to observe proprieties. The sheik did not seem surprised by his wife's underhandedness. He quickly made financial amends. In the end Elspeth felt that the youngest wife's punishment would be more severe than the police would have inflicted and would probably be physical. Why had she been so keen to get money? She lacked for nothing, but she undoubtedly had no funds of her own. At least the problem had been resolved and the wealthy Saudis hopefully would return to Kennington hotels in future.

Throughout the week Elspeth could not get Kristin Müeller out of her thoughts. In her job Elspeth dealt with many families from all over the world. In cases such as the Saudi's, she resolved the issue and then almost always put the people out of mind. Why did Kristin come back to her so often? At first Elspeth thought it was because of her problem with Lizzie. Later she was almost certain it was something else, something Kristin had said about her mother that had nothing to do with Lizzie. What was it?

Elspeth talked to or emailed Richard several times a day and frequently asked if the case in Bruges had been solved. The answer was always negative. Richard expounded on the inefficiency of Roger Bouchard, who, in his opinion, should have stayed in Bruges and cleared the whole thing up. Elspeth wondered if it was also a condemnation of her inability to find the murderer among Richard's weekend guests.

The affair in Edinburgh took Elspeth until Friday afternoon. Lord Kennington offered the use of his personal jet for her return to London, but she declined. She rang Richard and suggested he fly from Brussels into Edinburgh rather than London and that she would meet him with a hired car. She rang Biddy to confirm their arrival time.

When Elspeth met Richard at the security gate at

the airport, he looked tired. Earlier she had glossed over the reason for the weekend but during the drive to Biddy's farm, she told him of her purpose in inviting him to Loch Tay.

*

Since their marriage over three years before, Richard had judiciously stayed out of Elspeth's relations with her children. He came along to family events with them and treated them with kindness but not deep affection. He made no excuses for his distance, other than saying he did not want to compete with their father, who still lived and worked in Hollywood. Elspeth often felt that her children did not approve of her new marriage or the way she lived with her husband. Both travelled frequently and were often apart. Richard kept any show of his love for Elspeth hidden when he was with her children. He was fond of Tom and Tim, who called him Richard, not grandfather. Before Elspeth's break with Lizzie, Richard often took the twin boys on excursions around London, much to their delight, and had promised them a trip on his boat in Malta when they were nine. All that had stopped when Elspeth had found out the truth in the murder at the Kennington Bermuda a year earlier.

Richard had never stepped in to heal the breach between Elspeth and her daughter. He had advised Elspeth that time would help, and he had held her emotionally when she occasionally fell into self-pity over the situation. Elspeth always wondered if this reflected Richard's parents' Edwardian coolness towards him and his brother. He seldom spoke of his parents.

When he did, it was from a distance. Once Elspeth had asked Richard's brother David why this was so. David had explained that Richard had taken his parents' iciness painfully, particularly when David and Richard's nanny had died when Richard was eight. Shortly afterwards, Richard was sent away to school. Elspeth thought of her own parents, who had lavished love on her and even now indulged her in ways that still comforted her.

But now Lizzie. Why had Lizzie at the age of ten announced that she no longer wanted to live in Hollywood and that she wanted to go to boarding school in England? Granted both her parents were British, not American, but they lived comfortably among Americans. Peter, Elspeth's younger child, considered himself an American, but Lizzie had renounced all claims to that affiliation from an early age although she had been born in Southern California. Elspeth had missed her daughter when she had gone away. She had delighted in the summers and holidays when Lizzie came home, often with a friend, but Lizzie was always eager to return to Britain. Elspeth thought that taking the job with the Kennington Organisation based in London would allow her to grow closer to her daughter, who was finishing university at the time. But Lizzie soon attached herself to Denis Foxworthy and married him before Elspeth could form any stronger ties with her daughter. Moreover Elspeth was often away from London.

Could one day, one conversation reconcile them after the twenty years that had come between them? At least could it just be a beginning?

Richard listened as Elspeth poured out her troubles

but had little to contribute. He merely said, "Let Biddy help."

Elspeth put her arms around him that night at the farm and he held her lovingly. "You will do all you can," he consoled her. "Lizzie will have to give way a bit if your meeting is going to work. You can't make her do that. My dearest love, don't be disappointed if you don't get all you want."

She had slept lightly, lying close to him, but a loving husband could not replace a distant child. If only it could be so.

*

Mornings at the farm were busy. Biddy always woke early and was at the henhouse collecting eggs when Elspeth found her.

"Why is it that I'm more afraid of my own daughter than I am of the miscreants who come into the hotels? I have faced down several murderers with much less fear than I am feeling about today's meeting with Lizzie."

Biddy put the eggs in a basket and said, "Two of my hens aren't laying. I usually give eggs with the Macphersons, but with the soufflé for dinner, I can't share. Come, 'Peth, and let's talk over coffee. It's warm this morning. We can sit outside in the sun."

Only a true Scot would think the weather warm. I've become soft, Elspeth thought. She wrapped her jacket more snugly round herself and warmed her hands on the steaming coffee mug.

"What happened between you and Lizzie a long time ago?" Biddy asked as they settled on a bench outside the kitchen. "I think her reaction to your discovery in Bermuda was only an excuse to cover a wrong she felt when you lived in California."

Elspeth sipped her coffee and thought. "I'm not sure, but I think you're right. Lizzie has always kept her distance from me, even in childhood."

"What about her relationship with Alistair?"

Elspeth thought of her first husband, Alistair Craig. She also remembered their unresolved relationship, particularly after meeting him in India several months before. She had never considered that her growing discontent with her first marriage when Lizzie was a child might have affected her daughter so profoundly.

"Do you think Lizzie's desire to leave Hollywood at such an early age had something to do with Alistair?" Elspeth asked, staring over the rim of her mug.

"Or both you and Alistair. Lizzie may have felt overpowered by all the dazzle in your lives."

Elspeth screwed up her face. "I don't remember any dazzle in my life."

"Didn't you often entertain some of the stars?"

"Alistair did. He is an excellent chef. We had a housekeeper, so my job was just to make appreciative noises when the stars showed up. Stars like talking about themselves."

"And where was Lizzie in all this?"

"The stars always said something like 'what a cute little girl', and then they would ignore the children if they were still about."

"Whilst you and Alistair were doing your dance around the celebrities. Did you pay a great deal of attention to Lizzie when she was young?"

"I thought so at the time."

"But you also were off doing your private detecting."

"Do you really think Lizzie felt neglected? I certainly loved her. Perhaps I didn't show it enough. You may find it strange, but I have learned so much about loving from Richard that I didn't know when I was married to Alistair. At first I was as much in love with Alistair's image as I was with him."

"Do you think Lizzie picked up that you and Alistair were in different worlds and neither world included her? Or was she raised by a nanny?"

"Karlene Clare was a marvellous woman," Elspeth said. She knew she sounded defensive.

"Ask Lizzie today how she felt growing up in Hollywood. And why she wanted to leave. It's a start."

Biddy agreed to fetch Lizzie from the train and bring her to the farm. The day had stayed warm and sunny. Elspeth waited by the loch, sitting on her grandmother's favourite bench, remembering the many times in her life that she had discussed problems there with various members of her family. Several times she rose and paced and then sat down again, trying to compose her thoughts. Finally she heard the noise of Biddy's Range Rover coming down the gravel drive. Elspeth held back, breathing consciously to still her heart.

She saw Lizzie coming down the path. Elspeth took in her breath. She had forgotten how much Lizzie resembled all the Robertson/Duff women, her mother

Fiona Robertson Duff, Biddy, and Elspeth herself, all with a strong chin, sculptured nose, and intense eyes, although Lizzie's eyes were dark brown, not deep cobalt blue like the others. Lizzie held her head high, as Elspeth often did. Lizzie must have seen her mother, but she did not wave.

Elspeth let out her breath and moved towards her daughter. Unable to contain herself, Elspeth ran forward and, even while fearing rejection, embraced Lizzie. Lizzie stiffened and then her body loosened. She threw her arms around her mother and began to sob on her shoulder. Elspeth reached up and stroked Lizzie's light brown hair, as she had when Lizzie was a small child. Neither spoke. Elspeth let the tears work their way out before she led Lizzie to the bench.

Elspeth drew a clean handkerchief from her pocket and handed it to Lizzie, who had wiped the back of her hand across her streaming nose.

Lizzie laughed. "I remember your clean handkerchiefs," she said.

"I used to keep several in my pocket."

"Did I cry that much?"

"Just in case," Elspeth said. "For tears or scrapes."

"The former being mine and the latter Peter's?"

"For tears from you both, and more often for Peter's scrapes."

The love Elspeth had felt in those years washed over her. How could she have let barriers grow between her and Lizzie? Why had she never asked Lizzie the reason she had fled to England when she was a child? Neither Elspeth nor Alistair had gone away to school.

Elspeth had been a day student at the Blair School for Girls, which did have boarders, and Alistair had attended a local grammar school in the Lowlands. They had put their children in a ridiculously expensive school in Los Angeles, because Alistair insisted, but the children lived at home.

Elspeth wondered how to begin.

"Did Biddy talk to you on the way from the station?" Elspeth asked.

"A little. She said you were as fearful of meeting as I am." Lizzie said.

"What are you afraid of, my dearest? Am I such an ogre? If I appear to be, I don't mean to be."

"You always seem so competent, so perfect. I never could meet your standards."

Elspeth gulped. "My standards?"

"The way you always look and carried yourself. Your clothes and your confidence."

"Do you know how much of a sham that is?"

"Sham?"

"Oh, yes, darling. You knew Magdelena Cassar, at least slightly. Ask Richard what I was like before Magdelena dragged me off to Paris and made me spend the summer with an impoverished French countess, whom Magdelena paid outrageously high wages to take the ragtag girl from the Highlands and make her into a well-turned-out gentlewoman. In my heart I still feel most at home here on the farm and at your grandparents' house on Loch Rannoch and still love to ramble in the forests and on the braes the way I did as a child. The rest is only icing hiding a quite ordinary cake."

"You always made me feel inferior. You spoke so beautifully and made everyone else in the room seem tawdry, even Daddy's actor friends."

"Is that why you wanted to come to the UK for school?"

"Partly. I wanted to be like you, but how could I be if I stayed in LA? The girls in my school were so 'valley girlish'. I didn't want to fit in. I wanted to be British like you, to speak properly, to dress beautifully, to be sophisticated and elegant."

Elspeth listened without speaking. She realised that she had never shown her children her vulnerable side. Richard and Biddy were the only ones with whom she ever confided her deepest doubts and fears.

Lizzie went on. "I knew I couldn't be as grand and graceful as you are, Mummy."

"Was I so distant?" Elspeth asked. "I love you, Lizzie, and always have."

"But I was not first in your life. Nor was Peter. Nor, I think, Daddy for that matter. You seemed far away all the time. Untouchable."

Elspeth swallowed hard. Was that how she had been in Hollywood? She remembered her growing disappointment in her marriage and her increasing disdain for the shallowness of her life and those around her. She thought she had hidden it from her children. In doing so, had she shut down her emotions as Lizzie had implied? Elspeth wished she could go back and change things.

"When you came back from Bermuda," Lizzie said, breaking Elspeth's thoughts, "you were so smug about solving the case there."

Smug? Ouch, that hurt.

"Did you know how your investigation would affect others? My friend? Me? Did you even consider that?"

Elspeth leaned over and took both of Lizzie's hands in hers. "It's my job. I didn't commit the crimes, but I had a responsibility to uncover the murderer. Murder does taint everyone involved, profoundly. Usually in my work, I'm not connected with the outcome. I'm sorry that the Bermuda case did involve people you know."

"Have you ever been connected to a murder case where you were emotionally drawn in?"

"I've never told you about Malcolm Buchanan. I should have. Malcolm was my fiancé when I was at Cambridge. He was murdered the day we became engaged. The case wasn't solved for thirty-seven years, until I went back four years ago and found the murderer. I had lived with the pain of his death for all that time. Yes, I have been emotionally drawn in."

"You never told me."

"It seemed irrelevant to my being your mother."

"Was it really, Mummy? If you were living with pain, did that take over your life? Is that why none of us could reach you?"

Elspeth knew Lizzie was speaking the truth.

"Who else knew about the murder at Cambridge?" Lizzie asked.

"Richard. He helped me at the time. Also my parents and Magdelena Cassar. Biddy of course was aware of it." Elspeth said. "Oh, Lizzie, Malcolm's death was a sore that never has healed completely, not even now when I know who murdered him."

"And was the murderer convicted?"

"No, the murderer was dead by the time I solved the case."

"But you can understand how my friend was affected, can't you? She still can't absorb what happened. She cries often."

"I do understand," Elspeth said gently.

"But you still go on with your work. Why when what you do hurts so many people?"

"Crime hurts people. That's why it must be prevented. I do what I can."

"Do you think that has made you unfeeling?"

"Sometimes I have to be."

Lizzie withdrew her hands from Elspeth's and looked away.

"Don't you have enough money to live without working? If not now, won't you inherit money from Magdelena Cassar soon?"

"Yes, quite a good deal. How funny. Biddy asked me the same thing about retiring."

"And Richard?"

"We have our own way of dealing with our careers," Elspeth said. She did not want to tell Lizzie that her arrangement with Richard was strained at times. Elspeth felt certain things were inappropriate to tell either of her children, although she was more open with her son. Perhaps the time had come to show Lizzie more of her life.

"Lizzie, can we at least continue talking? I never have let you in on my personal life. Now may the time to begin, so that you know I am as humanly flawed as anyone. Let's start by my asking your advice on things in my life in the same way that you have asked me in the past. Parents sometimes find it difficult to think of their children as grown. I do. I ask Peter about my computers. May I ask you about young people I deal with? I don't always understand their minds. You could help me. You'll also see some of the dilemmas I face in my daily dealings with people at the hotels. It could be a start for you to understand who I am. I'm not as aloof as you seem to think."

Lizzie rose and walked over to the edge of the loch. Elspeth stayed still, but her heart was pounding. How could she reach her daughter? She felt she had bungled this try. Lizzie picked up a stone and skimmed it across the water, the way Elspeth had taught her many years ago.

She turned back to Elspeth and said, "Only nine. You always did more."

"It's my one sport," Elspeth said. "When I was young, I skipped stones for hours on end. I always did so when I had a problem to solve. I did it so many times that I learned how to read the water and judge my throw. But I'm hopeless at tennis and croquet, which you are good at. And I throw up every time I even get near to Richard's boat."

Lizzie laughed. She returned to the bench. "Let's try to be friends, Mummy."

They didn't speak as they climbed the path up to the main buildings of the farm. They walked hand in hand, the way they used to when Lizzie was a small child.

Elspeth could feel her own tears of pain at her separation from her daughter and relief that a way had opened for her to end it.

Elspeth put her new resolve to the test shortly after she and Richard returned to London. Their landline answering machine was blinking madly. Elspeth gave the number to very few people and therefore the message must be important. She tapped the button and Pamela Crumm's voice came on.

"Elspeth, this morning I had an urgent call from a Jean Luc Novikov, who seemed to know my place at the Kennington Organisation. He said that he and Kristin Müeller wanted to speak to you as soon as possible. They are taking the Eurostar to London this morning and asked where they could meet you." Pamela had as usual set up the meeting at the Kennington Mayfair, with the time remaining flexible.

The recording had been made at eight that morning. Elspeth and Richard had been on their way home from Scotland and not at their flat most of the day. Elspeth checked her watch and saw it was well past four in the afternoon. She rang through to Pamela.

"I hope, my friend that you are at home and not at your desk on Sunday. Richard and I have been in Scotland and have just returned. What's this all about that Jean Luc and Kristin needed to see me in person?"

"They said it was about the murders. But I assume that the two of them wanted an excuse for a day together."

Pamela always could find romance if any existed at

263

all. Elspeth suspected that the ageing, bent and small woman, with a beak for a nose, and large round glasses had fantasies of being young, attractive, and eligible rather than being wedded to the running of the Kennington hotels.

"Can you reach them?" Elspeth asked. "Let's say half past four in the lobby of the Kennington Mayfair for tea. Can they make it by then?"

Richard pointed to himself and mouthed to Elspeth, "Me too."

"Pamela, tell them Richard is coming too. His interest in the events in Bruges is even greater than mine."

"I'll tell them, not ask them," Pamela said. "Half past four then. I'll book a quiet table in the tearoom at the hotel. The bill has been arranged for by me since your case in Bruges is still unresolved. Eric would prefer you get to the bottom of the murders as soon as possible."

"But the police have taken over," Elspeth protested.

"We cannot have murders committed just outside our hotels. You know how Eric feels about these things. He doesn't trust the police but he trusts you."

Eric Kennington frequently put Elspeth in similar situations. The disadvantage of her no longer being in Bruges did not cross his mind.

On ending the call, Pamela said, "Good hunting and enjoy your tea."

Elspeth put her head back and let out a cry of frustration.

23

"Will it never end?" Elspeth said.

Richard came up to his wife and touched her cheek. She rubbed her face against his hand.

"Will what never end?" he asked.

"Just as I solve one problem, another one crops up."

Richard had seen Elspeth's happiness when she had come up from the loch with Lizzie. Elspeth's usual edginess had faded into a large smile, which lasted most of the trip back from Loch Tay. After Pamela's phone call the strain was back. Richard had long since accepted this tension in Elspeth because he could not change it. Any mystery ate at her until she resolved it.

Richard had been sufficiently disappointed with Roger Bouchard that he was secretly glad Elspeth was back on the case of the murders in Bruges.

They arrived by taxi at the Kennington Mayfair shortly before four thirty and found Jean Luc and Kristin waiting for them in the main lobby. Kristin came up and hugged Elspeth. Jean Luc shook Richard's hand. The table Pamela had booked was waiting for them.

"Are all Kennington teas the same?" Kristin asked as she selected one of the cream teas.

"Lord Kennington tries always to have local food on the menu, but he knows that many travellers prefer the comfort of sameness," Elspeth explained.

"Cream teas are a wonderful sameness," Richard

added with a grin. He spread clotted cream and jam lavishly on his scone. "The strawberries for this confection are grown in France especially for the Kennington hotels all over the world."

Elspeth, unlike the others, ordered cucumber sandwiches. She accepted her tea and got down to business.

"The powers that be tell me that you have something to tell us that can't be done on the phone."

Kristin looked up at Jean Luc as if for confirmation.

"I was afraid that my calls might be monitored," she said. "Jean Luc agrees. He suspects my father is having my activities secretly listened in on. My father may not be as astute technologically as Jean Luc's, but he has a staff who is. I have something to tell you that may not please my father. Jean Luc suggested a day out and then rushed me on to Eurostar, which brings London so close."

"Kristin was with her father in Paris and convinced her father that she wanted the day by herself. I took the TGV up from Marseille last night and we made arrangements for today."

"Has your father been excessively protective since your mother's death?" Elspeth asked Kristin. Richard wondered where Elspeth was going with this.

"Only a little. He is trying to convince me to stay in Hamburg with him. I don't want to. I think that is why he indulged me and came with me to Paris."

"Did he have any other reason to go there?" Elspeth asked.

"No, Papa prefers to stay at home. He has extensive

offices there and every kind of communication device
that his assistants can think of. It was my mother who
travelled. But that is why I want to talk to you, Lady
Munro. I want to talk about *Mutter*."

Jean Luc was making good work of his second
scone. When he turned to Kristin, a bit of clotted cream
lined his mouth. Kristin smiled, picked up a napkin and
touched his lips. Richard recognised the tenderness of
her touch. He had never expected to spawn a romance
between the children of his guests during the weekend in
Bruges, but if Jean Luc and Kristin had found happiness
then at least one good thing had come out of the
meeting. Jean Luc looked at Kristin adoringly.

"Tell them, Kristin," he said.

"My father and I have been questioned thoroughly
by the police in Bruges. Captain Schrott came to
Hamburg personally to ask us what we had seen on the
day of my mother's murder and if we could think of any
reason why she might be other than a victim of street
crime. I could think of nothing at the time she
questioned us, but afterwards I began to wonder. Now I
think *Mutter*'s murder was caused by her own activities
and not by random violence. I have no material proof,
which I am sure the captain wanted. Jean Luc thought
you would understand, Lady Munro. At the hotel in
Bruges, you kept asking questions about us all. You
must have believed that someone in our party was
guilty."

Richard watched Elspeth look at Kristin and cock
her head slightly. He had seen Elspeth use this
expression many times before. She seemed to signify

assent but tacitly to ask the person to continue. Richard presumed that Elspeth must have practiced the look in front of her mirror in order to perfect it so completely.

"*Mutter*, you see, liked to, how shall I say it, to stir the pot more than *Vater*. My mother may have looked like a *hausfrau*, but she had the soul of a gypsy. I told you that she was frequently away from home. I don't know if this contributed to the bad feelings between her and my father, or if the bad feelings drove *Mutter* away. My mother was always restless when in Hamburg. She preferred Portugal, where she said people were more intriguing. That was her word. She mixed with a fast crowd there. I never liked her associates and would keep my own company most of the time when I was visiting her in Oporto. I fear she may have got into bad company."

"Are you suggesting that this bad company had something to do with her death?" Richard asked.

"I think so," Kristin said.

"Did any of this involve your father or Viktor Novikov?" Richard asked.

Kristin shook her head. "I don't think so. It seemed all *Mutter*'s doing."

Richard turned to Elspeth, who picked up his visual cue.

"Tell us about her associates," she said. "Do you remember any of their names?"

Kristin frowned and then shook her head.

"Think hard, if you can," Richard said. "Their names may be important in our finding your mother's killers."

Jean Luc touched Kristin's hand. "The names will be safe with Sir Richard," he said. "My father says Sir Richard has a reputation for integrity and honesty. I am certain you can trust him and Lady Munro as well."

Kristin looked like a trapped animal. She hesitated and finally said, "I'm afraid."

"Don't be, my dear," Elspeth said in a motherly voice that Richard had never heard before. "Above all we want to protect you."

"They might discover that I gave you their names. They are a bad lot."

"You don't need to return to Portugal," Richard said.

"They found my mother in Bruges, didn't they? They could find me anywhere."

"Tell me why you think they would attack you?" Elspeth said in the same soothing voice. "Do you know something about your mother's murder that you haven't told us?"

Kristin looked to Jean Luc for help. "Tell them, Kristin," he said.

Kristin curled her lips under her teeth. She raised her head and then took a deep breath.

"We came to London to tell them. Don't lose courage now," Jean Luc prompted.

Kristin looked at him, her eyes wide with fear.

"All right," she said. She paused. "Sir Richard and Lady Munro, the morning my mother was killed, she had a phone call, I think from Portugal because she was speaking in Portuguese. I don't speak that language, but I have enough Spanish and Italian to know that my mother was very upset. She would say a long sentence and then say '*Não, não, não*', that's 'no. no, no' in Portuguese. When my mother gets, got, angry, her face turned dark red. When she rang off, she shouted something that sounded like 'imbecile'."

"Do you know who was on the other end of the line?" Elspeth asked.

Kristin continued to bite her curled under lips. "I was curious. Once before I saw my mother like this, about a month ago in Oporto. She was speaking Portuguese that time as well."

Elspeth took a bite of one of her cucumber sandwiches and chewed slowly, clearly forming her next words carefully.

"Kristin, do you know what happened to your mother's mobile phone? Did the police give it to your father?"

Kristin answered Elspeth's question slowly, as if considering her reply. "They may have. . . but wouldn't it have been destroyed if it was in her handbag and went into the canal? She always carried her bag if she went out."

"The police might be able to reconstruct the phone number of the call that came from Portugal if they had the phone or its number. Please ask your father or see if you can find the phone or give you the number."

"I'll try, but I can't promise."

Richard broke in. "During her last conversation, did your mother use any names, even a given one like Mateo?"

Kristin gave no reaction to the name, but Jean Luc

did.

"Mateo? My father used the name several times with my mother," he said.

Elspeth turned to him. "In what context?"

"My father said he thought it was time that Mateo be put to rest. My mother agreed. Does that make any sense?"

"When did they say this, before or after they learned Frau Müeller was dead?" Elspeth asked.

"When we were packing to go home last Sunday from Bruges."

"Think carefully, Jean Luc. Do you suppose they believed Mateo had been put to rest or that he should be put to rest? Is there a difference in French?"

"There would be in French, but they were speaking in English. We often speak English together to keep in practice. My mother is a great linguist."

"Repeat their words exactly," Richard said.

"As closely as I can remember my father said, 'I think it is about time Mateo be put to rest', as I said. My mother said, 'Mateo should have died a long time ago.' And then my father said, 'Thank God the whole affair will be over soon,' or something like that. I didn't know what they meant. I had forgotten all about it until you mentioned Mateo."

All his career Richard had dealt with people and felt he knew when they were lying. Jean Luc was telling the truth. The young man seemed genuinely puzzled by what his parents had said and could shed no more light on it.

The waiter came with more tea and passed around a

platter of fresh scones, strawberries and cream. Jean Luc took another but Kristin and Elspeth shook their heads. Richard, who in middle age was watching his weight carefully, regretfully declined as well.

When the waiter left them alone, Elspeth turned to Kristin. "If you think of any names of your mother's associates in Portugal, will you send them to me at the Kennington Organisation?"

"Or you can take them to the British embassy in Paris or our consulate in Hamburg, if you want to know they are secure," Richard said. "You can address them to me at the Foreign and Commonwealth Office here in London. Mark them most urgent and confidential and I should get them the next day or two."

"I will consider that," Kristin said in a small voice. "But please, there is danger. My mother sometimes laughed at it. She said danger made life exciting. Now she is dead."

"Have we helped you with what you came here to do?" Richard asked Kristin. "I fear we have done very little."

"I needed to tell somebody else about my fears, someone in authority."

"Then you must trust us," Richard said. "My wife has worked on many difficult cases, some where murder was involved. She is always discreet, as you can imagine she must be in her job here at the hotels."

Elspeth added, "I promise I won't go to the police until you want me to, Kristin. My daughter will tell you that too many people can be hurt if I fail to keep their feelings in mind. I'll promise I will do all I can to cause you no harm."

Kristin looked down at her plate sadly. "I wish I could have said that my mother was that sensitive. You are lucky that you and your daughter get on so well."

"We don't always," Elspeth said. Elspeth's face showed no emotion other than a half-smile. What an odd juxtaposition of personal traits she had, Richard thought. Only her competence showed now, and not any of her usual doubt. Richard admired her for this; Kristin seemed comforted.

Jean Luc eyed Kristin. "Won't you tell them why we came here, Kris? Won't it be easier? Putting it off won't help."

Kristin squirmed. She obviously wanted to take Jean Luc's advice, but some feeling was holding her back. She looked round the room as if she was suspecting someone to be watching her.

"She's been terribly jumpy all day," he explained.

"Kristin, if I took you into the back rooms of the hotel where we can't be seen or heard, would that make it easier? The manager keeps several conference rooms there that are secure. We could pretend we are going to the ladies' room. One of the doors into the management offices is near there. I have a passkey. Richard and Jean Luc can come round the other way and I can let them in."

Kristin's eyes made another survey of the tearoom. "All right," she said but she seemed reluctant.

Elspeth answered Richard's light knock on the door that was hidden at the end of the hall to the men's room, and she let Jean Luc and Richard in. She led them down a wide hallway to a small conference room and explained that she used it frequently. It had no outside windows and the walls were sound insulated, which Elspeth explained made conversation within safe. On the sideboard was a neat stack of Kennington hotel stationery and engraved envelopes beside them. A porcelain container with the Kennington hotel crest held felt-tipped pens similarly marked. Richard had heard a great deal about this room and the many confrontations Elspeth had previously had in it. He never had been there before, but Elspeth had described it in sufficient detail to him for him to recognise it without being told where they were.

Kristin looked wide-eyed at the opulence of the room, the fine detailing of the furniture and the original paintings on the wall. Elspeth had told Richard that the flowers were always yesterday's but only the expert eyes of a florist would have known.

"Is this better?" Elspeth asked.

"Do all Kennington hotels have rooms like this?" Jean Luc asked.

"The larger ones do. The management finds it useful to entertain guests in private here." From the nuance of Elspeth's voice she suggested that the meetings were not always pleasant ones.

"Do you ever get used to this luxury?"

"It serves its purpose. If one is going to be direct with guests, it's best done in an imposing atmosphere. But let's hurry. If Kristin thinks someone is watching us, we shouldn't stay too long away from our table."

Elspeth drew a sheet of stationery from the stack and handed a pen to Kristin. "Richard can put this in his inside pocket when we leave. We'll keep in the safe in our flat until the morning, when he can take it back to Brussels."

"To Brussels?" Kristin said. Fear crossed her face. "I hoped only you would see it, Lady Munro; that somehow you could use the information to help find my mother's murderer without anyone else knowing I had given you the names. If these people ever found out that I knew about them, I think my father and I would be in great danger of being killed as well."

"Can you tell us why?" Elspeth asked.

Kristin began to cry. "Because of the money."

"What money?"

"My mother said it was all about the money. She said she held the power because she knew about the money. I don't know what she meant, because she said this to me once when she was a little tipsy. I don't think she remembered in the morning."

"All the more important we know their names. I promise we will not use them or contact them until we talk to you first."

"*Courage, ma chèrie*" Jean Luc said, falling into French.

Kristin looked around at each one of them. Finally she said, "All right. These are the only ones I remember. I may not spell them right."

She wrote down three names, folded the paper, put it in the envelope Elspeth gave her and sealed it. Elspeth handed the envelope to Richard. He carefully tucked it in the inside pocket of his jacket and patted it to show Kristin it was safe.

In the taxi on the way back to their flat, Elspeth turned to Richard.

"Are you thinking what I am thinking?" she said.

"That Helga Müeller, not Ulrich or Viktor, was Mateo?" he asked.

Elspeth bobbed her head slowly up and down.

"And where does that put us now?" she said.

24

Over dinner at their flat Elspeth and Richard discussed the options that lay open to them if their assumption about Mateo was correct.

"I feel obliged to honour my commitment to Kristin not to reveal these names to anyone, but I will use them if I need to. Still I'm perplexed on how to proceed. At the least I need to find out who these people are," Elspeth said. How would she do so securely? She could try the internet, but she as yet had no idea what she would find there or the information's veracity. The people on the list might verify that Helga was Mateo, but she already had assumed that no one on the list was the murderer. Their names might or might not be important later once the murderer was found.

She looked up and found her husband watching her.

He said, "What do you suppose Jean Luc meant when he said his father said, 'I think it is about time Mateo be put to rest', and his mother replied, 'Mateo should have died a long time ago.' Perhaps focusing on Helga's contacts in Portugal is diverting us from the Novikovs' interest in Helga's death."

"Are you suggesting that one of the Novikovs was involved in Helga's death?" Elspeth asked.

"I've suspected Viktor in both Alexandre de Saint Phalle's and Helga Müeller's deaths from the start," he replied.

"Jean Luc's words imply something different, more

a sense of relief than guilt on Viktor and Hélène's part. If Jean Luc reported the conversation accurately, their comments would seem to establish their innocence."

"But it also means Viktor and Hélène had a good idea that Helga was Mateo," he countered.

Elspeth bit the corner of her lower lip. "But what about Alexandre de Saint Phalle? Did he know that Helga was Mateo? As yet I don't see how Helga's death and Alexandre's are connected. I think if we could find the connection, we could identify the murderer."

He cocked his head and frowned. "You don't believe that both of them were killed by a criminal gang, do you?"

"No, but if for the moment it diverts the police from the hotel in Bruges, I'll have more time to find the truth. I need to return to Paris this week on other business and I think I'll pay a visit to Dagmar when I am there. She always implied that she knew who Mateo was. Now that we do, I feel more confident in confronting Dagmar again."

He chuckled. "Everything comes back to our troublesome Dagmar."

"So it seems," she said.

Elspeth was not being fully honest with Richard, but for good reason. She suspected that the Mateo network, even without its head, could soon be exposed and stopped. Richard then would have fulfilled his mission which had prompted the fateful weekend in Bruges. He was inclined to leave the murders to the police. Still Elspeth's job was the security of the hotels.

If word got out that two unsolved murders had occurred outside the Kennington Bruges, people might consider the area unsafe and cancel their bookings there. If she found the murderer or murderers and if she could prove that the reason for the murder was internal to Richard's group, Lord Kennington could assure his guests that he had done everything possible to make sure his hotel and environs were safe. Richard was not concerned about this. He might even advise Elspeth to let the matter drop.

They passed the rest of the evening pleasantly in each other's company and did not mention the murder again. Before Elspeth was up the next morning, Richard left for Brussels. She mumbled a goodbye from under the duvet, and he bent and kissed her, saying "Stay out of trouble, my dearest."

Elspeth had no intention of staying out of trouble. She felt she had to find the murderer soon. She also knew she must value Kristin's concern for the safety of her father and herself.

Knowing her daughter would be up with the children, Elspeth rang their East Sussex home. Her daughter's tone was no longer icy.

"Lizzie, I heard what you said in Scotland. Would you be willing to help me with one of my current cases? I need some outside insight. I also think you will be able to understand more fully why I do what I do."

"I'm not trained as an investigator. Aren't there people in the Kennington Organisation that can be more helpful?"

"I don't think so. Here's the problem. If you were a young person and you discovered that your mother was an international criminal on a grand scale, how would you feel? And if your mother were then murdered, where would you turn for help? You see, if you turned to the police, you would be exposing your mother and, in the process, destroy the trust that your father relied on for his livelihood. The daughter came to me and asked for help. She thinks that she and her father are in danger from her mother's colleagues. I'm working on solving the murder, but how do you think I can help the daughter? Do you see my dilemma?"

Elspeth hoped that by involving her in the personal side effects of the case, Lizzie would see that her mother was not heartless.

"How terrible," Lizzie said. Real pity filled her voice.

"Since the daughter confided in me, I feel obliged not only to find her mother's murderer but to protect the daughter. Let's call her K."

"Mummy, I had no idea you dealt with things like this. Are such things common in your job?"

"I frequently have to deal with people innocently affected by crime, but in this case I feel personally obliged to help K. Perhaps it was our talk in Scotland that has made me think this."

"Can you invite her to stay somewhere safe? Would Biddy take her in until the danger passes?"

Elspeth was pleased by her daughter's sympathy. "I can't ask Biddy. For many reasons I must keep my job separate from my family. I can't foist K on Biddy or anyone else close to me. They might be put in danger if I do so. Can you understand that? I wish at times that I could, particularly in K's case. What I need is someone like you to give your opinion on how K is feeling."

"She must be terrified."

"She is."

"What does she think about her mother normally?"

"They didn't get on."

"Did she know all along that her mother was a criminal?"

"She was away at school in Switzerland until recently. It was only after she left school at the end of last term, that she began to suspect." Elspeth was not sure this was true but it served her purpose.

"What was her mother's crime that was so terrible?'

"Her mother was responsible for laundering money to help pay for the illegal movement of weapons grade nuclear material from the former Soviet Union into Western Europe. The material could easily find its way into the hands of terrorists."

"But surely Interpol would have found her. Are they involved?"

"Not yet. We only recently found out that K's mother was the person laundering the money. Our discovery doesn't help K."

"How ghastly," Lizzie said. "I don't know what to say. May I think about it and ring you back?"

"Of course, darling. Now tell me, how are the boys?"

After ringing off, Elspeth let out her breath with the hope that Lizzie might now begin to understand the difficulties of her mother's job. At least Lizzie had not said that she thought her mother was just trying to cover up things to maintain the image of the hotels. Other people had accused Elspeth of this in the past with some accuracy.

Elspeth dressed slowly but without great thought to what she put on. She was due at the hotel in Paris the following day. She wondered how best to contact Dagmar. The de Saint Phalle's address and phone would be in the Kennington Organisation database, but Elspeth would need permission from the top to access it. She knew Pamela would be at her desk so, chewing on a slice of toast, she tapped the automatic dial button for Pamela's direct line. She got Pamela's voice mail, which was unusual. Pamela did not ring back until half an hour later, which was unprecedented.

Pamela spoke breathlessly into the phone, which was completely out of character.

"Goodness, Pamela, what is the matter?"

"HHL is on a rampage," she said. HHL was their code word for 'His High Lordship', a joke between them. Pamela explained. "The dam is about to burst in Bruges. *The Guardian* news chief in Brussels called to ask if he had any comment on the murders of his guests the weekend you were at Kennington Bruges."

"Yikes," Elspeth said.

"Eric wants you in Bruges to make things right and to handle the press now that the word is out. Better yet, he wants you to solve the murders without delay and cover up all you can."

"But my meeting in Paris?"

"He wants you to return to Bruges immediately. His plane is waiting for you. I'll put off your meeting in

Paris until you return."

"Will I have my usual full authority?"

"He wants the job done. Ask for anything you need. Most important, keep me posted about any new developments. He'll keep asking."

"Then I need to be able to go to Hamburg, Marseilles and Paris as well. Will I be authorized to do so?"

"Deal with Brussels first. Himself is more than usually upset."

"I'm on my way," Elspeth said. In her job she always had a bag packed, ready for immediate departure.

The flight to Brussels was just long enough for Elspeth to ponder her possibilities. She did not want to alert the police about Mateo's identity and more particularly the names in the sealed envelope in her safe at the flat. She decided that stirring up the members of the Mateo Organisation would be her last resort. Yet she did want to see Captain Schrott and find out if Raffaello Conti was in any condition to talk about what he had seen the morning Helga Müeller was killed. How far would Raffaello's observations help Elspeth find the murderer was a question, but it needed to be addressed. Next she would contact the news chief of *The Guardian* in Brussels and find out what exactly he had learned about the murders and if his news story would harm the reputation of the Kennington Bruges. After that she had no plan.

A large Mercedes with liveried driver was waiting for her at the airport in Brussels and took her directly to

Bruges. Elspeth hardly noticed the flat landscape dotted with red-roofed farms as they went by them.

"Take me to the police station before we go to the hotel," Elspeth said once they entered the outskirts of Bruges.

Captain Schrott greeted Elspeth with a worried look.

"We haven't progressed very far, I'm afraid," the policewoman said. "We brought in several of the gang members whom we suspected, but they all had unbreakable alibis for the time of Frau Müeller's death and swore they knew nothing about Monsieur de Saint Phalle. We have done all the usual things to find the murderer and questioned numerous people, but we have no new leads. It's frustrating."

"What about Raffaello Conti?"

"He is still in hospital. The doctors say he has only a twenty percent chance of surviving. The hospital called today and said he was conscious and we could talk to him. Do you want to come along?"

Elspeth wanted to speak to Raffaello alone but that now seemed impossible. Therefore she accepted Captain Schrott's invitation. Elspeth had told her driver to wait.

"You come in a very posh car," the police captain said.

"I'm on official business and my boss, Lord Kennington, wants fast results. When he sends me to Brussels in his private jet and gives me a car and driver, he means that I am on the hook."

"So your expensive car comes at a cost?"

"Always."

Raffaello's head was wrapped in a surgical dressing and his right arm was encased in a cast. He had the far-off look of a person who was heavily drugged. His blackened eyes slowly focused on the uniformed police officer behind Captain Schrott.

He said something in Swiss German. Captain Schrott translated for Elspeth. He said he had not done anything wrong.

"May I question him?" Elspeth asked. She wondered if Raffaello would recognise her. "He may find me less threatening."

The captain nodded.

"Raffaello, do you know me?" Elspeth said in English.

His head wrappings prevented him from nodding. His lips were still blood encrusted and Elspeth sensed he had difficulty speaking.

"The lady from the hotel," he rasped.

"I work for the hotel, Raffaello. We want to know about the woman who was killed and thrown into the canal."

"Canal," he said groggily. "I do nothing."

"Did you see anyone go near the woman?"

"I do nothing," he said again this time more loudly, as if Elspeth did not understand.

Captain Schrott stepped in and spoke in rapid German. This time Raffaello shouted. Elspeth assumed the message was the same.

Elspeth made one last try. "When you left your brother when the woman came out of the hotel, where did you go?"

"To the toilet," he said. His consciousness seemed to be clearer. "I not see the German woman. I do nothing wrong."

Elspeth could not remember if there was a public toilet near the hotel. She looked at Captain Schrott for confirmation. The captain nodded. "There is a toilet near the fish market."

"Is your brother still here in Bruges?" Elspeth asked Raffaello.

"The nurse say he come every day. He do nothing wrong."

Raffaello closed his eyes slowly and fell back into semi-consciousness.

Elspeth turned to the captain. "I want to see his brother. His name is Giorgio."

"We have already questioned him. He had nothing useful to say. Like Raffaello he says he did nothing wrong."

"The same words?" Elspeth asked.

The captain considered the question. "Yes, the same words."

"Do you think they agreed on what to say?"

"I don't see that they could agree. Raffaello has been unconscious since the beating," the captain said.

Elspeth remembered her own head injury two years before. She had been in a coma for three weeks but did come in and out of consciousness at the end.

"You can ask the doctors," the captain said as if reading Elspeth's thoughts.

"I will. But about Giorgio, does he really come here

every day?"

The captain motioned to the nursing sister, who came to Raffaello's bedside.

Elspeth asked, "Has he ever come in and out of consciousness, particularly when his brother is here?"

"Only once," the sister said.

"Did you hear if he said anything to his brother?" Elspeth asked.

"He said something. His words were not clear, but I think his brother understood," the nurse said.

"Did you hear anything, any word or a name?"

"Perhaps the word 'love' and later 'tell her'. My mother was Swiss, so I understand a bit of Schweizerdeutch. That is all I could hear. It sounded like the last request of a dying man," the sister said.

"And did his brother reply?"

"He gave him encouraging words about recovering, but the patient fell back into unconsciousness before his brother finished. After he left, I sat here because I hoped the patient would come to again. He never did, that is until today. It is sad for a young person to be near death."

The captain broke in. "How often does the brother come to see the patient?"

"Every afternoon at three. He stays until the end of visiting hours at seven. He sits and holds the patient's hand and whispers to him."

"What does he say?" the captain asked.

"Just words like 'come back' and 'we need you'. Sometimes he just puts his head on edge of the bed. I think he is crying."

Elspeth looked at her watch. It was two o'clock and she had not eaten since her light breakfast in London.

"Captain, I want to come back at three to see Giorgio, but I must check in at the hotel before then. Would you share lunch with me at the hotel? You can fill me in on your investigations."

The captain beamed. "With pleasure. I could never afford to eat there."

"I'll see that we get a private room so that we can talk freely." Elspeth was glad that she now could demand a room in her official capacity. She also wanted a secure place to call Pamela after she had spoken to the police captain.

Elspeth rang ahead to the hotel and lunch was waiting for them in a small private room. Elspeth had chosen a light lunch of roasted chicken, fresh tomato soufflé, a spinach and pecan salad, with an apple and apricot tart with whipped cream for dessert. She had also ordered a small urn of fresh coffee. The captain ate with obvious enjoyment; Elspeth as always ate lightly.

"Do you eat this way every day?" the captain asked.

"I try to be cautious. The food is always this good but I don't want to blow up like a balloon. Tell me, captain, what you have discovered about the two murders."

"We have been after two rival gangs that have terrorised the area around the good hotels, but we still have no proof that they killed either Monsieur de Saint Phalle or Frau Müeller. But one of the gang members we questioned said he saw someone from the other gang attack Raffaello. The boy we questioned is about fifteen years old and not a reliable witness. He may have been purposely implicating the rival gang. All the other leads have gone cold. You will understand that this is very difficult for us. Bruges makes much of its money from tourists. We cannot get the reputation for violence in the tourist areas."

Elspeth slowly chewed and swallowed the last of her main course before speaking. "An English newspaper has heard about the two murders and wants to publish an article about them, I am here to stop the article from blaming the hotel. Would you work with me to minimise the sensationalism and to see that the report of the murders is downplayed?"

The captain licked her desert fork appreciatively after sampling the tart. "What can I do?" she asked.

"I'm going to Brussels to talk to the news chief. Will you come with me?" Elspeth asked.

"In your car? I will be spoiled afterwards, but I will come. Do you have any ideas of what to tell the paper?"

"I wanted to talk to you first. I'm sure you don't want the paper to say that the police are baffled. Why not say you are pursuing several leads and are hopeful of apprehending the suspects soon and also think these are isolated incidents? That's vague enough to put the newspaper off. We want to make the whole thing sound as non-threatening as possible for future guests here. And if I can, I want the investigating reporter to write good things about the police and the safety of tourists in Bruges."

"That is a good idea," the captain said.

Elspeth seldom ate dessert but could not resist the

tart. She cut into it and savoured the rich flavour of fresh fruit and rich cream. One bite only, she thought, knowing that was an impossibility.

"It's not exactly a lie," Elspeth said. "I still think the murders are connected and that they have more to do with the victims than the gangs. I plan to talk to all the people who were with our party over the weekend. I strongly believe that the murders were committed to keep Alexandre de Saint Phalle quiet and to stop Frau Müeller from committing a crime that Alexandre may have known of."

"Do you have any evidence to support this?"

"I have a strong sense that has served me well in the past," Elspeth said. "I'm going to continue investigating the crime from the viewpoint of the hotel. In fact my employer insists I do. If I can prove that the murders have nothing to do with the hotel or the criminal element outside the hotels, we all will rest more easily."

"This is true," the captain replied. "You will keep me informed, yes?"

Elspeth decided not to tell the captain about Mateo. Surely Richard, with all his skill at diplomatic finesse, would agree.

Over coffee after dessert, the captain asked, "When do we leave for Brussels?"

"As soon as I question Giorgio. I thought I would find him and ask him here to the hotel. I find these environs facilitate a certain comfort that makes people more willing to talk. Giorgio watched the hotel for three days. I had the doorman keep him out. He might enjoy coming in."

"Do you use the hotel often to manipulate people?"

"Frequently."

"I envy your ability to do so," the captain said.

Elspeth laughed. "The hotels are good tools and I've learned to use them to my advantage."

With the captain's concurrence Elspeth went alone to the hospital and arrived just before three. She waited in her car for Giorgio's arrival. He came on foot and was punctual. As he mounted the steps at the front entrance, Elspeth stepped from the Mercedes. Giorgio looked startled when she called out his name. He pivoted on his foot like a dancer and stared at her. Finally recognition came over his face.

"You are the lady from the hotel," he said. "The one who ask me about Raffaello."

"I am Elspeth Duff," she responded. "I do work for the Kennington hotels. I'm sorry about your brother."

"The police tell me you find him after he beaten."

"I came across his body and called the police. I didn't see what happened."

"He maybe die," Giorgio said, his voice flat.

"I hope he doesn't. He was badly beaten."

"Why you come here?" Giorgio asked.

"I want to talk to you. Can you tell me about Raffaello?"

"I know nothing to say."

"Will you come to the hotel for some coffee or a beer?"

"They not let me in. Raffaello and I try go into the hotel. The doorman he make us go away."

"They will let you in if you are with me. Please come. I would like to ask you about the night Raffaello was hurt."

"But my brother . . ."

"The nurse said he is not conscious. Please come. Perhaps I can help."

"You are not doctor."

"No. I am an investigator for the hotels. I am working with the police."

"I have no words for you. I do nothing wrong."

Elspeth was getting impatient, because she wanted to be in Brussels before the story was sent to the copy editors at *The Guardian*.

"Come. Let's go where we can't be heard. It's just a minute away by car."

"Is that your car?"

"A hired car."

He looked admiringly at it and at the driver. "May I ride up front?"

"Of course." Anything to make him come to the hotel.

Elspeth took him through the main door and nodded to the doorman, who gave a discreet bow in return. When she and Giorgio were settled in the back room, she called room service and offered Giorgio his choice of beverage.

"Beer," he said.

"Which kind would you like?"

He asked for Falken Cool, which Elspeth repeated over the phone. She wondered if he were testing the hotel's ability to find one, since she had never heard of it before, but she was not an expert on beers.

"It will be a moment, but we will get one," Room Service said without a moment's hesitation. "Is there anything else?"

"Just more coffee."

The beer did not arrive for fifteen minutes, but when it came, it was in a frosted glass on a silver tray with a lace doily and a small vase of flowers. Giorgio looked impressed. "Your hotel have everything?" he asked. "I not find Falken Cool in Bruges before."

"If the hotel doesn't have something which someone has ordered, they find it," she said with a smile.

Whilst waiting for the beer, Elspeth attempted to put Giorgio at his ease. They had talked about Raffaello's condition and his brother's home in Switzerland, but Giorgio seemed uncomfortable in the grand surroundings, as he kept looking around the room as if to take it all in. He fidgeted.

This interim period gave Elspeth time to strategise. She decided a gentle approach might have the most effect.

"Please forgive me for taking you away from the hospital. I too am concerned about your brother's injuries. I was once attacked and had severe head injuries, so I know a little of how Raffaello is feeling. At the time I found it difficult to say anything that made sense. The nurse told me that your brother had spoken to you. Did he tell you who attacked him?"

"He say only few words. He do not remember."

"Did he say anything that might help find his attacker?"

"The police ask me same question. He say nothing."

"The nurse thought he said something about sending love to someone. Who was that? His mother?"

Giorgio laughed and took a long swallow of his beer. "His mother? No. She not see him no more. She say she wash hands, throw him out. She not like the work we do."

"And what is that?"

"She call it spying."

"Oh? I thought you were protecting Madame de Saint Phalle."

Giorgio squirmed in his chair. "Our boss he want us to watch, to tell what she do. Raffaello want to protect her. I think he love Madame Dagmar."

"She is a very beautiful woman. Many men have fallen in love with her. Did Raffaello tell you to let Madame Dagmar know that he loved her?"

"He is idiot. Madame Dagmar no can love him back. She not look at Raffaello. His father is Italian, and he is very *romantico*. My father is Swiss and, very how do you say, simple."

"I understand. Sensible."

"*Ja*, sensible," he said.

The beer must have been having its effect because Giorgio became talkative. He told Elspeth about following Dagmar from Paris to London and afterwards to Portugal and Rome.

Elspeth ordered another beer for him. He asked for crisps, which seldom appeared at Kennington hotels except in the minibars or in the bags brought in by guests. Room service brought a bowl of them.

When Giorgio was halfway through his second Falken Cool, Elspeth decided to ask the information she wanted the most.

"You and Raffaello were watching the hotel on the Friday when Alexandre de Saint Phalle was killed, which took place between about eleven o'clock in the morning and noon. At that time did you see anyone come out from the back of the hotel?"

Giorgio stared down at his beer. "I go to get lunch. Raffaello wait out front of hotel. He is solo."

"Did he say that he saw anyone?"

"He not say."

"Did he see Dagmar, Madame de Saint Phalle?"

"We do nothing wrong. We just watch and report to our boss."

"What did you report to your boss that day?"

"Raffaello talk to the boss. I come back with sandwich. Raffaello, he is, how do you say, nervous. I think he want action. He is man who like action, not just sit all the time."

Elspeth considered that Raffaello might consider another profession if he survived the attack. Surveillance was a sedentary business most of the time.

"Tell me about Saturday. You said you saw Frau Müeller come out of the hotel. Did you know who she was?"

"Raffaello said she is enemy of Madame Dagmar."

"How did he know that?"

"Madame Dagmar tell him. She say that woman is a very bad person."

Elspeth raised her eyebrows. So Dagmar must have

known that Helga was Mateo.

"Did Raffaello follow Frau Müeller when she came out of the hotel?"

"I not know. Maybe Madame Dagmar think German woman is killer of her husband."

"Did Raffaello see anything when he followed Frau Müeller?"

"He say he go to toilet. When he come back, he say he not want to go away from Madame Dagmar. Our job is to protect Madame Dagmar not follow the German woman. But I think he see her fall in canal."

"Did he say anything else about Frau Müeller? Did he see anyone following her? Did he see Madame de Saint Phalle?"

Giorgio thought for a moment. "Madame Dagmar come out of hotel, so we follow."

"Where did she go?"

"She go into centre of city. Go to church and after walk back and forth and look in shop windows. Then she go back to hotel."

"Did she come out of the hotel before that? Did she follow Frau Müeller and that is why Raffaello left you to go after them?"

"I not see," Giorgio said. Elspeth felt he was telling the truth but cursed that she could not question Raffaello. He seemed to hold the key to what happened at the time of the two murders.

Elspeth rose. "May I come with you to the hospital? We can go back in the Mercedes."

"OK," he said with a sloppy grin.

Raffaello was unresponsive. The only sound was the machines that were attached to him making steady noises. Elspeth could see the heartbeat was weak. The nursing sister was with him when Elspeth and Giorgio entered the room. "He is restless," the sister said. "Sometimes he seems to be aware I'm here. In Schweizerdeutsch he said 'tell Dagmar' several times and then 'love' and once 'your love' or possibly 'for love'. Even when he is awake, he can hardly speak, his lips are so damaged, so his words are garbled."

"I stay with him now," Giorgio said. "Goodbye. Thank you for beer and ride in car."

Elspeth returned to the Kennington Bruges, where she was to meet Captain Schrott. The captain had not yet arrived, which gave Elspeth time to ring Pamela Crumm and to tell her what she had learned.

"The lead to Raffaello doesn't sound very useful," Pamela said. "But in the meantime, 'Himself' has been in touch with the head of the Flanders Tourist Office and asked him to put in a call to *The Guardian*. Eric also has contacted the paper's European editor, who has promised to hold the story for a few more days if we give them an exclusive when the murders are solved. You needn't go to Brussels today, but if *The Guardian* has the story, others will get it too."

The dreaded press, thought Elspeth. How often in her career had she dealt with the less honourable among its corps?

"Pamela," Elspeth said, "can you book me a room in Hamburg tonight and get me a flight from Brussels in about three hours' time? I'll have the car take me to Brussels to catch the plane."

"I'll have a car and driver meet you in Hamburg," Pamela said. "What are your plans there?"

"I want to see Ulrich Müeller one more time."

"Then I'll have a car pick you up again in the morning. I understand the Müellers live outside the city. What time would you like the car to come round?"

"I'll let you know as soon as I speak with Herr Müeller. Kristin says he often works from home."

Elspeth next rang Captain Schrott. Elspeth had decided to tell her as little as possible about her interview with Giorgio. She merely said that Giorgio had seen nothing and that Raffaello continued to be incoherent. The captain sounded as if she were disappointed she would not get to ride in the Mercedes to Brussels but promised to stay in touch with Elspeth.

25

This case has to be near its end, Elspeth thought wishfully. Several theories whirled through her head but none of them seemed conclusive. She needed two more vital pieces of information.

When Elspeth called from her hotel in Hamburg, Herr Müeller's bank of assistants stonewalled Elspeth's request for an interview. Finally Elspeth asked for Kristin.

"Fraulein Müeller is not in this office," the harsh voice said at the other end of the line. "I will take your message."

"Tell Herr Müeller that Lady Munro called. There is no message," Elspeth said in as haughty a voice as she could muster. It produced no softening in the assistant's tone. Maybe she was anti-British. Elspeth did not leave her number.

She opened her Blackberry and scrolled down to the number Kristin had given her. Kristin answered immediately.

"Jean Luc?" she said hopefully.

"Regretfully not," Elspeth said.

"Is it you, Lady Munro?"

Elspeth acknowledged her identity. "Kristin, are you still in Paris?"

"No, I'm in Hamburg."

"So am I. Can you set up a meeting for me with your father? I need to speak to him alone and as soon as possible. His assistant wouldn't put me through."

"You must have talked to the Nazi Frieda," Kristin said. "She's excessively protective of my father. Now that *Mutter* is dead, I expect she will make overtures to my father. What a terrible thought to have Frieda for a stepmother! But why not join us for lunch? Frieda won't be there. Do you have a car? We're five kilometres outside the city."

"Yes, the Kennington Organisation has provided one with a driver."

"I'll make sure the man at the gateman knows you're coming. One o'clock then?"

Elspeth did not know what to expect for the Müeller residence, but a fortress never did enter her imagination. The house was a mansion, obviously new, on several hectares of land. A brick fence, several metres tall with broken glass on top, surrounded the compound of buildings, including a multicar garage, a stable and Herr Müeller's offices. The trees seemed to be old and the gardens well established. Was this a great house that replaced one destroyed during the Second World War or was the older house simply torn down to be replaced by something that suited new owners?

The guard at the gate was not in uniform but from his posture he could have been. He checked his clipboard and found Elspeth's name. He gave instructions to the driver in German and let them pass.

The interior of the house was as grand as the exterior. An invisible servant opened one of the main doors and Kristin came out to meet Elspeth.

"*Mutter* not *Vater* wanted the security," she explained. "Although she grew up in what was West Germany at the time, she was terrified of the communists. Her mother was badly abused by the Russians when they came into Berlin in 1945. My mother inherited her mother's paranoia, I think. Growing up in this house was difficult. All my school chums were intimidated when they found out where and how I lived. I never brought any of my friends from my school in Switzerland here, although I am sure many of them were very wealthy and might understand."

They walked through a huge entrance hall that rose two stories high. A grand curved staircase was at the end opposite the front door.

"Come into the sitting room. My mother said it was the only room where one could feel human," Kristen said.

The sitting room resembled those in almost any English manor. Chintz slipcovers abounded, and the tables were dotted with silver framed photographs and porcelain objects, all too cluttered for Elspeth's minimalist taste. A small fire burned in the grate, adding more to the atmosphere than giving heat. A King Charles spaniel lay asleep on a small sofa. He opened one eye and viewed Elspeth disdainfully.

"Will you sit?" Kristin asked. "My father will be here in a few moments. Frieda makes sure he is always prompt, and he insists that we eat when the food is hot. Come. Tell me why you are here? Does it have anything to do with our meeting in London on Sunday?"

"I've not opened the envelope you gave me, but, if

one of my assumptions is correct, I may have to. Do I have your permission to pass the information on to Interpol if it becomes necessary?"

The door opened and Ulrich Müeller entered. "Interpol?" he said without greeting. "Why Interpol? Surely the police in Bruges are capable of curtailing gang violence in that city. Captain Schrott assured me that she was close to finding the people who killed Helga."

"I saw Captain Schrott yesterday. She has questioned a number of suspects, but still has no definitive answer. That's why I'm here, Herr Müeller. Richard and I both feel some responsibility in solving this case."

At that moment a servant announced lunch. They moved from the comfort of the sitting room to the grandeur of a dining room that was panelled in dark wood and lined with inferior but old oil portraits. Three places were set at one end of a highly polished mahogany table surrounded by at least twenty heavy wooden chairs with embroidered backs and seats. Lunch was served immediately. After they finished a thick broth, a servant brought on covered silver bowls and a large slab of meat was placed in front of Ulrich ready for carving and serving.

"Our food here is hearty," Ulrich explained. "Both Helga and I prefer/preferred good German food. Kristin is always on a diet and picks at what we serve. You will enjoy this sauerbraten made from Helga's own recipe. She used to make it herself before we had servants. Do have some boiled potatoes with it. They are from the estate. The food may not be as fancy as yours at the Kennington hotel, but it is more filling."

He served Elspeth a large plateful. Out of politeness she tackled it and found it amazingly good, although she could not finish the generous portions.

"Now, Lady Munro, tell me why you have come. And what is this about Interpol?"

Kristin looked up at Elspeth with a supplicating look. Elspeth briefly touched her finger to her lips, hoping the gesture would indicate her intention to keep Kristin and Jean Luc's confidences.

Elspeth decided to approach the problem head-on. "Herr Müeller," she said, "were you aware that your wife ran the international money laundering ring that uses the name Mateo?"

Ulrich Müeller coughed and spit out some gravy. It drizzled down his chin through his beard. He picked up his napkin and wiped it away.

"You are making a big mistake," he said.

Elspeth shook her head. "No, I think I'm not."

"Is it Sir Richard that came to this conclusion? I told him that I suspected Viktor Novikov was Mateo."

"And Viktor Novikov accused you. Tell me why Viktor broke off negotiations with you to become partners. Was it because Viktor suspected your involvement with Mateo, that Mateo was your wife?"

Ulrich Müeller had not been as successful in his business without developing the ability to avoid answering a question.

"You make great assumptions."

Elspeth stared at Ulrich without flinching. He

303

looked down at his plate and cut another large bite of the meat, piling cabbage on top of it.

She continued. "I don't know for sure, but I suspect Frau Müeller became involved with this dirty business on her own, and you only became aware of it when Viktor Novikov broke off talks about partnering with you. Viktor, of course, would have made a thorough investigation into your affairs and those of Frau Müeller. I expect you had never paid much attention to your wife's affairs. You must have thought you provided well for her and that she had no need for anything you did not give her."

"I always gave her a great deal," he said. "She had everything she wanted."

"I think she could have had a need for excitement that just being your wife couldn't fulfil. Some people need to be on the edge," Elspeth said, laying her knife and fork on her plate. "I expect this was why she started the Mateo organisation . . . and why she was killed."

Elspeth glanced around at Kristin, who was staring intently at her father. "You know what Lady Munro is saying is true, Papa."

Ulrich Müeller froze. His normally jolly face was stoic.

"I want to see that no harm comes to you. I suspect that your wife's associates in Portugal may be dangerous," Elspeth continued. "They may think that you and Kristin know too much. They have a great deal at stake. I've no idea if your wife had a deputy or had set up a mechanism for their dirty dealings to continue if anything happened to her. Or if they have any desire to avenge her death. They may also be concerned that you know them and will reveal their names to the police."

"We are well protected here," Ulrich said.

"But you cannot stay inside your compound forever, Herr Müeller."

"I am sure that Helga's associates did not kill her," he said defensively.

"I hope you're right," Elspeth said truthfully. "But I suspect they are dangerous people. To be truly safe you will need to report them to Interpol."

Ulrich eyed her, steel in his eyes. "And condemn my wife? Can you imagine what that would do to my business? No one would trust me after that."

"No one will trust you if it gets out that Frau Müeller was Mateo. It will, you know, particularly now that the police are involved. Police Captain Schrott is dogged even if she has found nothing so far. I would suggest that you work quietly with my husband and with Interpol to round up the rest of the Mateo organisation, which would alleviate your need for such fearful defences to protect you and your daughter. Richard has many contacts and is a trained diplomat. He knows how to do things discreetly. Herr Müeller, you can trust Richard."

"*Ja*," he said but gave no commitment.

Elspeth sensed that Ulrich was a stubborn man who needed a great deal of convincing. "He is in Brussels this week. I'll give you the number to his private line."

Ulrich said nothing. He poked at his food, which Elspeth thought was uncharacteristic. He surveyed the paintings of unknown people who looked out into the world blandly and whose troubles had died with them.

"Herr Müeller, I think you have little choice, but I'll leave it to you."

"*Ja*," Ulrich said again. This time resignation filled his simple word.

Elspeth looked over to Kristin, who was studying the remains of her meal. Kristin glanced up at Elspeth and nodded her head slightly. Elspeth could not interpret the gesture.

"I need to leave after lunch," Elspeth said. "Thank you for letting me come."

On the trip back to the Hamburg airport Elspeth rang Richard but did not reach him. She phoned Pamela Crumm next and found her at her desk.

"I need to get to Paris as soon as possible. Can you book me a flight this afternoon or evening and tell the hotel that I'm coming?" she begged.

"Of course, ducks. Ask and it will be given to you. Any luck in Hamburg?"

"Nothing concrete at this point, but I feel I'm getting very close."

"Are you close enough to let me in on your thoughts?"

"Do you mind if I don't? Can you stall with Eric?"

"Luckily for you he's out of town and won't be back until day after tomorrow, but he will call in. What shall I tell him?"

"That I have one more person to visit in Paris. If I'm correct in my suppositions, I should know who the murderers are."

"Murderers plural?" Pamela asked. Elspeth could almost see Pamela's eyes widen behind her large round glasses.

"I think so."

"Good."

"Good that there are multiple murderers. Pamela, I didn't think you were so ghoulish?"

Pamela burst out laughing. "No. It's good that you are so close to finding out who they are. Eric has been in a frightful temper over this whole thing. Next time, Elspeth, when you go out with you husband for a weekend, try not to get involved in more murders, particularly near our hotels."

Elspeth laughed. "I'll try but I don't promise."

Elspeth could hear the keys on Pamela's computer clicking.

"You are on the Lufthansa flight to Paris, leaving at a quarter past five from Hamburg. I'll confirm your stay with the hotel in Paris once we ring off. I expect you may have to settle for a small room as the hotel is completely booked, but I'll make it happen."

Elspeth had known Pamela Crumm for over ten years, but she never ceased to be astonished at the strings Pamela could pull with a few taps on her computer keys. Elspeth's first-class ticket was waiting for her at the airport.

26

Pamela had been right; the accommodation was tiny. Elspeth had no idea that Kennington hotels had such miniscule rooms, hers being the size of most common hotel rooms, not as generously proportioned as the ones Lord Kennington normally provided in his hotels. The room was tucked under an eave in the roof, which did not seem to have restricted the interior designer's creative freedom. Elspeth peered out over the rooftops of Paris through the oval window and thought the view compensated for the lack of space. The evening boulevard below was crossed with ribbons of car lights, yellow and red, and shop windows blazed out their fine wares. Paris cast its unique spell, even to such a seasoned traveller as Elspeth.

Elspeth was travelling with only a carry-on bag. Her clothes were now crumpled. She called room service and was assured clean and pressed clothes within the hour. The room, despite its miniscule proportions, had all the amenities of a Kennington hotel. The management had had time to set up the room to Elspeth's specifications. She poured her favourite lavender and sage bath oil into the bathtub which was tucked cleverly in a corner under an eave, and she soaked until the water became cool. Then, donning her freshly ironed clothes, she went down into the lobby and into the hair salon. What her bath had not done to refresh her spirits, the shampoo and blow dry did. Feeling distinctly less travel worn, she made her way into the dining room. The maître d' greeted her by name and welcomed her back to Paris. How good it was to be in a familiar environment and as herself not just Richard's wife. Now she had to prove her worth by placating Eric Kennington.

She waited until the next morning to phone Dagmar. Elspeth wanted her visit to Paris to seem unrelated to the murders and hope this strategy would gain her access to Dagmar's home.

Elspeth was surprised Dagmar and not a servant answered the call.

"Dagmar, Elspeth Duff here. I'm in Paris on business at the Kennington hotel and thought we could meet together for lunch. I'd like to see you and meet your boys."

Elspeth held her breath, hoping that Dagmar would invite her to her home rather than expecting an invitation to lunch at the hotel.

"Elspeth, how nice to hear from you. I need someone to talk to about Alexandre. Do you have time to come out here? We live in the sixteen *arrondissement* near the Bois de Boulogne."

"I would love to get out of the hotel this afternoon."

"Two o'clock? Is that all right? The boys will be home from school at three and we can talk before then."

"Two o'clock it is."

Dagmar gave the address on the boulevard Flandrin.

Elspeth had seen the houses near the Bois many times but had never been in one which was tucked one street away from the park. She did not know what to

309

expect. Dagmar had warned her about the policeman at the doorway. Alighting from her taxi, Elspeth gave her name. The stoic young policeman took a notepad from his pocket, checked the name and asked for identification. He rang Dagmar from his mobile and announced Elspeth's arrival. He told Elspeth that the de Saint Phalle apartment was on the second floor and showed her to the lift. Elspeth wondered if such police duty was challenging at all. She doubted it.

Dagmar opened the door and showed Elspeth in. The entryway was small but its furniture exquisite, perhaps Louis XV or Louis XVI to Elspeth's untrained eye. Dagmar led Elspeth in through double doors to a large sitting room, again formally furnished.

"This is our stuffy drawing room," Dagmar said. "Alexandre furnished it to impress people. Are you overwhelmed? Probably not if you spend a great deal of time at the Kennington hotels."

Dagmar the unexpected. She was wearing jeans, well-used trainers and a tattered tee shirt saying 'I ⬜ NY'. Her hair was pulled back in a ponytail and she wore no make-up, not even a splash of lipstick. Dagmar needed no aids to enhance her beauty, but the lack of them put five years on her age. Again Elspeth saw no signs of grief.

Two overstuffed and brocaded sofas straddled an intricately carved marble fireplace surround. Between the sofas an ornate coffee table was strewn with photographs.

"I've been going through them," Dagmar explained. "It's time I got rid of the bad memories of Alexandre. I am burning them. I find great satisfaction in watching the photographs curl up at the corners, turn brown, wrinkle and disappear into the smoke that goes up the chimney."

Dagmar offered Elspeth a seat and yanked a bell pull by the fireplace.

"I suppose you being English, you would like tea," Dagmar said.

Elspeth did not correct Dagmar's assumption about her national origin although she would have liked to. Dagmar was sophisticated enough to know the distinction between the Scots and the English.

"Why are you here, Elspeth? To talk about the murders or is this merely a social call?"

Elspeth girded herself against Dagmar's disdain.

"Both, I suppose, since our earlier acquaintance centred around the murders."

"I'm sure I would have heard had the police in Bruges uncovered anything. Have you? Or are you still poking around?"

"I spoke to Captain Schrott after breakfast," Elspeth said. "I told her I was coming here. She asked me to let you know that Raffaello Conti died this morning from his injuries."

"Stupid boy," Dagmar said. "He would stick his nose in where it didn't belong. Now he's paid for it."

Elspeth had not expected this reaction.

"A rather high price, don't you think?" Elspeth said and then checked her irritation.

"Did he say anything about me?" Dagmar asked.

"Should he have?"

Dagmar snorted but did not answer. She rose and went to the fireplace, where she stirred up the browned reside of the photographs among the ashes.

"Did Raffaello see anything, Dagmar? You talked to him after your husband was killed."

"Are you implying he was trying to blackmail me? No, Lady Munro, he didn't."

"Did he see who murdered your husband?"

Dagmar's face paled. "No," she cried.

Elspeth could not make out if Dagmar's reply was a denial or a wish to push the thought away. Dagmar looked down at the fire and then turned back to Elspeth.

"No, he didn't. He wasn't near Alexandre when he was attacked."

"How do you know?"

"I . . ." Dagmar stopped.

"Did you see the attack? Is that it?"

"You think you're very clever, don't you?" Dagmar spat out.

"No, not particularly, but unfortunately in my career I have dealt with several murderers. They are the ones who think they are clever."

"You can't prove anything."

"There was another witness," Elspeth lied.

"Who? I saw no one."

"Then you did witness your husband's murder."

Dagmar sank into the sofa across from Elspeth and burst into tears. "I don't know who they were."

"They? How many?"

"One," she whispered.

Elspeth couldn't tell if Dagmar was telling the truth.

"How did you see them, your husband and the attacker?"

Dagmar began to cry silently. "I watched from an upstairs window."

"What happened?" Elspeth said softly.

"Alexandre came out the back door to the alleyway."

"Why did Alexandre go downstairs?"

"He said he had an appointment—with Mateo."

"But you knew the man was not Mateo because I suspect both you and Alexandre knew who Mateo was. And that Mateo was inside the hotel already."

"How could I know who Mateo was?"

"You asked someone at the reception at the Belgian Embassy in London if Sir Richard knew who Mateo was. I heard you. Other than Richard, your husband and I were the only people at the hotel in Bruges and who were also at the reception in London. I think you were speaking to Alexandre about Mateo."

Dagmar raised her beautiful head defiantly. "Did you see Alexandre in London when I spoke?" she asked. "You can prove nothing if you didn't."

"Dagmar, won't you tell me the truth? It will save you dealing with Interpol. They will not be as pleasant as I am."

A terrible feeling struck Elspeth. Perhaps her assumptions about the murderer were wrong and that Dagmar had engineered the killing of her husband. Elspeth drew in her breath and waited for Dagmar's reply. Dagmar looked at Elspeth. Dagmar's eyes were unreadable, but her lovely mouth was set hostilely.

Finally she spoke. "Do you know who Mateo is?"

"Was," Elspeth corrected. "Yes, I do."

Dagmar looked puzzled at Elspeth's remark. "Mateo was responsible for Alexandre's death," Dagmar said.

Elspeth wondered at the lightness in Dagmar's voice, as if she were saying something of no consequence.

Elspeth slowly let out her breath. "How?" she asked.

"Alexandre was ready to betray Mateo and tell your husband who he was. Mateo had been blackmailing him into silence for years."

"Over what?"

"A business deal. Mateo asked Alexandre to add a box of radioactive material with one of his shipments from Ukraine to Germany. Alexandre was desperate for money at the time and agreed. After that, Mateo would not leave Alexandre alone. When your husband asked Alexandre, Viktor and Ulrich Müeller to go to Bruges for the weekend, Alexandre decided to end his relationship with Mateo and tell Sir Richard exactly who Mateo was. Mateo had to silence him. When Alexandre came back from the morning meeting with Sir Richard, he told me he could not wait any longer, but he had agreed to see Mateo before lunch."

"And how did he get out of the hotel?"

"He used his key card which worked for emergency exits."

The security tapes would show this, Elspeth thought. She was sorry now that she hadn't been on the case earlier because the tapes must by now be destroyed.

"That's the reason you were standing looking out of the window, isn't it? To see what was going to happen between Mateo and Alexandre."

Dagmar looked down at her feet and nodded her head.

"What did you see?"

Dagmar swallowed visibly. "Mateo was there with two men who looked like thugs. The men attacked Alexandre. Alexandre tried to fight back, but they overpowered him. Alexandre fell down. One man laughed. He took off Alexandre's tie and gave it to Mateo, who slipped it around Alexandre's neck and choked him."

"The tie you bought at Hèrmes the day I saw you there," Elspeth said almost to herself.

Dagmar laughed almost hysterically. "There were many times I wanted to strangle Alexandre, but I never intended to use that tie. It was too expensive."

"Now tell me the truth about Raffaello. Did you see him when Alexandre was killed?"

Dagmar frowned. "No, he wasn't there."

Elspeth wanted to believe her, now that Dagmar was in a talking mood, Elspeth needed the answers to several more questions.

"What were you talking to Raffaello about the night Richard and I saw you in the park?" Elspeth asked.

"It's not important," Dagmar said.

"I think it is," countered Elspeth. "You were telling him your husband was murdered, weren't you? What was his reaction?"

315

"He was a silly boy. Even before the weekend he followed me around like a drooling puppy. I am used to this reaction from men, but I felt sorry for Raffaello. It must have been the first time he had fallen in love."

"He was in love with you or just infatuated?" Elspeth asked.

"I have no idea. I cannot get inside the head of all the men I have known who have pledged undying love." Dagmar shivered as if to brush the men and their feelings away.

"Did you tell Raffaello about Helga Müeller—who she was and what she had orchestrated that morning?"

Dagmar frowned and did not speak for a moment as if trying to digest what Elspeth had said. Finally Dagmar said, "I may have. I don't remember."

Elspeth knew she was lying, in fact she probably had been lying the whole time.

"And what was his reaction?" Elspeth asked as if Dagmar had answered her previous question in the affirmative.

Dagmar's face registered no reaction to being caught in a lie.

"He swore he would kill Helga."

"I think he did," Elspeth said blandly and watched Dagmar's reaction.

Dagmar puffed air through her lips contemptuously. "Kill Helga Müeller? Don't be absurd! Do you have a witness for that too?"

Elspeth knew she could stretch her prevarication only so far. "The evidence strongly suggests he did."

"What evidence?" Dagmar said.

"His own confession."

"Did the police hear it or are you making it up?"

"He confessed to the nursing sister in the hospital where he died."

"What did he say?" Dagmar asked looking suspiciously at Elspeth.

"He said he did it for you." Elspeth's statement was stretching the truth, but Raffaello's words might be interpreted that way. "Did you ask him to do it?"

Dagmar looked worried. "You aren't going to pin the murder on me, are you? How like you."

Elspeth could not be sure what Dagmar was implying in this last remark. "No, I have no intention of doing so if you will tell me all of what happened that night you were with Raffaello in the park and also your relationship with him."

"I had no relationship with him!"

"None at all? Hadn't he been following you for weeks if not months? I'm certain his brother can confirm this. In Bruges you seemed to want me to believe you had not seen Raffaello or Giorgio before, but that wasn't true."

"I suppose Giorgio told you that."

Elspeth stared at Dagmar and nodded.

"Damn him! Where is Giorgio now?" she asked.

"He was in Bruges only yesterday. He wanted to stay with his brother. I expect he was with him at the end. But, of course, now he is free to come back here and contact you."

"Why would he do that?"

"Raffaello may have told Giorgio what happened

the morning Helga Müeller was killed. Giorgio may think you'd want that information kept from the police."

"Are you suggesting he might want, what is the word for it, hush money?"

"He might. Wouldn't it be better for you to tell me everything that passed between you and Raffaello the night your husband died?"

"Damn you too!" Dagmar's grasp of curses in English seemed to be limited. "Are you one of these Scottish witches?"

At least she got Elspeth's nationality right this time.

"I have been accused of it before," Elspeth said dryly.

"It's amazing such a nice person as Sir Richard could have married such a bitch as you."

Elspeth jerked back. For some reason Dagmar's taunt hit home. Elspeth blanched. Yet her mission superseded her personal feelings.

"Will you tell me or shall I call Interpol?"

"Are you threatening?" Dagmar's face was now mottled, destroying its loveliness.

"Yes," Elspeth said, meaning it. "I am not accusing you of murdering Helga, but I think you egged Raffaello on, using his blind love for you as a weapon."

"I did not make him love me. Men just act crazily when I am around."

Elspeth was trying to stay cool, but she was tiring of Dagmar's constant verbal diversions.

"What were you arguing about the night you met him in the park? Richard and I could hear you."

"Were your passionate embraces so shallow? You

looked like you were enjoying them."

Now Elspeth bristled. "If we had been enjoying them, we would have gone to our room. We were following you."

"We?"

"Yes, we."

"Were you afraid to go out alone?"

Elspeth thought of worse curse words than Dagmar had used but decided not to be dragged down into Dagmar's quicksand.

"Did you go to the park because Raffaello appealed to you or did you contact him? Did you want to know what he had seen when Alexandre was killed?" Elspeth asked coolly as if Dagmar had not cast aspersions.

"What did you and Sir Richard hear?"

"Enough to know you were angry. What were you angry about? Was it Alexandre's murder or was it your hatred of Helga Müeller?"

She turned from Elspeth and did not reply.

"I have one more question," Elspeth said. "Was it you who sent the messages saying BE WARNED?"

"What if I did? After Alexandre's murder everyone needed to be warned, didn't they?"

"Then you did," Elspeth said.

Dagmar smirked scornfully. She rose.

"I have nothing more to say to you, Lady Munro. Will you please go now?"

The policeman at the door helped Elspeth get a taxi, and she made her way back to the hotel. She felt personally bruised. She found little satisfaction in her interview with Dagmar, whose beauty seemed to be wasted on such an unpleasant woman. Elspeth now was convinced that Dagmar was directly involved in Helga's death. She wondered if Dagmar had exploited Raffaello's passion and had driven him to murder the German woman. Elspeth wished she could believe all that Dagmar said, but she knew she would have to take the kernels of truth from her interview and put them together with the other evidence she had gathered. She did not have enough solid proof to present her theories to the police in Bruges or Interpol, but she thought she was right.

27

Richard was absorbed with other matters when Elspeth's call came. It took him a moment to disentangle his mind from the matter at hand and focus on what Elspeth was saying. He could tell she was upset.

"I have seldom been so personally attacked," Elspeth confessed after she described her time with Dagmar, "and I need comforting."

"My dearest," he said. "Dagmar is unspeakable. Do you think it was she who killed Raffaello?"

"No, I don't think so. She may be self-centred and perfectly nasty, but I don't think she's a killer. Who said she was like Helen of Troy? Was it Viktor? I think that's an apt description. But I doubt Helen of Troy was so vulgar. Dickie, this case stymies me. I think I know what happened, but the only witness I have so far is Dagmar. I wouldn't call her particularly reliable. In any case, Raffaello, who might have been forced into a confession, is dead."

"His brother?"

"He seemed innocent when I questioned him."

"Elspeth, I've never heard you so personally upset with a case in a hotel, not even FitzRoy's murder in Malta or when you were arrested in Bermuda. What's bothering you?"

She did not respond immediately. She let out a deep sigh. "It's that I didn't have any authority from the first. Why should anyone accept my legitimacy as an investigator with power of my own? All the people involved see me first as your wife, not an unbiased security advisor to the hotels. If I were on the other side of the fence, I suppose I would wonder who this nosy wife was and why she thought she had the right to ask so many questions. My role has left me in a nebulous position. I'm beginning to think I should bow out."

Richard had seldom heard defeat in Elspeth's voice. "Come to Brussels," he said. "I'll be working at the flat this evening."

"That would be lovely, Dickie. A hug from you right now would be a gift from heaven."

*

Richard bent over his papers and then looked up at the secretary they had assigned to him. She was a pretty girl, a redhead, with a tight, clinging blouse that showed more cleavage than Richard was comfortable with but which was at the moment trendy. He thought of the many girls who had worked for him. Elspeth would have admonished him for calling them girls, but to him they were. Despite the ways of the current age, he suspected these young things were still out for a husband. He was used to the way they looked at him, a seasoned diplomat, who looked as he aged more and more like Lord Mountbatten of Burma, although the 'girls' might not even know who the famous royal earl was. Richard was amused by the admiring looks these girls gave him. His first wife smiled at their adoring glances at Richard and promptly arranged for them to meet suitable men. Richard could not imagine Elspeth doing so. A pity, he thought. Much was lost when women insisted on being liberated.

He had just handed the secretary a folder that he wanted returned to the office in the morning before he was scheduled to arrive, when the doorbell rang.

"Get that will you," he said to the secretary.

She rose and brushed her miniskirt down. Its length was just short of indecent. He could hear her open the door.

"May I tell him whose calling?" she said. Her tone was protective.

"His wife," Elspeth's voice came back.

Richard swallowed a laugh. Elspeth had spoken in her most imperious tone, ones she had cultivated as a girl herself for one of the melodramas her mother directed at Blair School for Girls.

Richard did not need to see the secretary's blush. He imagined it starting from the cleavage. He could hear her stammer.

"Oh, I'm terribly sorry, Lady Munro" she said.

·When Elspeth came into view, Richard understood the secretary's dismay. Elspeth was dressed in one of her most handsome business suits and wore four-inch-high heels, which made her tower over the girl. Elspeth was holding her head high and looking down her nose. The girl shrivelled into her scanty clothing.

"Eh, ah," she said. "Sir Richard, I must be going." She grabbed the folder, picked up her coat, and fled from the flat.

When she was gone, Elspeth burst out laughing. "What were you doing with someone like that in your flat?" she asked, humour filling her voice.

"One of my worshipful subjects," he said. "Come here, my dearest. You've no cause for worry."

Elspeth rushed into his arms.

"Of that I am positive," she said in the same tone she had used at the door, but then her voice changed to supplication. "Oh, Dickie, I can't find any proof!"

"Let's talk about it," he said, stroking her hair.

She raised her head on his shoulder. "Let me use the loo first," she said.

"I'll get you some sherry," he said. "Too bad my secretary isn't here to do it for me."

Elspeth playfully boxed his ears. "At least you didn't ask me to do it," she said

He chuckled and let her go.

When sherry was poured and Elspeth had returned, they settled on the sofa, which was hard and without pillows.

"I think I need to go to Portugal and talk to the people on Kristin's list," she said.

"Wouldn't that be terribly dangerous?" he asked. "If they were somehow responsible for Alexandre and Helga's deaths, they might have no compunction in killing you. I won't allow it, my dearest."

Elspeth straightened up to her full height and stared at him. He knew he had said the wrong thing.

"Or at least if you go, I'm coming with you," he said in full retreat. "After all this is my case too. I can meet you in Portugal on Friday evening. I'm busy here until then. Does the Kennington Organisation have a hotel in Portugal?"

"Not yet. I think Eric is planning one, but Pamela

can find rooms there. Eric will be paying for it, so our accommodations will be luxurious. He always asks me to keep an eye on the competition if I can't stay at a Kennington hotel."

They ate at a bistro tucked around the corner from Richard's flat, where the food was good and the atmosphere non-pretentious. The owner was delighted to greet Richard's wife and gave them a free glass of wine.

Richard cradled Elspeth in his arms when they went to bed, and soon she fell into deep sleep. The rhythm of her breathing comforted him, but he did not sleep well, thinking Elspeth's plan audacious and wishing she had agreed to leave the matter to Interpol. But that would not have been like her and he loved her as she was. At least she had conceded to his accompanying her. Marriage to Elspeth was certainly not what he had initially expected.

28

Before making her way into the City of London and an interview with Lord Kennington that Elspeth knew would involve demands as to why she had not solved the Bruges case, Elspeth went to the safe in her office in the flat in Kensington and withdrew the envelope Kristin had given her. She sat biting the edge of her lip and pivoting the envelope on its corners between her fingers before opening it. In Brussels she had not told Richard the fear she was feeling. If her theory was correct, the people she so boldly had declared she would meet in Portugal could very well take extreme umbrage over her interference. She knew she was stepping beyond the usual parameters of her job. Had she not felt so conflicted about her role in the case, she would have gladly handed over the subsequent interviews to the European Commission or to Interpol, but she felt responsible to both Richard and Eric Kennington. After all she was both Richard's wife and Eric's special security advisor. The solution to the three murders in Bruges would not have been so complicated if she were surer of her role in finding their solution. She thought she had to prove herself, to show she was not just Richard's dutiful wife who was snooping around a bit on her own. She had great respect for the police and the hotels' security forces in most cases. Captain Schrott was undoubtedly capable, and Frans Bootds as efficient as most Kennington hotel security officers, but the case was hers to solve.

Yet Elspeth was nettled. She had deliberately withheld information from both the captain and Frans and in doing so must have impeded their investigations. Was it pride on her part or foolishness?

She ripped open the envelope and looked at the names written in upper case letters before remembering she had promised to inform Kristin before doing so. Kristin had supplied three names: EDUARDO TOMÀS COSTA DA SILVA, JORGE XAVIER MORILLA FIGUIERA and WILHELM VOGLER, all living near Oporto. The last one certainly was not Portuguese, but Oporto was an international city, like most of Europe's larger cities. Herr Vogler probably was one of Helga's German contacts. Kristin had not provided any specific addresses.

Elspeth went to her computer and searched the internet. She could find nothing relevant under the names listed. She debated calling Kristin but then remembered that Kristin had given the names under duress and more than likely would not want to be reminded of her indiscretion. Elspeth had no wish to contact Dagmar again. But what about Viktor Novikov? She did not want to return to France, so she googled Viktor's firm and found the address of his London office, which was near the Kennington Organisation's central office in the City. Best, Elspeth thought, to contact Viktor's London branch before she faced Eric Kennington.

The receptionist answered in French and then English and informed Elspeth that Monsieur Novikov was unavailable.

"Tell him Lady Munro called," Elspeth said.

"Just a moment," the receptionist said and sent Elspeth to canned classical music. Several moments into a Brahms violin concerto, Viktor came on the line.

Such was the power of a title, Elspeth thought. Her egalitarian side growled.

"How is the investigation progressing?" he asked. "I understand you visited Dagmar in Paris but had little to report."

News travelled fast.

"We still have not solved the murders, but I have another lead. I wonder if you could help me? Do you know a Wilhelm Vogler in Portugal?"

"I do, but he lives just outside Oporto."

"Can you tell me how I might contact him?"

"Give me a moment, but I strongly advise you stay away from him. He is, was a close friend of Helga Müeller. Ulrich would not like you to contact him. For all I know, it could be very dangerous."

"So I understand," she said.

She heard the clicking of computer keys.

"Vogler used to have several legitimate businesses in the Oporto area. I suggest you approach him saying you are interested in property there. Here's a phone number there you can call," Viktor said. "I'd advise that you use it judiciously."

"I will," Elspeth assured him, although she guaranteed nothing. Plans for contacting Wilhelm Vogler turned in her mind. She did not want to involve the police or Interpol as yet. She wondered what Richard would make of Viktor's warning and then decided not to tell him about it.

She caught a taxi to the City and waited impatiently as it made its way through Central London traffic. She should have taken the tube for speed but did not want to mix with the general populace on the underground. She arrived at her appointment with Eric Kennington with five minutes to spare.

Pamela Crumm was waiting for her outside the doors to the lift.

"He's foaming," she said, "but I have ordered some of his favourite cakes, which should sweeten him up. Try to be as positive as you can."

"Thanks for telling me," Elspeth said.

She walked into her employer's office with her head held high, as if she were returning in triumph, not defeat.

"Elspeth, where the hell have you been?" he asked without greeting.

"All over most of the western world," she said, and then regretted her flippancy. She expected him to be angry, but he laughed.

"Does that mean you've caught our criminals?"

"I'm close," she said optimistically. "I need to verify one last thing, but I'll need to go to Portugal this weekend to do so."

"Do you want to tell me?"

"Not yet, in case I'm wrong," she said.

"Have Pamela make the arrangements and don't be wrong," he said. With an impatient flick of his hand he dismissed her. Pamela cracked the door from her adjoining office and motioned Elspeth in. Pamela had obviously been listening surreptitiously to their short conversation through headphones on her computer.

"That was brief," she said after she closed her door. "Which is for the best. Now tell me the details."

"Pamela, I want to make arrangements to get a handgun in Portugal," Elspeth said.

"A handgun? What on earth for? Besides I'll have to check if carrying small arms in Portugal is legal, which I doubt. Elspeth, m'friend, I hope you're not considering getting in harm's way."

"I only want some protection."

"Can you handle a small gun?"

"My uncle taught me how to shoot a rifle when I was a child and I learned how to handle a revolver at Scotland Yard. I had a pocket-sized pistol in Los Angeles—with a licence. As a private investigator I was allowed to carry one although I never used it."

"Packing a pistol hardly fits the Kennington image," Pamela said frowning.

"I don't plan to fire it," Elspeth said. "I just want to have it as a backup. I'll need to get it there, since I can't take it on the plane. Also I need a hotel in Oporto—for me and Richard."

"I'll do what I can," said Pamela. Her voice sounded doubtful. Elspeth's request was not a usual one. "Come have an early dinner with me this evening," Pamela said in a rare personal invitation, "I want you to tell me what's really going on and why Richard is going with you to Portugal."

Pamela was a small woman and rich enough that she had everything in her penthouse flat on the south bank of the Thames scaled to her size. Elspeth took the glass of the proffered crisp white wine and settled into a chair Pamela had for taller guests. She poured out the whole story of the case, and for the first time left nothing important out. Pamela sat in a smaller chair sipping her wine. She did not interrupt.

"Aren't you getting a bit over your head, Elspeth?" Pamela said when Elspeth was finished. "Eric and I never again want you to place yourself in a situation where you might be harmed. One nasty incident is more than enough. We don't want you out of commission for six months the way you were after the attack in Singapore."

"That's why I want the gun."

"But if you pull out a gun, won't Wilhelm Vogler be likely to have one too?"

"I hope not. I don't plan to threaten him. I only want information about where he and his cohorts were when Helga and Alexandre were murdered. If he stalls or in any way appears to be lying, it will be time for Interpol to step in. But I don't want anyone else to intervene as yet."

"Why are you taking Richard with you?"

"Like the gun, for protection and also because he insisted. It would be helpful if you could arrange for a driver with a fast car."

"Aren't you afraid?"

"A little, but I'm more perturbed about the elusive quality of this case. I want to solve it, not let it go."

"Don't overstep your duties for me and Eric, Elspeth. We would prefer you alive and safe."

But I'll find the bastards, Elspeth thought in a most unladylike way.

Elspeth spent a long time preparing for her trip. She wanted to get everything in place beforehand and to present herself to Wilhelm Vogler in a manner that would appear nonthreatening but that would solicit the information she needed. She decided to say that she and Richard were business associates not husband and wife. She would have to convince Richard because he did not like her lying, even for a good reason. She chose a name for a fictitious import export firm, Duff and Munro, and printed up business cards with her name and Richard's but without his title. She selected a wardrobe that was casual but business-like and also would afford her the freedom of a quick exit if needed. She had a jacket with deep inside pockets and hoped Pamela would get a gun that would fit in one of them without a bulge because she did not want Richard to know she was carrying the gun. A casually thrown scarf in the way she had learned in India would hide any anomalies in her figure.

Satisfied that she had all the props in place, she rang Detective Superintendent Tony Ketcham at Scotland Yard to ask a favour. He greeted her with the heavy and tired voice Elspeth had noticed the last few times talking to him.

"Tony, can you make arrangements for me to use the firing range at the Yard? About an hour is all I need."

"Do you have a case that will be of interest to me?"

"Possibly but nothing I can tell you as yet. But I do promise not to use a gun in the UK."

"If I had more time," he said, "I would drag things out of you, but things are rather busy these days. Call DS Jane Dawes. She worked on your Malta case and always wanted to meet you. I'll patch you through, but first I'll clear your entry to the firing range for you."

Elspeth was glad for her association with the Metropolitan Police. Good as her word, Elspeth only needed an hour to refresh her skills with a handgun, and DS Jane Dawes fawned over Elspeth and her awkward first attempts at firing the pistol. Elspeth tried several guns in order to make sure she could adjust to the one Pamela would get for her in Portugal. Satisfied, Elspeth thanked DS Dawes and made her way back to their flat in Kensington. She could think of no more preparations before she reached Portugal.

Having an hour free, Elspeth rang her daughter and was pleased at the eagerness with which Lizzie answered the phone.

"Mummy, will you come down for the weekend? Tom and Tim have produced a play and want their grannies, their grandfather and Richard to see it."

"Er," said Elspeth, not wanting to tell her daughter her plans for the weekend. "I have to be out of the country on business on Saturday. Will you tell the twins that I want to see the play and Richard and I will be down as soon as possible? We might even be able to make it Sunday evening if we are back in the UK."

"They will be disappointed," Lizzie said. "Did you solve your problem with the young woman you spoke to me about?"

"Not yet. Do you have any thoughts?"

"None really. Only that your work seems quite horrible. Can't you give it up?"

"Right now I can't. Too many people's lives hang in the balance," she said. She did not explain that hers might be one of them.

"Can you come on Sunday evening? Denis's parents will stay until then."

Elspeth had met her son-in-law's parents several times. They were of the County set and in Elspeth's opinion led unexciting lives. The latest bridge and golf scores did not interest her.

"I'll try," Elspeth said. "I'll call you Saturday night or Sunday morning. I won't know before then."

Lizzie still did not seem to understand. Elspeth wondered if she ever would find a way beyond this impasse with her daughter.

29

Richard had never liked being part of Elspeth's escapades, even when they were young. He was always amazed, however, that she had an uncanny ability to get out of scrapes, even now. He was not keen on going to Portugal or in challenging someone there who very likely was involved in the murders of Alexandre de Saint Phalle, Helga Müeller and possibly Raffaello Conti. Why had so much gone awry during his meeting in Bruges? On second thought, however, Elspeth had uncovered the identity of Mateo, which was the real purpose of the weekend and under normal circumstances would count it as a success. Richard liked dealing with crime at a distance and regretted that Elspeth preferred direct confrontation. He suspected that she would cook up some devious scheme to question Wilhelm Vogler.

Richard had little time to arrange for the trip to Portugal and caught his plane to Oporto at the last minute. Since taking on his new job at the European Commission, he frequently hop-scotched across Europe and had a bag packed for any occasion, a skill he had learned from Elspeth. She had said 'business casual' and he had gathered together the little clothing of that type that he had in Brussels.

Late that evening Elspeth met him as he emerged from the security section of the Oporto airport. His heart always filled with joy when he saw her standing gracefully and with a big smile of welcome. When he was free from the barrier, she hugged him. He could feel the tension in her back despite her usual straight posture and loving eyes.

"I've set up an appointment with Herr Vogler tomorrow afternoon at his estate outside Oporto. Pamela has booked us into a hotel in an old villa here in the city, and we have a driver who speaks passable English. He is waiting outside in an outrageously large Mercedes," she said as they walked through the terminal arm in arm. "I wonder about Pamela's penchant for such vehicular beasts."

"Elspeth, are you comfortable with our meeting with Wilhelm Vogler? What have you told him?"

"Not a lot. I said we were interested in the European import export trade, which is technically correct."

"Did you mention Helga Müeller?"

"Not yet."

"How do you plan to do so?" He had made up his mind to go along with Elspeth's scheme, at least in the beginning. Elspeth frequently planned appointments that were more dangerous that he would have done.

"I'm sure he will ask how we got his name. I was vague on the phone, but I suspect that many of Mateo's clients are at first. I don't know for sure that Herr Vogler is the one who took over from Helga. I had a feeling that he was sounding me out to see if I were genuine or a bit crooked."

"And which did you indicate?" Richard asked, although he had an idea how she would answer.

"You guess," she said with a grin.

Over breakfast the next morning, Elspeth laid out her plans. Richard listened to them and finally said, "What is your backup if he doesn't believe you?"

"Flee like the wind," she said laughing. "I asked Pamela for a fast car."

"I hope it's armoured."

"Knowing Pamela, it probably is. She's concerned for our safety."

"What if Herr Vogler admits to being in Bruges?"

"I want him to tell me why."

"Is there any reason he should?" Richard asked.

"Perhaps. If Helga was killed because she was Mateo, her associates might be as interested as we are in finding the killer."

"But I thought you said Raffaello was the probable killer."

"It's only a hunch. Someone killed Raffaello for a reason, most likely to silence him. He must have seen something he wasn't supposed to. He may even have indulged in a bit of blackmail. He was undoubtedly waiting for someone at the fish market before I found him. The alternative is that he was killed because he was responsible for Helga's death. We may never know for sure. Whoever killed Alexandre planned it beforehand, I feel. Whoever killed Raffaello didn't."

"And Helga's murder? Was that pre-planned?"

Elspeth frowned. "If it was Raffaello, he must have had a reason. He may have killed her without premeditation, but someone may have provoked him into

337

doing so."

"Dagmar?" he speculated.

"Possibly. I just wish we had heard more of what Dagmar said to Raffaello that night in the park."

"She was angry from the sound of it," he said, remembering the sound of Dagmar's voice from afar.

"Why I wonder?" Elspeth puzzled. "Was it Alexandre's death? Then why did Dagmar say she hated Alexandre and was glad to get rid of him? Still, I don't think Dagmar is guilty. She may be disagreeable, but she doesn't have the personality of a murderer."

"Could she have asked Raffaello to avenge Alexandre's death? That's assuming of course that Dagmar is telling the truth about seeing Alexandre's attackers."

"Dickie, our suite was directly above Dagmar's. Do you remember that we heard her singing? We could see the canal from our windows, not the back of the hotel. How then could Dagmar have a view of Alexandre being bludgeoned from her room? The problem with this case is that I come up with one theory and then, on further thought, I can think of any number of reasons why I'm wrong. I sincerely hope that our meeting tomorrow won't be as confusing."

30

The following morning the loud peeling of church bells roused them. Elspeth rolled into Richard's arms, kissed him and quickly rose.

"I need to get one or two things before we go out to see Wilhelm Vogler," she said, hoping her voice implied that they were of a private nature and she would not be questioned. "Stay in bed. I shouldn't be more than half an hour and then we can have breakfast in the courtyard below."

Elspeth had rung Pamela the night before to get instructions and Pamela told her where her 'packet' could be retrieved. Elspeth had checked the city map and knew it was close to the hotel and she wanted to go alone, in case Richard objected. The morning was crisp, and a host of merchants were setting up stalls in an open-air market in a nearby square. Elspeth took a moment to admire the plethora of fruits, vegetables, olives, fragrant loaves of newly baked bread and fresh fish. She noticed it was nearing eight o'clock, when she was expected at the gunsmiths. She found the shop on a side street and went through the metal gate that protected the door.

A Portuguese man, who was stooped with age but had keen dark eyes, said in understandable English, "Good morning, Senhora Duff. You are on time. Come into the back room."

A packet bound in a soft green cloth lay in the

centre of a worktable. The old man slowly unwrapped it with his arthritic hands and revealed a small Beretta Tomcat pistol. She picked it up, caressed it and looked down the barrel.

"Perfect," she said.

"I cleaned and oiled it for you. It will shoot very straight. Also I will give you a box of bullets. How many do you need?"

Elspeth had not considered using the gun at all, but she also wanted to be prepared. "Five should be more than enough, along with the seven in the gun now." If she could not get them out of any situation with a dozen bullets, she would be in deep trouble.

The man went to a large, wooden cabinet with carved doors and drew out a small box of bullets, some of which he gave to Elspeth.

"The other senhora from London said you will need it for today only. If the door is not open when you return, ring the bell. I work here in the back until late this evening."

"Will I need a license?"

He grinned, showing irregular yellow teeth.

"Not unless you are stopped and questioned. If you have a problem, have the police call me. But I prefer you do not let them know anything. Be careful."

Elspeth lifted the gun again, spreading her legs, took the pistol in two hands, and mimicking the stance she had been taught many years before. She recognised the balance of the weapon and the ease with which it handled.

"I will," she said.

He wrapped the gun back in the cloth and put it in an ordinary tote bag that said 'Exclusive Portugal Holidays' in English on the side. He handed the bag to her and said, "Enjoy your stay in Oporto."

Richard was up, shaved and dressed when she arrived back at their rooms. He had shed his business suit for an open necked shirt and dark blue blazer that hung smartly on his trim figure. Unlike so many men, he had grown more handsome as he had aged, Elspeth thought. She went over and touched his cheek lovingly. He looked more like a retired admiral than a disreputable businessman, but for today that would have to do. Not all criminals, especially those in the high echelons, looked the part, as Elspeth so well knew from her job with the Kennington Organisation.

"Did you get the gun?" he asked.

"How did you know?" she cried.

"I'm not clairvoyant although you may think so. Pamela just rang and asked. Are you comfortable carrying a gun? Don't you think we might be searched when we get to Herr Vogler's estate?"

Elspeth had thought of this. "If we are, we will plead that we felt the need for protection here in Portugal. The most they can do is take the gun away."

"And brand us as being a threat," he said.

"We are pretending to be on nefarious business," she countered.

"Are you sure you want to go through with this?" he asked.

"At this point, do we have any choice?"

"We could have Interpol take care of the whole thing."

"But I still only have suspicions, no proof. Bear with me, Dickie. Despite the gun, I think we will be received with a welcome from Wilhelm Vogler."

The reception at the entrance to the villa was not exactly welcoming, but they did not search Richard and Elspeth nor ask for any weapons they could be carrying. A mangy looking man with a rifle stood at the guardhouse at the tall steel gates. He spoke in rapid Portuguese to their driver and then spoke into a disreputable looking mobile phone that he took from a case at his ageing leather belt. He said '*sim, sim*' several times, disconnected his call and spat on the ground. He turned again to the driver and gave instructions. The gateman went into the guardhouse and must have pressed a releasing device because the gates swung open.

The drive meandered through lemon groves lined with olive trees, whose grey leaves shimmered in the sun, which gave a sense of serenity and peace. Despite the beauty, Elspeth could not relax. She took Richard's hand and felt irritated by her need for his support. He squeezed her hand, raised an eyebrow and smiled quizzically.

"Almost there," she said and thought her remark inane, but talking alleviated the dryness in her throat. She had decided to rely on as much truth as possible but to twist it so that Herr Vogler would interpret it wrongly. After her experiences in both Cyprus and Singapore, where she had been physically attacked in the line of duty, she felt abhorrence towards any threat of violence towards her person. She fingered the gun, which she could feel pressing against her hip, but it gave her no comfort.

The building compound was half a mile from the gate along the narrow, paved road. The estate was devoid of workers, perhaps because it was Saturday. Elspeth felt the eeriness of this unpopulated space despite its loveliness. If there were a problem at the house, there would be no one to call out to for help except their driver. In the rear-view mirror, Elspeth could see his weary eyes.

When they reached the cluster of buildings, Elspeth saw another guard at the door to the main house. The bulge under his coat was unmistakeably a gun of some sort. He lolled against a column of the covered entry and was picking his teeth. When the car got closer, he straightened up, pulled his crumpled jacket down and motioned the driver to the main door. The driver approached him and rolled down the window. From the subsequent conversation it was apparent that Elspeth and Richard were expected. The guard watched them with little interest as the driver let them out of the back doors of the car.

The main door opened for them. What appeared to be an old-fashioned footman in a short jacket, stripped waistcoat, and sharply creased black trousers appeared from behind the door and motioned them into the house.

Elspeth put their false business cards on the silver tray he was holding.

"Come please," he said in broken English.

They followed him through an entryway that opened on to an opulent garden, large palms shading beds filled with brightly blossoming flowers and deep green foliage. The footman led them through the garden to a room with three storey floor-to-ceiling glass walls that looked out over the grooves.

"Senhor Vogler say wait here," he said. He indicated a pair of rattan sofas with bright yellow cushions. A tray with a jug of lemonade, an ice bucket and three glasses stood on the table in front of the seating. Beyond the sofas was a vast and empty desk with a computer at one side but no chair. On the other side of the desk were several photographs on a table, but they were not visible from where Elspeth and Richard sat.

Elspeth arranged herself so that the gun was not obvious but where she could reach it quickly if needed. Richard watched her do so and shook his head and sighed.

"Don't get up," a voice said, as one of the wall panels of the solid wall opened. Elspeth looked up to greet her host and then looked down to see a man in a wheelchair. He had a mass of white hair, a neatly trimmed beard, and unruly white eyebrows, one of which was bisected with an ugly scar.

"The result of a car crash on one of your British motorways," he said as if they had asked for an explanation. "I was the lucky one. I survived. Neither my wife nor son did."

This opening was not what Elspeth had expected. She drew in her breath. "I'm sorry," she said but instinctively knew he had put his guests at a disadvantage with his grisly tale.

"Now tell me what you really have come for," he said. "Not just to inquire about the import export business in Portugal. You could find out about that on the internet or from the Portuguese Embassy in London."

"I, we," Elspeth stammered, not knowing quite how to begin.

Wilhelm Vogler, or at least she assumed this man was Wilhelm Vogler as he had not introduced himself by name, raised his good eyebrow.

Elspeth gathered her wits and began again. "My associate, Richard Munro, and I had an appointment in Bruges with Frau Helga Müeller, but she didn't keep it."

"So you knew Helga?" He used the past tense, which indicated he knew of her death.

"Only to know that she agreed to help me and Richard," Elspeth said.

"And how did you get her name?"

Elspeth had not anticipated this question. Richard came to the rescue.

"We heard about her from Alexandre de Saint Phalle," he said. "Alexandre told us he had business dealings with her."

Elspeth looked over at Richard and was amazed how quickly he stretched the truth.

"Did he?" Vogler asked.

"Do you know Alexandre de Saint Phalle?" Elspeth asked in the present tense. To the best of her knowledge there had been no public announcement of his death.

"By reputation only," Herr Vogler said. "Ms Duff, you indicated that you and your partner wished to break into business with the former Soviet Union. Doing so is very risky. I sense you know very little about it. I could not find your firm on the internet."

Elspeth cursed her lack of foresight. She had not posted anything on the fictitious Duff and Munro Company online. She thought quickly.

"We want to stay quiet about what we are doing, and admittedly are new at it."

"I suggest," Wilhelm Vogler, "that you should be careful in your business plan. It sounds unformed."

"We were looking for Frau Müeller's advice. That's why we were disappointed in Bruges."

"Did Alexandre de Saint Phalle tell you what Helga's business was?"

"Vaguely," Richard said. "We had hoped Frau Müeller would tell us more."

"I am amazed that Monsieur de Saint Phalle told you about Helga," Wilhelm Vogler said.

So Herr Vogler did know something about Mateo, Elspeth thought. She pushed farther. "Is there a way to contact Frau Müeller? She does not answer the mobile number she gave us." Elspeth hoped her voice sounded innocent.

"Ms Duff and Mr Munro, I suggest you leave Portugal and forget any ideas of contacting Frau Müeller. She unfortunately is no longer alive. But you must have known that if you came here to find me." For the first time his voice sounded harsh. "You are out of your league here. Business with the Soviet Union is brutal and not for novices."

"No longer alive?" Richard said in a most convincing voice.

"Quite dead," Wilhelm Vogler said. "I think you have made your trip here in vain. May I offer you some lemonade before you leave? The heat of the day will be up soon, although I see you came in a comfortable car."

Elspeth would not give up that easily. She glanced over at Richard, who was staring at her. She looked back at Wilhelm Vogler.

"Shall we stop the pretence?" she said.

"Yes, Ms Duff, I would prefer that."

"We were in Bruges when Helga Müeller was killed. We are trying to find why."

"Are you from the police?"

"No," Elspeth said. "And what is more, we do not want to involve the police. I represent the hotel where Helga Müeller was staying when she died. We do not like violence associated with our operations and want to cover up as much as possible. Can you help me, Herr Vogler?"

He burst out laughing. "Well, I hope you are better at covering up murders than you are at posing as a businesswoman. And you, sir, as well. Are you retired from the Royal Navy?"

He shook his head. "No, I am a civil servant and Ms Duff is my wife. She asked me to come along."

"For protection?" Herr Vogler asked with a hint of humour. "I can hardly be a threat in my condition. As you can see, I live alone and, being incapacitated, have a staff to help me. Do I know anything about Helga

Müeller's death? Only that she will be missed as a friend."

"Do you know any other of her associates here in Portugal?" Elspeth asked.

Associates? Do you mean in a business sense? No. I knew her when we were growing up in West Germany. She came often to see me when she was here. Sometimes she brought her lovely daughter, who was the same age my son would have been. I had no business dealings with her. I suspected her business dealings, if she had any, were negligible and probably just fraudulent enough to satisfy her. She had been that way ever since she was a child in school, engaging in petty theft or lying. She did it as a game in the end, stealing things and then selling them, which she had done as a schoolgirl. Her husband was very rich and she wanted for nothing. But that didn't fulfil her. She needed stimulation and her small crimes were basically harmless. It may be that her mother suffered terribly in Berlin at the hands of the invading Soviet troops in 1945 and had resorted to thieving to stay alive. Helga's mother was not sane, and Helga had a touch of that insanity too, I fear. I always felt sorry for Kristin and hoped she was free of her mother and her grandmother's curse. I never have been quite sure."

Elspeth was confused. This information did not fit with what Kristin Müeller had said in London.

"Do you know Eduardo Tomàs Costa da Silva and Jorge Xavier Morilla Figuiera?" Elspeth asked. "I may not have pronounced their names correctly."

Wilhelm Vogler frowned. "Eduardo Tomàs Costa

da Silva and Jorge Xavier Morilla Figuiera?" he said pronouncing them differently. Then he laughed. "How do you know those names?"

"Kristin Müeller mentioned them to me."

He laughed again. "She would be one of the few people outside my household who would know them. They are my valet and head gardener."

Elspeth shook her head to clear it. "They are not business associates of yours or Frau Müeller's?"

"I have been retired since the accident in the UK. Before that I was an interior designer in what was then West Berlin. I have a few properties that I own and manage but no business associates now. I think you have been misled, Ms Duff, or should I say Lady Munro?"

Elspeth raised her chin, hoping by doing so she would restore her own dignity. "How do you know who I am?"

"Helga and I were in constant contact up until she died. She called me from Bruges and told me about your conference, Sir Richard. She was frightened and justly so after the murder of Alexandre de Saint Phalle."

"What was she frightened of?" Elspeth asked.

"Her husband," Herr Vogler said. His eyes held Elspeth's for a long moment. "Are you surprised?"

"Yes, rather," said Elspeth. "Why was she afraid of Ulrich?"

"Because she knew too much about his business. I don't know what happened in Bruges, but I have lost a close friend. I'm glad you two are pursuing the case and that you came here to ask me about Helga. The police have not contacted me although I may be one of the last people to talk to her."

"Are you suggesting that Ulrich may have killed Helga?" Elspeth asked.

"I have no idea," he said. "If you find her murderer, I would appreciate you letting me know. The crime seems to have been hidden from the press. I spend a great deal of my time on my computer, and I have seen nothing about the murders. I would not have known about Helga except Kristin called me and told me. Now let's have that lemonade?"

As they made their way out of Wilhelm Vogler's glass-walled sitting room, Elspeth felt the weight of the gun in her pocket and felt foolish. She would have to explain herself to Eric Kennington and Pamela Crumm on Monday morning and would have to admit to her failure. She would be reprieved only if she could solve the case over the weekend, but she no longer was sure where to turn.

They settled into the Mercedes, and she rolled down the window. Wilhelm Vogler sat in his chair framed by the grand wooden door and waved goodbye.

"Best of luck," he said. "Do find whoever did this."

As they rolled away from the house, Richard put his arm around Elspeth's shoulder.

"How are you feeling?" he asked gently.

"Like an idiot," she said resting her head on his shoulder. "With guns and armoured cars and dragging you here, I feel a halfwit. And now I am going to have to explain it away to Eric and Pamela."

"You were misled," he said into her hair.

"Purposely, I think. But why would Kristin give me the three names?"

"Perhaps she knew that her mother was so close to Vogler, that he would shed some light on Helga's murder."

"But why the act in London? Was she playing to Jean Luc?" Elspeth speculated.

"I think not. She was playing to us and using Jean Luc," Richard said. "What he told us was that his parents said it was best Mateo was dead or something to that effect. The Novikovs may have suspected Helga was Mateo. Dagmar would have told them that."

"But Helga was not Mateo," Elspeth burst out. "We were just supposed to believe that because of what Kristin told us." She had no idea what had precipitated the thought.

"So the identity of Mateo remains a mystery still," he said.

"I don't think so. Among everyone we have talked to, only one person had no reason to lie to us."

"Who," he asked.

"Wilhelm Vogler. He told us indirectly who Mateo was—Ulrich Müeller. If you factor in everything, that makes the most sense."

"But if Ulrich is Mateo, why was Helga killed?"

"Probably for exactly the reason that Herr Vogler told us. Helga knew too much about Ulrich's business. Not the precious metals business, the money laundering. That made her a liability, particularly since you were inching towards the truth?" She swung round and faced him. "You were getting too close to Mateo at your

Friday meeting with Ulrich, Alexandre and Viktor. Viktor told you that Ulrich was Mateo, but Ulrich countered that Viktor was. Alexandre, of course, knew that Ulrich was Mateo because he had dealings with the Mateo organisation. Ulrich needed to silence Alexandre, who had betrayed him, and consequently killed him. I think after Helga heard of the murder, she confronted him, much to her peril."

"And he killed her?"

Elspeth bit her lower lip. "I'm not absolutely sure, but he could have. I suspect Raffaello saw him. The boy should have gone to the police, but instead he must have approached Ulrich for hush money. What a silly thing to do when Ulrich had already killed twice. It all fits together."

"But I still don't understand about Kristin," he said.

"Nor do I exactly. Either she is in league with her father, or she is terrified of him. He may have intimidated her and insisted she go to London to lead me on a wild goose chase."

"How can you find out?"

"I won't ask Dagmar," Elspeth said with a grin. "She has far too frequently tried to push herself into the middle of this case, only to lead us far afield."

Richard laughed. "How like her. She always loved dealing in speculative gossip, even if she only heard the edges of the facts and repeated them as truths. Now, my dearest, what do you plan to do next?"

She rested her head back on his arm. "I suggest that at this point we turn everything over to the police, fly back to London and go see Tim and Tom's play."

Elspeth called Captain Schrott on Monday morning and poured out her suspicions, but after she hung up uneasiness filled her. Her whole premise was based on believing Wilhelm Vogler and the circumstantial evidence she had gathered from her various interviews after the murders. In the end if Ulrich were Mateo, he would need to be trapped into a confession. Elspeth did not want to confront him again and would leave that to the Bruges police. Richard had agreed to call Interpol, who would investigate the money laundering. Their task was made easier now that they had a name.

But what about Lizzie's earlier admonishment? What happened to the people left behind? How would Kristin live out the rest of her life with a mother who was murdered and a father who most likely had killed three people if not more?

Kristin's future needled Elspeth. The young woman might be in danger from her father. Elspeth wanted to know the real reason that Kristin had given her the three names. She had indicated the three men whose names she had written down might be following her. But that was nonsense. No one could be more benign that Wilhelm Vogler and his servants. Elspeth was not ready to accept that Kristin truly believed that Herr Vogler, his valet and his head gardener were a threat. Unless Wilhelm Vogler was the liar. Elspeth sensed he was not.

Before going to Portugal to meet Wilhelm Vogler, Elspeth had not contacted Kristin, as she had promised she would. Kristin had left a mobile number but had indicated it might not be secure, so Elspeth did not now want to call her on it. Elspeth wished she had Jean Luc's number, but she did not. She rang Richard, who had flown to Brussels that morning, and asked for Viktor Novikov's number at home.

A servant answered the phone and informed Lady Munro that he would see if Madame Novikova was at home. A minute later Hélène was on the line.

"Have you found the murderer, Lady Munro?" she asked in a sleepy voice and then she yawned. It was past ten o'clock in France and Hélène obviously was still in bed. Elspeth wondered briefly about such an idle life.

"I believe we have," she said.

"It was Ulrich Müeller, wasn't it?"

"It seems so," Elspeth said.

"Then Viktor was right all along. Your husband should have listened to him. If he had, perhaps the murders could have been prevented."

"But that's really not why I called. I'm trying to find Jean Luc. He contacted me and I lost his number," Elspeth lied.

"Is it about Kristin Müeller? I never liked that girl. She is touched by her mother's madness and father's dishonesty."

"Why do you say that? She and Jean Luc seem so close," Elspeth said, although that may have been the reason Hélène disliked her. No woman would be good enough for her son.

"Don't be fooled by Kristin. She has a strong streak of Germanic determination despite her pretty face. Perhaps you could tell this to Jean Luc when you talk to him. He won't listen to his mother."

Hélène gave Elspeth Jean Luc's mobile number. "He's in Paris and I expect with her," she said before ringing off.

Would Eric Kennington tolerate her making one more trip to Paris? Elspeth still had unfinished business at the Kennington hotel there and wanted to see Kristin, even though the case was now out of her hands.

Paris in October might not offer chestnut trees in blossom, but the city never failed to enchant. Elspeth watched from the window of the taxi and thought about asking Richard for a weekend in Paris alone with him once everything was resolved to her satisfaction. She longed to stroll along the Seine without a care.

She arranged to meet Jean Luc and Kristin in the lobby of the Kennington rue du Faubourg Saint-Honoré. She had invited them to meet there at three o'clock, specifically wanting to talk to them without benefit of a meal. When Elspeth arrived, Jean Luc was holding Kristin's hand and whispering to her. Kristin sat bolt upright and did not smile when Elspeth entered. Elspeth led them into the bar, which was empty except for a couple sitting in one corner. Elspeth took them to a table in the opposite corner.

Kristin asked for a Perrier with lime and Jean Luc a beer. Elspeth joined Kristin in her choice.

After the drinks were served and the weather sufficiently discussed, Elspeth turned to Kristin.

"I know I told you that I would ring you before opening the envelope you gave me, but circumstances took me to Portugal this weekend and I dared not call you on your mobile," she prevaricated. "So I took the liberty of contacting Wilhelm Vogler."

Kristin looked up from her glass. "You said you would not," she said with a frown.

Elspeth had seen the same expression on her daughter's face when Lizzie found fault with her mother.

"Herr Vogler seems a pleasant fellow," Elspeth said. "Not at all what I expected. Why did you say he was threatening?"

"I . . ." Kristin began but stopped.

"He isn't, is he?" Elspeth said. "Why did you deceive me and Sir Richard? You must have known the other names you gave me were his servants, who I suspect have never threatened anyone nor even left Portugal. I can't think that Herr Vogler goes much beyond the confines of his estate considering his condition."

Kristin stared at Elspeth but did not answer the challenge.

"Did your father instruct you to come to London?" Elspeth asked. Again she was met with stony silence.

"Are you aware, Kristin, that your father may possibly go to jail for the rest of his life for murdering Alexandre de Saint Phalle? You know he did."

Kristin paled but again said nothing. Jean Luc turned to Elspeth, horror in his face.

"It is not possible," he said.

"Unfortunately it is. He was arrested this morning in Hamburg. Kristin, you must tell me the truth, although I think I know it."

"How could you know it?" she said hostilely

"Long experience in detection and a confession from someone," Elspeth said although the latter part was not true. She watched Kristin carefully for a reaction.

"Your father killed Alexandre de Saint Phalle, and I think you know it. Monsieur de Saint Phalle was about to tell Sir Richard that your father was arranging money laundering for people who wanted to move nuclear waste from the old Soviet Union to Germany. Alexandre knew this because he was involved. He needed to be silenced. That Friday morning after my husband's meeting with Alexandre, Viktor Novikov and your father, your father invited Alexandre to go out behind the hotel. As they were guests at the hotel, their room keys let them both out without setting off the alarm. Your father beat Alexandre and then strangled him." Elspeth knew she was stretching the truth, but she needed an admission from Kristin to make her case.

"I have nothing to say," Kristin said raising her head and sticking out her chin.

"Your father told you to remain silent. Did he threaten you?"

"I do not like my father but he does not bully me."

"But he is a criminal. Your mother knew it, which gave her power over your father. Once he had killed Alexandre, he easily could have killed your mother too."

"He didn't!" Kristin shouted.

"No," Elspeth said. The truth filled her with sadness. "You did."

"You can't prove it."

r"I can."

Ann Crew

Kristin turned and fumbled with her handbag. She drew out a small gun. "Let me go," she said pointing it at Elspeth.

"I think not," Elspeth said.

Kristin's hand was shaking. "You can't keep me. I'll shoot you, Lady Munro, with all your fancy airs. You don't know what it was like to have a mother like mine. She was vicious and controlling."

"And you took the opportunity to kill her and have it blamed on your father. That was very cunning of you."

"How did you know?"

"As in all detection, I used a process of elimination. Raffaello saw you. Is that why he was killed too? Who killed him, you or your father? You told your father, didn't you, that you had killed you mother? Afterwards Raffaello approached your father for money."

Kristin raised the gun. "Leave me alone. I am going to walk out of here and neither you nor the police will find me again."

"You cannot hide forever, Kristin. The world is too small these days, and you will need access to money. The police will see that all the accounts in your name and your father's will be blocked, even the ones offshore. You can always plead for leniency, particularly if you testify against your father. You might even say your father forced you into killing your mother."

"He didn't. I had my own issues with my mother. They weren't his."

Kristin rose and held out the pistol with both hands.

Throughout the exchange between Kristin and Elspeth, Jean Luc had remained silent. The colour

358

slowly faded from his face. He jumped up and charged at Kristin. The pistol discharged and Elspeth felt a searing pain in the upper arm. Kristin turned the gun on Jean Luc.

"Stay out of my way," she yelled.

The man at the table in the far corner rose quietly and came up behind Kristin. He grabbed her around the shoulders causing her to drop the pistol. The man, who Elspeth knew was from the *Sûreté Nationale*, turned her around and spoke to her in rapid French. Elspeth had enough French to know that he was arresting her, but on what charge she was not sure. Possibly assault with a deadly weapon. The murder charge would come later. The French policeman expertly pulled back Kristin's arms and snapped handcuffs on them.

Captain Schrott, who had been the other member of the couple at the far table, came up to Elspeth, who was gripping her arm. Blood seeped from her wound. She pulled one of her clean handkerchiefs from her pocket and handed it to the policewoman.

"Please bind my arm, Captain. It stings dreadfully. Jean Luc, go ask at the reception desk if there is a doctor in the house. If not, there will be one on call."

The captain ripped open Elspeth's sleeve with an expert hand.

"It is not a deep wound," she said as she tied the handkerchief around Elspeth's arm.

"Did I get enough evidence for a conviction?"

The captain nodded. "Probably. Your conversation was recorded through the listening device you had installed at your table. I was wearing an ear bud and heard the whole thing. You're a very brave woman, Ms Duff."

"All in a day's work," she said and then fainted.

Epilogue

"What I regret most was that one of my favourite jackets was destroyed by the shot and was beyond repair after Captain Schrott was finished ripping open the sleeve and binding me up," Elspeth said to her husband as they were strolling down the quay along the Seine two weekends later. Her arm was still in a sling, but she had fashioned one from a grey, brown and blue patterned Hermès scarf, which Richard had bought for her earlier in the day. It matched her tweed coat tailored from material she had bought on the Isle of Harris.

Richard marvelled at his wife. She may not be the perfect diplomatic wife, but she was all he wanted. He was as in love with her as he had been from the first but understood her far better. He would never again compare her with Marjorie or even expect her to be his hostess at diplomatic events. She had not failed him in Bruges, but she had admitted her discomfort.

He often wondered how she often stumbled on to the solutions to her cases in the end. He might tease her about her Scottish sensibilities, but he sometimes thought she pulled answers out of an imaginary hat. Yet her theories seldom proved wrong. He still was baffled about Kristin. He had never once considered the girl's involvement in the murderers.

He enfolded her good arm more closely in his, and asked, "Whatever made you suspect Kristin Müeller?"

Elspeth put back her head. The cold November

breeze off the river ruffled her stylish hair. She turned to him with a whimsical look and cocked an eyebrow. "In Portugal when I began speculating that Ulrich had committed all three murders, I couldn't make the pieces fit neatly together, the way they do when I find the right solution. Helga must have known for a long time about Ulrich's being Mateo and therefore how did it benefit Ulrich to kill her? They obviously had established a relationship that worked for them. Nothing that happened in Bruges would have changed that. His killing Alexandre was presaged by Alexandre's possible revelation of his identity to you, thus betraying him. Even if Helga had guessed that Ulrich had murdered Alexandre, she already knew he would be indirectly responsible for multiple deaths if the spent radioactive metals he imported did get in the hands of terrorists in Germany. I suspect that Ulrich was the cause of other deaths too and Helga was undoubtedly aware of them. The more I thought about it, the more I became convinced that the cause of Helga's death wasn't because she knew of Ulrich's crimes but that someone hated her. Only one person fit that description—Kristin."

"Weren't you stretching?" he asked.

"In getting her to confess, yes, I was. Yet I could find no other plausible explanation for Helga's death after we talked to Wilhelm Vogler. Kristin expressed her hatred of her mother at every turn. I didn't at first link this to Helga's murder. But Hélène mentioned the madness in Helga's family and hoped Kristin wasn't touched by it. She was such a pretty girl, who looked like an innocent, but who had a gene for deception and crime that first showed up in her grandmother."

"Unfortunately. What a pity."

"I think I would have come to the real solution sooner, if it hadn't been for Dagmar. She kept muddying the waters, first with the 'BE WARNED' notes, and then with her unfortunate relationship with Raffaello Conti. He was terribly in love with her, if one can read his last words correctly. He must have wanted money to impress Dagmar and that's why he resorted to blackmail."

"Then why the words of anger the night she went out into the park and we followed?"

"Dagmar must have been fed up with Raffaello and Giorgio following her. She must have known that Alexandre was having her shadowed to see if she strayed."

"Do you think she did?"

Elspeth smiled sadly. "No. Her main concern was her boys. Alexandre provided a good home for them; she didn't want to change that. She spoke loathingly of Alexandre but at the same time she was dependent on him."

"And her first husband? Did Alexandre kill him?"

"I doubt it and I seriously think Helga made up the story of his being gay to provoke Dagmar. Even if he was, Dagmar must have loved him."

"What do you suppose will happen to Dagmar?" he asked. "Hopefully she will no longer force herself onto diplomatic circles."

"Do you want my best guess? She will follow her heart and take her boys back to Denmark, where she will buy a farm and retreat from all the unpleasantness of her former life. She will have all the monetary security she needs unless Alexandre's affairs are in such bad order that his estate will be worthless. Even so, I imagine there are farms she can afford simply by selling some of her jewellery."

"And the rest of us will be spared her misguided gossip," Richard said with some relief. "Have you heard anything from Captain Schrott?"

"She called me yesterday and told me that both Ulrich and Kristin are due to come to preliminary hearings later this month. Neither has confessed fully, but what Kristin told me at the hotel here in Paris will be used against them both. She said you and I would have to testify. She'll be calling your office next week."

"Have you spoken to Lizzie?"

"She rang me just before I left London and asked how my case with K was coming?"

"What did you tell her?"

"That the case had not worked out as I would have liked. I left it at that. She didn't push me, because at that moment there was a long howl from Tom or possibly Tim. She said she would ring me on Monday. Did I tell you that I'm off to Hong Kong on Tuesday?"

"For long?"

"Only a week."

"You must be glad to get back to your real job," he said, waiting to see if she would respond to her role as his wife.

She dislodged her good arm from his, kissed two of her fingers and touched his cheek.

"That," he said taking her carefully in his arms, "is

not the proper way for a man and a woman to kiss along the banks of the Seine."

He proceeded to demonstrate what he thought was the real way.

Bruges and London and Portugal and the Outer Hebrides were all forgotten; Dagmar, Alexandre, Ulrich, Helga, Viktor, Kristin and Jean Luc disappeared into the mist rising from the river. Only the Paris meant for lovers remained.

Author's Notes and Appreciation

When I visited Bruges in 2016, well after writing the first draft of this book, I wandered through the centre of the city to the places I had imagined through my earlier research into this beautiful city, finding spots that fit the action I had portrayed. There, of course, was no Kennington hotel, but there was a likely site that I used for its location. It was near the picture on the front cover.

Although, like Elspeth, I speak no Flemish, most people I met spoke English, as do so many Europeans. So many nameless people helped me during my visit. I had notebook, sketchpad, and camera in hand and furiously jotted down and visually recorded the spots I had tagged for the novel. My son has suggested I share some of the photographs and sketches on my website, *elspethduffmysteries.com*. After the book is published, I will do so.

As always, I want to thank Alice Roberts, my brilliant editor, and eagle-eyed Bev Mar, who does the final proofreading.

My mysteries could not continue to be written without the support of Ian Crew, who constantly urges me to publish what initially was written for my amusement alone.

Ann Crew is a former architect and now full-time mystery writer who, before the pandemic, travelled the world with her iPad, camera, and sketchbook gathering material for the Elspeth Duff mysteries. Hopefully she will be back on the road soon. She lives near Vancouver, British Columbia.

Visit *anncrew.com or elspethduffmysteries.com* for more.

Made in the USA
Monee, IL
28 April 2022

94918018R10207